NANTEOS:
The Dipping Pool

JANE BLANK

With thanks to Anne, Eifion, Eirian, Gwenith, Helen,
Ian, Jeanne, Jeremy, Lefi, Nigel, Richard, Shane and Carol

First impression: 2020
© Jane Blank & Y Lolfa Cyf., 2020

Cover design: Tanwen Haf

ISBN: 978 1 78461 877 3

Published and printed in Wales
on paper from well-maintained forests by
Y Lolfa Cyf., Talybont, Ceredigion SY24 5HE
e-mail ylolfa@ylolfa.com
website www.ylolfa.com
tel 01970 832 304
fax 832 782

Chapter One

F AR AWAY TO the west, the sun sets behind the bald hills below Devil's Bridge, the sky thin and purple as the skin under an old man's eye. The darkening land is pocked by lead and silver mines, even the horizon deformed by the lumps of waste and scarred by adits and trenches. It is *Calan Mai*, a spirit night, and many climb the mountain road at dusk. The foul weather of the last winter has ruined it, made great claw marks across the surface. Fast streams in flood, following wheel ruts downhill, have pulled away the stones, making the road almost impassable. No matter. The feet, nailed in leather clogs or bare and strong, pass on. There is a hum bubbling up from the people. They clump together, then groups split – teasing out like carded wool; then huddle again, all the time making a determined progress upwards. Sometimes distinct voices separate out; many are laughing. But as the front of the group turns the final corner, silence takes them. Directly ahead, and black like a crucifix against the sky, is the tree of *Siôn y Gof.*

Though it is now too dark to see details: the discoloured bone, the teeth – raw, intimate; the fetishes and charms of animal bone, feather, leather and glass that the people have hung around it to banish evil; the occasional glimpse of these as a torch catches them, the screech of the slowly swinging cage and the memory of what is here, are worse. One woman crosses herself; another puts an offering on the ground at the bottom of the scaffold and backs away.

But they can see the great bonfires now, just make out the crowds surrounding them. With a new energy, they turn their backs on him and make their way towards the light.

*

Before they reach the fires, there are dancers in the dark. The old *crwths* and harps of the strangers play harmonies and rhythms not of these mountains. Wooden boards have been laid and the women of the travelling people, up from the camp at Tregaron, stamp at them with their clogs. They wear their long hair loose, their clothes colourful even in the torchlight, skirts sewn with coins. Though their dancing has a little of the travelling fair to it – the ribbon flicking, the high-pitched whoops and shouts, it is unfamiliar to many on the hill tonight. The women's feet stay in contact with the ground. They do not skip and reel, but swirl and stamp. They rap the ground sharply with their steel toecaps, like ewes stamping a warning. Their arms curl above their heads; some clap and sing in their strange language with hard, nasal voices. Authority wraps around them in a thick perfume as they lift their wide skirts high, seeming to be without shame, even their knees visible in the torchlight as they spin.

Branwen is drawn towards them, passing a blind fiddler who sits alone on a low stool, his violin lying silent across his knees, the ravaged eyes closed. His body is perfectly still, though his head moves, weaving like a horse's trapped in a stable too long. Her friend Cari's body presses against her in the dark.

Someone has picked up a drum. Here there is no regular beat as Branwen is used to from the music of her own people at weddings and feast days. This drum is played fast, with hard fingers – a breathless beat. She cannot keep herself still any longer and Cari takes her hand and draws her in towards the music. Some of the people her friend passes grab at her – squeezing her arm, her shoulder. One woman runs her cupped hand down Cari's hair, from scalp to the end of her copper-coloured plait, exclaiming in admiration. In the group of travellers almost no one is covered tonight, the women's hair dressed only with a feather or flowers. The harpist and *crwth* players sit on a large rectangle stone in the centre.

Standing to one side is a man with the round drum. People are clapping their hands – but it is not applause. A woman, her face even in the torchlight gnarled and broken with scars from some pox or pestilence, opens her mouth, releasing wave upon wave of a high, pleading, demanding call. It could not be called singing. She is one of the few to wear a headdress, eyes hidden under a short, black veil which does not cover her mouth. Beyond the makeshift stage other dancers have beaten the coarse grass flat. Each seems to move alone – turning, stamping, weaving their bare arms above their heads like snakes, disturbed from their tunnels and writhing towards the light. Sometimes they too utter shrill calls or warble from the back of their throats.

Cari drops Branwen's hand and joins them. For a couple of minutes the seemingly random clapping appears to solidify into a single beat that drives her friend's movements; a man's voice calls out her name. Cari's face and arms are white as a scrubbed root and mark her out as she turns and worries her body to the music, her skirts heavier and duller than the other women's. She holds out her arm, hands open in Branwen's direction, eyes fixed on her friend. She weaves nearer and Branwen feels a nudge at the base of her spine, then again, harder this time and suddenly she too is in the ring. Cari smiles at her, then turns her body away.

Branwen's feet are moving, slapping down on the beaten earth around the boards, her hips dipping from side to side, then swivelling, making figures of eight. A strange tingling, a delicious itch begins inside her. Will she wet herself? But it is not quite that...

Cari takes Branwen's hand and passes her under her arm; again and again she turns and spins her friend until Branwen is dizzy, the music becomes only the beating drum for her now – the drummer's relentless fingers and the wooden block he holds, tapping devilish against the frame. She moves away, whirling herself ever faster, her arms reaching out into the dark, hair loose and flopping over her face, clinging to the coloured grease Cari's smeared on her lips. The faces of the group blur and merge, mostly dark, their hair and the men's caps also dark, yet there is one that steals her attention, each time her eyes return to the same spot in the crowd as she spins. This face is light – broad and light, the hair a halo. She stumbles and veers towards another dancer who catches her around the waist and, laughing, holding onto her hand, spins around and around with her. But however often she looks, that figure is still there, standing alone, the face seeming to float unattached in space, like the moon.

The music stops suddenly; a roar of clapping and shouting as the men lay their instruments flat on the huge stone and straighten up. The drum carries on for a few minutes, slowing until it is just a pulse – one short, one long, the beat of a heart. One of the *crwth* players reaches for a flagon and leans back to take a long draught and someone in the crowd throws a full skin at the harper for him to drink. Branwen's feet slow and she catches her breath, leaning forward over her knees. For a moment she thinks she'll be sick, but Cari appears at her side, linking their arms together and pushing her body into her, nudging her away.

"Happy?"

Branwen nods, laughing, but as yet unable to speak. Before she leaves the circle she looks again for the pale face of the golden man. He has gone.

Now the men have the cattle ready for the drive between the two fires and Cari and Branwen join the new crowd of people forming around them. An old man next to her mumbles, a repeated complaint. "When I was a youngster they used to throw a calf right into the fire, or a ewe if there was trouble in the herd or flock. This new way; no good at all. And what are they doing letting Gypsies up here on a spirit night, no good; no good at –"

Another man snaps at him. "Hush, Iwan; some of the lads'll watch over the beasts overnight and drive them through the ashes in the morning. Only a bit of fun anyway."

The old man stares at him, his mouth open and black. He worries at the corner of his rough waistcoat. "Just a poor shadow of what it used to be – a small herd driven *between* the two bonfires. Rubbish!"

The other man shrugs and lets himself be swallowed by the crowd. The largest of the fires have been allowed to die down and here two rows of men are forming between the burn sites, their backs to the embers, facing one another. Again, the old man, shouting this time. "Bloody dangerous! Used to be they'd drive the beasts right into the flames. It was part of it, them burning. Cleaned the land for a good crop. But a man could get knocked down and trampled this way. You'll get burned yourself – stupid devils!" he shouts uselessly into the night.

Other men with their sharpened sticks, clubs and dogs, the animals whipped up by the shouts and cries of the people and too excited to fear the fire, form a tight arc behind the cattle, driving them forward. The bullocks bellow in terror, a couple at the front locking their legs, refusing to move ahead. But those behind them, tormented by the snapping and snarling of the dogs and desperate to escape the clubs, barge forward. One animal at the back turns to fight, lowering his head, getting under one of the taller dogs and tossing it into the air. His horns have been sawn away and are blunt and one of the heavier mastiffs fastens on his throat. Others, distracted from their task by the blood, join in and the beast is brought down. The men laugh.

The old man seems to have adopted Branwen, his fingers tight as a cockrel's foot around her arm, keeping her back – not that she needs any encouragement to stay away. "There you are – one beast's killed; dead already! No blessing'll come of it if they don't go alive right through the burning fire like they used to!"

The remaining bullocks pass between the two lines of men who face each other, their backs to the fire, keeping the animals moving with their clubs and spikes. The beasts pass through the human corridor and into a ring of people, waiting to stop them bolting into the dark. Many hold torches, waving them and shouting whilst the dogs catch up with the small herd, moving into place around them. Soon the drovers part the crowd, calling on their dogs and driving the cattle back to the makeshift pound on the edge of the bog.

The old man hacks up onto the ground, shaking his head. "That won't have done anything. Hardly a beast even had its flank singed. We'll not be in for a good summer." Suddenly a man is stumbling and thrashing his arms, the hessian sack fastened across his shoulders having dipped into the flames behind him. His friend scrabbles to loosen it and pull it away but the man's flailing arms force him back. Another tries to knock him to the ground and smother him, only succeeding with the help of others nearby. Though he is unharmed from the waist down, the flames have risen up, ravaging his face and hair. "There we are; there we are – bad luck, I knew it!" Old Iwan, jerking and bouncing with anger points as the injured man stands, his arms out like Christ on a cross, screaming as rhythmically as a badly-fitted wheel turning.

Cari eases Branwen's arm out from under the old man's hand as he remains fixed on the brutal pantomime. "Come away, Branwen." Her voice is an urgent hiss. "We can't do anything for him!" She leads them away towards the sound of a fiddle. It's like nothing ever heard before – faster than the fastest jig, but not a sunny and joyful sound like fair day in Aberystwyth. Cari's face is alight. "It stirs me! There's nothing like their music, Branwen. Nothing. Something wicked in it."

A woman comes around the inside of the circle that's forming, holding out a small bowl of beaten metal. The sound of coins hitting it is almost in time with the music. The blind fiddler stands unmoving, his head bent, resting on the violin on his left shoulder, leaning in like a mother would towards her sleeping child. His hair is long, dark and curling and, in the manner of all the strangers, he wears no wig, though his clothes are quieter than many. Others of his group move around him, yet it is he, in his stillness, that catches the eye. She cannot see the fingers on his left hand, the neck of the violin is lost in shadow, but his right arm opens and closes like a wing as he draws the bow across the strings. As he finishes there is a beat of silence, the notes evaporating into the night. The coin woman comes out of the darkness and takes his violin from him as he bows his head once, then stands, rocking slightly from left to right. Neck flexed back, face lifted towards the sky, he moves his head from side to side like a fox searching out a scent. Then he turns suddenly from the ring and walks into the dark, the woman at his side rushing to catch him by the arm.

Branwen turns to Cari but her friend hasn't been watching. Following her gaze she sees a huge form loom out of the dark. A well-bred horse, coat gleaming as the torchlight catches it.

"Cari?" She nudges her. "Cari, who is it? Who's that man?"

"Edward Gruffydd of Nanteos. We call him Cai. He said he'd come for me."

"Oh, I..."

But Cari has already moved away. The man and horse, all one form in the dark, come towards her. There is a powerful smell of leather, of polish, of horse sweat. He jumps down and she loses her friend in his arms. Finally Cari pulls away and they turn towards her. Cai Gruffydd. She has seen him from afar.

"Your pardon, maid." He lifts his hat to her. His mouth is

broad, the teeth white in the torch's light. "You came here together?"

"Yes, but I can find my own way back."

He shakes his head. "We'll take you home."

"No, there's no need. I've friends here who live nearby. I can go with them."

"Then let's see you to them. Where do you live?"

"Y Pandy, Ffwrnais."

He whistles through his teeth. "You walked up tonight?"

"It's not so far; not if you don't mind leaving the road sometimes. I know all the tracks." Cari says nothing. Cai stands behind her, his arm around her waist, his palm flat against her belly as she leans back into him, tickling the horse's cheek under his bridle.

"Your parents let you out on a Spirit Night?" he asks.

"There's only my father. My aunt lives near here, if the weather was to turn."

"There they are!" Cari points at an old couple near the ale tent. "Twm and Sara, Tŷ'n Cwm. I'll ask them to walk home with you!" She disappears into the dark.

All but the man's jaw is hidden under the shadow of his hat. "I've heard of you, Edward Gruffydd. Cai."

"And I of you... Miss Rhys?"

Branwen nods. "Branwen."

He smiles. "They say you help run your father's mill. As capable a young woman as there is."

Her voice is urgent, flattered. "I like the buying and the selling; the bargaining. 'Tis a shame the cloth guilds keep so tight a rein on us."

"Indeed. They strangle your trade, I hear."

"We should get together with our neighbours; buy and sell our own cloth – then we can set our own prices, we –"

But Cari is back. "They'll see you home, Bran. See, they wait for you by the beer wagon." She points and Branwen can just see them, Twm waving with his stick. Cari kisses her on the cheek and pushes the brim of her hat up. "You alright?"

Branwen nods vigorously. "Good to meet you, Mr Gruffydd." She makes a small curtsey.

"And you, Miss Rhys."

"Miss Rhys!" Cari laughs and jumps up onto the horse, wriggling herself comfortable in front of the saddle.

Cai, one foot in the stirrup, looks back. "Until our next meeting, then." He touches his hat to her before swinging up onto the horse's back. Within moments they are lost to the dark.

For a moment Branwen stands watching the people and dogs moving in and out of the firelight. She is about to join her neighbours when she feels the hand on her arm. It is he, the stranger, the watcher on the edge of the dancing circle. "Sorry to frighten you. I was afraid to lose you again in the crowd. Henry Davies." He bows to her, as, shocked, she looks into his face. There is light everywhere about him – caught in the hair released from his hat; captured in his face, in his coat – clean and of some bright colour, perhaps yellow. "You are alone now I believe and the 'party' almost over. May I see you home?"

She shakes her head, immediately annoyed with herself – nothing but a dumb beast! She forces herself to respond. "I thank you, Sir, but I'm not alone. I have neighbours waiting for me." She gestures towards Twm and Sara, taking a few steps towards them. "Will you not join us?"

He looks over to the two old people who are waving at her again "Ah, I fear I go a different way, much as the idea would be a delightful one. You are…? I beg your pardon but I didn't catch your name."

"Branwen Rhys."

He bows again, glances towards the beer wagon. "I must take my leave." Before he does so he lifts her hand to his lips. His gloves are softer than moleskin to the touch and smell sweet – some soap or preparation. "I hope to have the pleasure of your company another time." He bows, low this time, like a gentleman leaving a ball. She has no chance to reply before he's gone.

"What a night! I feared there'd be trouble from those Gypsies, 'Egyptians' they call themselves, don't they? I said so to Twm, but it seems I still have my purse on me after all!" Sara takes Branwen's hand. "Who was that man with the fancy clothes?" Branwen shakes her head. The old woman grunts. "Ah. There are often wolves hiding in the shadows at *Calan Mai*. Come home with us, girl."

She is not sorry to be leaving and neither Sara nor Twm talk much as they trudge home. Sara has a fine strong torch which has to do for the three of them as Branwen's is long since burned out and Twm, because of the hump on his back, needs to find his way with a stick. The night is clear and it is not impossible to see the ground. She is nearly asleep from the waist up, only her legs and feet concentrating, her thoughts moving like debris in a whirlpool: Cai Gruffydd and the horse, the dancers, the fiddle music and, more than all put together, the man with the white-gold hair.

"Here we are then, *cariad*." They are at the gates to Tŷ'n Cwm. "You'll be alright just around the corner?" Sara holds the torch up to her face.

"Yes, of course."

"Best to borrow this. It has a few more hours in it yet."

Branwen takes the torch and bids goodnight. On her own the flame, so comforting before, writhes and shudders in the breeze, accentuating rather than calming the shadows. Her feet are loud on the loose rocks of the track and she has to resist the urge to look behind her, knowing from childhood how thin the line is between panic and comfort.

"Branwen?" She stops. A male voice behind her. "Branwen? Wait a moment." The voice draws nearer and she hears the low chunter of a horse. Man and horse dissolve out of the darkness into the arc of her light. It is he. She feels a strange sensation, as though her body is split in two. Her legs seem to want to run, yet her body turns eagerly, holding the torch aloft. The horse whinnies, perhaps alarmed at the fire, as he dismounts.

"How do you take this road now, Sir? I thought you had to go another way." She is bold, surprising herself.

"Perhaps I'm lost." She can half see his grin. "Perhaps I sought to be lost... in a pair of beautiful eyes!"

She turns quickly so that he doesn't see her own smile. The time to her gate passes like the flutter of a moth's wing. Once there they are so tangled in conversation that perhaps a half-hour passes, maybe only ten minutes, their voices little above a whisper but the content made bold by the dark. At last they hear a noise from within the mill house – her father will discover them!

"I must take my leave again I fear," he says, stepping towards her, his arms outstretched.

She dodges through the gate. It's between them as she says, "Thank you for your kindness, Sir, in bringing me to my door."

He bows deep to her, like she'd seen a soldier give to a lady, kisses her hand and turns quickly away, still leading his horse for as long as she follows him out of sight.

Her father is standing just behind the door waiting for her. "Where's Cari?" She shakes her head. "I told you not to walk home alone, especially on a night such as this." She looks at him, puzzled. "May Eve, Branwen. You shouldn't be alone on a night such as this."

"I wasn't on my own. I came back with Sara and Twm, Tŷ'n Cwm."

"I heard only one pair of clogs."

"They left me to come the last bit alone. They lent me the torch." She gestures through the window to where it still burns, safe in the pig's old stone shelter.

"But I heard voices and a horse, though only one set of footsteps."

"Ah, you've found me out, Dada… My friend doesn't wear clogs but good leather boots." Her father looks at her for a moment, then turns back into the room, his face hidden as he bends to bank up the fire, arranging the turf with care. He lingers at the task; does not turn around. "He works for Lewis Morris, Dada. He's had education in south Wales." Still her father does not turn. "He's been in England! He even knows some German from the engineers – they say 'v' but they write 'w', like the English write 'f' but say 'ff'. Oh, and he can speak English too!"

At last he turns around, straightens up slowly. "Your face is shining, though the flame of the candle goes nowhere near it." Though she looks down, she cannot hide her smile in her hair. "I would you do not see him again, child."

"But why? We do no harm!"

"What can he want with a girl such as you?"

"I'm no stone breaker or ore carrier! You have a mill –"

"Owned by the Pryses, and even if it wasn't, it would hardly be enough to tempt a man such as he. What's his name?"

"Henry Davies."

"A Welshman at least," he mutters, turning away.

Her face hot, Branwen moves to challenge him. "I'm not engaged to the man, for pity's sake! He offered to do me the kindness of walking with me on the way back to his lodgings. We talked together. That's all."

Evan snorts. "Indeed."

"Yes. I think sometimes we forget there are such gentlemen in the world; gentlemen who go out of their way to be civil."

"You say he lodges with Morris?"

She nods. "I believe so, yes."

"Well, Mr Morris is living at Pant yr Eithin, on the top road." He looks hard at her.

"Oh!"

"Do not smile, Branwen – you flatter yourself. It's a pride that may undo you." He turns away and takes a few steps towards the door. "That man in his expensive boots can have nothing more to say to you. *Nos da*, child."

He makes his way outside to the privy as she climbs the ladder to her room in the loft. As she crouches over the pot, she runs through their conversation, their glances, stolen in the torchlight. Through the single layer of planks she hears her father come back in and get into the closed cot by the fire. Henry Davies; the name shivers through her. His hair, blond and so different from everyone else in that circle by the fire; a special man, like a white bell in a wood of bluebells.

Chapter Two

CAI WAITS UNDER the shelter of the farm wall, his strong cob cropping the tough grass. The air is rank with fog, noises from the poultry on the yard behind woven into it, seeming to come from every direction, every height. Although the estuary is only a field away, the eerie call of a curlew comes as if from another world. This is a dangerous place, even in summer, the tide coming in unseen, deep and fast, up the channels. Sheep are often drowned, even men. A deathly smell hangs in the grey air, seaweed rotting perhaps; the bodies of the formless creatures that live in shells? Suddenly, the mare stops chewing, raises her head – ears taut, but not able to fix properly on some sound far out on the marshes. He takes up the slack reins and holds them under her chin. She seems to have her bearings now and stares into the mist, ears pointed straight ahead. For a moment he is alarmed by her shrill squeal – but there is nothing to be seen. He walks down from the slight rise of the farm road, following the line of the horse's concentrated gaze onto softer ground.

Then he feels it – up through his boots – a vibration deep in the ground. His horse squeals again. The whole bog is shaking. He backs up fast, back to the shingle track, the animal pulling against the leather, tossing her head. Only at the last minute does he hear them coming as a massive form bears down at them. He swears as his horse panics, wrenching his arm and rearing up. The shape veers away just in time and his horse wheels around, almost pulling him off his feet. This time she whinnies – some sort of recognition as the mass now in front of them, seeming to dissolve out of the fog, becomes a heavy horse and its rider.

"You bloody fool; you could have trampled us! Why're you riding like that in these conditions?" He looks up the huge flank looming out from the grey. The rider's face is mostly hidden. "No saddle, no bridle – a ton of horseflesh! I'm talking to you, man – you could have killed us!" Tal doesn't answer as he slides down from the animal's back, pulling the covering from his mouth. Passing the halter into his left hand, he holds out his right. Cai stares him down. "You could have killed us both."

"Sorry for it." Tal wipes the hand on his britches and holds it out again.

Cai takes it this time. "Edward Gruffydd, bailiff at Nanteos. Cai to most. Sorry to call so late."

Tal grins. "Heard of you. Taliesin; Tal. You're here for me?"

"I am."

Tal nods. "Give her something to eat," he calls over his shoulder as he walks his own horse through the yard, disappearing into the stables. Cai takes his mare to a half-full hay net and waits outside. The yard is quite dry, considering the weather, a slight camber helping to drain off the rain and there are good cobbles underfoot. Suddenly he is aware of a shape, deadly still and fixed on him. The fowls and ducks, even the geese have largely ignored them, but it is the tense stillness of the white, black and grey dog that catches his notice. At least he's wearing long boots and has a crop. The animal's body quivers with tension and it is beginning to flex its legs, hunkering down, the back low and straight, head pointing at him like a stone.

A short whistle; Tal appears in the doorway and the dog becomes fluid, moves to shadow his leg. "Here, let me take her for you." There is a smile in his voice as he moves towards the mare, only a slight raising of its lip betraying the mood of the dog at his side. Then, "You've come from Nanteos today?" Tal says over his shoulder, gesturing with his head for Cai to follow.

"I have."

"Long way to come on so foul a day. You won't go back tonight."

"No. I lodge at Ynyshir. I have business with the bargemen at Garreg tomorrow."

Tal whistles through his teeth. "A fancy bed you'll have there." He looks up a moment, "Untack her for you?"

"Thank you." As Tal works on his horse, Cai looks around the stables, stopping by the rows of tack, clean, oiled and mounted on the walls. "Ah, this is what I wanted to see." The great jaws of the work horse keep up a regular chomping. "You're ostler here, are you not?"

"I am."

"Powell sent me." He waits. "You're to come to us."

"What says Johnes?"

"They have agreed it. They met last market day at Aberystwyth, so I'm told."

"Powell himself!" Tal whistles again. "I'm an important man, then." For a moment he straightens and looks at Cai, but, getting no response, bends again to the horse. "Ay, I'd heard Powell was hiring ahead of trouble; I'll not get into a fight for any landowner – why should I give a damn whether it's Old King George or Thomas Powell owns the land over the ore. All like their own way if they can but come by it!"

"You're not asked to. You're there for the profit – training horses and men with the new harness. You're there for the silver and lead."

Tal laughs. "Silver I can do."

"Accommodation too."

Tal stands. "No bunkhouse for me, I give you thanks!"

"Not the barracks. A cottage; your choice. Whatever you get here – Powell will beat it. Johnes speaks highly of you, you don't come cheap." At last he has Tal's attention, the younger man leaning back against the big horse's flank.

"What deal have they made over me?"

Cai shrugs. "Who knows what deals the gentry make over brandy when the drapes are closed."

"Wait for me in the tack room while I see to the beasts. We may share a pipe." Tal gestures into the gloom where a door stands ajar beyond the stalls. "I have a fire, though 'tis a shame to need one in May... and a flask."

"As do I." Cai smiles. "French brandy."

"Brandy! I'm afraid you will find my liquor a bit rougher on the gullet."

Cai gestures to a piece of tack, "May I?" Tal nods, turning away to finish off with the horse and put her in an empty stall. "Did you make these, or just do the design?" Cai calls to him.

"Mostly both. Done leather working from a child." As Cai examines the kit, Tal comes to stand beside him. He is hardly up to the bailiff's shoulder, constantly moving, though Cai is still. He takes one of the intricate bridles from Cai's hands. "I can't take these with me – know that." Cai nods. "But I can make others for you."

"Do you know anything of mining?"

Tal laughs, "Try not to! Try and stay under the sky. Be long enough in earth."

"Quite so." Cai puts the halter back. "We need to do better with the horses at the surface and fetching the ore out. They tell me you ride the horses when they're at their work."

"As you've just seen. You can get so much more control from their backs. Even heavy horses on the farm or in the forestry work so much better if you ride them – if you're not scared of going bow-legged."

Cai laughs. "This is why I'm here. There's so much more we can do. Everything, well, almost everything we do is done by hand in Cardiganshire. You'd be interested in developing this for us?"

Tal nods. "Wages?"

"As I said. Let's say… treble what you get here?" Cai looks at him, the deal hanging in the air between them.

Tal grins. "How much brandy have you got left?"

"How much can you drink?" Tal spits on his palm and they shake. "You boasted a fire, did you not?"

"I did. Follow me."

Chapter Three

"I T IS KIND of you to take an interest – I know you humour me, Edward." She looks at him and smiles. "A house is nothing without its grounds, its gardens. These will be as beautiful as the house. No, more so, for they will live and breathe and no one can tire of them. Thomas builds Nanteos; I will build a paradise around it."

"It is not far short of that already –"

"But I will grow such fruit, such flowers for the house! Nanteos will be known even in London. Maybe I will open to the public, like Stowe?" She laughs. "That's one of the reasons I said 'yes' to Thomas all those years ago: the chance to develop a country estate." She pauses and looks directly at Cai. "Don't be embarrassed – I liked him as well of course, even from the start. He smelt of fresh air. And he had something of the dashing Welsh brigand about him, though his father's letters of introduction were smooth as snakeskin!"

"I thought snakeskin to be rough?"

Mary laughs, with her head thrown back; a real laugh that looks out of step with her fine, rare clothes. "I see you do not pet the snakes enough, Edward! Have you no shoes of snakeskin? No scabbard, belt or snake-pelt tunic?"

"No, I –" He laughs. She's teasing him again, her smile broad, despite the uneven teeth that many women would seek to hide. "I'll leave the snakes in their London cages, I think," he says.

"You do that, Edward." She does her ribbon up firmly under her chin. "Did you say that a message has come from Sheffield?"

"From the grinding mill, yes."

"And was it the information you required?"

"Yes. But I don't know whether their methods will work for us; the gradient on our river is so much steeper than the Sheaf and the flow varies so much more. I'm looking forward to seeing how they manage things for myself."

"Indeed. Well – you will just have to do with it what you can. Vat ve need is Germans; more Germans!" He laughs at her effort to mimic an accent. "Le Brun, Edward; what we need is a man like him for this generation."

Cai laughs. "He did very well for this family so I understand." They come to a stop by the foundations of what will be a furnace for the hothouse plants. Birds fill the air around them, swallows and martins worrying the sky, with the black swifts fastest and highest of all.

"I hope they don't think to dirty my new dress," she laughs. Cai doesn't reply. "Where have your thoughts taken you?" she asks. "You will be our Le Brun; our man of new inventions; of the water-powered... 'jackhammer' is it you call it?" He smiles. "We will hire you out around the country – I will be the envy of all the mine owners' wives; I will have my very own wizard of the waterwheel, Edward Gruffydd!"

"It would be satisfying to have investment and make the changes necessary. We still have women and children hitting at the ore with hammers, for pity's sake; some of our smaller mines only have hand-operated windlasses! We work the lode here in Cardiganshire little better than the ancients! Time's slipping away Mary, and I achieve nothing of any importance; both the Duke of Cumberland and the Young Pretender were younger than me – only twenty-five when –"

Mary laughs aloud. "I can just see you entering into Edinburgh, what was it... 'sword in one hand, Bible, no... cross in the other' and the Butcher Duke; oh my word!" She laughs again. "Dear, dear Edward, no one could accuse you of being lacking in ambition. You're so earnest; how did we ever deserve you?" She looks at him in delight.

"Ah... I think I may have been carried away with my own importance a little there." He smiles. "Maybe John Powell would make a more suitable hero."

"Poor John. To die out in The Cape like that –"

"He was an agent for the Royal Africa Company, wasn't he?"

"Yes. He was Thomas' father's favourite... sad times indeed. Sad times."

She takes his arm and turns them towards the house. She is nearly as tall as Cai, her stride not far short of his, even hampered as she is by her hoops and skirts. She stops before they reach the house, standing to take a last look at the river and the gentle slope of the valley beyond it. "Thinking again of Thomas when I first met him in London... We all knew he was sniffing for an heiress of course." Cai stiffens. "Oh, don't be shocked, for heaven's sake! What ambitious young man is not out to catch himself a fortune?" She takes a firm hold of his arm again. "But I was happy to play that game with him. He would come to my father's house and look me in the eye (I could hardly keep from laughing!), yet he was so easily distracted from his task of wooing for a wife. He loved to drink even then; food was, still *is* his pleasure of course and any of the beautiful women, maid or fine lady, would always draw his gaze." She grows quiet for a while. "Why am I telling you this?" Cai smiles and shrugs. "But when we played music together... oh, he looked at no one else. Unusual combination that in a man: hunting, shooting, yet music too. Anyway, as my mother always said, 'If your husband's eye *doesn't* follow a beautiful figure around a room, what good is he to you?'" She releases his arm and pulls her short cloak close around her body.

"Will you go in, Mary?"

"I should, I'm sure, instead of breathing in this river air, but I won't. You remind me of him." As she says this, she turns to look at him, drawing closer as if expecting an answer. He steps back slightly. "You're like a young Thomas Powell – but more serious. Look at you now." She laughs. "You're half afraid of me! You are charming – like him, but as though some of the candles are blown out. No, not blown out – placed in the corners, flickering in the shadows instead of beaming from a chandelier." She looks hard at his face. "Oh, what nonsense am I speaking now – ignore me, Edward. Let's go in."

She turns towards the house but he draws back, taking her hand and making a slight bow. "I have much to attend to, Mary."

She smiles, taking his arm again. "'Til tomorrow then. You may see me just as far as the door in that case."

As they walk towards the house five red kites cruise overhead, their wide wings fragile, tails blown in the breeze. "Look at that for heaven's sake – five of them! That gamekeeper, what does the man do all day? Ah, what was it... Yes, I remember. Shakespeare's 'hated kites'. Do you enjoy Mr Shakespeare, Edward?"

"I don't have much time for reading, though it seems he knew much of human nature."

"How so? I agree with you, of course, but upon what evidence do you base your assumption?"

"That Scottish King –"

"Macbeth himself," she says with relish.

"Yes. He was content, before he met the witches that is, not to wish for what he could not have. Once the idea was set however, it consumed him."

"Em, what was it... I have it! 'Full of scorpions is my mind, dear wife.' What a line! What an excellent example to pick, Edward. You received quite an education from that tutor in... where was it?"

"Pontrhydfendigaid."

She laughs. "In general I do quite well with my Welsh place-names, so Thomas tells me, but that is certainly one I'll go to my grave without!" She smiles. "And then in England, a most worthy school Thomas found for you. Shame that university wasn't possible – you'd have enjoyed it, like any handsome young man. Instead, however, I'm delighted that Thomas was most energetic in finding opportunities for you to study men of industry at work and –"

"I'm grateful for that."

She stops and looks hard at him. "I wasn't asking you to be grateful, Edward. You bring all you've learned back to Nanteos with you and, if proper funding can be secured, it's the estate, the mines in particular, that will benefit." They walk on for a couple of steps, then she stops again to watch the kites, now joined by a buzzard, more squat, compact. "What it must be to be a bird, do not you think? If we could see as they do, from such a height, we would be different, I think. Edward?"

"I beg your pardon... I was just looking at the stable site."

She sighs. "If Thomas had his way, the stables and kennels would be finer by far than the house!"

He laughs. "He would make the most of them, to be sure."

"Indeed, he is happier outside than in; a most reluctant squire for all his fine ideas on building. I do wish that he had engaged a more prominent architect, however. Mr Morgan is a skilled man but, as a local, lacks the authority to advise him and correct his errors. He is a grave man, more suited to be an inhabitant of Gray's Inn than to be a provincial architect. Do you notice, no hair is ever out of place, the thin locks still sporting much brown, though he is past fifty?"

"We are lucky to have him in the town."

"Agreed. Oh, just look! For goodness sake, look at how close they build to the tree!" He doesn't answer. "Those men at work on the left wing are drawing too near, far too near the great oak tree. Despite everything that has been said!"

Mary is already striding straight towards the building team. He watches her for a moment, a half-circle of men, tools still in their hands and glad of an opportunity to stop work, gather around her. He smiles and leaves across the lawn.

"Mr Morgan, good day to you," she says brightly.

"And to you, Mistress Powell." He lifts his hat; she nods her head in acknowledgement.

"I will get straight to the matter that bothers me. Keeping this tree, so near to the house – can it be achieved?" He looks openly at her, though he doesn't speak straight away. "Mr Morgan, please answer me in as direct and truthful a manner as possible; do not spare my feelings."

"No."

She looks sharply at him. "I beg your pardon, Sir."

He speaks deliberately, putting each word down as carefully as a brick in a wall. "In a word, Mistress, no. Since my last visit, the building works, the plans, have been 'modified' quite considerably and the west wing moved. It will not do: the tree must be removed and the root killed. I don't recommend digging it out from the ground as this will disturb the building just freshly completed. I'm sorry for it –"

She holds up her hand. "Thank you. It is as I feared. I will deal with it." She sweeps inside. Thomas Powell is in the new library. He turns and stops work as she enters, though he worries at the desk with his thumb as she speaks. "How do you fare with the accounts?"

He shrugs and mimes pulling at his hair. "I often think mining in Cardiganshire is sustained more by wily promoters than by dividends. We're still living on the good name Sir Hugh Myddleton made for us a century ago! Thank goodness the investors still believe in silver, though there's precious little of it to be found with the lead these days." Seeing the concern on her face he adds, "Worry not; your husband will not be defeated by a mere ledger!"

She comes further into the room and goes to move a chair. He gets up to help her. Once seated she waits for a moment. He is looking closely at her. "The tree, Thomas." He raises his eyes to the ceiling, opens his mouth to speak. "No, Thomas – you must hear me. We build too near." Again, he seems about to speak and she holds up her hand to stop him. "It is a danger to that whole wing; or rather I should say, the house is a danger to the tree for it must come down."

"I have told you before; we keep it – all is landscape, Mary. Landscaping – you must know this? We must keep the structure. Several important men have commented on how picturesque Nanteos is."

"I'm all for beauty, Thomas, and there's nothing more beautiful in my mind than the grace of an ancient tree to set off the beauty of a fine, new house; indeed the tree will give dignity to the building, stop it from looking rather bald perhaps, but there are practical considerations. It's a great shame as the tree's been here for, perhaps, three hundred years –"

"Four hundred, surely!"

"As long as that? Then a tragedy indeed that we have taken it upon ourselves to build so near –"

"You mean that I've built so near? It's I who am master of this project, Mary!" By now he is out of his seat and pacing in front of the window.

"There's no need to blow out your cheeks and grow scarlet over it, Thomas. It must be done. You've built too near the oak and it must come down." He moves to speak but she hasn't finished. "Or of course if you prefer, the walls could be torn down and rebuilt elsewhere instead."

"Neither of these is acceptable! But then you know this, Mary. Leave the blasted tree for now, I charge you. I have more than enough to do in preparing our case – it seems every ragged miner, every squatter and beggar, has an opinion about who owns my lead and silver. They go secretly to that swindler Lewis Morris with precedents and outlandish claims that the land is common land; common they say! We Powells have owned it for generations, well at least since my father's time. Out come the begging hands and you can be sure that Lewis Morris fills them with the King's coin. I'm told he keeps a ledger and records their outlandish claims;

writes down what he bribes them so he can claim it back as expenses in his role as Mines' Surveyor, he –"

"Thomas, I know you're burdened most sorely by all this; it's just that swift action now will surely save such profound problems later with regard to the tree and Mr Morgan is only just outside –"

"Desist, I beg you, Mary! God's teeth; I'll speak to the man when I return from London."

Mary pauses, tugging the lace on her sleeve straight and taking a deep breath, audible in the tense room. "Thomas." Her tone is measured once more and she makes the effort to speak more calmly. "I do not deny – how could anyone – that Nanteos is already the most beautiful of houses, part of which of course comes from your inspired design, so much enhanced by your choice of location. I say only this: the new wing will cramp the tree and alter its course over time and that, with one severe gale, our handsome house could be badly damaged, even before it's finished." He has returned to his seat. She raises her hand, palm upwards to placate him. "You know I leave the building to you, but I do have an interest in the grounds and I only warn –"

"Very well, Mary." He takes up his pen. "I'll consider it."

"I –"

"I have said, I'll give it some thought. You're no fool; neither do *I* want to be found a fool when a branch comes through my fine lead one winter's night."

She nods. "Well, we'll see if such a thing is achievable. As you say, when you return from London – if it's not too late. Thank you, Thomas." But he has already turned back to his papers. For a moment she remains seated, though it is clear that the conversation is over. As she leaves, he glances at her, making a small gesture for her to close the door on her way out. In the inner hallway she pauses a moment as is her custom and listens to the house. Outside the hammers ring, iron against stone; so much of building work seems to involve hitting things! But here, inside the mansion, the scrape of metal on metal as a hearth is cleared; the voices leaking from the kitchen; all the sounds from all these rooms belong to her.

Chapter Four

IN THE HILLS, lead is king. All the trees are underground – gone to make props after being stripped of their bark. For mile on mile the land has a crumpled, sickly look, the colours wrong, the curve of the surface ridged, wrinkled and puckered by the hollows and tips of mines. From the mines on high ground lead spreads its tendrils downwards through the valleys, poisoning the rivers, like a fungus moving unseen, spreading through the soil. Though most of the high ground is of little use for food, there are clusters of buildings belonging to each mine. Women with bandaged hands using hammers break up the rock, children picking out nuggets of lead like plums from the waste. At the Powell mine it's not raining and the ore cleaners are, for once, glad of the fact that they sort outside in the open air. The stream is running well to clean the newly-dug rock, so progress is good and there is a smell of summer in the breeze coming in from the distant bay, a trace of salt with it and almost warm; not the spiteful bite of the last few months.

At the head of one of the deep shafts Tal is working with the heavy winch horses, going over the same manoeuvre with them again and again, using a lightly-loaded kibble dangling down from a short rope to get the animals used to the new harness. A couple of the women carriers watch him, their full baskets resting on the ground for a moment.

"New are you?" The woman is old to be carrying, but still looks strong – her shoulders and body broad, legs short. The hair escaping from beneath her hat is orange as autumn heather, her face brown with freckles. Tal nods. "Working for the Powells now, is it?" Again he nods, coming around the side of the animal's flank. "Short aren't you?" she says, looking around at the other women who laugh. Tal smiles and carries on adjusting the tack.

"Dark, isn't he." Not a question, but a statement from one of the younger women who comes nearer. Sinews strain at her throat and collarbones; she has not put down her load.

"What're they calling you?" The older woman has come towards him, studying his face.

"Taliesin. Tal."

"There's a miner here already with that name. He's not dark like you, though; he's from round here. No, not like you at all; he's a big lad all round." She turns to the other women and winks. They laugh.

"Your basket's heavy," he says to the younger woman as she shifts to adjust her burden.

"It is." She stands proud, turning around for him to see it.

"Why do you not rest it a moment?" Tal moves towards her, arms ready to help her.

She takes a step backwards, cheeks flushing and shakes her head. "Only have to pick it up again, wouldn't I?"

"Don't bother yourself about it; be too 'eavy for you, my darling," the older woman says, looking around and playing to her friends again. More laughter. Suddenly she leans past him and fixes on something in the pass below. "Eh, girls; Powell," she says. "Bollocks." She helps her friends on with their baskets which most carry on their backs. Tal goes to help her, bracing to take the ore basket and lifting it to chest height. "Yer stronger than you look, new boy." She laughs but, instead of putting herself through the straps, she takes the load on her head. For a moment she stands, her feet splayed outwards, hips waggling to settle herself under the weight. The women move off, each bare foot planted deliberately, backs braced and bent forward with the strain.

Tal watches the rider come up towards the mine buildings. The man stops every few yards to talk to someone on the way, gesturing a lot with his arms and crop. Then he seems more purposeful, riding straight up the track to the mine head. Tal waits for him. Thomas Powell's horse is a powerful cob, fat hind quarters brushed to a sheen. Though only late spring, the animal has lost almost all of its winter coat, if indeed it needed to grow any in the pampered stables at Plas Nanteos. He stops a comfortable distance from the winch horses.

"You the new man? Ostler?"

Tal nods and, stepping away from the windlass, proffers his hand. Powell laughs and reaches towards him with his own, though he doesn't remove his glove or dismount. "Taliesin," he says.

"Is there another name?" Tal shakes his head. "Ah, well, Taliesin is a long one, long enough for an ostler, I'd warrant; double the required length you could say; enough to do for Christian and surname. Yes, it'll do very well, though the paymaster may need another one by and by. Goes well, does it?" He gestures broadly with his crop, taking in the horses, the winding gear, even a generous patch of sky with his wide arc. "What an enterprise, eh? Bet you've not seen the like of it, eh, young man?" But Tal has turned away, looking up past the brow of the hill. Powell follows his gaze. "A monster!"

"The way it holds the sky…"

"It would take some killing."

"Bait. Poison in bait perhaps. The only way." Tal has not lowered his eyes, though he shields them now with his hand as the eagle changes direction. "But why do it?"

Powell snorts in scorn. "That thing's big enough to take a ewe!"

"There are many sheep."

Powell looks hard at him for a moment, but it seems he had not meant insolence; his attention far away, locked on to the angular shape as it makes off, far, too far for even the sharpest eye. "Easy to see you don't own land. You'll be bringing the wolves back next!"

The bird out of sight, Tal turns back to the harness. "I heard tell that once an eagle took a fox; not a cub – a grown vixen."

"An interesting match indeed! Who was the winner of such a contest?"

"There was no contest. The eagle broke the vixen's back and carried it away. Four legs limp and only a useless mouth snapping at the end of a hanging neck."

"Good God, you sound as if you saw it yourself!"

"Only a cat is a match for an eagle in the air. The claws hold on while it uses its fangs. It can twist up and use its back claws to rip open the bird's belly."

"God's teeth, man! How did we even start this discourse? I came only to check on progress with the winches!"

Tal smiles slightly. "There is progress."

"Will it save me money? Will it let us go deep?" Tal looks past him and nods a greeting to Cai as he rides up. Thomas turns around in the saddle. "Ah, here you are, Edward." He turns back to Tal. "Will it let us go deeper?"

"I cannot tell. Cai will know, if anyone."

"Eh?" Confused by the name just for a moment, he nods. "Of course. Well, Edward, how are you thinking now?"

"Too soon to be sure." He dismounts and goes to inspect the harness. "Good. You've set it on the diagonal… Yes, that might work."

"Do you know, this… Taliesin, isn't it?" Tal nods. "… would have the wolves back in Cardiganshire." He laughs, but Tal continues with his work. "Would you not, young Tal? Would you not have the wolves back from times of old? Humour me – speak, lad!"

Tal straightens up. "No Sir; no wolves for me I give you thanks. I love my own throat too much."

Thomas laughs. "Good man!"

"Yes, we need to stop the horses being able to lunge forward and crash the load – we've lost ore that way before now, and damaged kibbles; yes, and men." Cai's face is serious.

"Training's important too," Tal adds, quietly.

"Of course. Another reason you're up here."

Thomas rubs his hands together. "You two seem to have things under control. Good." He gestures for Cai to come alongside his horse, leaning down to speak, "Has he replied since the last time?" Cai nods. "Let's meet him again. Not around here, remember – as we said."

"Machynlleth – next fair day. He should have hold of the underground plans as well by then."

"He'll bring them? Dangerous for him. We must be paying well!"

"Copies. That's why he's needed the time – and yes, we pay royally for his 'services'."

"And the names – those that Morris bribes to speak out

against our interests? The rats he pays to say that I don't own that land?"

"The list of names too. If we can trust him, that is."

"What? You doubt him?"

"Of course! He's betraying his masters – why not us?"

"Because we're paying the bastard a fortune, that's why! You don't think he'd speak of this to anyone, do you? Eh?"

"You mean, is he some sort of agent for the Crown? Some spy?"

"Good God – you think he's a spy?" Thomas seems about to fall from his horse in panic.

Cai holds up his hands to calm him. "No. No, I'm saying nothing of the kind. Even a polecat like Davies isn't that clever. No, think not of it; it was only that you cast doubt on how true his information to us is – and of course we can't be sure of it, we'll just have to trust him. That's all." Thomas has dropped his crop and Cai hands it up to him. "Leave Davies to me; all's under control. Do you not need to go to Aberystwyth this afternoon?"

"Yes. Yes; I must get myself back down." Thomas straightens up, gathers his reins and adjusts his hat. "Good man! Yes, I'll leave it to you." He looks around him. "A good day for some hard work. Well, I'll be off. Mary wishes me in Aberystwyth tonight – 'shiny and handsome', so she says. Shiny I can do, but handsome..." He laughs heartily. "You coming down, Edward?"

"No. We're working on another load – the ships are only in 'til Friday."

"Good man. 'Til tomorrow then." He looks behind him. "Ah, there you are, young Tal. Good work. Keep going; one foot in front of the other." Tal nods and lifts his hat as

Thomas rides away, slowing to acknowledge the homage of his workers by touching his crop to the brim of his hat as they stop for him to pass.

"Seems a good enough master," Tal says, spitting out the reed stem he's chewing on.

"Yes, good enough with the people. Can take advice – but doesn't like spending money."

"Who does?"

"Lead needs it. They say, but for powder, we work the mines no differently from the Romans – a disgrace! There is hardly a drainage wheel in all Cardiganshire and the roads are so bad everything must be moved by pack horse and mule. Thank God for the barges on the Dyfi or we would all starve!"

"You seem to have a burning for the trade yourself. More so even than the owner."

Cai looks hard at him, but he doesn't seem to mean anything by it. He is looking out through the gap in the hills to where a small patch of water can be seen. "Ever been on it?"

Tal shakes his head. "You?"

"Once, to Liverpool. But I will go again, and further next time."

Tal nods. "You're taking more ore out soon?"

"Yes, in fact I must go and check the loads. They put too much in – it's a false economy overloading the animals –"

"A good mule's a precious beast –"

"Exactly so. They would cripple them with too much weight. In some mines backs are broken." Cai swings up onto his horse. "I'm glad you agreed to join us, even if you do refuse to give up your other work on the farm."

"There's plenty of light for me to do it all – summer's almost here."

Cai laughs, tips his hat and rides down to the sheds where the mules are kept ready for loading.

After making some more adjustments, Tal hands over to one of the winch hands, a thin boy of eighteen or so, his hair orange, skin almost translucent. His thin arms look as if they would snap at any minute, but he's proving strong as a wire. Cai had told him about this one. 'Don't be fooled by his looks: Gwyn's tough, in the head too. Kept his calm last time the mine was flooded. Got the ostler to hitch up the horses to a winch in an old shaft and went down in a bucket to shout the men back. Seven got out that way and only a couple drowned.' He would be just right to train up with the new harnesses.

Tal watches him for a few minutes. Satisfied, he puts his hand on the horse's halter to rest them. "Any trouble and I'll be down in the sheds for a while. After that you're on your own."

"You in the barracks?"

"No. Got a hut just above Tŷ'n Garth. Prefer my own company of an evening."

Gwyn laughs. "Better alone than in a bunkhouse. Wouldn't mind though if I was sharing with a load of women."

Tal smiles – the lad looks as if he'd bounce off most of the women he's seen around the mine. "Anyone in particular in mind?"

"Oh, aye – that tall one with the dark, red hair that comes up 'ere sometimes with new horses, or running messages. Aye, she's a princess!"

"Cari – I know her." The boy whistles in admiration. Tal continues, "You have a good eye: she would fit just as well in a dainty parlour as a mule train!"

"She's above the likes of me, I know it. You could have her, though." He looks thoughtfully at Tal. "Well, I don't know. Yer 'andsome enough, but yer a bit short in the leg."

"Thank you!" Tal laughs. "If I ever want myself puffing up, I won't come to you! You all ready with these now?"

"We are." Gwyn gestures to a couple of younger boys. "I'll get these lot trained up too – be handy to have a few of us 'as knows how to handle the new 'arness."

"Good. I'll leave you to it, then."

Tal goes down towards the horse sheds. Though open on one side they give more shelter than the ore-dressing buildings give to the people. He's put one of the mares up to rest for a few days. He knows her foal must be near, though the teats don't give milk yet, but the old man looking after them doesn't seem to remember when she was covered. As he draws near he hears shouting and a horse's high scream. Hughes has got the young gelding in a corner, striking at him with a driving whip. The horse is sweated up, eyes rolling. As he shouts out, running towards them, he sees the animal spin around and throw its weight down into its hind quarters. "Get back you bloody fool." Hughes turns to look at him as the huge horse rises up. Tal thumps into him and rolls him away as the front hooves come down. The man is struggling to his feet as Tal pulls the whip from his fist and throws it behind him. "Get out of here!" The horse screams and rears again, coming down in the same place, coming down just where Hughes had stood only seconds before. The gelding squeals and contorts himself, crouching as if to kick out. Tal waits, taking care not to look at him. After a while he steps slowly towards the animal which pulls and twists on the rope. He plants himself just out of reach, arms out but still. He talks quietly, keeping his tone even. The animal snorts and stamps. He must stay with the horse until it calms – once it loses confidence in them there'll be no using him; no one'll be safe to work with him. Hughes sidles in behind him. Without fully turning his back on the horse Tal says quietly, "Get me water and a handful of feed, will you? Not much. Don't come in with it, just put it by the door to the stall."

Hughes leaves, his face mean and hard, though still grey with shock. Tal keeps talking, easing himself down to sit on a bale, just out of the horse's reach. Making himself small he shows the animal that he's no threat, but stays near enough to show he's not afraid of him either. Sailor. He's not worked with him yet. Though not as big as Benjamin, he's seen him under harness – a fine youngster with lots of promise, interested in everything.

Hughes returns, slides the bucket and hay net around the door to the stall and leaves, muttering to himself. Tal needs to calm the animal and then get the rope tied tighter, that way the horse has less chance of breaking free or rearing again. Taking the water bucket, he approaches the head. Sailor's watching but stands his ground. As he draws nearer with the water the horse shows his teeth, flattening his ears against his head. Tal keeps going, putting the bucket within reach, standing for a few moments. Then he goes back for the hay. Again, he approaches, giving Sailor no chance to kick out at him. This time the horse's ears are up, he's hungry. Tal stands just beyond his reach and offers him the food from his hand. The animal snorts and moves uneasily on his tether. Tal pulls the bunched hay, releasing a sweet scent. The horse chunters deep in its chest and takes a step towards him. It nudges the hay and Tal lets it fall to the ground, brushing it with his foot so the horse can get to it. Once he's prepared to eat and doesn't feel the need to depend on his hearing, Tal knows he's coming down from his panic. Still talking, he fetches more hay and moves briefly and calmly into the horse's space to put a handful in the wall bracket. Sailor lets him do it, stopping his chewing whilst the man is near, resuming as he leaves. Tal sits on the bale for a while as the horse eats. When the gelding's weight is on all four legs, tail swishing and his eyes on the hay, Tal moves again. Though Sailor doesn't stop chewing, he moves away from the man as he approaches. Tal takes the rope and reties it, gathering up the slack but not pulling on the animal. Enough for now. He goes to check on the mare.

"Who do you think you are, lording it around here. Bloody Gypo!" complains Hughes. The old man's already starting to get a bruise on his cheekbone where he hit the ground.

"I saved your damned head, man. Gelding was going to smash it like an egg."

"Needs bloody whipping, that does – sending for meat."

"What happened?"

"Went to double-barrel me! I bloody showed him!"

Tal looks at him. "You should know not to back an animal into a corner. Once there they've got nowhere to go but rise up or lash out. Keep your whip for the wagons and put him on a tighter rein next time." Hughes mumbles angrily under his breath. Tal continues. "I'll take him to work in the forestry for a while; he's not fit to work the winches – he'll hurt someone in that state."

"I'll bloody hurt 'im!"

Tal ignores it. "Where's this mare then?" Bonnie is lying in the straw as they approach but gets to her feet easily enough.

Hughes, his tone gruff and snapping, shouts at her, jabbing at her flank for her to move over from the wall.

"No need to do that. Why're you putting yourself between her and the wall? It's maybe a ton of animal you've got there; she could burst your ribs for you!" Tal puts his hands on her belly, plenty of life in the huge space inside, though still no milk. "Can you walk her around outside for me?"

Swearing under his breath, Hughes leads her from the stable. She is reluctant to leave her hay, snatching a mouthful as she goes. "Get on with you, bloody ugly mare!" Hughes kicks her hock hard with his boot.

"Right, that's enough. You wouldn't dare kick the gelding if he wasn't tied up! You're a bully, old man." Tal takes the rope off him. "Shouldn't be in this job."

"It's not your place to 'ire and fire! Who d'you think you are anyway, bloody stinking Gypo?" Tal looks at him. "Eh? What you looking at?"

Tal takes the mare out into the space in front of the sheds.

"What you doing? Eh, I'm talking to you!" Hughes shouts after him.

Chapter Five

BRANWEN IS JUST about to turn off the low road from Tre'r-ddôl and onto the short track home when she hears a shout. A light trap is coming fast, the long whip dancing and the pony hardly touching the ground. She stops. The man's voice again and she can see Henry Davies, dressed for town. He pulls hard on the pony's mouth, stopping exactly at her feet just before she'd had to spring up onto the wall to get out of their way.

"Branwen from the fulling mill. How perfect! Come aboard." She shakes her head. "How so? Your father won't even miss you. You will be delivered to the door in a fine pony trap. What could a father possibly object to?"

"No, I thank you. I have errands to run."

"Nothing that cannot wait for you to ride a smart trap into town on a fine day. I'll have you home in a couple of hours."

She looks around her, half disappointed that no one is there to see her climb aboard such a vehicle, even though it may have caused her trouble. Certainly, no one having seen her she has more options in terms of explaining to her father where she's been. She's ridden on a cart before, of course – but this is different. The small, padded seat seems to react to every bump, springing up. The wheels, thin and light, are almost without noise. Even the pony moves differently, his trot light, travelling as much upwards as forwards with every step. There is no jarring; the trap bobs along the ground. It moves so fast that the breeze pulls up her skirts and, though she's wearing stout clogs, she has no stockings. She bends over her lap, firmly holding down the hem and Davies, watching her out of the corner of his eye, smiles. They come through Ffwrnais, the village by the waterfall.

"They're building a smelting works here." He reins the pony in, just beyond the bridge. "Look at that power!" The waterfall thunders down, alive with spray. They have to raise their voices. "They'll smelt iron ore with charcoal. Ship it in from England."

"Why bring it here, to the old silver furnace?"

"Cheaper to bring iron ore here than ship trees or charcoal there. The water will power the bellows – an excellent project; exciting times indeed!" He looks at her, face rapt, lips open. "Yes, I'm a big part of all this, of course – lead, iron, all part of the same thing." He gestures wide with the long whip, startling the horse – he checks him, irritated, laughs to see Branwen, her hand clinging tight to the rail. "Plenty of charcoal – we can take all this down." This time he makes an expansive gesture with his left hand, leaving the whip quiet. "All this wood to use; new men, new ideas, new machines! They're even driving hammers with water now." Branwen looks at him. "Yes, men like me are much in demand. German engineers, Cornish miners, men from the south such as me, men of business, we'll transform this place. It's a disgrace how backward you are –"

"Me?"

"This whole area." He gestures expansively with his free hand again. "Loads lifted up from the mines with hand-worked windlasses!"

"My father has a wheel to drive the fulling hammers."

He looks at her. "At least he adds a bit of value to something. But why would he not fully process the wool here? Why have the whole cost of transporting the unfinished cloth, something heavy and low in value, to the English markets just for them to make money, to have someone else make a king's profit on finishing it, making it into a high value material that people will buy?"

"A good question. There are rules; guilds control the market and not everyone is allowed to work on every stage of the cloth. The Shrewsbury Drapers' Company –"

"Ha! Peasants, they are easily controlled." He looks sideways at her. "You speak quite well, though." He stirs the pony on. Not even a flick of the whip is needed as the animal turns back onto the road. They pass through the tiny village of Eglwysfach, the handsome Ynyshir Hall just visible. He points. "There; that's the house for me!" She laughs, he joins her. "I have big ideas – true. But the house is not so grand. Many a family has gone through draughtsman, solicitor to gentleman in a matter of only a few generations. I have made a good beginning at the project. I mean to make money here and use it to start up somewhere new."

"What is your father?"

"Was… smelting: copper and lead; but not just anyone – he was an engineer."

"Where were you living?"

"Margam, south Wales – near the coast. Like here, ships can bring in raw materials. The smelting works is near the coalfields – cheaper to move the ore and the fireclay to the coal than the other way around." The road curves sharply and suddenly the Dyfi estuary, with views to the long ridge of hills behind Aberdyfi, is in sight. Branwen exclaims with delight. Again, he reins the pony in. "You haven't seen this view before?"

"Yes. Well no, the cloud was always low, well, for some reason I haven't noticed it before. The colours! Hardly to be believed!"

"Would make a fine picture, no doubt."

"The noise does somewhat spoil it; and the barges –"

"And the bargemen with their filthy clothes and filthy tongues." He flicks at the pony with his whip.

"What are they loading?"

"Can't see from here – not ore. Bark perhaps? Come, we have better places to be, and I'll be late!"

"You have a meeting?"

"Indeed I do."

She waits a while, but he is not forthcoming. "With whom?" He tips the side of his nose and she laughs. "Apologies; I'm always asking questions; it is a fault."

"I don't think so."

"Well, then?"

"Well, Mistress – you shall not be told – except that two, no, *three* important people feel it worth their while to treat Henry Davies to a good dinner at the Black Lion!"

"How do you have business so far away from the mines and your lodgings? Why do you not meet them nearer home – in Aberystwyth, perhaps?"

"Your friends are right – you are a one for questions. You shall have an answer of sorts... I do not do business only for Lewis Morris and his masters. I will rise and I'll make money for myself, however I may."

"Mr Davies, you're a most interesting man!" The pony is

enjoying himself on the straight run into Glandyfi, his neck fully stretched and the three white socks lifted high in a trot. "A shame he doesn't have all four white feet!" she says.

"He would have cost me double to rent, if so!" They slow briefly to dodge the carters and mules turning on and off the road down to the barges.

"This seems a squalid place to live – always dark under the shadow of the hill."

"Who would care – there's money to be made. Look at those full barges, all on their way to the ships at the mouth of the estuary and then out to sea. Then, the world!" He looks at Branwen and her expression doesn't disappoint him.

"I've never really thought about where it all goes; just seen the mule trains leaving from the mine, not ever asked." She leans back to watch the busy river port out of sight. "Have you ever been to a far-off land?"

"Does England count?" He looks at her, she nods vigorously. "And there's talk of my skills being needed in Saxony and Württemberg." He looks at her, her face eager for more. "But of course, I cannot neglect my affairs here. Important plans are to be made." The Dyfi comes close to the road as they cross the low-lying land on the approach to the town, stinking tanneries lining the outskirts. The fine grey buildings are ancient, more like the buildings of Dolgellau, flavoured from north of the Dyfi rather than the towns in the south. "I'll drop you at the livery stables." Davies pulls abruptly off the road.

"Oh… but what shall I do?"

"Do? Does not a young woman always have some trinket to buy?"

"To get home?"

"I'll take you, after my meeting; I've said as much."

"Yes, thank you." She seems reluctant to move away, though he has already gathered up the reins.

"Well? Don't you have shopping to do?"

"No, but I can amuse myself with exploring the town. I have no funds, not expecting to be here today."

His smile is cynical as he reaches for his purse. "An excellent ploy to get money from an admirer. There." He tosses a coin at her. "Return within an hour and wait for me here." He moves down the lane towards the stables.

The accent of the town is peculiar, rich with both the tongues of north and south Wales. The clothes too are a mixture of several counties, some of the bonnets even seem to hail from England. She passes the Black Lion. It is hardly an inn at all, not a place she would expect so successful a man of business as Henry Davies to attend. Though the windows are small and it's dark inside, she sees a man grinning at her over his tankard and quickly steps backwards. She blunders into another man and bobs a hasty curtsey, "Beg your pardon, Sir!"

It's Cai and Thomas Powell, Nanteos. Cai touches his cap. "No harm done, except perhaps to the shine on my boots." The older man laughs.

Cai seems about to say something else but Thomas has already moved away. For a moment she stands there, a certain disturbance in the air where they'd stood. Their clean clothes, perhaps? The scent of them – perfume on Thomas Powell's wig? To have a wig scented with perfume! She pulls herself together and, putting her head down, treads carefully up the street. As ever there is much to see in this busy town. Two- and even three-storey houses faced with dressed stone line the main road, though she can see through the gaps that those in the meaner streets behind are low. She walks the length of the main street, stopping by the *maen gwyn*. It is not what she'd imagined but a lump of quartz; natural, not fashioned, the size of a small mounting block. Some said you touched it to bring fortune; others, that you should avoid it to escape the bad luck it would bring. A lump of stone could do nothing. Only words or actions could make a spell.

Drawn by a high squeal, Branwen turns down an alleyway. Behind the buildings of the wide main street are a warren of squat sheds, little workshops and hovels. The side door of a large barn is open. She peeps inside but can see nothing at first. There is the sound of a horse in distress, an angry, unfamiliar scream coming from the barn. She hears the noise again, then a loud whinny, the sound of hooves striking wood. She moves towards the sound – her feet seeming to make the decision for her. The entrance to the barn is in shadow and she can stay unseen until she is right inside. Now there are men shouting too and the voice of a different horse. Two men hold a mare steady on a short rein with pincers clamping her nose. Another holds her tail to one side, pulling on an iron hoop. Two others hold a handsome stallion between two long chains, standing either side of him. The mare is hobbled so that, as the stallion rears to cover her, he's in no danger. He squeals again, each time accompanied by the men's laughter. His neck snakes forward and he bites the mare on the back of her neck, his teeth and rolling eyes striking white in the gloom. The stallion's penis is an object of much interest and comment. He whinnies long and loud, ending with the same piercing squeal. A bystander shouts, "Make sure you swab that dirty mare down properly; we don't want 'im catching anything." A lichen-haired man lunges at the mare with a rag and they bring the stallion forward again; once more he rears up, comes down on the mare and she screams again as he bites into the back of her neck. Branwen backs away, standing for a moment back on the lane.

"A strange entertainment for a fresh maiden such as yourself!"

She spins around. A tall, lean man, expensively dressed, makes an exaggerated bow to her. She blusters something. He puts his hat back on and offers his arm. His face is like polished brass. She shakes her head and makes to go.

"Woa, woa, little filly." His expensive cane blocks her path. "Perhaps you need an explanation for what you've just seen, from a man of the world; a JP, no less?" As he speaks he pulls his lips tight, as though hiding bad teeth.

"Indeed, I need no explanation, Sir, I thank you."

Cane still outstretched, he pulls a full purse from his breeches. "I'm sure after such a dramatic 'interlude' you must be in need of some refreshment. I see there's a pleasing hostelry right there." He turns to point and she slips past him.

"I thank you again, Sir, but I need no refreshment, neither do I need an explanation. I have a donkey which I bred myself."

He laughs, a high rhythmic sound that somehow matches his elaborate clothes. "A donkey breeder! Well, well, what a woman of business, to be sure."

With a brief bob of a curtsey she slips away. Her guts jump as she finds herself back on the busy main street.

"A guinea for your thoughts." The man is tall and stands with his back to the sun. Her hat has only a small brim so she has to shield her eyes to see him.

"Do I know you, Sir?"

"I wish I could say you do! Will you take a drink of ale with me and make it so?"

Though she shakes her head, she can't help a smile betraying her. Certainly, a smooth way he has! He is very handsome, dressed well, his complexion healthy. "I'm busy, Sir, and do not drink ale with those I don't know."

"You give a clear answer and I understand your meaning. In that case, would you walk a little way with me in the sunshine, in full view of the passers-by?"

"I will do."

They walk back on the other side of the wide street. Self-conscious, she finds it hard to move in a natural way and takes small steps to try and conceal her clogs beneath her skirts. "Parliament house and the Prince of Wales," he says, stopping suddenly and pointing.

"Parliament!"

"Well, a sort of parliament; a Welsh parliament."

"Yes, I have heard something. A tragic end I think?"

"Nothing has ended." He smiles at her and bows. "I think we must part company; people will see us together and it may become awkward... for you perhaps."

"No one knows me here."

"Still, you clearly value a good name and have the fine wits to keep it. I'll take leave of you and find another... friend." He disappears through the door of a nearby tavern.

What is it about her that draws strangers? Or are the men of Machynlleth all bold in this way? Her laugh of surprise comes loud and she covers her mouth as she walks towards the parliament house. It seems a sad, rundown place though the idea of a prince sitting proudly and making laws there instead of in London is a fine image, a good tale to tell around a fire on a winter's eve. She adjusts her clothes and hat. Surely it must be time to go back? She can't afford to miss Davies, not that, as a gentleman, he would go without her of course.

The pony is already tacked up when she gets back and he has a parcel in his hand which he gives to her without speaking. "To keep safe for you on the journey? Is it breakable, Sir?"

"You may open it now, if you like."

"For me!" He nods and climbs aboard the trap, a boy removing the pony's nosebag. He reaches over and helps her up. She hardly has time to settle herself before he starts off and she has to cling to the rail to steady herself. The package is not tied, but whatever is in there is rolled in the canvas cloth. She unravels it; he glances at her as he steers the pony around the traffic. "Oh!"

"You like them?"

"I can't accept them!"

"Try them on."

"But I cannot accept them." She hurriedly folds the material around the shoes, holding the parcel towards him.

"Nonsense. I cannot have my passenger wearing rough clogs." Self-consciously she tugs her skirt down. "Try them now, if you please – it would give me pleasure. Perhaps you don't like them?"

"No indeed! They are better than any I've seen, Sir –"

He grabs at the shoes in her lap. "Well, I can't have them insulted; I'll take them back, give them to a more grateful maid."

She snatches them up – perhaps as much to stop him scrambling around in her lap as to own them. "Forgive me. I meant no offence."

His eyes back on the road he says, flatly. "If you're not going to give them back to their owner, you better put them on." Biting her lip in concentration, she kicks off her clogs and rubs at her feet. "You will not clean them like that! Just put the shoes on, madam – you try my patience. If you don't get on with it, I'll be forced to stop the trap and fit them to your dirty feet myself!"

She laughs and carefully eases her feet into the quality leather. The buckles are no longer shiny, but the slight heels are as new. "Well, your verdict, if you please?"

"Wonderful!"

"Excellent. A truly profitable afternoon!" She goes to take them off, smoothing out the wrapping material on the seat between them, ready to cover them up again. "Do not!" He snatches the cloth from her. "Do not even think of inflicting those wooden boots on us again. In fact –" He makes a motion to throw her clogs out of the trap. She exclaims and tries to reach them but he holds them high and she's not sure enough of her balance to let go of the rail. "I cannot bear the monstrous things in this gig any longer! Well?" He looks at her, grinning. "One, two –"

"If you insist, Sir!"

"I do." He laughs and throws the clogs into the bottom of the trap. On the journey back he pretends to watch the road, a smile always threatening to break out as he sees Branwen admiring herself in her new shoes. "It is fortunate that you're not the driver."

She looks alarmed. "I? Drive? No, Sir – I've not learned it!"

"You've hardly looked up at the 'fine hills' you so admired this morning. All is your dainty feet, pretty ankles, and, quite frankly, grubby shins."

"Oh!"

"Not that I mind them in the least." He is grinning broadly now as he looks straight ahead.

She is still red-faced when she says, "You tease me, Sir. I was wrong to accept so expensive a gift from you."

He pulls up at the same spot he found her. She gets down, leaving the left shoe, dislodged by the step, hanging off her toes. "They are too big I fear!"

"No indeed!"

"Indeed they are." His voice has a note of accusation.

"No, well, nothing that a handful of straw in the toe won't mend." She gathers her clogs and the packing material and straightens up. "You are angry, Sir."

"Not I."

She shrugs. "What may I do? I cannot grow larger feet?"

He smiles reluctantly. "I seldom err when I judge a woman's size. Merely that. I do not enjoy being wrong." He tips his hat, flicks the whip and leaves. She watches the trap out of sight, but he doesn't turn around.

It is almost night as she finally approaches the mill, the moon casting everything in a smoky light. Solid objects like the cart loom larger, but the branches of trees, moving in the slight breeze, are like phantoms. She has been away so much longer than the two hours she agreed! The light is on full in the windows of the mill cottage and, as she approaches, she can hear men's voices. She breathes more easily. Her father will be drinking, will have lost track of time and maybe not even have missed her. She moves quickly to the stable. If she does her duties by the animals she can wander in and her father, with luck and plenty of spirits, will think she's just popped out.

She settles the donkey and the calves and is on her way across the yard to check the hens when she is stopped by a sight that makes her spine freeze. Out from under the feed shed comes a column of rats. In line and silent, only the slight sound of their claws on the stone cobbles betrays them. They do not move like any rats she's seen before; there is nothing random about their passage across the yard. They seem liquid, backs curled, arched, their heads fixed straight ahead and led by one that, in this strange moon night, looks white. They pass her, about eight feet away, their tails held off the floor, moving down towards the river.

Chapter Six

THOMAS POWELL'S LETTER from London has clearly been rushed – he writes almost as he speaks. This time it is all 'The Attorney General is against us; the dispute now filed in the Court of Exchequer!' ... 'That wretched Lewis Morris and his prospecting – he's bribing the cottagers and tenants to testify against us! Even squatters on the wastes grow bold, coming on to my land and digging open rakes everywhere.' He drags the embarrassment of the election defeat and the terrible financial cost up yet again. 'Even now I cannot seem to escape from the ignominy of that overturned result. Tregaron annulled! Of course, Tregaron is a borough; how could they disqualify me!'

Yet, surely better to try again? How could he be so sensitive as to refuse to stand again – this time most assuredly he would have prevailed against the wretched Pryses to be MP of Cardiganshire once more? What did her grandfather always say? Fear of failure is the truest path to the very heart of failure itself. He'd been MP and Mayor of London in his time and had taught her well the value of perseverance.

She sits back in the chair and studies her room. Small. A small estate in Cardiganshire. A fine, new house, granted (oh, beautiful project!), but an empty nursery. Compared to her sister, The Duchess of Atholl, nothing. Yes, and what of it, Mary? What of it? You were the one with 'a face and neck like a warming pan', so, what did you expect? She pulls her mind back from running along those ruts through a muddy field of... is it envy? Not quite. Regret that she'd put herself here, in the 'wild west' as some called it? No. There had been so few other offers and she was not to know that the marriage would not bear fruit. Oh, but it has! She smiles ironically; real fruit she has and will have in abundance from her gardens and glasshouses. But first she must kill Thomas' tree. She puts the letter back in its envelope, marked as always with the Machynlleth stamp, though how such an austere town on the edge of north Wales with, in effect, only one main street (however wide), could be more important to the addressing of letters than the newly-thriving Aberystwyth is beyond her. She turns away from her writing desk, takes her cloak and goes outside.

The men are already assembled and clearly in good spirits, though falling quiet as she approaches. They remove their caps, though she notices, not very far. "All ready?" she asks Jenkins. He mumbles, studying a scar on the top of his hand. "Well then, let it begin." Jenkins only nods. She finds herself speaking again. "Please take care not to damage the new stone carving at the corner of the house." Jenkins looks quickly at her. "I'm sure that you will take every care, of course; you are most careful in everything you do." She catches a smirk pass between a couple of men at the back of the group but it is unlikely to be anything she has said; they are most likely Welsh speakers who would not have understood her.

One of the men has picked up his axe and Jenkins puts his cap back on. At last he speaks. "The Master –"

"What of him?" She answers sharply, then waits. He does not finish the sentence. "As you know I'm sure, my husband is in London. His wishes are clear however." She looks boldly around the circle but there is no overt challenge. "Right, well, I'll leave you to your work." As she gestures to the oak, seven pairs of eyes follow her arm. There is wind in the tree and it moves, waves passing through it. She is suddenly aware of the whispering in the leaves.

The foreman, a man surely in his fifties, though slim as a youth, climbs back onto the masonry giving orders. "Can't keep an eye on the men if you can't get up to the work," he'd said in the beginning when she'd asked him his age, concerned for his safety. But the real brains on site seems to be a big, slow-talking man. His pale blue eyes and regular features would have made a fine squire of him, yet he seems determined to avoid any title. It was he, however, more than the foreman who raised questions for the architect.

"He's not put it on the plans. See there," he'd said to her, never touching the paper with his bare, black fingers but always with the end of some twig. "The tree should have been marked, right from the beginning if it was to be kept on." He'd looked up, bending forward slightly to scan the front wall. "Moving the wall twenty paces wouldn't have been a problem if we'd known the tree wanted keeping." He'd straightened up, looked directly at her, then turned away.

"You're not from these parts?" she'd asked him. A slow smile, but no answer. "Neither am I – of course; obvious I'm sure to anyone." He'd nodded and, still looking into the distance, moved his hammer from hand to hand. It was clear their tête-à-tête had come to an end. It was rare for men to talk to her properly, especially men of his class. Today, however, he hangs back, standing with a relaxed stillness at the edge of the group until the foreman's call, when he swings up to where his wall has reached the first floor.

There is a new team drafted in to fell the oak, men she doesn't recognise. Day after day they work on the tree, taking it out of the sky piece by piece as, next to it, the wall slowly takes its place. As she takes her walk she sees figures with hooks and saws slung from their belts standing high in the tree. She calls Jenkins to her again.

"It's perfectly safe, Mistress Powell. They use ropes these days, you know. Everything is safety now."

She watches the men managing every branch down. Before each one falls, they call to the team on the ground who guide it with ropes, standing back out of the way at the call of *"Perygl!"* Another group works on the large branches as they fall to the ground, taking off the thinner growth from the sides. Boys drag away the small pieces to a great burn pile in the meadow. She is unable to settle properly until it is finished, though on the third day she sits down at her desk to inform Thomas of what she's done, the light tone and garnish of good news (a small vein of silver has been found along the new lead seam and there may even be more to be had – who's to know?) a careful sweetener. When he returns, seeing the job on the tree done to such satisfaction, he will surely thank her.

A hole appears in the sky where the oak had been. What fanciful nonsense to see the sap as tears, the creak and groan of the mutilated tree as they work on it with the ropes, saws and axes, as any manner of complaint!

But at night she is aware of the truncated figure, naked in the dark – the topmost branches and much of the side growth gone now. The blunt, sawn branches are like arms without their hands. *Titus Andronicus* – Shakespeare again; the man has a relevant reference for every situation! That particular play had not been recommended reading for her of course, yet she had made it a point to inform herself, hiding a small copy from her father's library within another volume. It had not been difficult to do as it was not one of his longer works. She opens her eyes, sits up in bed and draws the candle towards her. All over the estate trees were being felled – had been felled these last ten years and more for his handsome staircase, the panelling, even the humble floorboards. Why then should this one specimen have captured her imagination in such a way? The wood, once dried, will surely come in useful and maybe some of the trunk could even have the honour of being the Yule log. It was a worthy venture; had been a fair contest: horses heaving on the ropes, a team of men straining and struggling to bring it out of the sky. The rhythm and voices of axes, the low and the higher pitches of the hard men and boys seem to invade even her sleep and the stump, raw and bald, was awful to her; seeming to bleed, to ooze, black like the back of an open mouth screaming.

In the morning she is up early and out to face the world. The chains are ready for the trunk to be dragged away to the saw pit and she is standing again by the stump when she becomes aware of the man with blue eyes beside her.

"What is that stain on the stump?" She points with her gloved hand.

He shakes his head. "Some idiot has nailed it; ruined it. The mark goes all the way through; quite spoiled some of the wood for planking I reckon." His native English is good; she remarks on it and he smiles his faint smile, tips his hat and moves away. Looking at the spoiled wood she is angry at the lack of respect shown this tree. Someone had taken a hammer and driven in a nail – for what? A fence, a poster, to nail the corpse of some pest or another as a warning?

Fires for the tree burn all day and night and afterwards a sweet, unpleasant smell hangs over the west of the house as she has the sawdust spread where her paths are to go through the new pleasure gardens. But, apart from the scars in the grass and the injured stump, all is finished, as she'd planned, in a matter of weeks and before Thomas' return. As she sits at her desk to order specimen trees for the woodland walk, she feels vaguely uneasy; it seems perverse to pay so much, to take such delight in the planting of some spindly sapling after she's spent so much effort on cutting down the most majestic of trees. She is somehow a fop, rather like the squire who mercilessly whips his hounds but hand-feeds a lap dog in his carriage.

Chapter Seven

B RANWEN IS TALKING to her donkey as she picks her way up the damaged road.

"The mule trains are ruining it; they should come down from the mines and mend it, put down more stones and rake out the ruts. Fiends they are."

The hedges are sickly with hawthorn blossom, the air full of the dust of flowers. The river is nothing but a stream running through bog here. She crosses it easily, using her special technique – only one foot down at a time, springing from tussock to tussock and taking off as soon as she lands. Cari says she's half-goat and it's almost true – she hardly ever gets her feet wet. She stops for Siwan to drink, at first a loud slurping but soon just snuffling her nose in it, playing with it. There is a dull sound, so different from the roar of the falls, that thunder of water near the weir, though the stream is still moving, even here, hidden somewhere under the marsh plants. 'Water has many different voices,' her father says. She finds the path again. Up ahead is an old shepherd's hut – good stone, but gone part to ruin for as long as she can remember. It seems that someone has been repairing the roof and the door is open for the first time. She calls out; no one answers and there are no fowls scratching around. There is no garden, the rough grass around the dwelling filled with cuckoo flowers, riddled with plantain and yellow rattle. She looks around her;

no sign of anyone and she can't resist drawing nearer and peeping inside. It is lit from both a window high up and a front window – surely someone with money to spend, but why here on the high road from Ffrwrnais to Tre'r-ddôl? Maybe someone has got hold of the frames and glass from another building?

Almost everything inside is handmade from wood except for a big brass dish, intricately worked in an unfamiliar pattern, that is propped up against the wall opposite the window. Light blazes from it. The floor is the usual beaten mud, with a ladder leading up to a sleeping platform. It's a good building, the wood of the first storey resting on a stone shelf jutting from the wall. There is no chimney, and no fireplace – but then it isn't cold now and easy enough to cook outside. She walks carefully around the building and, sure enough, there is the fire, the iron triangle holding a cooking pot. She goes nearer and looks inside – nothing much left in there but snail shells across the grass! She laughs. Snails! Who would eat these, a poor feast indeed? With that strange feeling you get of being watched when you're snooping yourself, she straightens up, glancing quickly around her. Nobody. She reties her shawl, gathers up the grazing donkey and goes back to the track.

The path has started to drop again and she stops to check on the load and for one more view across the estuary. Though she is roughly at the same height as she was before, she has come about a mile over the hill and the angle is different. She can see open sea beyond the sand dunes and just make out some of the buildings in the port of Aberdyfi, a dirty grey strip in the distance between the hill behind the town and the coast. She takes a drink from her bag.

Across the shallow valley in a field below a man is working his dog on the sheep. The animal moves in hoops and arcs, like the flourishes of a skilled pen. "If his feet were dipped in ink there would be circles." She has spoken aloud again, the donkey's jaws still for a moment as it listens to her. "Sorry, Siwan, carry on," she says. The sheep below are all smooth and flowing, like froth moving on the river. One separates out, the dog's curve suddenly ending as it sheers off, fast in a straight line, in pursuit. 'A wizard, acting out his magic,' she says, but only to herself this time.

The man has his back to her so she can relax – he is concentrating so hard on the animals he won't turn around to see her on the hillside above. He's wearing no shirt – possibly the shape in the long grass at his feet is a pile of clothes. His whole back is brown, the muscles moving as he lifts his right arm to gesture with the stick, his left hand to his mouth in a whistle. The dog hurtles back at the heels of a terrified ewe, her woolly back wide and flat as a table, as she bolts towards the rest of the flock. She sees him slam his staff into the ground, his body curving in an arc as he leans out from it, making himself wider. The eight-or-so ewes are together now in a hollow under the trees by the stream, the dog, heron-still, crouching before them. The man bends to pick something white off the ground, straightens up and, giving the animals plenty of space, crosses to the gate. Once it's open wide, he gives another few high whistles and the dog moves again, low, almost a crawl, towards the sheep. They stir and shift away from him but there's a natural bank that channels them towards the gate. One leaps up onto it but immediately takes fright, throwing herself back down again, almost knocking another over. The dog weaves behind the stragglers' heels – down in the channel, then up for a moment onto the bank. As the leaders come to flat ground they fan out, but now the dog, though quite far behind them, is out in the open too and, seeing the gap in the hedge, the sheep hurtle towards it, their heavy wool rolling and wobbling, their stick legs stiff. Another whistle and the dog stops. The man closes the gate, calls his dog and they pass out of sight. For a few moments she continues to watch the sheep. It doesn't take them long to settle and spread out, heads down to the fresh pasture. What a thing to see!

As she comes down the sunken lane amongst the trees someone is heading towards her. A man, young from his gait, with a lean dog at heel. A stranger? She pulls her hat down further, the brim serving to shade her face a little. Siwan plods on regardless, the panniers wobbling from side to side as she picks her way down between the stones. Branwen looks out for the passing place, a break in the banked-up wall and waits. Leaning around the edge she can see the stranger is speeding up to stop her having to wait too long; good manners at least. He draws near and she takes a strong hold on her stick but, even though he has a dog, the donkey still doesn't seem concerned. He stops as he passes and touches his cap to her.

"Obliged."

She smiles. The dog has attractive colouring – the spotted legs giving it a refined look. "A handsome animal."

"He is." He nods at Siwan. "And yours."

"There's blue in your dog? An unusual colour. What's his name?"

He grins. "Llew. He's a strange one. Doesn't seem to mind you, though."

For a moment they stand; she keeps her gaze just beyond

his shoulder, though he's looking openly at her. "Are you new to these parts?" she asks.

He laughs. "Been passing through all my life, but new to settle, yes. Yourself?"

"No! I was born here." She makes a vague gesture to the hill behind her. "My father has the Pandy at Ffwrnais." She has told him too much – bold and stupid that she is.

Again he laughs, touches his cap. "Honoured to meet the daughter of the fulling mill, who was born and bred and lives here still, going with her well-fed donkey on some adventure surely!"

She looks hard at him but he's trying to keep from laughing. "I'm going with spare wool to the hatters in Tre'r-ddôl." Again! Why is she spewing out her business to him in this way! His shirt is open to the waist and it is hard for her not to look at him, not to follow the matted track down from his chest, across his belly and into his trousers. If he was anything like a gentleman, he would have covered himself. "I must go. Siwan's getting restless," she says, though the donkey is standing patiently, resting her weight on three legs.

"Of course." Glancing at the contented animal he grins and moves up the track a way so she can come out of the passing place. "A pleasure to meet you both." This time he lifts his hat. His hair is very dark and curly, but they are big, not tight, curls. That explains the large dark eyes and severe cheekbones.

"What is your work?" she blurts.

He seems amused. "Horses mostly; sometimes sheep – as you can see." He puts his hand to his dog's head.

"Yes, I know, I saw you... happened to see you as I was

coming down. You are like a wizard with his familiar – I have never seen it before, using a dog like that to drive sheep!"

"I thought it. In fact there are two holes burned in my back underneath this shirt where green eyes singed me, judging me a very poor shepherd I expect."

"No indeed – that is far from the truth!" But he is teasing again and her hot cheeks turn to laughing with him. "You are good at making people say what they shouldn't." He looks at her. Someone needs to make a move. She tosses her stick with a flourish into her left hand and closes her fingers around the donkey's head collar.

"Taliesin Wood!" he shouts to her back as she moves away.

She carries on for a moment, then stops, turns around and shouts back. "Branwen. Branwen Rhys."

He cradles his hat in his hands, acting like her shouted words were a thrown apple he has caught in it. She turns quickly before he sees her laughing and makes her way downhill, her feet light as down.

Chapter Eight

From her window Mary watches Edward and Thomas in conversation, walking together in front of the house. At least Thomas has forgiven her for the tree, though his temper hasn't been right since he came back from London. Without his wig, his hair is tight-cropped and glossy, and there is still some dark in it. He has a taut head and neck, broad and muscular. A most unlikely squire he looks with his slightly bandy legs, his knees bending outwards over his boots when he walks. She smiles as she watches the two together. What is the saying? Yes, 'As close as two Gypsies on a horse!' What an easy way there is about him when he is with Edward! The two walk in step; Thomas, his legs shorter, taking long strides and looking rather comical. Edward, gesticulating, his face alight with interest; Thomas head down, stooping, glancing quickly up at the younger man, nodding, looking down again, hands behind his back. She could write the script for them, she's sure. It would have plenty of Thomas' customary 'God alive' and 'God's teeth' and be dominated by galena carriage costs and market prices – perhaps, too, from watching Edward's expressive hands in action, one of his beloved waterwheels features in the conversation today.

She waits for her husband in the hallway. Thomas strains to kick off his riding boots, red in the face with effort. "Good

God alive, get me some new ones, these cut off the circulation completely!"

"A letter has come from Mabws Hall, Thomas. Come through when your circulation is returned; I've called for refreshments." She goes on ahead of him.

Once settled in the drawing room, he looks up from his letter. "I need to talk to young James Lloyd about the election. He's offered to come here, but I would relish a chance to see Mabws. All are speaking about the place. I wondered would you come with me, Mary? It's been a long time since we called on anyone together."

"It's a long trip, I think, to go as far as Mabws Hall and back in a day."

"Do I see a twinkle in your eye, wife? Yes, a stay at a good inn maybe is in order, if one is to be found, or perhaps we'll be their guests." She kisses him on his bare head, the hair still thick. "Ha, it doesn't take much to wring a kiss from you." He squeezes her hand.

"It never did, Thomas!"

"And maybe there will be more of the same if I visit you tonight for help… You saw I cannot cast off my riding boots unaided. I'm sure I have the same trouble undoing my breeches these days – I need almost to wear spectacles to do so!"

She laughs. "You know my strengths so well! I was ever adept at that job."

*

That night, Mary finds herself strangely nervous as she sits before her mirror. 'Thank goodness for the merciful candlelight, and the fact that Thomas is so long-sighted now,' she catches herself thinking, a faint smile lifting her cheeks, plumping them nicely. There is still some sort of glow coming off her reflection when she looks from certain angles and her skin, always having been on the oily side, is not so much subject to wrinkles as that of some women. She has had her maid Elin dress her hair; rub a little scented cream into the back of her neck and down between her shoulder blades – one of Thomas' favourite haunts in times past. But she is careful not to seem to try too hard. A desperate woman of a certain age is not endearing, she knows, and too much perceived effort by her might even make Thomas nervous himself! She moves her head from side to side, the shadows catching her face like clouds moving over a sunlit field. She has avoided the excess weight so many of her contemporaries carry, though her lean cheeks now seem more hollow than sculpted. 'I will lose my nerve if I sit here longer!' she tells herself firmly.

She uses the commode one more time, careful to wipe with the toilet water, and gets into bed. She will be reading something light when he comes in, pretend to be engrossed, let him seduce her in his own time. She finds a notice for a meeting inside the catalogue. The date has long passed but she remembers speaking to one of the organisers and giving a small donation when she was last in London. The Magdalen House; she had meant to follow it up and take out a subscription. She had even thought of approaching the trustees in order to help in a more active role, but the building of Nanteos had taken over and she found herself in the capital less and less. Resolved to follow up on the fate of the project the following day, she puts the information to one side. Where is Thomas?

She slips from under the bedclothes and opens her door a little way. Her hair is down and she is anxious not to be seen by either Edward or the servants as she scans the corridor. No sign of Thomas. His door is firmly closed, though there is perhaps light behind it still. What to do?

It seems a waste – of the bathing, the brushing, the scent – and more than that, her own nervous excitement. She is aware of her body tonight in a way that is unusual now: the feel of the deep rug through her toes, the pleasant sting after the cleansing between her legs. 'Be brave, Mary; be resolute!' Though she does not dare face the possible rejection in presenting herself, all in readiness outside his door, she finds the courage to ring for Elin. As she waits for the girl to appear, she scribbles a note. 'Dearest Thomas; a fine bottle of Burgundy is warming by the fire and I find myself at your convenience. Do join me, if you are disposed to do so.' There. Done.

A quick tap and Elin is in the room, her dress rather crumpled around the bodice and her face one big question. Mary doesn't explain but gives her the note and instructions. "Knock briskly and be sure to give it into his hand with the message 'My mistress sends her compliments'. Don't wait for an answer." As Elin turns to go she sees that the dress isn't fastened properly, surely explaining its dishevelled appearance from the front.

Elin reappears almost immediately. "The Master was awake, Mistress, and asks me to tell you that he will be along directly." She looks at her feet as she relays the message and Mary smiles wryly, remembering only too well how comical the affections of older people seem to the young.

"Thank you, Elin. I will not disturb you again tonight."

Alone again, she puts herself back in the bed, arranging her still mostly brown hair across the pillow. Though she feels she needs another trip to the commode, she doesn't have the patience to go through the ritual with the scented water again. Anyway, there may not be time.

Thomas arrives almost immediately. He has clearly actually been in bed as his gown is imperfectly covering his crumpled nightshirt. She will not mention that she knows he has forgotten their arrangement. Instead she turns the coverlet down a little way and says, "I'm sorry not to send for you earlier; I found I had some pressing correspondence to attend to. Shall you bring the wine to bed with you, husband?" Her voice is light and soft.

Afterwards, they sit up for a while finishing the wine. "You know, Mary, I always wonder, after you've received me into your bed, why I am not here every night that I'm at home!"

"Yes, I understand that sentiment. But for me, the reality of taking off my clothes and being uncomfortable in a cold bed suffocates any ardour I imagine I might have!"

"Exactly so! The practicalities sometimes seem insurmountable these days – something I would never have considered in my youth. And the prospect of rising and going to my own chill cot after the 'event' – quite puts me off before I've even started!"

"Yet you used not to go."

"You used not to make me."

"Ah… because you used not to snore so!"

"And if I did – you didn't mind."

"True." She curls into him, burying her nose in his hair and he holds her hand, playing with her fingers. Suddenly she winces and pulls her hand away. "Sorry, Thomas, it's painful."

He rolls over to face her. "My thumb. I trapped it and now there's a lump there. It seems to dislocate."

"I wondered at you not playing much any more. I thought perhaps there was something wrong with the action of the new instrument?'"

She shakes her head. "All my fingers ache, ache at the joints now. I'm sure all will be well soon."

"This climate! The water gets into everything, even the bone itself." He takes her hand. "You have a queen's fingers."

"And a milkmaid's rear!" They laugh.

"Did I really say that to you?"

"You know it." She pushes back a lock of hair from his forehead. "I liked it," she says. Though she wishes very much to empty her bladder she doesn't move, grateful to preserve this moment in time as Thomas' breaths lengthen. As he starts snoring, she shifts her thigh ever so slightly where his leg has gone heavy and weighs on her. She grits her teeth against the pins and needles as her circulation returns, an almost delicious torture which she suffers in silence, squeezing her fists tight. She falls asleep facing the long window, watching the strip of sky visible between the drapes as it turns to the deep blue of a summer night that never becomes completely dark.

★

They rise early the following morning and are in the coach before the pink has gone from the sky. It is a rare chance for them to be together. After a pleasant drive they arrive at the village of Llanrhystud. Mary holds Thomas' hand with a light touch, his warmth causing the quiet smile on her face. "What a busy settlement this is, Thomas!"

To their left a grain mill draws from the river and smoke drifts in from the coast, hanging in the air. "At least it masks the stench of that stuff!" Thomas' hand indicates the piled carts of seaweed on the roadside, a team of men just beginning to work on it with their pitchforks, spreading it on the broad, flat fields. "The Lloyds own all this." His gesture takes in the village and the land from the invisible shore to the edge of the mysterious mounds beyond.

"What are those strange hills over there, Thomas – do you know? Some sort of ancient castle ruins? Roman remains, perhaps?"

He shakes his head. "You're the historian, Mary! Let you scour maps and archives for the answer."

"A most diverting project that would be, certainly. Perhaps the ancient Britons had some sort of homestead there? It would be most interesting to explore with a trowel at some point –"

"When the walled gardens are complete; the pleasure garden planted; Edward's wretched pond dug to feed his wheel and hammers, the court case settled in our favour and the blasted election paid for –"

"And won."

"Of course – and won. Then, dear Mary, there will be money enough for a hundred spades, let alone trowels and I'm sure James Lloyd of Mabws will be persuaded to let you dig away to your heart's content under the hillocks there. Maybe there'll be treasure, one of those beaten sheets of precious metal they find –"

"Or a torque." He raises his eyebrow and she laughs. "A metal armband, worn they think on the muscle of the upper arm. What a –"

"God's teeth, that smoke smells appalling; it's worse that
the seaweed! Lime roasting I would bet. I hope he has had
the sense to build his hall well away from the path of this
stench!"

They turn off the main road, crossing the river and passing
a patch of grass on which two neat women, each wearing
her pauper's badge, are spinning. They look into the passing
carriage and Mary waves.

"What a prosperous, well-governed little village this is,
Thomas," she says. "They are even putting in a new bridge!"

Having left the village behind, the narrow valley winds
on and on, following the shallow River Wyre up to Mabws
Hall.

"This is nothing but a stream, Thomas – no bigger than
the Paith!"

"Yet so much further from the coast road. Most
inconvenient one would have thought, and the road is low
and surely subject to flooding."

As they turn off the track along the tree-lined drive, Mary
hastily secures her gloves and bonnet. "Their drive is very
short – I had not realised it would be so short!"

"There is not much of an avenue. Perhaps fifteen trees are
possible – at most."

The coach turns in a wide arc and they pull up below a
steep bank. Only the service buildings can be seen properly;
the side of the house, though shallow in depth, rearing up
above them. Mary looks at Thomas and grimaces. "But where
is the vista?" This is no Nanteos, where the fine, wide drive
twists and turns; where one passes a lake and, suddenly, the
house appears – ochre-fronted, washed in sunshine with a
wide, gentle valley in front.

"Perhaps this is not the main approach?"

"I would hope not!"

Thomas gets out to consult the driver, returns. "Ah, it's as we thought. The hill being too steep for us to approach from this direction, we've come around the side, by the trade entrance if you like. But the view of the house is very fine as one approaches from Tregaron, for example. So he says."

"I dare say you're right. Let us go and see for ourselves."

Mary brushes down her skirt and secures her gloves. "You did say that he was no relation of the, I have to say it, rather unsavoury, *Herbert* Lloyd, didn't you? What a nose that man has – like the mountain Vesuvius!"

"'And teeth like a forest of old oak' was how you described him once, I believe. Yes?"

"Yes – they're no relation?"

He laughs. "Yes, no relation. As far as I know. Sir Herbert's a most useful contact, however, whatever you think of him!"

"His habits and character are even more unpleasant than his aspect and he relishes the role of Justice far too much, I hear. Come, let's think of something else."

They follow the road up a slight incline and suddenly there is Mabws, its blue stones noble in the sunshine. The carriage pulls up. There is still no sign of their hosts. The house is on a plateau around which a semicircle of hills rises up. It is neat and somehow austere.

"It reminds one of the Edinburgh buildings, Mary," Thomas says quietly. They continue towards the main door and then there are James Lloyd and Anna Maria at the corner of the house, walking towards them. There is no formality. Where are their servants? Where is the butler?

They are holding hands. Mary squeezes Thomas' arm and he responds, whispering in her ear, though his smiling face remains to the front. "Not married long, I believe!"

"So kind of you to visit us here, we are honoured to have you." James proffers his hand as Anna Maria steps forward to kiss Mary. She is as tall as the older woman, a dark-haired, dark-eyed young woman with a pleasant smile. She takes Mary's arm as the two men walk around the house to the front entrance. Mary stops them, looking up at the swallows, martins and swifts tearing up the sky.

"Delicious, truly; it is a veritable delight!"

"Indeed it is."

"What a lovely, sunny plateau; an island, with your lovely parkland around you!"

"Yes. It is rather like being on stage; on a Grecian stage perhaps."

Mary nods. So, Anna Maria is a well-educated young woman as well as attractive. "An amphitheatre. Yes indeed. The flat plain on which the house stands and the way the gentle hills rise around it on three sides."

Anna Maria's expression is animated as she turns to face her. "Yes, oh yes, an amphitheatre indeed – I will use that comparison again, if you have no objection, of course."

"Of course not. May I?" Mary gestures to the edge of the plateau.

"Please."

They walk to look at the drive from above. "A delightful valley – a dell really. Why, you could even create a grotto! It would be ideal for terracing. You could have your own 'hanging gardens'; and almost due south. Good heavens, with some thought and care, you could even think to model the whole side of the valley on a Tuscan garden. Is there a stream to feed it?"

"Well, yes."

"Fountains! How wonderful –"

"Yes, what an idea. I'll speak to James!"

There is a shout from behind them – James waving and coming towards them across the gravel. There is no sign of Thomas. He joins them as they survey the scene. Anna Maria rushes to tell him of Mary's suggestions.

"Your reputation as a garden designer is well founded, I see." Though he is smiling, his tone is thin.

"Oh, just a pleasing hobby of mine… the wonders of gardening in foreign climes; the wonderful possibilities when one can rely on sunshine!" She looks at James but he doesn't reply. "They are fortunate of course in Italy to have both sunshine and rain, though I hear in Spain they manage beautifully with very little precipitation. I have not been lucky enough to travel as far as Spain. Have you had the chance?"

"No. In fact I do not know Italy either. I have not yet travelled abroad. My father lacked the funds, though a tour was discussed before our marriage. I prefer English design."

"English design is most elegant, I concur, but in itself is much influenced by continental design – as indeed is our architecture, of course. Palladio –"

"Ah, the famous Italian! What a well-informed older woman you are to be sure." He turns away to look down the valley.

Mary waits for a moment, lips itching with a suitably sharp riposte, but she says only, "Shall we go back to the house?"

She is already moving away. James turns around to offer

his arm to her, taking his wife's hand as he does so. "I'm afraid your husband is still inspecting the stables. I believe it will be difficult to tear him away."

"I'm sure you're right!" She takes his arm and they move towards the house. James seems disinclined to talk but Mary stops before they go in, planting her feet firmly and retrieving her arm. "But why orientate the house so?" James looks at her in surprise. She repeats her question. "This faces east, if I'm not mistaken. In my Greek theatre image, this view would be the close, the near part of the half-circle. Here the hill rises up just beyond the lawn whereas, if you were to face that way," she indicates south, "the sunshine would be yours for most of the day and I'm sure you would enjoy an even more expansive view!"

"But we use the old house as a foundation – we are almost finished! The driveway comes this way, here to the frontage."

"Yes – of course, I understand the practical reasons. We have done the same at Nanteos – built on the site of the previous house, kept (for now, at least) the drive and so on, but it is most assuredly not too late for you to think again, to create a vista still more lovely than the present one by arranging for the main door to be around the other side?"

Thomas is to be seen, hurrying across the drive. James, his jaw set, hails him. "Thomas, your wife is not only garden designer but architect now, I see!" Thomas smiles amiably, though he clearly hasn't heard properly. He is out of breath from climbing the rise up from the service building to the plateau on which the house stands. "You must be a proud man!"

Thomas still smiles. "I beg your pardon; didn't catch what

you were saying..." He is bending over his boots, hands resting on his knees, catching at his breath.

"I was remarking that your good wife speaks in a most learned manner about building and, so *my* wife tells me, about landscaping too. I understand the modern improving landowner is not content with a mere garden; no, landscaping is the thing, prospect, aspect – really a very different scale to that which sufficed for our fathers."

Thomas has regained some of his composure and smiles. "Mary reads very widely and has a mind for design. Many ideas come from her travels, of course, and do not perhaps sit as easily here in Wales as they would do in warmer climes, but many of her London friends have fine seats and both the means and the will for experimentation – such is the strain on my poor pocket." He laughs.

"Who is your architect at Nanteos?"

"Ah... There's a thing... I forget the man's name..." Thomas looks at Mary who answers for him.

"Thomas has engaged a wonderful local man, a Mr Morgan. He has a most sound knowledge of how to maximise the advantages of the site."

"Oh – a local man! How brave of you." James looks brightly from one to the other but neither Mary nor Thomas seem eager to elaborate. "Perhaps the ladies are in need of refreshment?"

Thomas nods eagerly and they move towards the wing of the house that is already habitable. At Mabws the fine oak stairs rises straight through the middle of the house, the carving somehow antique. Though the oak flooring is elegant, the building lacks the fanfare and flourish of Nanteos. The women remain in the front parlour as the men go through to what will be the library.

Anna Maria leans towards her guest, her voice low, almost a whisper. "James designed the house himself."

"Ah, I see now." Mary nods, rising to take a look through the window at the view from the far side of the house.

"Do you know Mr Hogarth?" Anna Maria asks suddenly.

Mary smiles. "I can't say I do; except to know that he makes himself most useful in raising money for the Foundling Hospital."

"He has a little pug dog of which he is most fond and when the hydrophobia was rife in London lamented the beating to death of stray dogs most keenly."

"Did he indeed? What a good man William Hogarth must be, if perhaps misguided." She comes back to sit by a dainty table on which a maid has prepared tea.

"London is such an exciting place. Do you visit often? Do you see the King and Queen Caroline abroad there?"

Mary laughs. "I'm sorry, but I'm out of touch these last twenty years or so. I've been back to London since my marriage of course, yet there are always so many elderly relatives to call upon or who are calling upon me, that I hardly have time for what you might call the 'sights'. I have too many chins to be a lady of fashion!"

"I've been to London of course – many times." Mary nods politely. "My husband says your younger sister is a duchess!"

"Yes. Jane is Duchess of Atholl."

"I'm not sure I know where that is... but, a duchess!"

"A title is a burdensome thing to wear."

"Oh, Mary, I would wish for such a burden, however heavy!"

"Indeed!" She smiles. "How are you finding married life?"

"I cannot think what I did all day before I was married!

How I could imagine my thoughts or actions important before I was married. I do so enjoy being a wife."

"I'm glad of it." Mary is quiet as she finishes her seed cake.

"You don't offer advice?"

The older woman laughs. "Advice? Not I!"

"James says you're rich, well, that it's your money builds the house. Oh, I'm sorry –"

Mary smiles and puts down her plate. "Does he, indeed!"

"I hope my comments don't seem out of place?"

Mary laughs again. "Not at all – you're young and no doubt artless. I would say (though this is merely a comment, not advice) that I found time difficult to manage after my marriage. I hadn't realised how much my own mother did; how much time was required to run a household and entertain according to one's station – and of course I did not even have children to draw on my time." Anna Maria looks quickly down, brushes imagined crumbs from her skirt. Mary continues in order to cover any awkwardness. "But of course it's something one becomes used to, learns to manage – and now I even have time to be involved with building and the design of the grounds and park. Now all is well. This house and estate are, of course, your inheritance." As she gestures to the lovely scene outside the window, Anna Maria smiles. "And you build a new hall here at Mabws. This is enough as your 'project' for now, I'm sure."

"It's no Nanteos, that's certain; but it is beautiful, though yet to be finished!'

"A far cry from your husband's more humble seat at Ffosybleiddiaid." The younger woman nods. There is silence for a moment. "Do you have many friends nearby; any women of your age and class? Do you know for example Eliza Lewis of Llaner... erm, how on earth do you pronounce this – it eludes me!

"Llanerchaeron?"

"Just so – bravo! Yes, daughter of Thomas Johnes of Dolaucothi?"

"I know *of* her certainly – who does not, but I can't say I've really made her acquaintance."

Mary chuckles. "A shame indeed. I'd hoped to solicit some gossip from you. Well, apart from dressing and occupying your paupers well at Llanrhystud, what other charitable pursuits could be occupying your time, I wonder? It's easy to be busy and useful in London, of course. The Lock Hospital, for instance, is always seeking support and, if you're interested in the welfare of women, as am I, there is so much to patronise. You've heard perhaps of the Welsh School out at Middlesex?" Anna Maria nods. "And all talk is of a hospital for fallen women, a Magdalen House that is to be established. You've heard of this too?" Anna Maria shakes her head vigorously, moving her chair in closer. "Ah, I'll tell you about it – what a wonderful opportunity to invest in the needy..."

*

"Did you have a pleasant journey here, Powell?"

"We did indeed; no tawny wanderers stopped our way!"

"Glad to hear it. There's been trouble up in Borth though, I hear; the Gypsies even attacking each other!" He laughs. "They are masters of the highway in some districts, robbing and abusing the unwary, then melting like bubbles into air, never to be seen more."

"Most difficult to apprehend them to be sure. A capable

crew of scoundrels in many ways..." Thomas clears his throat. "The Mabws money is made through shipping you say, Lloyd –"

"And soldiery/military pursuits. Ah, and milling, seaweed and lime-burning at the coast – someone brings forward an idea, we Lloyds invest in it! You're lead and land, are you not?"

Thomas nods. "And silver, when we can get a whiff of it. We could do with more, of course; builders' rates are extortionate these days and we landowners and men of business are improving roads across the county; good roads don't come cheap, eh Lloyd? I noticed you're rebuilding the bridge in the village: a most worthy undertaking. Good man, yes... A sensible decision surely – you don't want your lovely new bride taking a dip in the stream!"

Lloyd laughs. "Quite so, though bridges don't come cheap either." He refills Thomas' glass. "You're a wise man, Sir, if you don't mind me saying it."

"How so?"

"You married an heiress!" They laugh.

"You too have made a wise choice, Lloyd. Your wife is both beautiful and heir to all of this." He gestures to the ceiling.

"Yes. And, best of all, Powell – do you know what has made her the happiest of all?" Thomas shakes his head. "She didn't even have to change her surname!" They laugh and drink for a moment in silence.

Suddenly Thomas says, "I hope I can rely on your support in the election, if I were to stand?" Lloyd says nothing, rising to refill their glasses. "Lloyd?" He gets to his feet.

"Yes. I remember the 'debacle' surrounding your Tregaron win... and subsequent defeat in my father's time. The House of Commons Committee… did it not find against you? Was there not a fight; the mayor involved somehow?"

Powell stares at him for a moment. Then, with a dismissive gesture of his hand, says, "All that was a long time past. The committee ruled that Tregaron was not a borough after all – what nonsense! It was a fair win Lloyd, but then the Jacobite interest confused everything, bribery of course… But, as I said, all that was a long time ago, your wife's father and I 'head-to-head' like two young rams…" He clears his throat; takes another gulp of port. "To the future I say!" He raises his glass towards Lloyd and drinks deep again. "Congratulations to you and your admirable wife on a most impressive new hall here at Mabws." Lloyd raises his own glass and sips. "Anyway, what was I saying? Ah, yes. A new generation, new building, fresh alliances – I trust I can rely on your support if I were to stand in the upcoming election?"

With a faint smile Lloyd turns briefly away to face the window before answering. "I must say to you, really most plainly, though of course with the greatest of respect, that I entertain both Vaughan and Pryse here at Mabws. Both Trawscoed and Gogerddan carriages find their way here to my door. If you understand me, Powell?"

Thomas' gaze is direct. "Then I must take my leave of you, Sir. It's a long way back to the relative comfort of Nanteos."

Thomas' face is hard, jaw set, as they return to the drawing room.

"… but of course, there are opportunities here too. I hear, for instance, that an Edward Richard does well with his school at Ystradmeurig – oh, the gentlemen are here!" One look at Thomas' blotchy face tells Mary it's time to go. She gets to her feet.

Anna Maria hastily stands up. "Will you not stay for dinner, Sir? I should have proffered it before; indeed I meant to and to have offered accommodation for the night, but I didn't send the letter in time. My apologies. We two have been so busy in conversation. Mary is so fascinating that I –"

"They're going, Anna." Lloyd makes a shallow bow to Mary and turns from the room. At the doorway he rings for their carriage to be brought up to the front door. Mary and Anna Maria exchange glances as Thomas stands in the middle of the room studying the carpet. As they wait for the carriage, Anna Maria shares some of their conversation with the men, her voice is light and bright and she is careful to present a mild and edited version. James listens politely, adding relevant comments here and there.

Mary studies her husband. Though she sometimes drops in a clarifying word or phrase to the conversation, she is uneasy. "Perhaps you would like a glass of water before we go, Thomas. Thomas?" He shakes his head. There is something of the Samson about him, a compact, miniature Samson with the world against him.

Anna looks at her, then at Thomas. "Of course. A glass of water. Would you like to sit for a moment?" She turns sharply to her husband, "Ring the bell for water please, immediately."

Lloyd saunters again to the bell and gives an order to the servant. Thomas, having been put to sit down and made to drink the water seems perfectly recovered as the coach arrives. Mary kisses Anna Maria warmly. "It has been such a pleasure to talk with you. I will send you the information you require in order to subscribe. Please make sure that you visit us soon at Nanteos… if your husband is busy, you are always welcome alone – an overnight stay would give me much pleasure, oh and plenty of time to bore you with my plans and schemes!"

Anna Maria laughs and squeezes her hand, coming out with them. Thomas bows and kisses her hand as he says goodbye, tipping his hat briefly to Lloyd who hands Mary into the carriage with, "Thank you for your visit; I'm sure some of your very many ideas may be useful at some point."

"Nonsense." Mary smiles at Anna. "You will make up your own minds." Mary leans out of the window to look back as they leave. Though Anna Maria is still waving vigorously, James has turned back into the house.

"Well, husband – what ails you?" Thomas grunts. "I will have it out with you. What happened between the two of you?"

"Did you speak to her about the election? Did she seem persuadable to my cause?"

"Ah... I fear I have to apologise, Thomas. We talked so animatedly about London and the advances happening there. She was so full of enthusiasm, I –"

"You didn't raise the election at all?"

"We were to stay much longer. I thought that –" She looks at Thomas. His face is pale now, though this only makes the broken veins on his cheek more prominent. "You're not well, Thomas." He squeezes her hand. "What happened to you in the drawing room, when you were standing there? Thomas?"

"There was a taste of blood in my mouth, like blood with iron in it and a wave passing across inside my skull; hot and cold, then dizzy." Her intake of breath is audible. "Only for a moment, Mary; only for a moment."

"You will not be going to London again next month to fight

the case for the mines' rights, Thomas." He goes to object. "No! Let Morris dig around in the dirt up at the mines, damn him. Neither will you be standing again for MP this time." He goes to speak. "No, you were right to eschew politics all these years. I was wrong to encourage you again, against your better judgement and I now forbid it." She looks at him. He is trying not to laugh. "Thomas, do you hear me?"

"Indeed I do, Madam. I would not dare defy you!"

It is her turn to laugh as they make their way back to the coast road.

Chapter Nine

IT IS A relief for Branwen to move away from the mill, to come up out of the damp from the river which always has a smell – like the breath of some predator, or a creature newly-dead. It is good to come up out of the tunnel of trees, friends though they are, to pull up and away from the river's presence and suddenly to see out, feel the wind tear at her hair rather than hear it growl high in the canopy above. She rests herself and the donkey, looking out across the valley of clear-felled trees, across the marshes, out across the estuary to Aberdyfi where there are several big ships at anchor.

She moves fast uphill, her hat far back on her head so that she can see better and catch the sun on her face. The banks and hedges are colourful with the white flowers of hawthorn. 'Never bring the thorn boughs inside, it will bring bad luck.' "I will if I want to," she murmurs, "but then, Siwan, I *choose* not to." 'More dog than donkey, that animal,' her father is always grumbling. 'You spoil her. She should go off with the hatters to the markets – once'd be enough to fix her, she'd be glad of the light work she does for us then.' But there was seldom need to bring the donkey to behave with the stout stick she always carries – though it had come in handy across the back or skull of the occasional dog. There is not much of the wood left now, most of the trees having been felled for mine props or burned for charcoal. Siwan isn't heavily loaded today and is quite happy picking her way between the stones and low stumps, the ground beyond the track impassable with tangled branches and sticks, waste from the bark trade. The donkey slows, lifts her chin up and pulls air over her big yellow teeth. "What is it, Siwan?" They stop for a moment. Soon enough, from around a bend in the road a young woman appears. With her shawl the same colour as her hair, she's immediately recognisable. "Cari!" The woman waves back. Branwen and the donkey break into a trot, the animal's dainty hooves covering the difficult ground at pace better than the girl's clogs. "What news? What are you on the road for?"

"You know me; errands mostly. I'm cheaper than a man on a horse –"

"And you know everybody!"

Cari grins. "What about you and Siwan?"

"More wool for Tre'r-ddôl."

"Oh, are you a rhyming *barddes* now – 'more wool for Tre'r-ddôl'!" They laugh.

"Oh, and a message for Mother Lewis."

"You need to watch her, Branwen – she'll recruit you! She's worse than the press-gangers."

"No danger there. She says I'm too small for that journey – more shrimp than woman."

"Charming!" They laugh. "Anyway, watch yourself, the mule train's coming this way. I passed them loading up. Looks like a good haul this time."

"You fancy yourself as a mine engineer now?"

Cari puts on her best Yorkshire drawl, "Get that wheel back in work, you lot, that lode won't drain itsen!"

"That's good! You speak English perfectly!"

Cari snorts. "There's English and English – like with us." She puts on a Welshpool accent, *"Ti'n iawn, beeeech?"*

Branwen laughs. "You should have been on the stage – and with your figure. How is it you can do all these voices?"

Cari shrugs. "Travelling with the horses I suppose. You hear all sorts – *Sipsiwn* are the best. They even speak English, some of them, as well as Welsh."

"Egyptians? I thought they had their own speech?"

"Yes, they do, but they pick up everything else along the way."

"Can you speak in their tongue, Cari?"

"Not really – but it sounds like a spell – a bit of magic in it; they talk around things, people say."

"What do you mean? Like what?"

Cari thinks for a moment. "Yes, right, listen to this: what's an egg-sucker?" Branwen thinks hard, then shrugs. "Cuckoo," Cari says, grinning. "What about a wart on the face, a lumpy one?"

"No idea."

"A wild sheep!"

"That's good," Branwen says. "What else?"

"Erm… what do they call a boil?"

"Don't know."

"A '*gajo*'s head'." Cari laughs.

"What does that mean – *gajo*?"

"Someone who isn't a Gypsy. They probably look like a boil with their fair hair!"

"How rude! What else?"

"Funny sayings – I know one, 'After the fair'." She looks expectantly at her friend. "Have a go, go on."

"Erm… it's all a mess?"

"No." Cari shakes her head. "Try again."

"It's all over, you're too late?"

"Yes! And they have special names for trees and things. Right… yes, what's a 'dancing tree'? No? A poplar!"

"That's good."

"And a yew's the 'dead tree'."

"That's an easy one!"

"Never speak out loud under a yew tree – it'll hear you."

"Watch out, Cari… quick, move, I can hear the mule train coming."

"Get out of the way – now, Branwen; get off the path!" The donkey has stopped grazing, her head up, ears pointing skywards. The clanging of the bells, strange and metallic; distant shouts, the bark of dogs and the long-drawn complaint of one of the mules. "Get back out of the way!"

Branwen and the donkey are backed up against a bank. "I am!"

"Not enough – they'll trample you. Get right over the bank and up the slope away from the road, come on!"

They look for a shallow bit of bank and half-pull, half-push the donkey over. She isn't too reluctant to move, frightened as she is at what she can hear fast approaching. They scramble up the hillside and sit to wait out the ore train. It can be seen now, the first mules and outriders have appeared on the far ridge and make their way along the skyline; more and more appear.

"Why're they coming this way?"

"To Garreg, I expect – to load onto the barges for Aberdyfi."

"Yes, but why not Aberystwyth, Cari – it'd be far nearer." Her friend shrugs. "Maybe the wind or the tides aren't good over the next few days. Must be much rougher out of Aberystwyth than Aberdyfi, you'd think."

Cari laughs. "Your turn to know it all now! Are you a master mariner suddenly, Branwen Rhys?"

Branwen laughs. Siwan is restless and she stands up to get a better hold on her head collar. Though still not visible on the road yet, there are no more figures to be seen on the ridge and the noise comes nearer by the second. "They're coming!" she shouts and Cari scrambles to her feet.

A long line of heavily-laden mules, tied together with strong rope, lumbers round the bend. The animals fill the road whilst each side, knee-deep in the waste from the forestry, ride the men. Their horses are small and rough-coated, tough mountain ponies with sure feet. Dogs patrol the line. The bells are deafening, must be literally so for the mules wearing them suspended from their tack and from metal arches across their shoulders. Cari and Branwen shout to be heard.

"Why do they have these dreadful bells?"

"Cai said they can't stop; the load on the animals is so heavy the front ones just can't stop. Only hope is that everything else can hear them and gets out of their way!"

"Makes sense. Wouldn't pet those dogs!"

"No chance. Take your hand off!"

"Your arm, more like!"

The men work the column constantly, whipping the dogs in, barging their horses' flanks into any mule who staggers off the middle of the path, putting the whip to the rump of any animal not keeping up.

"Worth a bit to rob this."

"Wouldn't like to try it."

"Never heard of it being done."

"Nor me. We could turn highwaymen!" Cari laughs and waves to one of the outriders who has lifted his hat off to them. "Ah, he's handsome. Nice!" The circus takes many minutes to pass, the road churned up, even big, embedded stones dug out and rolled over. At last the noise, like a cloud of noxious smoke, has drifted away.

"It's hard work for the mules." Branwen's finger strokes the donkey's cheek under her harness.

"They don't last long I heard."

"I wouldn't like that job."

"At least the panniers are empty when they come back up. I need a pee." Cari opens her legs and crouches, her skirts like a bell around her.

"What's happening with you and Gruffydd, Cai Gruffydd?"

Cari looks sideways at her, a slight smile playing the corner of her lip. "What makes you ask?"

"Saw you eyeing the rider."

"My eye does no evil, does it?" Cari laughs. "I continue to make him my project. Now that is a catch for a woman."

Branwen nods. "Handsome, clever, Powell money behind him – I don't know, I think I could do better!" They laugh. Taking a deep breath, she blurts out, "Cari, I think I'm in love!" Her friend sucks on her back teeth. "Really, it's something like no other, like... I know not what!"

"You have a sweetheart?"

Branwen reddens. "Well, he's not that yet, but maybe... oh, I knew the moment I saw him, at *Calan Mai*."

"*Calan Mai*! Never trust anything that happens on a spirit night, your feelings on a spirit night – especially your first time! The dancing; the fiddler; the fire, the beasts –"

"I know, but I have seen him since; ridden with him in the trap."

Cari stares at her. "The man drives a gig?"

Branwen nods eagerly. "Oh, let me tell you about the first time. We were at the fires for *Calan Mai*. We were dancing, then I saw him, out on the edge of the crowd. His face had no shadows and his bright hair was like an angel's. He was standing alone. The flames by then were mostly yellow, the same as his hair. No, it wasn't yellow – it was more… so fair and light it was almost white. Only his eyes seemed dark – hidden sometimes by the flames, when the breeze shifted I could see them. They seemed to fix on me. Later he walked home with me –"

"Cai said we shouldn't have left you –"

Branwen doesn't take any notice of her. "His Welsh was fast but flat – when I told him that he laughed and he said, 'Flat maybe, but rich and deep like the land in the south.' I must have looked at him strangely because he laughed again and said, 'You're not a travelling girl then? I took you for a Gypsy, the way you were dancing, but indeed, I find myself mistaken.' 'Indeed no, Sir,' I said. 'I am no traveller girl! We have the Pandy at Ffwrnais.' He liked me; I could tell in his soft voice as we spoke together, coming down off the mountain, and in his steady arm, pressing mine close against him, to protect me on the rough ground. Every time I think of him, a chord pulls tight, going from my belly down." She puts her palm flat against her groin. "A strange thing, like when you pull on the tendon behind a dead hen's foot and the claws curl."

"When you say his name or speak of him you look down and smile shy; as if he was there watching you. See, you're blushing now!"

Branwen laughs and nods. "He says he'll take me to Glamorgan." Cari looks quickly at her, then bends to adjust her clothes and shoes. "Sometimes I can hardly look into his face. He's so fair; his hair is filled with light and it seems there are no features just the blue of his eyes. He's like an angel."

Cari snorts and stands up. "You really are bewitched this time! You sound like a cheap pamphlet at a fair: 'Rhymes to a lady-love'!"

"Oh, Cari, if you could only see him! There is a way to him…" She tells her friend about the drive, his plans, his gift of the shoes.

Cari listens for a while in silence. Then, "What interest can a man like that have with a girl like you?"

"That's what my father said! Cari, how can you say that – you who're going with Cai Gruffydd!"

"Cai's a natural son. He has no real position; he's not above me."

"He's still of Nanteos and you're a horse trader's daughter. He won't marry you. Oh, I wish I hadn't told you about Henry Davies now!" Tense as two cats on a wall they look at one another. Siwan shifts restlessly.

"I wouldn't stay around here with him anyway," Cari says. "We'd go away somewhere where no one knew us. Cai knows about the mines and about how to get water to work the machinery to drain them properly and about ore trucks on rails; I know we'd be welcome anywhere…" Her voice trails off. She looks at her friend.

"I must be on my way."

Cari nods, crossing the gap between them and giving the younger girl a tight hug. "Be careful, Bran."

Branwen turns away, "Come on, Siwan; stop messing

about." She tugs the donkey's rope ready to move on. As they pick their way back to the road her friend still stands watching her.

"I'll see you, Branwen Rhys. Mind the brigands – both red and fair!"

Branwen pulls her hat down low over her ears and waves without turning around as she reaches the track leading to the mine.

Chapter Ten

Up at Tŷ'n Garth, a big farm on the gently sloping land overlooking the sea, Branwen is just checking her panniers are ready for the load of spun cloth to be finished at the mill. The farmer's a big man, chest and shoulders more like a labourer's, but his voice is high. He has a habit of shouting all the time, like he's giving orders into the wind aboard a ship, a habit that is much imitated by the half-dozen or so who work for him.

"Good fine cloth for you. Tell your father there'll be more in a week. I've got some new weavers in – I don't bother hiring workers for the farm any more unless they're skilled weavers as well."

"This is good work – they must earn well." After examining it, Branwen returns the corner of cloth to the bundle.

"They earn what I pay them – and I only pay them what I have to. Your father puts up the mill costs, got to get it back somewhere. I pay them what I need to."

"We have to ask more for the fulling; the agents set the price as they wish and we have to sell to them. The Pryses put up the rent too."

"Well, there's plenty of good workers around these days, more than ever, and the more people are looking for work, the less you can pay them! A win all round: the more mouths there are, the more demand for food, the more I can charge for it from the farm. Keep breeding I say, it's good for business!" Branwen looks sharply at him and he touches his cap. "Sorry – your father wouldn't like it, me talking like this. You're easy to talk to; not like some slow dairymaid."

"I must be going back."

"Oh, stay for the sport. The roof's leaking and we're moving the ricks – setting the old hay barn up as another weaving shed." He gestures across the yard. Beyond the buildings she can see the men coming over the brow of the hill, the dogs, seeming small as rats at their heels. "There'll be food, nothing too heavy for a refined maid like yourself." He has hold of Siwan by the head collar, but is already losing interest in her as the men and dogs approach.

The yard is soon full of men and their small dogs and several come to bother Siwan, snapping towards her legs, though not quite daring to bite. The donkey lifts her hooves like a dancing master, trotting on the spot and it is only a matter of time before some terrier dog or bitch will find a foot in its face. "Get away!" This is what the stick is good for. Branwen thrashes it about under the donkey's belly, aiming a couple of kicks at them herself for good measure. She pulls Siwan towards the stabling at the far side of the yard. Through the noise of the yard she picks up a couple of appreciative whistles and shouts she knows are for her. She shuts the door of the stall and takes a breath. Made for the work horses, the door is high and the stable generous, filled with straw that is hardly soiled. She takes off her hat for a minute and scrapes her now damp hair away from her face. The outer door fits well and not even a rat-sized dog could squeeze under it. Siwan is making use of the water trough. She peers in; yes, quite fresh, good enough. Splashing her face and washing her hands she and the donkey listen to the din outside. "Well, I think you'll be staying in here for a while, my girl." The donkey keeps slurping. "I should stay with you really."

Shouting and furious barking; a yelp. *'Iesu mawr!'* She can't resist going back outside. A dog fight surely, well, a scuffle anyway, with some blood on the cobbles. Two men are pulled up face to face, one with a whining dog tucked under his arm. As she crosses the yard, no one seems to take notice of her this time and she is able to sit on the mounting block for a rest in the sunshine. Over near the barn stand two magnificent work horses, their rumps fat and gleaming.

The yard is heaving with men and their dogs now. The terriers are really just a snapping mouth on legs. Bandy legs at that. One comes up to sniff her. This one is even smaller than the rest, with a body no bigger than a rat's, though her legs are longer. The bitch throws herself on her back across Branwen's foot. She laughs. "Oh, I see. You want me to tickle you, don't you?"

She is aware of a pair of boots approaching and the dog twists around onto its feet. She straightens up, looking into the face of a man who grins at her. "Hey, don't go spoiling Tiny – she's got work to do!"

"I'm sorry to be sure. Never get between a girl and her work." She reaches out to pat the dog which squirms in the man's arms, desperate to lick her. She smiles. "I can't see she's in the mood to do much damage to any rat!"

"On no, maid; you should see her, she's the best there is. Come on, I'll show you an entertainment better than the fair!" 'Why not?' she thinks. As she goes with them towards the great barn, the work horses are being led in, their chains dragging on the floor. "To move the ricks," the terrier man says, following her gaze. By now Tiny is twisting to get free, wriggling desperately in the man's arms. "All right, girl. Down you go." She shoots off into the barn and Branwen loses sight of her in the chaos.

The great double doors are closed and the dogs already beyond themselves with excitement, barking and burrowing into the bottom of the ricks. She has to shout to be heard. "Won't they be able to get out under the door?"

"Good thinking, girl. We'll have it blocked off, you'll see. If you don't mind me saying, you should stand away awhile and tuck your skirts up tight around your legs." She looks at him. "No, I'm not joking with you. The rats'll run anywhere – up anywhere, down into any hole to get away from a dog. That's why we're in these." He pulls at his breeches where some twine holds the bottom tight around his stockings.

"I wondered why there was a need for such a fashion!"

"Well, there you are!" He smiles at her, touches his cap and goes to find his dog.

"Afternoon Branwen Rhys." Taliesin, teeth white in his brown face. His dog waits at his feet.

She feels her cheeks hot but is quick to answer him back. "Ratting? You've got the wrong dog, I think."

He laughs. "He guards the door. None of the other dogs has the discipline – watch." He gets the collie to lie down in front of the doors. Though the animal quivers with excitement, he stays on guard. "He's not above snapping at a rat, but he won't desert his post. What're you doing here?"

"Come to collect cloth for the mill."

Tal laughs. "And stayed on for the sport, and the food."

She nods. "I've put Siwan in the barn. Her hooves itch when small dogs snap around her legs."

"Well, pull your skirts tightly around your legs. We're going to move the ricks."

"You're the second man who's warned me – I will!"

Tiny's owner has joined the other men who hold their terriers in their arms out of harm's way as the horses pull the pallets with the ricks. The dogs struggle like rabbits in a sack, yelping and barking. They move the first rick, not far, but enough to dislodge the rats. They can hardly be seen. Moving so fast and near to the ground they run for their lives. A dog darts in, a squeak. Sometimes it takes longer to kill them, the less experienced dogs snapping at them or shaking them tamely in their jaws. Then the dogs slow down, their movements aimless, searching for more. No sign of the quarry; no squeak, no shadow scuttling quick, just beyond sight. Time to move the next rick. Some of the dogs, a bit calmer now, are restrained on the ground, one hand enough to cover the chest of the terriers and hold them back from their drive, their obsession to kill. The horse is fastened up and drags the pallet – a little way is all that's needed and they pour out, more than ever this time, surely swollen in numbers by those who took shelter from the first attack. The dogs are waiting, quivering, salivating, whining, barking, writhing in anticipation. Like roosting starlings scattered by a gunshot, the rats burst out in every direction. Something sickening about the way they move, especially in a group.

Some of the dogs are just playing with them now – rolling them on their backs, tossing them in the air. But a rat can jump and Branwen sees more than one right itself in the air and land on four legs ready to run. There are yelps as well as squeals as the rats fasten onto a dog's face. Men, holding spades aloft, strike at the creatures, but it's a dangerous game – as easy to kill a ratter as the rats themselves. Each one squeals as it dies – no rat is stupid and they run or fight for their lives, one fastening on the shoulder of a terrier and biting deep, a bite that will turn bad perhaps and wreak some sort of revenge long after the perpetrator itself is dead and buried in a pit.

The men are busy with their spades, but this is dirty, foolish work, the burst bodies filthy to clear up. Just to the right of her, three dogs have cornered an enormous rat. They dart in at it, snapping. The rat dodges and even comes at them, one at a time, but that leaves its back exposed and the other two dogs can lunge and snap at it. It is a horrible creature – sharp claws and thin legs under an oily body, the bald tail vile, but as it fights for its life, she's sickened.

"*Duw,* they can jump! *Maen nhw'n ddigon ffit i fyw!*" one of the men says to her as she inches open the door to slip outside. Llew has not abandoned his post, though he's standing up now.

Out in the yard the sun is still bright. She has lost her appetite for food and goes to find the farmer about loading the cloth. A girl at the house tells her he's supervising the pit for the rats. She catches up with him as the sloping field behind the house levels off. He's the other side of the hedge and waves to her. A couple of the labourers look up, leaning on their spades.

"Get back to work!" he shouts. "How does it go down there?"

"A fine day's work you would think, I'm sure."

"Would've liked to be there myself but these bloody fools were digging the rat pit next to the river – could have poisoned us all if that lot gets into the water as it rots. *Diawled*! Oh, sorry again for my speech, maid!"

"Think nothing of it…" She smiles. "But I need to get back now. Who'll come and load the cloth?"

"You'll not stay for food?" She shakes her head vigorously. "Oh, maybe a rat's had your appetite. Sorry to hear it." He turns and shouts at a man taking a swig from his bag. "You; loading up the cloth?" The man nods. "Yes, right you are. I'll send a couple of these fools down now. Off you go then and get the mule ready, they'll be right with you."

"Donkey."

"Eh? Off you go then, maid, we won't be long." He smiles, but his eyes are already looking past her to where his men may be slacking again.

As she returns to the yard some of the men and dogs are crossing to go out to the bottom field. "All over?" she shouts.

"Just about! Out for some rabbiting now while they get ready with the victuals."

She waves and continues to the stable. Siwan is rubbing her harness against the wall. *"Damo! Paid, Siwan!"*

"Had your fill?" Tal is there at the entrance to her stall, the big horse looming behind him and Llew skulking at his heels.

"They've gone down the field to have a go at the rabbits," she says. "Why aren't you with them?"

He shrugs, "Got the wrong dog for it. Anyway, I got sick of the taste of it – lived on it as a boy."

"The hatters pay well for the fur. Every man enjoys rabbiting, doesn't he? Why don't you get yourself a terrier? It's as good as fair day to some."

"I'd sooner have fair day. Anyway, why're you still here? Come to beg a rat skin or two to make a muffler?"

"No indeed! A rat pelt…" She looks hard at him. "You're teasing me!" She laughs.

"Maybe, but there again, you never can tell which maid might be partial to a muffler of good rat fur." He moves the horse into the stall next door; she follows. He takes off the tack, hanging it across the stable door and brushes the animal's thick coat, though it doesn't really need doing, the horse has hardly worked up a sweat. "Saw you on the road to Tre'r-ddôl a few days back."

"You didn't call out."

"You were standing some time. Had your hat tilted up and your eyes closed – enjoying the sun."

"Well, I was surely having a rest for a while; I'd come up from Felin-y-Cwm and my ankles were tired," she says.

"Your ankles?"

"Yes, my boots hurt."

"They hurt your ankles?"

"Yes."

"Both of them?"

"Well, yes, they… *damo*, you got me again!" Tal grins. Grooming done he rests, one hand on the animal's flank, studying her. "Why do you look at me so hard, Mr Wood? What is it you see? No, don't just smile… What are you thinking when you study me like that?"

"I'm wondering just which rat would match you best; what colour fur would suit those green eyes the best?"

"Cheek!" She laughs and throws some hay at him. He dodges. "I told my father about you."

"Should I be afeared?"

"No indeed. I told him about using the dog with the sheep. I could hardly believe it; the skill of it." Tal grins, shrugs.

"That's the gift of being able to travel around, I expect. You can learn things, change things; you're not trapped forever doing things the way others around you have always done them." He nods. "You're no fool are you, Branwen." She tries to be casual in front of him but he's smiling at her, his eyes big and dark in the gloom. "You will walk out with me to Aberystwyth next fair day." It is not a question.

She opens her mouth to put him down, but her hot cheeks betray her. "I must go. They'll be waiting to load the cloth." But she doesn't turn to go. He stands watching her. He is very still, yet has an absolute intent, just like his dog. She laughs. "Yes, I think I will be on the road to Aberystwyth that day. You may see me, perhaps."

"A deal then." He puts out his hand. To ignore it is to make too much of it, but to take it, hold it… She brushes her hand against her skirt and takes a step towards him.

The door squeaks on its hinges. "Branwen, Y Pandy?" Light jars in a band across the stable. Unable to see them for a moment, the man calls again.

"I'm in here." Relief at the interruption obvious in her voice, she slips into Siwan's stall to untie her.

"Ready to load?" the man says.

"I am." She follows him out. As the farm servants strap the cloth onto the donkey and fill the panniers, Branwen finds her eyes drawn again and again to the stable door.

At last Tal comes out and straight towards her. "Still here?" She laughs, holding her hands out as if to say, 'No, I'm a phantom – what do you think!' His turn to laugh, at himself. "I'm leaving too. Walk with you a way?"

She nods, not trusting herself to say anything. As they turn away from the farm she catches laughter and snatched comments from some of the men. Tal glances at her but she shoves her hat down firmly and pretends not to hear.

"Loose," and a whistle through closed teeth sets Llew free to leave his side and explore away from the track a bit. "Did you get the rat hides you came for?"

"You do love your own jokes, don't you!"

He smiles. "I spend too much time on my own, I think."

"You're an Egyptian, like those in the camp at Tregaron, aren't you?" She hadn't meant to say it. He stops. "I don't mind," she blusters, "I mean, I would love to have the open road as my view every morning, and, to please myself, not always to be on an errand carrying cloth to be stamped or having been stamped, or sometimes spare wool to the spinners or hatters or..." He still has not spoken, though they seem to be moving on again, "and to be free of rules, even on a Sunday."

He laughs heartily. She stares at him. "Free of rules! You don't know much about it then. We have rules for everything!"

"Do you? Like what?"

"Men's clothes, women's clothes – never wash together. A dog licks from a dish – smash it. Woman, never walk in front of a group of men. If a woman's skirt touches something, burn it/throw it away."

"I had no idea!"

"We might live in tents and carts, but there's no end to the rules we can make up."

"Most of them seem to be about women."

He nods, whistles Llew. "That's how we look to you *gaje*, I know – free as air!" He stands still for a moment, whistles again. "I know where he'll be. Come with me?" He looks towards a narrow track.

"I don't really want to take Siwan along there, not with a full load."

"No, sorry, you're right. Wait for me?" She nods. He grins and throws her a small pouch. "This'll keep you busy until I get back."

He takes off down the track and she opens the pouch – dried apple rings and pear halves. She tries not to eat them all whilst Siwan grazes. They're not away for long, but Tal doesn't look pleased and there's a mighty stink coming off the pair of them. "Where on earth 've you been?"

"He got into the wolf pit again and they've baited it up for foxes."

"Wolf pit? There are none!" But she can't help herself from looking around.

Tal, catching her, laughs. "No, you would have to go to Ireland for a live wolf now, I believe. They say the last one on this island was in the Young Pretender's time up in Scotland."

"How do you know all these things?" He shrugs. "What's a wolf pit?"

"On the way to Llyn y Gigfran. It's stone lined and was covered in bracken or some such with a sheep carcass for the wolves in the old days. Now usually it's a rabbit in there and used to catch foxes. One had died in there, don't know what Llew was enjoying most – rubbing on the dead fox or eating the remains of the bait!"

She laughs. "I'll look out for it next time I go up there."

"If it's as ripe as today you won't miss it!"

"Strange to think of wolves here. A different world, surely."

"I was planning to see you to your door and Siwan to

her stable, but we'll do you both the favour of going in the opposite direction, I think."

"We'll not argue with that!" Branwen laughs. "I thought Egyptians were clever, canny people, but I see there are exceptions." He grins. "Well, Mr Wood, I may see you on fair day I suppose – though only if you and your friend smell a deal more sweet!"

He backs away from her, back up the hill, raising his hat in salute, his dog following "'Til fair day, lovely Branwen!"

*

That night, all chores completed, she settles with her father by the low, peat fire. "You want *cawl*, child?"

She shakes her head. He goes back to studying the fire. "The Egyptians; do they settle sometimes? I mean, do some stop their roving ways and settle to live amongst us?" she blurts out. His back stiffens, though he doesn't turn around. "Some of them, they have work. Some of them can even read." He snorts in disapproval, but she continues. "They are able you know, Father – some can write, without help."

"I know it." His voice is stark, though he still has not turned around.

"How do you know this? Which Egyptians have you known, Dada?"

"I know enough. I know of one who can write silver words. 'A large sin can come in through a small door.'"

"What're you talking about? What words? What sin?"

"Hold your tongue, daughter. You hardly speak more than two words together for weeks, then you are a cataract of nonsense! Hold your tongue!" He turns back to the fire;

turns around again. "No good can come from speaking about the *Sipsiwn*, let alone to them. Get yourself to bed. Find your senses in sleep, I beg you."

But she does not move from her seat at the window and it is he, not she, who leaves the room.

Chapter Eleven

"**G**ONE TO EARTH!" The cry rings out as Sir Herbert Lloyd and Thomas Powell come up the track.

Lloyd turns to Powell. "Good. Now the real fun can begin!" The terrier men are already busy with their spades, filling in the holes around the den site, the hounds held back by the whip, leashed and taken out of the way. They rein their horses in. The conversation continues, though their eyes are drawn to the action on the ground.

"Edward has secured him. It was not cheap."

Lloyd's laugh is mocking. "You always did prefer bribery to blackmail, my friend."

"Blackmail?"

Lloyd nods. "After all, in betraying Lewis Morris, Davies betrays Lord Powis and ultimately old King George." He shrugs and smiles. "No matter to me, as long as I'm, 'appreciated'." He rubs his finger and thumb together, laughing. "I'm always happy to help a friend. As I say, bribery or blackmail... it's your money; you're the one with the heiress."

"That pot of gold can't last for ever."

"Shares is it? East India? South Seas? I always did wonder." Thomas nods, wiping his sweating face with his sleeve. Lloyd's horse is restless and worries against its bit. "Damn thing!" He yanks at the reins and shouts across to one of the boys. "Take him, will you, before I break my crop against the wretched beast!" Held securely by the bridle, the horse quietens and Lloyd slides neatly to the ground. Another boy takes Thomas' mount and he flings himself from the saddle, staggering for a moment before regaining his balance. Lloyd laughs, "Why, pray, do you always dismount in this ridiculous manner, my friend? Anyone watching would believe you to be a plough boy, getting down from a cart horse!" He speaks loudly, looking around him as he does so, noticing a couple of smirks from the Nanteos men standing waiting for them. He gestures wide with his crop. "One of your good men here will, I'm sure, bring a mounting block out in a cart for you next time; or maybe a couple of the stronger ones can lift you down!" He laughs.

Thomas is bending to study the terriers. Tiny he has seen before but today she is with a big dog, probably too large to make a good fox terrier. "Heavy dog this, Parry."

"He is, Sir. Don't know where he gets his size from with a mother like her. He's a great ratter – don't know what he'll do down a fox hole, though."

All around the den, terrier men are putting their dogs in. Tiny is put into the hole and disappears, the bottom of her pads the last thing to be seen. Her son is inconsolable, leaping into the air and twisting his muscular body around. "He'll bloody strangle himself! What's the matter with the silly devil, Parry? But I like his spirit!" Thomas laughs. "Why do we hold him back? He must get to work. Put him in, man!" Powell gestures to the hole.

"His mother's in there already, Sir."

"Do as you're told!" Lloyd barks. The terrier man hesitates, turns again to Powell.

"Wants to get to his mother, Sir." He slaps the dog hard

on the side, but he only jumps higher, snarling and tearing at the rope. "We've just put her in that one. It's his first trip out, Sir."

"You heard Sir Herbert – what's wrong with you, man?" Thomas is shouting now. Parry looks from one to the other. Nodding to Powell, he bends to untie the dog, taking care to keep his hands from the jaws that seem ready to bite anything. Grasping the dog firmly by the scruff, his other hand scooping up the legs, he walks around to the right, looking for another hole. There doesn't seem to be one. "For God's sake, man – engage him! What are you waiting for?"

"Sir – his mother's just gone in… It would be better to place him somewhere else in case he –"

"Can you not hear your master, blaggard?" Lloyd turns to Powell. "You might need to get yourself a new terrier man, Powell. I don't like the attitude."

"God's teeth! Just get the dog in the blasted hole!" Thomas roars, red in the face. Parry doesn't speak again but thrusts the struggling young dog into the hole.

A couple of men who'd gone around the other side of the den come back. "No sign of them, Sir. Maybe we didn't block all of the holes? Maybe the vixen's got out somewhere?"

"Damn! This is the third hunt we've had without anything at the end of it! Oh, here we go!"

The young terrier, covered in soil, has backed out of the hole and is running backwards and forwards in a frenzy of barking; in a bound, two men crouch just behind the entrance, ready to catch the vixen when she shows her head and now another figure can be seen, the bandy back legs of Tiny as she backs up, drawing the vixen out of her den – a deadly game but one she's an expert at. Now the vixen's visible as far as her shoulders and the men lunge forward to grab her. She's out. There's only a brief moment between the fox's head and teeth appearing and the animal flailing in the air, held at arm's length by one of the strongest men in the party as another two enclose her head and body in a sack.

"An excellent job; congratulations!" Lloyd's voice.

But something's wrong. Tiny lies still, her whimpering hidden by the snarls of the fox, the frenzied barks and shouts of triumph as men and dogs crowd in. Parry picks the bitch up. Part of her cheek is hanging open, fallen blood already cleaning a path through the soil, and her muzzle is torn. He holds the flap of skin down with his thumb as he tucks her under his arm, kicking away her son. "Get that bugger tied up!"

Thomas, turning at last from the glad sight of the fox, all but her tail safely captured in the bag, sees him. "Hey – watch those boots with my dog." But the terrier man only glances at him, before turning his back and moving away. "You; come here." The young man stops. "By God you'll take note of me when I talk to you!" Thomas covers the ground between them in a few strides. Suddenly he stops. "Why – the bitch's bleeding!"

"Yes, Sir. She's been bitten in the face."

"How so? She's one of our most experienced dogs, is she not?" Parry nods. By now a couple of the other men are standing near them. "Well, what's gone on then – how has she been bitten in the face – and a nasty one at that I can imagine?" Parry shakes his head. Powell looks around him. "Well?"

"The young dog was put in behind her blocking her exit; she couldn't back up when she drew the vixen out." The man looks down, worrying at a clod of earth with the toe of his boot.

"I see," Thomas replies. "I'm sorry for it." He turns and strides away, Lloyd approaching him, worrying his crop against his boots. "That vixen's had my best dog, Lloyd!"

"Poison, a fox's bite."

"I'm surrounded by fools!" Thomas mounts up and wheels around. "Kill that blasted thing, won't you! I don't want to see its damned brush again."

"Hold!" Lloyd goes over to where the vixen writhes in the bag. He gives it a kick. "I have a better idea. Get that noose around its neck again and break its legs – we'll take it back to the kennels, train the young hounds on it. Get a pliers and rip out most of the teeth too while you're about it."

The gamekeeper is holding the squirming fox by the brush, the rest of it still in the stout sack, now firmly tied at the base of the tail. "Shall I take the brush and release her to the dogs, Sir?" The man's shouting, his breath uneasy as he deals with the weight of the fox.

"Did you not hear me? Keep her to train the young dogs on."

"What do you mean?"

"I've told you. Disable her: pull the teeth, break the legs etc. and keep her in a pen; bait the young dogs on her."

"What about the brush? A finer tail on a vixen I've not seen for many a season!"

"Oh, you can take that – she'll likely live. In fact, better to take it before you bait her – won't be much use to you afterwards."

★

The following morning Thomas finds his way to Parry's room behind the stables. He coughs loudly by way of introduction. "How is the terrier bitch with you?"

"No good, Sir."

"Ah. You couldn't stop the bleeding?"

"The poison's taken hold." Parry's arm flicks towards the corner, a helpless gesture.

Powell steps into the room. "Ah, yes – a fox's bite…" He approaches the small figure on the pile of sacking. The bitch is lying on her side, eyes almost shut, her breathing rapid. He stands for a couple of minutes. "Hum, kinder thing to end it, I would say."

"I don't like to."

Powell nods. "A loss. A good dog – won't happen again." At the doorway he turns back. "Apologies, man – you were right."

Chapter Twelve

THE HUGE KITCHEN table at Nanteos is covered in blood. The long windows are opaque with moisture as Martha the cook, hair and face damp, stands in the doorway. For once she does not know what to do. Annie, the kitchen maid, in that way she has, appears at her elbow. The girl clings to the door handle, rocking it back and forth. Martha ignores her for a moment, then lashes out. Annie, biting her lip, rubs at her arm.

"Will I fetch water?"

Martha shakes her head. Blood has dripped onto the floor, run into the grooves of the slate paving. "What did Doctor say, girl?"

"For you to come. He sent for Roberts and Jenkins too – I don't know on what errand. He said for you to come 'immediate-ly'."

Mary shakes her head, as if dazed by a blow. "Where are they now?"

"The bedroom, I think – well, I don't know in truth, but they were on the stairs when Doctor said 'Girl; you, girl, fetch the cook'. So, I came here. To fetch you." Again, she has fastened herself to the handle and repeats the opening and closing of the door. Martha slaps her hard this time. She cries out and moves back into the servants' passage.

"For pity's sake, go and fetch a pail and start clearing this up, will you."

Annie opens her mouth to speak but Martha is already ascending the back stairs. Before she moves out onto the landing she stops. Bad sounds. The sound of an accident or death in the house – that mixture of hissing whispers, sudden strange noises, random cries and hush where there was none before. A door slams and Elin, Mary's maid, comes towards her. "The doctor – he asks for you."

"I know it. How is he? How is the master?" Elin shakes her head quickly. "Has he spoken yet?" Again, the girl shakes her head. "Where are you going?"

"To fetch brandy, or port or… or Burgundy."

"Keys?" The girl holds up the mistress' set. "Go on then." Martha tidies her clothes automatically as she walks down the first-floor passage. She doesn't often have business in this part of the house, but each time had meant trouble. She raps hard on the door and opens it. Thomas Powell is sitting on an upright chair. Both his sleeves are rolled for bleeding. He turns towards her as she comes in, but his eyes seem not to focus, or rather there is a delay in his reaction to her form moving across the room. The doctor nods at her; Mistress Powell turns from the window into the room. "You wanted me, Sir?" Martha says.

"I need the spiced poultice for the soles of his feet and the cupping and scarifying equipment. And send a fire shovel up too. You have them?"

"I think so. Maybe not the… scarify? What is that, Sir?"

"No matter. He will be cupped and his feet treated with poultice. Oh, and the coals held to his head. If that doesn't work then I must apply an enema."

"Has he spoken?" The doctor looks at her quickly, an eyebrow raised. "Sorry, I don't mean to rise above myself, but my father…" She stops.

Mary Powell comes towards her. "You do no harm, Martha." She swallows hard. "No. Since he came in this morning he hasn't spoken." She moves forward, seems about to speak again.

"Go prepare the physic, if you please," says the doctor. Martha looks at him but he has turned away, bent again to Thomas Powell's vein.

On her return to the kitchen she sees that Annie has made a start with the mop. "Fool of a girl – you make it worse!" The blood is fresh and sharp; a smell like nettles. "It's everywhere!" The girl stands limp, biting the inside of her mouth. "Use a dry mop first! For the love of God, do I have to do everything myself!" She sees that Mary Powell has followed her downstairs and watches from the hallway. "Mistress?"

Seeing her, Annie takes the opportunity to melt away, her mop and bucket disappearing with her.

"I'll take it up to him. It's happened before." Mary's voice is quiet, but steady. "But not as bad. No; never as bad as this."

"He said his eyes had gone only yesterday. A blanket in front of them from within, he said. I made him a bath for them."

"His eyes are increasingly affected. I asked him not to ride to the hunt yesterday. Oh, Thomas!" The two are silent as Martha first warms then decants the mixture for the poultice, using her apron to wipe the spills. Mary suddenly looks down at her feet and steps back from the table. She looks around, as if noticing the carnage for the first time. "Heavens! You have made a timely start!" She gestures to the carcasses dressed and already in their roasting tins.

Martha points at the other pile, heads, feet and tails still intact. "Got interrupted, I'm afraid."

Mary shakes her head. "I've already sent to cancel. There'll be no electioneering at Nanteos this season." She pinches the bridge of her nose with her fingers.

"Headache, Mistress?"

Mary nods. Martha goes to the cupboard for a bottle. "Oh, please don't trouble yourself. I'll ask Dr Watkins for something."

Martha smiles. "This'll do better." She takes a spoon, polishing it on her apron. Mary grimaces. The cook looks down to see the linen is smeared with blood. "Sorry, Mistress!"

Mary smiles, taking the spoon and rubbing it on her own skirt. "How many?"

"Two perhaps? I take three."

Mary smiles again. "In that case, one should be enough for me." She finds a clean patch of table to put the bottle down.

"My father was the same," Martha says suddenly. "Not his eyes, though – he could always see, even when the staring attacks came upon him."

Mary nods. "I'll take this up." She closes her whole hand around the small bottle as if to warm her fingers. "A strange thing… when the doctor is in a house there is no rank. He has perfect authority over us all." Martha nods. "This has happened before, when we were in London petitioning against the election result – years ago. He'll be well again." A smile breaks and leaves her face, all in a moment.

"The master should have won then – everybody knows it."

Mary sighs as she turns away. "They should never have taken Tregaron off him that time. He's been struggling to get it back ever since."

Chapter Thirteen

A FORTNIGHT HAS passed and Branwen is drawn to thoughts of the man with flaxen hair, like a painting of Christ in the great Llanbadarn Bible she was once allowed to see. Her insides are unquiet, like the air before a thunderstorm, vibrating strangely. Every morning when she wakes it's like fair day; every night as she puts her head on the pillow her skull is full of fresh air and she has to force her eyes to close. All night she is half-awake, as though her bed were a flimsy boat on a lake and she trying to keep from falling into wakefulness. But she has a plan.

At *Gŵyl Ifan* she begs to go out with the other young people. The nights are light until after ten now, a blue light that leaches to a thin dark. She prepares her father well in advance. He knows that Cari has gone to Llanbrynmair with the hatters so she cannot claim to stay with her.

"It's time to collect the cloth from Tŷ'n Garth again. Shall I go today and stay with Aunt Lizzie tonight and come back tomorrow?" She has gone to the mill to ask him, shouting over the noise. He is busy and merely glances at her. "Dada, I will need to go soon to get there before she goes to bed. I don't want to give her a fright."

"Wait until the end of the week. We've enough for now. I'll go with you, she'll be pleased to see me after all this time."

"But I think it must be today. We are letting the hammers

be idle too much. We have only enough to last us for three days and if we don't collect on time the farmer will surely go elsewhere for the fulling. Remember he has taken on extra weavers, Dada – they work for him in a special shed now. We must change to suit these new times. They're going to be bringing ore from England to smelt just by the bridge at Ffwrnais – all is moving forward, but for us. We stop our wheel and hammers too often because we haven't got the cloth, even when there's plenty of water!"

Evan stops his work and straightens up. He smiles and whistles thinly through his teeth. "Well, daughter, you speak like a man of business: all this talk of changes! Where do you get your big ideas from?" He laughs.

"Please, I'll be back before dark tomorrow." She is still, poised and taut, laughing with him but desperate for his answer.

"Go, then. Take care. Go straight to Lizzie tonight – fetch the cloth tomorrow."

"Of course." She is itching to say more, do more to thank him, but forces herself to walk away soberly; to prepare Siwan as though this was an ordinary trip. She is soon on the track. It is too early for the revellers to be out preparing for Midsummer and she takes a different road away from the bonfires and the meeting ground at the crossroads. She pulls at Siwan – if she can make good time she will be with her aunt before dark and no one will know the difference.

"My blood is alive with bees," she tells the donkey, "and my bones full of air." It is nothing for her, each step up the hill, the stones twisting and sliding away beneath her boots. She knows where he is, has visited his lodgings with her eyes closed on many a night.

Siwan is rank with sweat by the time she reaches the top of the valley though Branwen hardly feels the climb. She has a comb in her pack and some lavender water from last year. She lets the donkey rest for a while as she washes herself in the stream. After the first tangled agonies she sings as she combs. Even saying his name sends a bolt of lightning tingling through her. She sings it, playing with it, changing his Christian name, changing his surname and even, once, whispering 'Branwen' in front of it. But that is an uneasy feeling, a glance-behind-you moment, so bold it may bring ill luck, so she doesn't repeat it. The shoes he gave her are not dirty, though she polishes them on the inside of her skirt just in case. The last mile or so, though on the flat, is not easy. With every step it seems her nerves increase and now she doubts her welcome. What if he's not happy to see her? The thought stops her feet, Siwan plodding on for a moment and yanking her arm before realising.

"Ouch, Siwan – stop!" She must find a reason to call! But what? It must be something to do with lead… She keeps moving, but slow enough to think. Lead. What has she heard? What does she know? There must be something that would be useful to him or his master, Morris. The lodgings are up ahead; one more bend in the road and they will be seen. Her father and his friends talking late at night perhaps… now she remembers something about Thomas Powell of Plas Nanteos; something about the fact that more lead had been found under the wet ground, on the wastes at Ystumtuen and there was hope that the seam would turn back onto his land and not go off where the Crown could claim it. That's it – needing to buy up one of the farms on the edge of the common quickly in someone else's name! These things would be worth telling, surely? She checks her hair once more, smoothes a damp finger across her eyebrows and tidies her clothes. Then she takes a firm hold of Siwan's rein and, as casual as it is possible to seem, turns the bend in the road towards the house.

Someone is outside, a man, but not the striking figure of Davies. He raises his hand to his eyes as she approaches and hails her with a hearty shout. She waves back. Every step towards him is self-conscious and she is relieved when he opens his gate and comes to meet her, his steps surprisingly light and quick for one so portly.

"A fair maid, come with supplies!"

Branwen stops. "Sorry, Sir?"

"Ah," he steps away from her empty panniers. "Where are the victuals, girl?"

"I think you mistake me, Sir. I come with a message for Mr Davies."

"I beg your pardon." He bows, looking past her back up the road.

"May I see him… see Mr Davies, please."

He puts his hand out towards her, still looking along the road. "You may give me the message. I'll ensure he gets it."

"It's not written, I beg your pardon."

"Then, unless it's a full ballad, I can assure you I'll remember and faithfully recite it to him. I'm a poet myself, did you know?"

She gives a quick shake of her head. "Please, Sir – it's for his ears only!"

Morris nods. "I'd suspected as much." He stands up straight and looks carefully at her, his tone more serious. "Your name?"

"Branwen Rhys, Sir."

"Rhys – a noble name indeed. Branwen, you say?"

She nods. "My mother named me."

"Not many Branwens left in Wales. All are Elizabeths, Janes and Marys. Do you have brothers and work in a castle kitchen? Have you ever been across the sea?"

She laughs – a strange man, but not unkind. "No indeed, Sir, I do… have not. My father works the Pandy at Ffwrnais."

His raised hands are a gesture of appeasement. "I jest, maid – forgive me." He steps back and glances down the road. "You have business with my assistant, Henry Davies?" She nods. "Your father knows you visit us here?"

"Of course! We have business with him." He nods; seems about to speak. Siwan pulls at her harness. "Will he be long, Sir?"

"No… no," he says, his previous jollity returning. "I expect him very soon." He gestures towards the back of the house and pats Siwan on the rump. "Please see that your friend is comfortable and come back out here – I'll make sure you get a formal interview and a chance to impart your message."

Branwen goes to the back of the house with Siwan and ties her to a metal ring on the wall by the water trough. The donkey slurps her water noisily. Branwen bends to kiss her neck and whispers, "We're going to see him, Siwan, we're going to see him!" She doesn't go back around the front of the cottage but waits for a while.

A servant comes out with a full soil pot, looks sideways at her as she empties it into a shallow ditch and swills it at the water pump. She sings but doesn't speak. When she's done, she turns to the donkey. "Well, what are you here for, eh? No fleeces or spinning here for you. Hope you don't think you're going to be eating our hay? Do you eh, beast?"

Branwen is about to greet her, but the girl looks at her sharply and leaves. "A strange one that, Siwan," she whispers in the animal's ear. "You have fur, really, don't you – not hair. A horse is silky; you're furry as a bear!"

The girl has come out again. "He's here. Mister Morris said to call you." This time she has nothing in her hands and stands with them on her hips. "You can leave it here." She gestures to Siwan.

Branwen thanks her, arranging her hat and shawl as she moves away.

"Eh!" the girl calls. Branwen stops. The serving girl comes towards her, her face hard. "You're a long way from home?" Branwen shrugs and goes to step past her. "Ha, you'll have to do better than that!" Suddenly she has hold of Branwen's breasts through the bodice, squeezes them hard, laughing.

Branwen slaps her arms away. "What do you do?"

"Them won't do for 'im. Them's smaller than a flea's arse bulbs!" She brings her big breasts together until they swell out over her kerchief in the middle. Branwen stares at her. "Go on then, get on your way." Branwen opens her mouth to speak, looking for a clever, cruel or even indignant reply, but none comes out. "Don't come back 'ere," the girl says. Her tone has changed and her face is serious. "Where you from, anyway?"

"Near Garreg/Glandyfi – well, Ysgubor y Coed."

The girl nods, a grave gesture that looks more concerned preacher than low servant. "Don't come back 'ere; for your own good. That's what I'm saying to you, anyway." She shrugs. "Anyway, it's up to you…"

Branwen waits for a moment, but it seems that there is no more to come. Feeling both the eyes of the donkey and the girl on her back, she goes around the side of the house. She sees him immediately in the group of men, some of whom are on horseback, others on the ground.

Morris is looking out for her and shouts, "Here is that fine maiden come for you with urgent news, Davies." He is not quick enough to turn away and she sees his tongue filling his cheek and a crease of laughter around his eyes. She stops, awkward and suddenly embarrassed, pulling her shawl around her. But Davies is gallant and steps away from the others, giving the reins of his pony to one of them and removing his gloves as he comes towards her.

Morris cries out again. "You have an admirer I see, Henry Davies! Or maybe the girl would prefer a man with a bit of a pot?" He strokes his paunch tenderly, like a pregnant woman. "Maybe she's come for me?" Some of the men laugh and one says something, but she doesn't hear. A smile lightens Davies' lips but he does not look back. "She's a pretty one alright," Morris continues, almost to himself as he turns to talk to one of the other men.

Davies holds the gate open for her, bowing slightly as she passes him. She can almost feel him as he walks close behind her up the path to the front door. It's open and he leans across her to push it further. "Go in, fair princess." He's laughing.

"Why do you say that?" She stops, her legs locking like a donkey's before even going over the threshold.

"Oh…" He puts his hand lightly on her shoulder, urging her forward. "Just the story Morris told me just now. You don't know the old story? No? Well, I'll tell it to you one day. Please, come inside."

The hallway is suddenly dark. Again, he is behind her, instructions to turn right into the parlour coming from his hand on her back, not his voice. He indicates a chair. "No, I thank you. I would rather stand."

She gives him the well-rehearsed message and he asks a few questions. Where was she? Exactly which day did she hear them talking? Did they mention silver? Was there anyone else there – perhaps someone who she hadn't thought to mention; someone perhaps silent, watching from a corner? Finally he adds, "You have been most kind in coming so far to tell me this. Can I get you something to drink?"

Her instinct is to say no, but she says instead, "In truth, I think I would like to sit down and yes, please, a drink." Her mouth is dry, her breath surely sour. He smiles and goes out of the room for a moment to shout for refreshments. She sits down by the open window, letting the breeze on to her neck.

He comes in without her hearing him. "I regret that I cannot entertain you properly here now. As you can see – we have business." He gestures to the men outside who seem to be drifting towards the entrance.

"Oh, no matter!" She jumps up. "I –" An older serving woman comes in with weak beer and some plain pancakes. As she lays them out, she keeps looking at Branwen, though she says nothing. Davies closes the door behind her. "Mr Davies, I –"

He holds up his hand to silence her. "Please, don't – you weren't going to apologise for disturbing me now were you?" He smiles, folding a pancake and handing it to her. "Please, do not. Your 'testimony', shall we say, has been most useful. More than that, I appreciate so much your coming all this way just to see me –"

"Oh, but I go to collect more spun wool from Tŷ'n Garth, Sir."

"I see. I am merely on your way? Fool that I am; I thought the information to be a trick. What do they say, an excuse!"

"No. No, it's not. I must be going. Now."

"Not at all. Our meeting will be over in an hour or so. Wait for me here and then I'll see you to your... surely you will not go home today?"

"No – I stay with my aunt after picking up the load and return home tomorrow."

He laughs. "An excellent plan! Shall we meet when we have both concluded business this evening – you with a loaded donkey and myself with a most satisfied smile, I'm sure?" She nods. "I'll walk with you awhile towards your aunt's home. And where does this aunt live? I am determined to see you on your way." She tells him. He thinks for a moment, then "Nanteos! Yes, we will go by way of Plas Nant yr Eos. I'll meet up with you there."

She shakes her head. "But that's not on my way, Sir. I won't be back before nightfall if I take that way to Aunt Lizzie."

"Not to worry. I'll be there to protect you from the wolves and brigands. I wish you to see the mansion with all the candles alight. You will humour me, surely?"

*

It's already dusk as Branwen nears Nanteos. She stops abruptly. There is something in the copse just ahead; something coming towards them. What is it, that eerie whir and buzz, the clap of wood on wood? She and Siwan freeze. A spirit, abroad on *Gŵyl Ifan*! The *Ladi Wen*? A shape comes nearer, rising and dipping over the ground; flashes of white and those noises, like nothing she's ever heard before. Like a huge moth the creature swoops, circles, its wing tips pale in the gloom and she remembers: *troellwr*! Another makes its awkward dance ahead of her and she smiles, lets her breath out in a rush almost of laughter. She urges the donkey on. What a night! Davies is already at the Nanteos turning waiting for her. He takes her arm in his. The road is low, running between shallow banks and he stops them, drawing her a little way off the path. They walk to the edge of the ridge. There below is the mansion, beautiful, like a picture of a fine ship or of a fairy's castle, golden light at every window. "I've been there, you know," he says. "You gasp, but it's true. I've been served meat and drink in one of the Powell's fine rooms."

She shakes her head. "They wouldn't have you amongst them, not you, who work for Lewis Morris."

"I wouldn't lie to you – but then, perhaps they mistook me."

She turns to look at him. He holds the torch away from her, this side of his face in shadow. "Do you jest?" she says.

He laughs. "Maybe then I am mistaken. Maybe it was just a fine dream I had." He gathers her arm into his side again. "But no finer dream than to walk through the dusk with the most beautiful girl in Cardiganshire on an enchanted eve." She has no answer to his compliment. He looks sideways at her. "For you are, you know. For all that you are small, you are fine-boned."

She snorts with laughter. "I'm not a pony!"

"Oh, but you are! You are quick and lithe as a Barbary horse, with a small intelligent head and a lively eye."

Again, she has no answer for him – she who can outwit any man, even the mine engineer. "I need to go."

"Your aunt expects you?"

She nods, then shakes her head. "She doesn't know that I'm to call today."

"Oh!" His smile is broad. "Then you may stay out all night, lovely Branwen. I can hide you at my lodgings."

"No indeed!" She pulls away.

He looks at her hard. Then his face softens and he reaches for her hand to tuck it through his arm again. "I jest, of course!" Branwen is still quiet, head down. He turns her to face him. "A jest, pretty maid. Old Morris would charge me rent for a guest and my purse is empty until my plans come to pass. You believe me?" He gently pushes back a strand of her hair.

She nods and smiles and they turn again to watch Nanteos. "How I would love to look out of those windows! To see inside the fine rooms, even just for a moment."

"Ah, if you continue so charming, maybe someone of your acquaintance will take you there one day." He looks at her and winks. "So, you will call again to see me tomorrow at my lodgings, on the way back with your load?"

She shakes her head. "I cannot."

"Your father?" She nods. "But it'll be on your way home. I'm at home all day tomorrow – I have to copy some of the underground plans. Morris won't be there... but there'll be plenty of people around to chaperone us, you can be sure of that, of course," he adds quickly.

Branwen smiles. "I must go on to Auntie Lizzie now." She takes a step away from him towards Siwan who's tethered nearby.

"Wait a moment!" He takes her arm and pulls her back towards him. As he wraps himself around her, she cringes away from the torch's flame, pressing herself against him. He laughs, holds her away from him and looks into her face. "Did I tread on your feet, pretty mistress?" She shakes her head quickly. "You like me, I think. You like Henry Davies; am I not correct. Am I?" He tickles her neck and she laughs, pulls away. "You are a little flirt, I see; come to a man's lodgings to give a 'message', then say you are going on alone. That makes you more interesting – but of course you know this. Come, I'll walk you back a way towards your aunt's cottage. We can take as much of the evening as we want in getting there, as far as I understand matters. As long as you can say you did arrive there at some time, when your father questions you tomorrow. Am I right?" She doesn't reply. "Ffrwd Ganol did you say?"

"Yes. You have an excellent memory, Sir."

"For those things I wish to remember, yes. And you will call on me on your way home tomorrow for me to serve you tea in the parlour?" He bends low to look past her bonnet. "Will you call to help break the boredom; stop me going entirely mad at my desk?" He pulls a face and she laughs. "Is that 'yes', Miss Rhys?" She nods. He takes her hand inside his arm again as she leads the donkey away from the ridge and down towards the hamlet.

Chapter Fourteen

CAI FROWNS AS he approaches Nanteos – they still haven't finished the new stable doors! Several men scramble to their feet as he jumps from his horse. One blusters, "There's been a letter from London; Mistress won't tell anyone."

Martha meets him in the hallway. "She wants to see you; make haste."

Mary is not in the morning room. Her voice calls him from the library where she's sitting in Thomas' chair. "He's gone, Edward."

He waits for her to say more. She holds a letter at arm's length, out to the side of her, as though it would burst into flames. "Thomas?" She nods. "What happened, Mary? An accident?"

She shakes her head. "His blood was always hot."

"He collapsed?"

"An apoplexy. He died right there on the street. Oh poor, dear Thomas!" She is still holding her arm out, away from her side.

Cai goes towards her. "May I?"

She gives the letter up to him, burying the hand in her other palm. She looks down at her fingers, worrying at her wedding ring, twisting it this way and that. Cai looks down at her for a moment before reading the letter. Her thin curls lie dull on her white neck. He raises his hand as if to comfort her.

She looks up. "Edward?" The skin is swollen around her eyes, though he can see no tears. "Come and sit by me." Pulling up a chair he sits to read, passing the letter back to her. She folds it neatly, pressing the seal back down and aligning the corners, running her finger and thumb firmly down it to reshape the crease. "Will you go and fetch his body home to me?"

★

Evan Rhys has gone to buy oil and for once Branwen's alone with her thoughts, the workers glad of the chance to tend their patches of land on so fine a summer's day. Even the mill machines are quiet, having been stripped and cleaned. The water makes a different sound now, the wheel stopped, it too having been cleaned, repaired and waiting for oil. Without the wheel the air is empty, that big block of noise in the centre of every day is missing and the small sounds have crept in from the edges of hearing. Her ears feel bald without it, even faint noises alarming and demanding and she finds herself jerking her head at the rustle of mice in the corner, the landing of a wood pigeon on the wooden outhouse roof and its plodding steps, the creak of its wings as it flies away and the terrible cracks of the wheel as the wood dries. Does anyone know about her? Did anyone see them at his lodgings? Has he told anyone about her? The damp dark of the mill building is oppressive and she goes outside to sit on the warm, low wall. The starlings are making their usual din, perched in their favourite tree – whistle, hiccup, trill and a high-pitched squeal that sets the teeth on edge. Will he keep his promise?

As she looks back at the house she sees something odd and awkward on the ground under the shadow of the eaves. A young bird, fallen from the nest? She bends down and it looks at her – eyes huge. It opens its beak wide and waddles towards her. There are no obvious legs; the swift shuffles forwards, using the long blade wings to balance. She could lift her foot and crush it in a moment – it couldn't even scuttle away like an ordinary bird.

"Him. You are a cock bird, I think." Slightly nervous, moving her hands very slowly, she intends to scoop him up, like she would a hen's chick, but he won't put his wings in. He doesn't move away from her, though; doesn't seem afraid. In fact, he comes towards her foot. Above them, the parent birds fill the sky with screaming. She straightens up again and looks around her, careful to stand still and not crush the bird. There are no adult birds flying near, casting an anxious, watchful eye on the lost young one. She watches the nest for a few minutes and one of the parents dives down, disappears into it, reappears like a shot bolt straight into the sky. The young bird is clearly forgotten. She bends down again – he seems to be trying to climb on to her foot. She opens her hand and he creeps on to it. Oh-so-carefully she straightens up, flat palm with the bird on it, his wings resting over the side. She laughs. Now she is mother to a black swallow!

Close up his feathers are many rich deep colours – not black at all and he weighs almost nothing, though is awkward to hold. She must find a box for him; give him water – when did he last drink? How long can a bird live without water or food? Putting him on the wall she goes inside, returning with a wet cloth which she squeezes by his mouth. At first he's stubborn, then she sees his throat moving slightly and he opens his beak a little, taking the liquid as she makes it drip. She fetches an empty crate from the store and lifts him in, putting a sack over the top in case of kites or buzzards and goes to find food. How could she possibly supply the diet of a wild black swallow? She is almost ashamed of herself – being so bold and stupid to try and rescue a young bird when they are all around her, useless and plentiful as bats.

But she finds herself unable to walk away from the crate, from the creature with the blunt head and hairy lips. Next, she tries him with some minced pork mixed with water into a paste, puts her finger at the tip of his beak. He clamps it shut. She tries wriggling her finger, smearing his beak with the mixture – nothing. He will die then. She tries again and is successful with the water, then makes another attempt with the food. Suddenly he opens his beak, the mouth yawning obscene, she thrusts her little finger, still smeared with the mixture, towards the hole and he latches on, sucking her finger down his throat as far as the first joint.

Laughing, she fights the urge to pull it away and waits until the bird himself releases the hold. Three more times she approaches the beak with food on her finger and he pulls on to it. When he lets go, the food is gone. She lies on an old shawl in a pool of sunshine at the side of the mill. As the breeze moves the branches, their leaves cast a patchy shade that stops her getting too hot. The bird waits a moment on the edge of the shawl, then creeps towards her with his wings out, lopsided, like someone with bad hips. She stretches out her arm to stop him going off towards the hedge and he keeps coming, tucking himself into her armpit. They lie like that for a while. She dozes, careful not to move her arm. Henry Davies... Ah, his very name shivers through her! His hair, his voice, the way he says her own name. The very smell of him...

She wakes with a jolt. They'll be gone soon. Her swift must fly or he'll be left behind. She takes him upstairs and opens the window just underneath the nest. Carefully she puts him on the ledge outside. If he falls but fails to fly he will die. She blocks the gap so he can't get back in. He shuffles along the ledge. She turns away, unable to look; is he to be forever a tame, lame bird, never to fly? She blocks his return with her folded shawl. But he is not even looking out at the sky, waiting instead to come back in. Almost relieved, she puts her palm down for him and he creeps on to it, balancing with his long wings outstretched as she goes back downstairs.

When her father returns she is still outside with the bird. "What the devil are you doing with that creature? He'll die! You'll get fond of it and it'll die, Branwen. Put it down by the wall – there's a stoat nest somewhere – it'll soon be gone." He puts down the oilcan, comes closer and peers at the creature. She holds it up near his face. The bird stares back with its huge pool eyes. Evan laughs. "Well, well. To see one so close. There is character in that small face, yes indeed." He chuckles as he goes inside.

She waits until the sky begins to darken before going in herself. The bird is safely in the crate but it is a big step, this first night, to take a creature away from the wild.

"I've a present for your new friend," her father says, peering under the cloth covering the bird. He has several big spiders pinched between his thumb and forefinger.

"Hold it at his beak, Dada, he might take it."

For a few moments nothing, then the bird opens its mouth and latches on. "'Rargo'l fawr!" He snatches his hand away, laughing. "Nearly lost it!" he says, holding it up in front of him, as if expecting to be a finger short. "You're like your mother, Branwen – she was always rescuing the lame and infirm. Used to joke that's why she picked me."

Branwen puts the crate on the chest near the far wall. "Don't want him to have a draught – from the door or the fire."

"No, he doesn't want to be on that floor." He studies his daughter for a while as she prepares food. "You've not seen that man, that Davies again?" Branwen shakes her head, bending again to her task, her hair hiding her face. "Branwen?"

"I have not."

"Don't even think on him. Do you hear me?"

She looks up, chopping knife poised over the slab. "I'm not a child, Dada – nor am I a fool."

He laughs and sits back into the settle. "That's true enough!"

Chapter Fifteen

THE BODY OF Thomas Powell lies at last in the vault at the ancient church of Llanbadarn Fawr and Mary, as his childless widow, must prepare to leave her home. In the few weeks that remain before her departure from Nanteos, she is closing down her life in Wales. An image comes to her mind in the rare times she finds to herself between the funeral and her leaving for London. She sees a long corridor in which she is walking as dusk falls. One by one she opens the doors that line the corridor – briefly, the light finds her face as she glances around the rooms, checking everything is in order, before she closes each door and moves on. How many times has she used the phrase 'settling my affairs' in the last weeks? But this 'settling' is more than just a matter of causing her possessions to be packed and transported; meeting with Edward to arrange for the mines, mills, quarries and farms to be managed in the interim, in the period before Thomas' younger brother William and his wife Elizabeth take over as master and mistress of Plas Nanteos. More than a matter of informing creditors, debtors, trades people and her social circle of her plans. Now, though she has shut herself in her closet more than once, stuffing her mouth with a cloth as she sobs, she realises her situation is not all bad. As well as the simple things that can give so much pleasure, such as eating what and when she likes, she is able now to say what she wishes, to speak to whomever she pleases. This is why she is here, sitting in the small parlour at Abbey House, Ystradfflur, home of Thomas' estranged sister, Anne Stedman, and her husband.

The conversation has already covered Mary's practical arrangements, moving on to how the estate will be managed during the time between her departure and the arrival of his younger brother. "What will Edward... Gruffydd (I think that is his surname) do now?" Anne asks, suddenly. "It will surely not be seemly for him to remain when William takes charge?"

Mary frowns and shakes her head. "I've asked him to come with me. There is such a future for him in England – as an engineer, I'm sure, and I do still have some funds. But... he declines. He seems to feel some sense of duty; or maybe he has a sweetheart – one hears rumours." She gets to her feet, peers at an archaic wall painting above the fireplace. "How curious! Virtue versus vice: a choice. Maybe even *the* choice." She smiles. The house is intimate and interesting; a mixture of ancient and modern styles. "Am I right in believing there's something of the old abbey in the architecture even now, Anne?"

"I think so... well, I don't know, Mary." She takes a deep breath. "I owe you an explanation; an apology even."

Mary shakes her head. "How so?"

"I've not been the friend I should have been to you." She pauses, perhaps waiting for Mary to deny it – she doesn't. "The damage was done between us even before you were married. Thomas and... Edward; well, Edward came between us, one could say. Not that I didn't think my brother shouldn't sponsor the boy: his schooling certainly; a trade, but then he should have been sent away; kept away from here. It hasn't been good for the family to have him always in plain sight – a man both something, and nothing; attached to the family so, yet with no proper place. And then so difficult for you on your marriage." Again she waits, this time looking expectantly at Mary who still gives no answer. "It must have been so difficult for you, Mary – the boy being there even before you first came to Cardiganshire."

"Nonsense! Sorry, I beg your pardon, Anne. What I mean is, why should it be difficult for me? As you say, Thomas' natural son was born before we married and anyway, I have no children of my own for him to threaten. Not that he could, of course, being illegitimate."

Anne sighs. "It was all unnecessary then, I see; all the bad feeling. My brother Thomas was always so quick to lose his temper when crossed and I'm so easy to offend." Mary laughs, nodding in agreement. "Neither of us was able to accommodate the other in terms of opinion and, since then, the road to Nanteos has become somewhat overgrown!"

"Perhaps we two should have forged the way through the brambles to one another's doors then, despite the men. We were feeble. I see that now."

Anne looks quickly at her. "Richard regrets that he wasn't able to be at home for your visit, but was most insistent I tell you that he will call on you in the next few weeks to settle our debt."

Ah, the debt! Mary lifts her hand, showing Anne her palm. "Please. That's not why I came. Let the debt sleep awhile. There'll be no more interest. Let the debt rest, like a bear in a cave."

Anne studies her sternly. "You're sure?"

Mary laughs. "You frown at me – I'm a curious specimen I see, rather like a dried-out seahorse in a case, or the hollowed-out hoof of a mighty elephant!"

"No, begging your pardon; it's just your generosity. I –"

"If I needed it, I would take the money – rest assured!" For a moment there is silence between them. Anne reaches again for the teapot as Mary continues. "As you must know I'm sure, my mother is still living and I'm her heir. There is very little a widow of some middling age, as I now am, will need, once she has inherited all her widowed mother has to give."

"But you have a sister."

"I do, but she's risen so high as not to have need of my mother's favour. Come, let's not talk of debt and death! Have you no other paintings to be studied; no rare books to puzzle over? I know! What do you do in terms of charity? My grandfather patronised Christ's Hospital and excellent work is being done with orphan children, fallen women and the like in the capital. I could help you make the acquaintance of –"

Anne smiles and holds up her hand for peace. "I'm so gratified to learn of the efforts being made in London, but really, there's no need to look for opportunities so far away. So much is being done here in Cardiganshire: Edward Richard of Ystradmeurig promotes a most celebrated seat of learning and Griffith Jones looks for support for his circulating schools.

"Yes, I'm aware. Excellent work but –"

"There's so much to occupy anyone who cares to patronise good works in our own county. We, the 'great' families of Cardiganshire could make a huge difference to these endeavours; humble though they might be."

"I'm sure you're right, Anne. I can only regret that I didn't look more keenly about me for good causes to support these past years." Anne smiles. Her cheeks are flushed; perhaps she is not used to being so forceful, articulating her opinions so eloquently? "What were we saying... Ah, yes. Have you no paintings or rare books to puzzle over?"

Anne smiles. "Would you like to see the abbey ruins?"

Relieved, Mary gets to her feet immediately, brushing down her skirts. "Indeed I would!"

"No, wait! I have something to both delight and puzzle you first." Anne goes to the mantelpiece and fetches down a small bundle. Holding one end of the oiled cloth she lets the contents roll free across her knee, reaching into the final fold to bring out a piece of old, dry wood, the remains of a bowl. "Made from the True Cross – or, some say, the vessel of the Last Supper itself," she whispers.

"The Grail Cup?" Mary laughs. "There are many claiming to be thus. When I travelled as a young woman, every other church had a sliver of wood, a phial of blood, a holy cup. Someone should surely put them all in one room – there may even be a dinner service."

"One should show respect to them all, I believe. One of them may be truly a relic of Our Lord." She looks quickly at Mary.

"Quite so; you're right I'm sure. I meant no disrespect."

Anne nods. "It's so plain an object – yet fitting, for who was more humble than our Lord Jesus Christ?"

Mary glances at her. Anne's face is bright with awe, no trace of irony to be seen, but happily no sign of offence either. She takes the piece of wood, delicate as an animal's skull. "It's been well used, that's certain. There's hardly any left!"

"They've found a well in the centre of the abbey."

147

"A fine discovery indeed. Perhaps this vessel was for the pilgrims to drink? Perhaps it was used to give healing water to the sick?"

Anne shakes her head. "The holy men of old would not have exposed the precious cup to such danger." She takes the object back and wraps it firmly in the oiled cloth. "Bleeding in women; it can save a life when the blood cannot be stopped, but not many know this."

"That malady isn't something which afflicts me often now." Mary smiles. They sit in silence for a few moments, then Anne gets to her feet and puts the parcel back on the mantelpiece. Mary opens her mouth to object, seeing the flames from the dry wood fire so near to the precious vessel, so easy for a careless servant to dislodge it, for it to fall, for it to turn to dust, but Anne remains on her feet, her hand outstretched. "Come, dear Mary, I've promised you a tour of the abbey, and that's what you shall have."

It is no cursory tour, however. Mary is determined to see everything she can, requiring translations of the many Welsh memorials, asking questions and mostly being forced to answer them herself, or at least offer an educated guess.

"Good heavens, Mary – you speak like an Oxford don! You know so much more than me about it and I have lived here all my married life!"

"Oh, dear – I always do that. I can talk for minutes at a time upon a chosen subject until my 'audience' is ready to take poison. I'm like a man in that respect. My father was the same, so they say. Forgive me!"

"When do you leave for London, Mary?" Mary shrugs. "I mean, I'm sure there's no desperate haste and with so much business to be settled. I'm sure that William cannot leave his parishioners in a hurry and that Elizabeth will have much to do to arrange for the children and the household to be transferred." Anne follows at her shoulder as Mary reads the inscriptions and tablets to the dead. Mary pauses long before one of them.

"'Elizabeth… aged ten years. In memory of this dear child, her most afflicted mother has caused this monument to be erected. She was a child of an understanding uncommon for her years, of a great memory and surprising application to learning.' What sentiments the poor family express here!" She gestures to the inscription. "Not just the grief for their daughter; what they say of her – an extraordinary thing, to value a girl so and to hold her in such high esteem for her intellect, her gifts of character…" She turns away from the tablet, her voice faltering. "Anne? Why do you…"

Anne shakes her head, wiping her eyes with the back of her hand. "Carry on. Finish it."

Mary reads on, then pauses for a moment. Slowly she turns around. "Your daughter?"

Anne nods. "A long time ago. There were other children too, though none who lived to be counted."

"I'm sorry," Mary says simply.

Anne stands awkwardly, her arms raised as though to embrace Mary, yet she fails to cross the ground between them. Mary's sobs have no sound; are obvious only in the bunched linen she holds to her mouth and the jerking of her shoulders. Anne glances behind her. There is no one to see them. She takes a breath and moves to Mary's side, putting her hand on her elbow. "Come, let's go back."

Mary nods. Suddenly she cries, "Oh my dear, dead Thomas. I had forbidden him to go to London – he'd not been well!"

"There's no forbidding a husband, Mary!"

"I know it. Oh, poor Thomas…"

"Will you return to the house? Come." Anne takes her arm more firmly, draws it through her own. "Come, Mary." She looks up into the tear-stained face. "I can warm some chocolate or spiced cordial – I can warm that too; and there are fresh biscuits."

Mary laughs through her tears. "You're bribing me with food… what an excellent strategy! How I wish we'd seen more of one another across the years!"

*

Anne settles them back in the parlour. The fire still burns fiercely, though it is a warm day and Mary can bear it no longer. Whilst Anne is out of the room she takes the holy cup and places the bundle in the middle of a small side table. No, there may be a dog here somewhere. She looks around her and, seeing a wide shelf protruding at chest height from the panelling, puts it safely there. She is back in her seat, serene and composed, before Anne returns.

"What will you do?" Anne asks as she serves her. Mary shakes her head. "I mean, will you maintain a small property here in Cardiganshire as well as one in London?"

"London will probably never feel like home again. But then… caring for Nanteos and developing the estate and those on it was what was important to me. Now that Thomas is gone… I have no purpose here, no role. Another woman will walk the corridors –"

"Elizabeth."

"Do you know her, Anne?"

"No, I have not had that pleasure. I'm acquainted with her, of course, as a sister by marriage, but we've exchanged fewer than fifty words on our own together. We found, as I remember, that we did not have much in common. I would like to know her better, though, perhaps –"

"Oh, and a pleasure it would be! She is like quicksilver –"

"Her temperament?"

"Both temperament and figure. She and William were often at Nanteos. You'll soon have the opportunity to make her better acquaintance, I'm sure. No, in answer to your question, I'll return to London and stay there. There are so many ways I can be involved. Girls –" Anne refills her cordial glass. "Thank you. This is good! Strong!"

"With plenty of the spices you said you like. You were saying... girls? London?"

"Ah, yes, I..." She takes a large gulp of her drink and adjusts her neckerchief. "Education for girls, of course – all girls. I hate to see young people wasted! There is so much to be done, *is* being done in this new age. Queen Caroline herself provides a fine example of how things could be managed if there was only the will. What, pray?"

Anne is smiling at her. "Dear Mary."

"What? Oh... please don't be sad on my behalf, dear friend. I will assuredly return from time to time and of course you will visit me in London. No, don't shake your head, you will. Most assuredly. You'll keep me company with tales from wildest Cardiganshire. Oh look, there's a thing – my glass is empty again!"

Chapter Sixteen

A LERT, EVEN PROUD, Sailor stands eighteen hands in the yard at the Pandy, his ears almost touching, quivering when Tal speaks.

"Look at him! What a monster!" Branwen cries.

"Well he's the smallest of the three. You should see Benjamin – now there's a gentle horse, and the mare at the mine – she's the biggest I've ever seen. Her shoes are like plates…" He stops talking suddenly, takes a deep breath in and frowns.

"The fulling vats," Branwen says flatly. "It always smells of piss around here. I don't notice it really."

"Piss? What piss? Why, the air here is fresh as a spring orchard!" He takes a massive breath in. "Delicious!" Branwen laughs. He leans down. "What do you have there? Is it alive?" She raises the bundle up towards him. For a while, Tal studies the bird's face. It is all huge black eyes and beak. "A witch's screamer!" he says at last. "May I?" He jumps down from the horse's back.

Carefully she hands over the bird. "We call them black swallows."

"Is he hurt?"

"Don't think so." She tells the story.

Tal unwraps the cloth. The bird seems calm as he spreads first one wing, then the other. The feathers part like a fine lady's fan. "Can he open them himself?"

She nods. "Well, I think so. He opens them when he's creeping about. I don't think he can stand up without them spread out."

His hand is around the bird's body, holding the wings firmly closed as he examines what are the creature's legs and feet. He laughs.

"I know," she says. "What a strange thing it is! It came out of the nest – not crippled but can't get up into the sky."

"What'll happen to it? They won't be here much longer now surely?" Branwen shakes her head. "Seems cruel just to hold it prisoner. Where do you keep it?"

"In a crate in the house. Yes, maybe you're right, Tal. It is cruel. No crueller than a weasel."

"But a weasel's quick."

"Where do you think they go after the summer?"

He shrugs. "Some say they sleep over the winter, like bats in caves; or change their form, dive into lakes and become fish. Does it scream?"

She shakes her head. "It never makes a sound."

He wraps it carefully and gives it back to her. They stand for a moment. Llew, having done his three-legged rounds marking the property, has come to sit by her. She rests her palm on the dog's silky head and studies his master's face. There is something of the bird about him – the angular cheeks and deep dark eyes, the wide mouth. She laughs. "Not a good sign I fear." He smiles. "A woman looks hard into my face, then starts to laugh. What is funny, Branwen, bird keeper?"

"Oh, I beg your pardon!" She shakes her head, a laugh escaping again. "Very well – I will tell you. You look like a bird." He laughs. "Not any bird, a hawk, a kite – something like that."

"Then it's a compliment you give me." He bows, grinning.

She laughs. "Would you care to come in – erm, some water perhaps? We have some fresh milk, I think."

"Is your father not in?" She shakes her head. "Would he mind me drinking his milk?"

"Well, he…"

Tal glances behind him to where the women tending the cloth on the drying frames have paused in their work and are staring at them; there is a hum of commentary from behind their hands. He lifts his cap to them and they laugh.

Branwen's face darkens. "Take no notice of them; anything to stop work for a bit! Come inside if you wish."

"Let them stare themselves blind, is it mistress?" He smiles and, taking a fistful of Sailor's mane, pulls up onto his back. "Sorry – we should get back to logging or we'll both be for hire next fair day. It's a special sort of woman who can raise a witch's screamer."

She opens her lips to answer him, but can find nothing of wit to say. She watches him take the horse across the yard, through the gate and up the track, without seeming to have moved to give any instruction. It seems a moment after his departure before the sounds of the mill, the wood and the yard return. She finds herself smiling. There is somehow a warm feeling in her, even though he's gone. "Branwen Rhys, stop it – you already have a sweetheart!" There – she has said it; it is out in the air.

*

For nearly two weeks she follows a routine with the bird. He seems to have no voice, though she hears his shuffling feet and the scrape of wings as he moves around the crate. Five or six times a day, as early as she can and as late as possible, she feeds him, gives him water and takes him outside to hear the other swifts and for him to feel the air on him. Though she's never risked him as high as the upstairs windowsill again, she puts him on the wall or on her shoulder, where she can feel his claws pinch and where he creeps sideways to hide in her hair. When she's away from the mill she can't wait to come back to him. 'Like having a child!' she tells herself. The adults are still overhead, though none come to the nests any more. Sometimes they fly so high they're like soot flakes; sometimes hurtling low across the roof, screaming.

She puts him in the crook of a dead tree – all the branches have been stripped and now there is only a stump. She reaches up but the bird is reluctant to leave her hand. She has to detach him with the fingers of her other hand and slowly, gently sweep him away from her. He sits hunched there – a perfect meal for a sparrowhawk. He shuffles around so that he faces her.

"You won't go while I'm here staring at you, will you?" She has spoken out loud again! "I'm going inside now. You must fly; you have to fly."

She turns to go, his gaze burning into her back. Inside she peeps at him through the window. He hasn't moved and is vulnerable, just like a piece of bait put out for a kite. She can bear it no longer. She comes out and around the back door, anxious to see him safe, but instead is just in time to see him rise into the air. Without any obvious flap of wings, with no hesitation or wobble, he goes forward and up in a clean line, right up into the sky. For a few moments she can make him out, lonely in space, then he reaches the other birds. Still, for a slow second she can follow him, then he is lost, becomes part of the shrieking sky. Her face is soaking – the tears, yes, of joy! But now too the realisation that she will never see him again and that, had she not bullied and abandoned him, he would still be here.

Later she tells her father. "It was without effort, like he'd known all along how to fly but... had chosen to stay with me awhile, here on the ground."

Chapter Seventeen

"THERE YOU ARE! I've not seen you for some time. Do you often haunt this spot waiting for me? This is almost the same place I picked you up the other time."

"No indeed – I was on my way home. It's getting late."

"The same story you always tell! What important errand awaits you this time, or is it just your father who expects you home?"

"No, he's not home. He's gone with cloth to the market at Llanbrynmair."

"Then you've no excuse not to keep a poor surveyor company on his ride into town."

"Why did you not call on my father, as you said you would?"

He raises his hands in a helpless gesture. "Forgive me?" She holds his gaze. "What a stony face! Oh dear, poor Henry Davies would have more mercy from a hanging judge. Mistress, will you not forgive me?" He fastens the reins and gets to one knee on the floor of the gig, his hands together as if in prayer. "Have mercy, oh grave, pretty judge." Branwen looks away, the only way she can hide the smile which betrays her. "I see you're back in those infernal clogs, is there nothing to be done with you!"

She laughs at last and he straightens up, leaning to help her aboard the trap, his hands are clean, even his nails shine.

This time the journey to Machynlleth passes like a dream. She does not look at the scenery; every small movement he makes holds her in a spell. He drives with his thigh pressed along hers, sometimes taking both reins in his right hand, the left on her knee. It burns; the muscle seems to throb under his touch. Breathing does not come easy and speech is almost impossible, though there is something hiding at the back of her throat; something more she needs to say; something more she needs to hear from him. He talks from time to time: his plans, informing her about things she's seen all her life but never noticed. He doesn't seem to mind that she hardly has an answer.

As they pass the piled bark near the tannery on the outskirts of town, something is wrong. No one is at their work. The same is true at the livery stables, yet the town is noisy. Shouting, both horses and men. A dog's howl. He ties his pony himself, not bothering to untack him from the trap, and grabs her arm. As they come out onto the street a woman rushes past her screaming, "Mad dog. Mad dog – get inside!"

The Black Lion tavern is almost empty, the few customers crowding the small windows that look onto the street. He looks quickly up the stairs. "Come up with me." She hesitates, slipping her arm from his hand. "Come; we were friends before we were lovers, were we not?"

The word explodes in her. Lovers! Yes; that is its name. She nods, dumb. As he goes to find the landlord she looks through the open door. There is a man in the middle of the road, a small dog, stabbed through with the spikes of a pitchfork and clearly dying. It seems to tense and then stretch, bending in the middle, like a fish hanging from a hook, though it hardly makes a sound. The man strains to hold it high, at arm's length. People approaching duck out of his way. A crowd follows him, shouting. Someone else is screaming. Davies returns and takes her arm again, pulls her up the wooden stairs.

Once inside he turns the key. It is not a comfortable room and the damaged floorboards hardly mask the noise from downstairs; in fact, light and movement can be seen in the cracks between the planks. "Now we are a little private at least." He loosens his cravat and goes to sit on the bed, easing off his boots by catching the rush mat on the heels. "Come and tell me again. What were you saying?"

"You didn't come and you haven't told me why."

He laughs "You wouldn't hold that against me, surely?"

"I waited all day for you to come. After we… that time we… well, the time I visited you on your own in your lodgings, you said you'd call on me; for my father to see you call for me. I made a good table for you," she says. He crosses to her and holds her against his chest, the buttons of his fancy waistcoat pressing into her cheek. He strokes her hair and she finds the curve and hollow of him, nestling in like a hen to roost.

"You're not angry with me, surely? You know Henry Davies is a busy man, a man of business. Of course, I would have loved to meet your father, you know that – another time perhaps." He stands between her and the door and, between gentle kisses, nudges her back towards the bed. As her knees buckle against the wooden sides, she shakes herself alert, sliding back away from him as he kneels on the feeble mattress. Shoulders and back pressed against the wall she draws up her legs, pulling at her skirts to cover them. There is something comical about the way he shuffles across the bed

159

on his knees, arms out awkwardly for balance. Something of the dear, black swallow about him. "You smile – I see you're teasing me."

She looks steadily at him. "I'm not your common mistress."

He laughs. "But indeed you are. Mistress' ire and pique!" She shakes her head. "Come, you were willing enough before; why so close with yourself here?" By now he has her shoulders in his fists. His expression is not unkind as he bends to look at her face, seeming truly to want an answer, to understand. He is kneeling on her dress and she pushes at his thigh as she moves away from him. "You have no answer for me. See, you squirm away! This isn't the maiden who crept sly around my lodgings so no one would hear. Come now." He grabs for her again, leaning forward as she tries to pull further away along the wall but her skirts are still trapped under his knees.

"Why did you not come?" she says. "I felt a fool. No –" This time as he tries to clutch at her she pushes him hard in the chest and tugs at her skirt. She is free at last, rolls to the edge of the mattress and stands up to confront him. "My father told me not to see you. I will have to lie to him again."

"Why so? Am I not a good match?" She doesn't answer, so he sits back, his shoulders against the wall, his legs outstretched, the thumbnail of one hand probing invisible dirt from under the nails of the other. He hardly looks at her. "Would he scorn me as a stranger, or does he listen to tavern lies and gossip like a common drunk?"

"He's no drunk! My father has nothing to say about where you're from but he... he didn't know that I'd come to you before. I told him you'd be coming to walk out with me in daylight; that you wished to meet him, had an interest in the

160

workings of the mill." Davies makes no answer. "If you'd come to meet me at home as you'd promised –"

"Promised?" He laughs, drily. "No! I never 'promised'." Davies looks up briefly, then continues his attentions to his nails, this time swapping hands.

"Well, if you'd done as you said, people would have seen us walking out. My father would have been a proud man if you'd come calling in daylight, as you said."

"I think he calls me stranger; I think you make excuses to quarrel. Tell me, you have another beau do you not?"

"No!"

He sits up on the edge of the bed in front of her. "How can I believe you when you tease like this? Come to find me, lure me to a tavern bedroom –"

"I do not... we came across one another by chance today, I didn't know what to say. I didn't tell him I'd expected you, that time before. I'm so glad I didn't, he'd have thought me such a fool."

"You play the wronged innocent so well; tell me, could you look into my eyes and swear you don't desire me?" Quick as a goose's tongue, Davies has his palm around her wrist, jerks her onto his knee. Other hand tight in the hair under her bonnet he leans back, looking her in the face.

"I think you do not love me," she says simply.

He twists her arm, pulling her sideways onto the mattress, shoving her in the chest. Then he's on top of her.

As he tears at his breeches, he uses his upper body to hold her down, his knees to push her legs apart. She squirms up the bed under him, trying to lift his weight enough to close her thighs, pushing up hard against his shoulders. "Stay still!" He draws up his knees either side of her and pins her arms down. "What do you do? Why do you play the tease?" He shakes her, suddenly releasing the pressure on her hips and she takes advantage of it, twisting her body and bucking, dislodging him for a moment. Hauling herself up onto her elbows, she throws herself backwards, away from him. Her head cracks against the wall, a blow low at the back of her skull and she cries out. The pain is sickly, and for a moment there is nothing but the pain, a spasm that blinds her. But Davies hasn't noticed and is on her again. He scrapes at her skirts, clawing them out of the way as she holds her head, hand squashed under her skull. As he pushes into her, her head gets trapped between two of the thick rope cords supporting the thin straw mattress. She tries to pull free, to sit up, but all she can do to protect the back of her head from slamming against the wall again is to use her palm as a buffer. Each of his jabs is a sickening pain, a fist punch to the stomach. His eyes are closed, his face turned to the side, the cheeks heavy and thick, swollen. The movement is repetitive, inhuman, like an arm of one of the hammers at the mill. He makes no cry, not even grunting as the movement peaks, the range increasing with the speed. He moves further back each time before thrusting forward and she feels her finger joints crunching against the wall under the impact of her skull. Only right at the end does he make a noise – a snarl, as though someone were twisting his arm in the socket, his jaws clenched together. He drops down on her, his face in her hair.

She holds still at first, then eases herself from under his arm. He grumbles, inarticulate as she slides from under him, then whines into the mattress, "No, don't move away. Lie with me a while, Branwen."

She is unsteady on her feet and sits quickly down on the side of the bed. He stretches out a foot, putting it across her lap but she moves away. She gets up and tidies her clothes – her bodice is hardly undone. She has no comb but does her best to make her hair acceptable with her fingers. She looks for the bowl under the bed – it is not clean but she bends over it, the urine stinging as it comes. She takes the rag to wipe herself, her knuckles disappearing into the mush of the hole he's made of her.

His hand gropes down the side of the bed and squeezes her shoulder. "Come back to bed," he says into the covers. She doesn't move and the hand flops down over the side of the mattress. She stands up. Hair tidy, clogs on her feet, she is ready to go. Face down, his breathing is heavy now and the back of his neck red and puffy, though his spreadeagled body is wholly relaxed.

She moves to the window, the tiny panes are warped and dirty. It's an engraving she sees when she looks out – black, white and grey; only the difference between space and bulk, and outlines. Sometimes colour flares, distorted in the flame of a torch; sometimes a lamp moves along the street. In here, something has happened that she's been working all her life to avoid. No one had caught her before; she was always the one not to be a fool, the proud one, a feisty daughter of a father who was his own man. Even at his lodgings she had managed to keep some control of herself. She opens the casement and the sound enters, almost a tangible thing, fresher and clearer than the tavern noises through the floorboards that have become background now.

"Branwen?" She jerks round. He is sitting up against the wall again, studying her. She shakes her head. He sits up straighter. "What's done is done. Why do you make it different from what went before?"

"Because it was," she says, simply.

He moves to the edge of the bed and begins to put his clothes in order. "You weren't worried before. You came to me like a weasel to fresh liver!" He smiles at his own wit. "Yet you still frown!" He looks at her for a response; there is none. He eases his feet into his boots and stands up. "Well, the hire of the room was not wasted, but I must admit, you are a sport I won't rush to enjoy again."

"Leave before me, if you please," she says, fighting to stand up straight and look him clear in the face.

"Why so?"

"I don't want to be seen with you again."

He sneers. "Now the strumpet's proud!"

"You are not what you seemed." Deliberately she turns back to the window, her back taut as a violin string, tuned to his every movement. But he does not come near her again.

"Who do you think would listen to you? Who do you think would come to the aid of a girl who's so loose as to go upstairs in a tavern with a man? What game do you play, pretty mistress – a line between your brows, your jaw set all severe yet your lips wet and pink and waiting?"

"There were mad dogs in the street."

"So you thought you'd come up here? You are more wily than the other village girls, that much is true."

"You have no interest in me? Not… beyond what was done at your lodgings and, and… this, this… ravishing?"

"Ravishing! You are certainly a strange one. To name it thus, after seeking *me* out before! You question me for all like a lawyer: What is my family? What are my plans? Yet you walk with me at night on your own, swoon when I so much as run my finger down the back of your neck, lie to your father – and your aunt, and now this! Go on, shout out. Have them come hammer on the doors and laugh in your face – the strumpet that changes her mind! Now that would be a sin indeed!"

She says nothing as he finishes dressing.

"They saw you come willingly up the stairs with me; some will have seen your hand on my sleeve as we waited for the landlord to get the key." He slams out of the room, fastening his coat as he leaves. Before he closes the door, he turns back. "And you can tell your father that I have no interest in his tease of a daughter. She carries the stench of the fulling vat about her."

She picks out his voice for a few minutes, laughing with some men, but she can't hear what is said. She is still watching as he leaves the tavern, glancing up at their window – an exaggerated tilt of his hat in greeting, visible once more as he passes a man with a strong lantern, then is gone.

The back of her head throbs and she feels sick, the dull pain creeping forwards into the front of her skull. She sits on the edge of the bed, legs open, a handkerchief pressed between them. Pink, watery liquid, seeps from her. As the seed gulps out, it is a dull, sinking recognition. But at least she will not fear a child: her body never softened itself to him and there can be none.

After hiding at the top of the stairs, waiting for the hallway to be clear, she slips downstairs and out into the street. The town is quite empty now, though she can hear shouting in one of the yards behind the inn. She slips into the barn. How will she get home? Then she hears the shouting directly outside, doors banging, dogs barking then a long, drawn-out dog's moan, running feet, a woman's scream, more shouts, like barked orders. She crouches down, her fists pushed up between her legs. Her mind keeps returning to the dirty room, like a finger crawling towards a bruise, pressing it.

Suddenly she sees it: a bear, looking at her, its face crooked in the unreliable light from the entrance torch. Before, bears had seemed like big dogs – sharp, pointed faces; wide jaws with dangerous teeth; shaggy, matted fur. This one looks at her, one eye missing. Its long neck is bare under the collar. The bear is sitting up straight, like a farmer at his table, both back legs stretched out, the front legs – more arms than legs, crossed over its belly. The smell is like nothing else: not stables, not kennels but a night smell, something caught on the wind after dark; something belonging to a wood at night. The chain seems too big for it, ridiculous, hanging from the worn, thin collar. Its claws are blunt and one of the ears is shredded, giving the silhouette a lopsided air. It growls deep from the belly. Perfectly still, it looks straight at her.

Chapter Eighteen

CAI AND CARI stop a little way from the bride's cottage. A group of brightly dressed young women pass them, each one looking at them from under her hat. Several fiddle unnecessarily with their clothes; others walk in an exaggeratedly slow manner, looking down at the floor, then across at them. They lean in to speak to each other, hands across their mouths. Cari calls out and waves. "Hannah!" One of the taller girls starts and looks quickly at them, raises her hand briefly, then hurries on. One is giggling, her body shaking, hand to her lips and is pulled roughly away by another. Cari looks sideways at Cai. "Well, what an effect you have on the young women of the district, Mr Gruffydd."

Cai laughs. "I think I know her from Nanteos – she helps sometimes when there's a party." They walk together towards the house, in time to see the front door open and the group of young women crowd inside. Cari hangs back. "Will you not join them inside?"

"No, I… no, I think not. Well, perhaps. Will you come in?" Cai shakes his head. "Or perhaps you could wait for the groom's party. You could join with them. We could rhyme backwards and forwards to one another."

"I don't know it, Cari. I've never learned it, though I've heard of the custom, granted."

"Don't they do this for weddings at Nanteos? For the gentry

weddings?" Cai shrugs. "What do they do then? What fancy habits do they practise? Or is it a secret that you can't tell a horse trader's daughter?"

He looks quickly at her, but she seems amiable enough, a smile on her lips. "I've been to none. My name is not the sort a fancy lady would put on a wedding invitation!" She doesn't answer. Instead she studies the house for a few moments.

"Come," she says. "Let's wait for them past the top of the hill. The groom's men will come that way to try and steal the bride – but they won't get her. She'll gallop away to church and they'll have to follow her."

Already the bridegroom's men are coming up the lane, the bride's supporters pulling taut the rope lying across the track. "Jump that, you whey faces!"

"That's Beth's uncle," Cari laughs. "He runs the Talbot in Tregaron!"

A couple of the bride's friends pelt the groom's party with fruit as they line up to jump the barrier. "Come on, jump it!"

The riders take stock, backing up the horses ready to jump. "Delicious! My favourite!" shouts the leader, taking a bite out of a wizened apple then tossing it in the hedge. His horse flies over, followed closely by a couple of others and then a fat cob who pulls up before he reaches the rope then cat jumps over it, the rider, a tiny skinny man, more leprechaun than horseman, swearing and clinging to his ratty hat.

Cari is laughing. "Come on, if we run through the copse we can head them off when they set off after the bride." She grabs Cai's hand and they jump the stream and go through the trees to wait at the crossroads. "Will you come back with me?" she asks, straightening her bonnet.

"What, now?"

"After we've seen them on their way."

"I can't Cari. I need to meet with the surveyor – we look to build a pond so that we can control the flow of water to the wheels and pumps – if we can get them installed." He lifts her onto a low branch and leans against the trunk. Her legs dangle in front of his face and she flicks at his cheek with her skirts. He smiles and brushes them away. "Sorry, Cari."

"Then I'll come to you. Have you moved out to your 'Bailiff's cottage' yet?"

"I've not had time – the funeral; going to Sheffield –"

"Then you're still in that room on the second floor – near the servants?"

"For the time being – suits me fine; I am in my bedroom as little as possible!" He smiles up at her but she is looking away.

"Then nothing has changed. Thomas Powell is dead; his brother takes over at Nanteos, but the loyal Edward carries on just as before." He looks at her a moment, but she doesn't seem angry – in fact, when she turns around there is a light smile on her lips and she flicks at her dress with a twig.

"I'll be in Tregaron next week," he tells her. "Powell wishes to meet with some of the tenants. There are those who are confused as to whom they owe allegiance. Some have even spoken to Morris!"

"And you want me to dine with you at the tavern, as before?"

"Well... he and I'll dine alone, no doubt. William Powell is up for a few weeks on his own at Nanteos before he goes to fetch the family to join him. He wants to 'clarify the position' as he calls it, but we'll be staying overnight, of course."

"Of course. And I am to come quietly to the inn and ask for your room after business is complete?"

"No need to be quiet, Cari – be as bold as you please!" He laughs but she doesn't answer. Instead her toe knocks lightly, though repeatedly, against his temple as she swings her foot back and forth. "Why do you kick me in the eye, maid?" He laughs.

"Why do you put your eye there for me to kick?" He grabs at her ankle and she pulls away, they wrestle for a moment, Cari holding tight onto a branch and Cai pretending to pull her down. Then she bends backwards and shoves him hard in the chest with her feet, dropping down to the ground and standing with her hands on her hips as he gets up, grinning and brushing down his breeches. "And the next day you'll walk me down the middle of the street on your arm and stop when you pass the Nanteos tenants and farmers, the tradesmen and mine officials – even the preacher will stop for you in the street. 'Good day, Mr Gruffydd!' They'll raise their hats to you, though you're really not a Powell at all, and you'll say, 'Good day, Owens, Jones or even Johnes. May I present my sweetheart to you?'" She makes a mock bow.

Before he can respond, horses appear on the road. They are going at a gallop, the riders clinging on with one hand and punching air, shouting and whooping. The bride herself is first past, facing backwards behind her 'guardian', laughing and making obscene signs to the groom's riders following her; then comes a huge woman on a skinny hunter, dressed in the bride's colours ("She's borrowed that to be sure!" Cari shouts), the apple eating man and his companions, and lastly the tiny man on his cob.

"So much more fun than a gentry marriage I would think." Cai laughs, picking up several of the blooms, ribbons and sweets thrown by the party as they passed. "A good horsewoman, the bride – no unseating her before she gets to church. How do you know her? Cari?"

She is fastening her hat, facing away from him as she follows the stragglers out of sight. He stands by her, takes the shining rope of her hair in his hand and, holding it to his face, breathes deeply.

"If I were to be married, I wouldn't do this."

He laughs. "Looks to be excellent sport!" He reties the green ribbon around her plait.

"What if one of them was to fall, to be killed on the wedding day; or, worse – crippled and drag their dead legs across the ground like a frog from under a cart wheel." Cai looks quickly at her, laughs in surprise at her grave expression. "The banns, the presents, the food – all of it, all of that fuss and money and then the silence of two people in a hovel looking at one another over a mean, turf fire."

He laughs out loud at this, slipping his hand around her waist and pulling her near. "Are you feverish, Cari?" She shakes her head and pulls away. He stops smiling and looks more closely at her. "Cari, are you ill? You look so pale…" He puts his hand to her brow. "Not a fever – perhaps we should go and dine somewhere. I could take a room –" She snorts a reply. "Have I offended you?"

"That is your answer to every hiccup, every snag, every awkward moment between us, is it not? 'Shall I hire a room? Put down a blanket on the hay?'" She waits, but he has no answer to this. "I can look you in the face with my head held high. You might well be Edward Gruffydd of Nanteos –" Her head waggles in derision as she says this, adopting a pompous, mocking voice.

"Cari, what –"

"– but I'm no cockle gatherer. We know more about horses than you'll ever know –"

"What did I –?"

"– and I have a proud family. We make our own money and no one tells us what to do." She stops and looks at him, biting her lip. He reaches out towards her, pulls her against his chest. She shoves him away. "There you are again; 'Cai Gruffydd's handsome face will cure it all', but I can see what you are and what you do here!" He holds out his hands in surrender. "Playing the innocent! You have no intention of marrying me –"

"Marrying you! Cari, what're you –"

"There you are! There you are, see, you don't deny it!"

"Cari." He grabs her by the wrists. "Stop a moment. What –"

She pulls away from him, shoves him in the chest. "It's as they say: you're waiting for a little heiress; oh, she may have a face like last year's turnip but she'll have the money to set you on your way. Look at poor, rich Mary Powell, there's a goose of a woman if ever I saw one, even if she *is* rich as a Turk!"

"Why speak of Mary like this?"

"You're like your dead father; who cares about the face or even the hindquarters as long as the nag pulls a golden carriage." She has gathered up her shawl, jerking it around her body with each sentence, knotting it at the front.

Cai looks at her. "What's happened?" he asks at last.

She stares back at him, her face to one side in defiance. "Why would you care, Cai Gruffydd?"

"Do you want to be married?" She scoffs. "No, answer me properly Cari – do you want me to marry you? I thought –"

"Marry you? Marry a gentry bastard – not in a thousand years." She tugs at the bonnet ribbon, breaks it and throws it on the floor. She is crying and Cai moves once more towards her. "Stay away from me. Go and find another stupid girl to tame the snake in your trousers." As she leaves, another party of riders comes careering around the corner and, as she stumbles to get away from the hooves, she screams at them "Go to hell!"

"Cari!" Cai goes after her.

"You can go to hell too. Get back to bloody Nanteos – get back in your fancy cage!"

Arms by his side he watches as she disappears from sight.

Chapter Nineteen

NOTHING IS FINISHED: not the house, the service wing, the stables, the gardens, the ornamental walk… all will now be handed to William and Elizabeth as some half-done thing, like an apple with a bite out of it. Mary shakes her head. How will they see Nanteos? Will Elizabeth have the enthusiasm and energy for it? Did a mother-of-three have the time? Would finishing the decoration of the mansion be as dull as altering another woman's cast-off clothes to wear instead of buying new?

Everything is packed now. She is leaving more furniture than she'd originally intended, but as the time came to make a decision each piece had looked so perfect where it was, had been chosen over the course of more than ten years especially for that recess, that view, that particular room – to take them with her would be to take an animal from its natural condition. She laughs, how whimsical she has become! How she romanticises the house, herself. How commonplace a thing it is after all to be a widow having to leave her home. Only that, for many women, their beloved possessions would now pass to their sons and wives; but there are no sons and wives for her. She shakes herself; shakes herself like the spit dog shakes a rat, killing the melancholy, the self-pity like the dog mauls the rat. What imagery again, Mary – desist from this self-pity, I beg you!

She gets up from *the* dressing table (she will not speak of it as *her* dressing table any more) and looks through one of the windows. Plas Nanteos is throwing everything it has at her today. It is as though the estate is thanking her for her care – that is one thing she cannot reproach herself for; during these last weeks the packing has in itself been an act of love. She has caused every part of the house to be cleaned and all Thomas' papers relating to the estate she has ordered herself, arranging and indexing them in a precise way that would have been unthinkable when he was alive. There had been some surprises too – many not at all pleasant. Those debts owed to the estate or owed by the estate and mines will not be a welcome discovery for William and Elizabeth; but that cannot be helped. She has left them her own papers too with all documents relating to the garden and the designs for the parkland and the small buildings planned there. They will be no good to her in London. Thomas' more personal papers she has with her; has not had the time (or courage, perhaps?) yet to visit these properly.

The carriage is waiting for her; has been there for almost two hours and her trunk and boxes are all aboard. Other of her personal possessions, including her instrument, will be safely stored and follow when she has prepared her new home to receive them. She looks again through the window. The tiny river in front of the house – so innocent, 'doesn't know I'm leaving'. She laughs ironically at herself, 'Always personifying the world, dear Mary' – Thomas had known her well. Goodbye to the long, low ridge and the noble trees.

A tap at the door – Elin. "Mistress –" She holds up her hand and Elin's form disappears. A last glance at the ridge. 'The sky unrolls its shapely clouds across a moonstone sky.'

Yes, that will do nicely, Mary. She opens her door, brushing the beautiful wood with her lips, then is out on the landing. She looks once towards Thomas' room, as though he could appear, gown open, hair on end, brimful with one scheme or another.

There is a murmuring from the hallway and a line of servants has formed for her. Elin wraps her cloak around her as she reaches the bottom of the stairs – she is leaving her maid here for Elizabeth and will engage another for herself once she gets to London, someone a little older. She will travel for the first few miles alone, then Edward will join her and accompany her for some of the way. They have much to discuss and she will be glad of his company.

Along the line now: Elin behind her with a pouch of money for each one. This time she faces out through the front door, but she remembers so well coming into the old house, the previous house, for the first time after her marriage. There was a purse for each one then too and, looking at them, most of the staff that were here when she was a new bride remain; she is proud of that as well – a sign of good, kind management over the years. Last is Martha. She takes the cook's knuckles, already curled tightly over the money, in her own hands and squeezes them. About her own age, Martha, though still a mystery to her, has become a confidante in these last months. She turns with her back to the door, says the right thing (thanks; kind wishes for the future, pledges to visit); then out into the windy sunshine, up into the carriage. They pour through the door and onto the gravel (surely the first and last time they will be allowed to do this!) and she knocks for the coachman to depart. She waves cheerfully. Now the lake, bald, its banks as yet unplanted; across the drive her thin saplings bowing to her from the woodland walk; the newly-built lodge and the handsome gates; then it is over. Tears come. She snorts, gurgles, blows her nose like a herring girl, laughing at herself through them. Mary Powell of Plas Nanteos is no more!

Chapter Twenty

It is thick with smoke and dark in Gruffydd Gruffydd's cottage as Branwen finds her way to a low stool in the corner, as far away as possible from where the conjuror sits by his fire. A heavy man, perched on the edge of the smoke-blackened settle opposite, gulps out his story. Alternately pulling at and squeezing, he plays on his cap like an accordion. "And they walk up the walls – bobbing their heads, grinding their teeth. Some seem blinded; some stagger – they are bewitched for sure!"

"Where do you live, did you say?" Gruffydd leans towards him as he speaks, his eyes big in the light from the fire.

"Tyddyn Canol."

"Where is that?"

"Near the mine at Bwlch Gwyn."

Gruffydd nods. "Are others on your neighbours' holdings the same?"

The man nods. "Jones' cattle roar and foam at the mouth! They cannot keep their calves in them!"

"From where do they drink?"

"Except for winter, when they are in the barns and we draw water from the stream near the cottage, they drink from the river. Why do you ask me?"

"How long have they been like this?" The man shakes his head lifting his arms in a hopeless gesture. "Weeks would you say?" The man nods. Gruffydd continues to press him. "Before they started digging again above Bwlch Gwyn?" The man nods. "Before, you say? Are you sure?"

"Eh... no, after. It was after they started blasting. I bought a milking cow from my neighbour and she was alright then. I thought he'd cheated me but his are worse than ours. Could it be the noise from the mines has upset them?"

Gruffydd shrugs. "Do you come just for yourself or for them too?"

"They sent me. They sent coins, but only I dared come."

Gruffydd nods. "You did right. I'll give you something..." He gets up and crosses to a small door behind the bed loft. As he passes, he smiles at Branwen, a look that lifts and tightens all the creases in his face, its surface as startling as a stone thrown hard into a still pool.

He returns with a small, rough-hewn box, settles back on the stool by the fire and opens it towards the man. "Take and keep it safe – above the fire if you have a shelf; if not, make one." He fetches a common teasel from inside the box. A small piece of paper is tied to it with a ribbon. "Give one of these to each of your neighbours and keep one yourself. When you close the box for the last time, don't open it again. Ever. Understand me?" He closes the lid and holds the box towards him.

The farmer nods, snatching the box in his haste to get up. "Thank you. I thank you." He looks about to cry.

Gruffydd gets to his feet and holds the door open for him. The man nods to Branwen and hurries towards the entrance. "One thing..." Gruffydd's hand is on his arm. The man freezes. "Move the beasts away from the river. Carry water from the high streams at the far side of the valley if you have to."

"But the river meadow's my best pasture... there are no fences to stop them getting to the water –"

"Build fences if you need to. Tell the others to do the same."

"It's not possible, they –"

"If you want the charm to work you will do as I say." He shrugs. "A blessing on you."

The man nods, repeating his thanks. "Go now," Gruffydd says at last, closing the door behind him.

A shower of coins clink into a metal bowl as he turns back into the room. "Now, young woman, what ails you?"

She tells him; all of it. The cottage is gloomy, the turf fire silent. Gruffydd says nothing, sitting in front of her and facing away. His thin back is bent towards the hearth and her own voice soothes her; after a while it becomes a tale told of another girl: A stupid girl; a girl who believes in fairy stories and fails to know the fox capering in children's clothes. As she comes to the end – the terrible ride home from Machynlleth, begged from the Ffwrnais blacksmith and his wife, her voice rises again. The woman had probed and probed, her tongue like a finger deep inside her ear, picking and picking at her story, a half-smirk on her lips. The spell is broken.

"What can I do to curse him? Help me, you must! Is there no cursed well – I've heard of one; there is, isn't there? Where is it?"

He turns around on the low stool. "A dreadful well?" He shakes his head.

"Where? Tell me!"

"There are none here."

She is on her feet, her voice shrill, feet dancing on the beaten mud. "Tell me – I don't believe you, tell me!"

"I will not. That is an end to it. The man will make his own curse." He turns back to study the fire. Branwen stands for a moment looking down on the bald, scaly ring right at the top of his head where no one would see it. She could lift the griddle that leans to the side of his stool and bring it down on his pate. "Put it down, child." She freezes. "Leave it. Come and sit here." He gets to his feet, the stool in his hand. Suddenly she is limp and loose as a freshly-skinned mole and slumps down onto the stool. He passes her, his palm lingering for just a moment on the crown of her head.

When he returns, he kneels in front of her, his back to the fire. He reaches for her fingers and opens them, placing the curved shoulder of a black wing in her palm. As she grips it, her hand fitting to its strange tension, her whole arm seems to vibrate, like a clumsy bow passed, hard and rough, over a string. He smiles at her surprise.

"It doesn't smell," she says. "I thought it would stink when you brought it to me." Holding the wing, she brings her arm up then across her body in a scything gesture.

"*Cigfran*. I knew the bird. He died a long time ago. Besides, there is no real blood in a wing." She stops her arm, though her thumb keeps moving, stroking down the feathers. "Pluck them out, as you need to, one at a time. Start with the softer, smaller ones at the top, then pull the bigger. One at a time."

"But what do I say? How do I curse him?" Gruffydd doesn't answer, seems unblinking with his white eyelashes and vein-blue eyes. "What if there aren't enough feathers for everything I must say?" Branwen again raises her voice to the conjuror, knowing she should not. Gruffydd moves away from her, holding up a flat palm as she tries to follow him into the far room. Still holding the wing, sweeping the air with it, she can't stop herself shouting after him. "A wing! Just feathers for what he's done. There must be something else!" When he doesn't return, she lowers her arm and sits on the settle, the black fan spread across her lap. She strokes the feathers with the side of her thumb. They are dry, not waxy; tough, not delicate. Only the top ones, the untidy downy ones, are soft.

Gruffydd appears at her side. "You frightened me!" But her voice is more accusing than frightened. Then, "I don't want to tear it apart." Gruffydd nods. "It seems wrong to break a flesh crow's wing for him; such a proud bird." She picks up the wing again and holds it like a lady's fan, blows the strange raven air across her face. She puts it gently down again. "What do I do with the feathers when I've plucked them out?"

"Lose them in water." She notices the bowl and moss bag in his hands. "Did you wash after the man?" She nods. "Is there a child?"

"No!"

Gruffydd looks hard at her for a moment. "When did he come for you?"

"I told you – market day, late in the afternoon. Why do you not speak his name?"

"If you wish, you can wash again. Put this on the floor in the fire's warmth and bend over it. It'll make you feel clean of him, though there'll be none of him left in you... not unless there's been a child made." He pauses. "I'll go outside."

Kneeling over the bowl she washes herself. At first she is shy of it, glancing constantly towards the door, but the moss is a wonderful sponge and a smell comes up from the hot dark water, drowned with herbs. The smell is of the bog in summer – rich, peaty, a slight tang of rot. She dabs, then sluices herself, taking the sodden sponge and pressing it hard between her legs until it hurts. Words start to form, then come from her mouth. There is a rhythm to them that increases, both in speed and volume and she finds herself on her feet, hurtling from wall to wall shouting and slapping the white-washed surface with her hands. She shouts his name, screams his name, howls his crime, calls down horror and pain on him. "May a raven have your eyes!"

*

Her father is waiting for her, *cawl* in the black pot; bread already cut. "Where have you been, Branwen?" She shakes her head. "You're still not well?" She nods, slipping off her light shawl. He comes up to her, holding her face in his hand, he looks intently at her.

She pulls away. "I've been to the *dyn hysbys*." She blurts it out. It is a relief to tell him.

He sits on the settle by the fire, ladles food for her, puts it on the small stool. She sits opposite him. "And how is Gruffydd?"

"Kind."

Her father follows the fire. It is warm in the room, though only a few peats glow. "Could he help you?" She shakes her head. He sighs. "Eat, Branwen."

She tries her food, but it tastes of nothing and there is no room for it to pass down her throat. She puts the spoon down as quietly as she can. The waterwheel is the only sound for a while. Then, "I saw a wolf, Dada." She sits upright in her chair. "On the way down the mountain." He looks up, spoon frozen before his mouth. "I know it was, Dada. Everything about it was different from any dog – looking straight ahead, not chasing after every scent, and silent. Suddenly I saw it below me in the valley, crossing an empty field, going uphill. It was trotting, but only the legs seemed to move – very long, bony legs, grey, the hair short and the body box-shaped. Other colours on the body too, not just grey – black too. He must have known I was there – it was a he, I'm sure. It was enormous, but lean. I was taking a short cut, trying to get home before dark. I scrambled over the rocks to the other side, trying to see him as he moved under the overhang. I hoped he would stop and look at me so that I could see his face, see the red tongue maybe, though it would have terrified me. He was getting towards the field's edge, just before the wall and the top of the hill, and I couldn't see him any more." She is quiet for a while. Without speaking Evan takes her bowl, returns the contents to the pot. "Do you believe me? You do believe me, Dada?"

He looks at her. "Have you told anyone else? Did you see anyone on your way down?"

She shakes her head. "But I would have liked to say goodbye; see him the minute before he disappeared." For a while they are quiet, the fire making comfortable the silence between them. "Do you believe me?"

He nods, stands. "Go to your bed now, child. Rest. It's late."

Chapter Twenty-One

Branwen waits in the yard of the hat factory at Tre'r-ddôl, breathing through a piece of cloth, miserable with the stench from the vats of boiling wool, rabbit and hare fur. She's been there for some time. People cross in and out of the yard looking at her and Siwan with mild curiosity, but none come up to her. At last Mother Lewis comes out and sees her. She marches over.

"What are you doing skulking out here?" Branwen shakes her head, hiding her face behind her hair. "We've almost run out, and a big order for the end of the month." She comes nearer. "What ails you, girl? Are you lovesick for some stupid youth? No?" Branwen shrinks away from her. The woman steps across the distance between them and peers into her face. "You're as green as a frog! Are you ill?"

Branwen shakes her head, miserably. "The boiling pots; the smell, I… it's even worse than the fulling baths!"

The woman takes a step back and looks her up and down. She seems about to speak but instead turns and goes back inside. Branwen manages to lead Siwan over to the wall and tie her up. She sits on the side of a stone trough at the far end of the yard, as far away as possible from the boiling cauldrons. After a while Mother Lewis returns with two other women and a boy and, though they look at her curiously from time to time, they say nothing to her as they unload the wool. Mother

Lewis takes her by the arm. Branwen tries to pull away, but the woman is insistent, though she doesn't say anything. She has a tankard in her hand and leads her to one of the warehouses. "Nothing smelly in here; sit down." She nudges Branwen down onto a straw bale. "This sickness; how long has it been upon you?" Branwen shakes her head and looks down. "Drink this, t'will help."

"What is it?"

"You don't want to know, except that it'll help you. Drink it." It is cold, slightly sour with a whiff of vinegar about it. Some leaves float around on the top. "Mint," says the hatter as Branwen takes one off her tongue. "No, eat it; bite it. Best bit for you." Branwen chews on the wet leaf as the woman studies her. "What, apart from the sickness ails you?"

"Nothing. I'm well."

"Do you shit loose?"

"No!"

"I didn't think so. Your dugs, are they sore?"

"Yes. They hurt me."

"Heavy?" Branwen nods. "Your mother is dead?" Again she nods, feels tears prick, though her mother has been gone all these years! "And your blood. The blood between your legs, when did it come last?" Branwen shrugs. "A while ago? Some months ago?"

"Some weeks."

"How many?"

She shrugs again. "What of it? Are you an apothecary?"

The woman laughs, the noise of flying geese. "No, maid!" She's quiet for a moment. "I think you should see Myfanwy." Branwen says nothing. The woman bends forward, speaking more quietly. "Myfanwy will see to you. I'll arrange it."

"I don't know her."

"I'd hoped you did not, being so young. You have a sweetheart?"

Branwen shakes her head, her belly squirms. "No, indeed!"

The woman looks at her hard once more, her face sad. "I feared it. You must then, and for certain, meet with Myfanwy, and soon." She gets partially to her feet, looking through the barn window into the yard. "I'll send the boy to you with word in a few days. He'll know only where and when to meet. Tell him nothing of why. Come, now; you're looking a bit better."

*

It is still dark, the damp air smelling of soil. No breeze, quiet. She sits on the wall to wait, her hands underneath her, protecting the cloak from damp off the stones. At first the garden is still, a thickness of solid shapes only – like an empty room at night, but before her eyes can detect it, the birds begin to greet the dawn. At first a robin's rattle, answered by others, invisible in the trees and hedges around. More of these with each passing minute, joined by the first blackbird's warning cackle. The light is coming now, almost invisible to the eye, more a high-pitched sound – the rubbing of a blade on stone at the margins of hearing. There is no sunrise as such, the morning depressed by an unbroken bank of clouds. Light comes like blood dissolved in water – a stain of brightness, increasing. It is minutes more before the first creature, a blackbird, breaks cover, flying straight and low, a rising stutter of alarm following him.

She keeps still, hardly wanting to breathe – it has something of the long sermons in church about it, this waiting, trying not to draw attention to herself; trying not to disturb the dawn. The realisation creeps up on her as the light begins to soak into the night, diluting the dark. The dragging, heavy feeling between the legs; that sensation of ants crawling under the skin; the full, deliciously tender breasts that usually come but once a moon – these were there all the time now. But no blood. Then, as the birds and creatures of the day begin to stir, she understands.

She goes to the river for fresh water – there is some sort of taint coming from the well now, not that her father complains, but she fancies she can taste it, and the water hasn't been clear since they found silver at the old Powell mine. There she looks in dismay, at first not believing what she sees. The birds had come since last night: a young snowbird, dusty grey, the white feather spots like maggots is lying on its side, the neck bent back and ugly. A jack-of-the-roof on its back, beak open as if to speak, its flat, spiked feet pointing to the sky; a tomtit, all colour gone from its feathers and silent eyes; a female blackbird, face down and drowned, lying like a rag in the rain. The birds had come since last night and lay by the edge of the stream that feeds the Einion. She stands staring at them, then bends down to take the blackbird from the water where it nudges against the bank. It is only the current that makes the wing seem to lift and weakly flap. She takes it up and folds the wings tidy. There is a flat slab of quartz just back from the water – like the *maen gwyn* in Machynlleth all those weeks ago. Before. She puts the bird to lie on her side, the legs stretched and tidy, one on the other. Now the jackdaw, its blue eyes dull as a fish. The beak is blunt and strong, the thighs feathered so the creature looks to be wearing breeches. Dead bird, lie there. Next the snowbird – so light, the beak a straight spike and, lastly, the tiny tit. She closes her eyes as she holds it in her hand. There is no detectable weight at all.

Her precious black swallow is alive somewhere surely, though long gone from the valley now. Alive in the air or asleep deep in a pool, waiting for the next spring to screech out, the 'witch's screamer' Tal had called it. But why have these other dear birds come here to die behind the mill?

Her father has gone to town again. The mill is not doing well. It seems there is more and more to do to get hold of the spun wool and sell the fulled cloth; less and less time to spend working the wool now. Behind her a magpie squawks and rattles, somewhere doing damage in the wood. She bends down and teases open the jackdaw's wing. The feathers separate like skeins of fulled wool. Was this bird a hen bird? She remembers the raven's wing at Gruffydd's hut. "I knew the bird," he'd said. She had opened the wing along the inside of her arm, fitted it to her palm and finger like the blade of a scythe. "The man will make his own fate," he'd said.

She feels it, a heavy, wet rope, coiling tight in her; sees the birds in a ring arranged around the well at the back of Davies' lodgings, beaks and sightless eyes pointing inwards. A dull, faraway sound as each falls in, poisoning his well.

She follows the spring upwards and there are others. Some have been there for a while – she leaves them, surprised that some fox or polecat hasn't taken them. Those that can be gathered, without falling apart in her hands, she carries back to the rock. The screamer of the wood is her prize. Newly dead, the feathers still hold their colour. What a marvel, that turquoise! She fetches a saddlebag and stacks the birds inside, head to feet; feet to head – the soaking blackbird is at the bottom. They are potted and packed like jugged birds and, at last, all together in Siwan's saddlebags, are ready. There is plenty of time to follow the valley up and cross the mountain to Henry Davies.

For the first time in weeks she moves with her old energy and is soon on the top road. What will be her story this time? What can she say if Morris is there to tease her? There will be no 'story'. She will say simply, "Your man has ravished me. I am undone." Yes – that is the word.

But there is nobody at the lodgings. She looks in through the parlour window. All is neat and bare. Going around to the back of the house she arranges the birds in a fan around the rim of the well. Starting with the smallest and ending with – what? A woodcock? Snipe? Each beak faces the same way and they lie on their side, legs tucked in. "Suffer them to come unto me; suffer them to come unto me." She hears herself as she nudges each towards the edge. There is no sound, no splash until she gets to the very biggest birds – crow and woodcock. Then only a dull, empty noise as they reach the water. The rim is empty. Only the pigeon has left some feathers behind. The coiled, wet rope inside her belly has gone dull and lies heavy and dead by her side. She wipes her eyes with her sleeve, careful not to get her stinking hands near her face. Tears. Poisoning him, this was to have been her revenge – but it is not as she had expected. She rises onto the balls of her feet and peers over the well wall. Down in the dark she can just see that something clogs the water. She's sobbing now. They should have been laid out side by side in a trench in the cool earth, their wings tidy, their dead spiked claws straightened and neat in respect. Now they bob lumpy and tangled; their wings hanging open, their dead faces hanging from their twisted necks. The tomtit will sink; all their sodden bodies will knit together.

She goes to the pump and rinses her hands again and again, smelling them, but the stench does not go away. She fits the empty, stinking bag back onto Siwan's back and leads her away. Each step helps to bury the sight of them in her mind's eye yet she feels… what? Is it shame?

As she reaches the crossroads she sees a young woman approaching. The woman hails her and she stops. "You're the mill girl." Branwen nods. It's the girl from Davies' lodgings. "Have you come from there now?"

"No. No, I've not been near the lodgings. I've had an errand to run."

The girl looks hard at her, shifting the basket on her back. "Took my advice then and didn't come near again. I'm glad of it."

Branwen touches her cap. "I must get back." She urges Siwan forward.

"He's gone of course."

Branwen pulls up and turns. The girl pinches one nostril and blows on the ground from the other, wiping her nose with a sleeve. "Morris too. But he went first, Henry Davies. Wasn't expecting it. They won't likely have gone far for lodgings as Mam says they're still going to the new workings – near the Powell mine. There'll be someone else takes the place on now – engineer maybe. I don't care." She looks at Branwen and seems about to speak again.

"Thank you."

"For what?" Branwen shakes her head. There is a moment

when she thinks of telling her. She will find out soon enough. "Are you alright, maid?" The girl takes a step towards her. Branwen nods quickly in farewell and moves away.

Chapter Twenty-Two

FOR TWO DAYS there had been an absolute calm. Trees, ragged and half-stripped now, held still in the damp, warm October air. On the third day it is dark at nine o'clock in the morning. High up the wind is moving fast, clouds heading east. The whole sky is grey – pale, dirt grey like the last of the water from washing the slate. Beyond the hills the sky is darker still, a warning.

She comes out of the mill cottage to a strange, yellow light. Near the ground there is no hint of a breeze, nor any sound of birds; not even a robin rattles its warning as she walks towards the barn. The sun is a perfect circle and she can look right at it through the grey air. Clouds pass over its surface, the strange diseased orange of rusty water. It is as warm as summer and close, but without the hum of insects or the din of birds. Evan has hired a wagon for the day to take the cloth into Machynlleth, passing it on to a broker who will sell it to the Drapers' Company for finishing, then to the London markets and beyond. Long gone are the days when her father would take the cloth himself to Shrewsbury, spreading it on the great tables for it to be fingered, smelled and prodded. She had hoped that one day she could arrange the delivery straight to the guild herself by joining with the hatters perhaps – getting around at least one step in the chain in which everyone who handles the cloth takes an ever-increasing cut, but this will not happen now. If only the Pryses would invest properly in the industry – but, as Davies had said, 'all the rich families in Cardiganshire are too busy with their hunts and parties; with building their mansions and fighting elections to develop the county for industry'. So busy selling the eggs that they let the hens starve. Hah! Davies… Henry Davies, damn his eyes! Oh, where is he now?

"Ready, Branwen?"

She nods.

The ride into town passes quickly enough, though there is little to see through the yellow fog. The crude wheels struggle against the road, setting her teeth on edge; every jolt and pothole is painful right up her spine and in her very joints. Why would that be? The womb hardly showed? It was hard to push away the memories of those other journeys, those times in the fine trap. The conversations, even his glances, the angles of his face, his gloved hands on the reins, are all still fresh and force themselves on her memory.

"You're quiet, daughter. Something ails you?"

She shakes her head. The secret. The secret. She wears it like an iron headdress, like the cage built for the murdering blacksmith hanged at the crossroads. She has swallowed it and the secret is solid and hard inside her, filling her up right to the throat so she can hardly speak. If she would speak, she would scream, "He did this!" But it would not be he they would see now, right in front of them. It was she carrying the shame, the blame. She was the fool, the stupid maid no better than the fallen girls you saw begging every market day – thin, weasel babies hanging off them; dark, rank milk stains on the cheap cloth of their bodices.

Before the tanneries at Machynlleth they have to stop for

a few minutes as a stallion walker struggles to get his charge under control. As they finally pass him the man calls out, "It's the devil's weather; he senses it!"

Her father pulls his hat down further over his face. "Stay away from men such as that, daughter: they have the same reputation as their charges."

In the town the people hunch forward as they walk, looking up over their shoulders at the sky, then hurrying on. Only the prophet man, a beggar from far away who preaches from a mounting block outside the Black Lion is animated. His eyes are wet with glee as he milks the sky with outspread fingers, "Now ye damned – repent! God will come at you from out of the mist, catch you up into the burning sky and torment you forever in hell!" Many times she'd seen him laughed and jeered at. He was good for sport, but not today. Her father takes her elbow as they approach him, steers her away fast.

"He won't make it happen by saying it," she murmurs, but he does not answer her.

They had sold their load on, leaving the hired wagon at the stables – cheaper to pay for a ride home from someone later than keep it for an extra day. Evan presses a coin into her hand. "Buy something, for yourself. Something to bring the light back into your eyes." She nods, but her fingers hardly bother to close around it. "I'll get what we need. Meet you back at the stables in half an hour? Won't do to linger here in this strange weather."

She nods and her father kisses her on the forehead before hurrying away. She stays near the wall as she goes down the main street – first on one side of the wide road, then up on the other. The mad dogs have been forgotten and a bear is dancing for a small crowd at the *maen gwyn*. She works herself to the front. The animal's fur is ragged, with bare patches. Its neck, the fur long ago rubbed away by the heavy chain, is comically skinny. A dark boy of about twelve controls the bear, tapping it with a blunt stick, giving simple commands and playing an unfamiliar tune on a whistle. The bear moves, lifting its limbs carefully, deliberately, like someone with rheumatism. The tip of the bear's nose is dry and beginning to crack. A small girl comes around the circle with a battered copper basin. The work on it is skilled, though it's seen better days. As she reaches Branwen she offers the bowl and Branwen watches her own pale hand move towards it; hears the coin drop. The routine is finished and people drift away. She sees the boy go towards the bear, comes within the reach of its powerful claws but the bear doesn't flinch away in fear of him. The boy strokes its shoulder. The animal drops his head down to one side and for a moment seems to rub comfortably against the hand. Meanwhile, the small girl picks through the coins in the bottom of the basin. It's a thin harvest, apart from Branwen's coin which makes her smile. She holds it out in front of her as she walks towards her partner and the bear. As he counts the coins, her fingers work absent-mindedly in the deep hair of the animal's back. Before they move away Branwen sees her give the bear an apple which he crunches at awkwardly, moving it around his mouth, perhaps to find the few remaining teeth. Perhaps that was her bear, the bear in the barn the night of her ruin? She is left on her own by the quartz rock as the three of them disappear down a side street.

*

That night the wind comes, sweeping the red from the sun, clearing the sick yellow light and putting the chill back. Its demented shrieking fills the mill yard, holding animals and people prisoner inside. The following day the world is right again. The white sunlight of October finds its way through the increasingly bare trees. A butterfly comes to warm itself on the flat, warm stone by the pool. A late wasp dips to drink. Branwen puts Siwan's harness on again and sets off to collect more of the rough-spun cloth for fulling. As she reaches the open hillside, she finds herself scanning the shallow horizon for a figure with a dog. A figure with a dog and perhaps a heavy horse. What will she say to him? She is tired in a way unfamiliar to her. The nagging sickness is better but her body is not familiar any more. Everything is keener: her sight, her hearing, the creak and grind of the mill machinery makes her wince. Away to the south there are people building a stone wall. There is no wagon in site – but there is no shortage of material up here and she can see women with stout baskets on their heads and a few pack animals. As she moves nearer her heart bangs in her chest. A well-dressed man, his back to her, his hair fair, acts as overseer, but he turns. Not Davies. Davies is gone.

She stops at the stream for Siwan. One of the women puts down her basket and comes to join her, paddling in the cold stream with her bare feet.

"Like stamping the laundry in the piss vat," she laughs. "Who are you then, girl?"

Branwen explains her errand. "Why do you build a wall on the wastes? Is it not common land?"

The woman laughs, bending low, her legs wide apart and splashing the cold water on the back of her neck. "Some are paid to say it is; some are paid by the Pryses, or the Powells or the Vaughans or Johnes... I know not who they are – to say 'tis private, this land." She gestures with her thumb at the overseer. "Can't on my children's lives remember which one of the devils he works for, but he pays me, that's all I need to know. The winch snapped and they've not had any rough ore up for days so I'm glad of it. Smashing lead out of rock or picking up rocks to build their walls or their roads, what's the difference? Eh, look at him – over there. You'd never know it – 'e's fifty if he's a day!" Branwen turns to where a muscular man with closed cropped hair, rough as a terrier's coat, is throwing rocks around with the vigour of a man ten years younger. "Molecatcher, just helping out for a day. Much admired by the women 'e is too. He said to me, 'Do you know, woman, now I'm in my middling years I find nothing is too fat, too thin, too old, too young, too red, pale or dark for my notice.' Oh we howled! 'Nothing is too old!' he says! What a fine fast talking man 'e is, with lovely blue eyes younger than his face."

Branwen laughs. "He should be wrestling bulls, not moles – look at his chest! I must go now."

"Aye, you get on your way, girl. The weather's promised spiteful."

Branwen and the donkey continue across the plateau for a while and she finds herself almost content. The road, though stony, is not too rutted here and she doesn't have to look down at her feet all the time. The October sun is quite bright and the donkey's fur is warm and smells wholesome as she plods along. The farmer at Tŷ'n Rhos is not there and the weavers themselves help her load the cloth, making a fuss of her and Siwan and giving them flummery and bread. She rests them both for a while, listening to the women talking, their backs against the sun-warmed farmhouse wall. It is easy to turn off from their chatter, their accents difficult to understand, the people and places they discuss unfamiliar.

"You're a quiet one!" one of the younger women says.

"Surely she's thinking of her sweetheart!" says another, looking at her expectantly, thinking perhaps that she will be roused, indignant, to defend herself.

But Branwen just smiles and, getting to her feet, looks around the group. "Thank you for the victuals; we must be going. It grows dark earlier now."

"I wouldn't let my girl go out on her own like that," one of the women says as she helps Branwen check the harness. "Pretty thing like you with only a donkey for company."

"Oh, don't worry about me," she replies. "This one's as fierce as any wolf if she's crossed. She'll defend us both." She leaves with the sound of laughter behind her.

The sky is sombre now, the colour of lead itself, but she hasn't got too far to go. The wind is increasing, bothering the tall, tough grass on the high ground. Despite her full load, Siwan is making good time on the homeward stretch. "You're imagining your warm mash and full hay rack, aren't you?" she says to the donkey. Across the valley is the gallows hill, that diabolical tree just visible, though if you were a stranger you would not really know, from so far away, what vile fruit it dangled. She stops. In the pass below, a coach with outriders and a laden wagon seems hardly to move against the dark bulk of the mountain. The rain has failed to fall, but threatens still in the layers of grey sky.

If it wasn't for the wind, she would surely hear them, the wheels struggling on the bad road. There is a passenger coach. It stops. Two women get out. Their clothes are dark and heavy but it is clear that the man who rides up to them has an expensive animal. Even at this distance she can see that the horse has a smooth gait, the man hardly moving on its back as he canters towards the women. Remaining on his horse, he leans into the coach, the door open – surely he talks to someone still inside? An elderly passenger; a child perhaps? He shuts the door and straightens up. On the wind she hears a faint whip crack and perhaps a shout, then the line moves uphill again. She watches as one of the women remains behind for some moments unmoving. What is she doing? The woman faces the hillside; perhaps she scans the top of gallows hill? The next wagon has almost caught up with her and she starts to move. Her walk is more a march, her head leaning forward and her hand lifting her skirts. She catches up with the man on horseback just before the brow of the hill and then Branwen loses sight of them.

Chapter Twenty-Three

TAL COMES BACK up the beach from the rock pools, wiping his knife on his breeches as he sits down beside her on the pebbles.

"Thank you for bringing me here." Branwen looks straight ahead, her cloak pulled tight around her.

"No need to thank me. No man says 'no' to Cari. Anyway, I have business here in Aberystwyth myself." But Tal does not look at her as he speaks, instead seeming to study the horizon. He will surely know about her now. Why else does a girl meet with Myfanwy away from her parents' house? She stares at the sea. It seems impossible!

"How does it stay there? Why?"

"Rises up, then stops. Well, most of the time. Twice in a day."

She picks up a black stone, worked and smooth. "This noise; how can someone think? So much noise, makes me feel dizzy."

"I like it."

She picks up one of the mussels in his tin. "Is this something the animal's made? These tiny pieces of rock and fibre hanging off them, a 'beard'? It's like a necklace, I think. How do you eat them?"

"Boil the water first, then drop them in. Never heat up the water with them live in it."

"But surely they cannot feel pain?"

"Maybe not, but how do we know?"

"Why would we care?"

He shrugs. "Costs nothing to boil the water first…"

Rooks, jackdaws and crows stalk the shoreline. Seabirds scuttle, drawn close, then back by the sigh of the waves. "Birds are different at the sea. Look." She points. "Even their voices are different from the land birds." They sit quietly for a while. "Why do people scream? My father told me once that everyone screams when they go to the sea."

"Have you never dipped your toe in it?" She shakes her head. "If you did, you would know. Even on the hottest day, you would scream, the same as everybody else."

She looks quickly at him but his eyes are still fixed far out over the sea. His sleeves are rolled up, shirt undone at the neck and his arms still brown from the summer. Llew has put himself to lie apart from them a little. He too watches the sea. "What're those creatures?" She points to a big rock offshore where huge black shapes pose against the sky. "Hags!" She laughs. "Waiting for night to come."

At last he turns towards her. *"Mulfrain."*

"An excellent name! What do they dine on?"

"Delicate cakes; baked meats; jugged hare…"

Branwen laughs. "I should know by now never to ask you anything."

"Fish." Tal grins. He leans back on his elbows and studies her.

Though she feels her cheeks grow hot she surprises herself by asking, "Will you stay in Cardiganshire?"

"I've no plans to leave." His face asks the question. 'Why ask? Is it that you care for me?'

She smiles. She can't help herself when she looks in his face, when she meets his eye. "Just asking a question. Sometimes you people stay for years, then... gone one morning, like dawn mist on a field."

"Who told you that?"

"My father."

He picks up a pebble, discards it, then another, tossing it into the air and catching it. Llew follows every move. "I'm not going anywhere, Branwen. Well, maybe I might go nearer to the sea." He stands up and offers her his hand.

They move further down the beach. Morfa Bychan. There is a sharp wind coming onto shore, carrying an unfamiliar scent. The stones are slightly warm as she sits down, though they are cold and wet just under the surface as she digs her knuckles deep down into the shale. At the water's edge is a group of gulls. Excited by something, they have made a crude ring, hanging back, taking turns to rush in, darting forward into the middle of the circle, necks and beaks craning towards something there. There is a brief tear in the circle and she sees a large chick. One adult bird stabs at it, grabbing the head in its beak and stretching backwards, pulling the young bird forward. Others peck at its body, screaming and squawking. Somehow the young bird manages to stay on its feet.

"An ugly sight!" Tal says under his breath.

Branwen is unable to look away. "No one to help him!"

"The mob – nothing I fear more."

"Come on, let's go, for pity's sake." But Tal is not listening; instead, he piles stones into a squat tower. She gets to her feet. "I'll go without you, then."

Tal's first stone goes far, passing across the group and into the surf. The birds stop for a moment, hunker down preparing to fly, but do not move their feet from the ground. One of the biggest throws back his head, beak pointing straight at the sky. "Never trust a creature with a yellow eye," Tal says. The call pulses from the chest and throat of the bird, regular and brash. Another copies. The second and third stones fall short but the group is uneasy and has lost its focus on the chick.

"Your aim is poor –"

"I am no David –"

"But then I don't think you meant to hit them." The last stone scatters the group, but she's lost sight of the chick. She is suddenly aware of a figure behind them. "Myfanwy! I didn't hear you come up behind us. You are Myfanwy?"

The old woman nods. "Well, I don't know why you didn't hear me coming. My flat feet made enough noise I would imagine. You were busy, no doubt." The woman's face is like a seed potato kept too long in the dark. She looks hard at Tal.

"This is Taliesin. A friend."

"I know who he is – course I do." Tal has got to his feet in respect but she makes no movement, only stares with heron eyes. "You have your own business in town, lad?"

He looks at Branwen who studies a pebble. "I do," he replies. He puts his hand lightly on the girl's shoulder, returns his hat to his head and leaves, boots crunching on the stones.

"Come on," says the older woman, "let's sit on the rocks over there. Nice and dry and better for my back; they're like a slab of lard cake." Neither speaks as they cross the beach to settle under the shadow of the cliff. Myfanwy sits carefully, pulls out her pipe and packs it meticulously, her few teeth worrying the stem as she looks out to sea.

"Will you not set it going?" Branwen says at last, gesturing to her mouth.

"No light." Myfanwy shuffles her rump on the rock.

"That is not the father," Branwen blurts.

Myfanwy sucks air through the cold stem. "I know it."

The girl follows a seagull chick as it crosses the beach in front of them. There is something wrong with its wing. It has its proper feathers on the sides and tail but on its head is a halo of down, like matted fluff on the back of a baby's head. It stands, just beyond the reach of the waves, looking towards the land.

"It's brown. Strange."

"Perfect to hide out where they nest, but not as good as the adults on a grey stone beach like this. This year's, by the look of it." The chick calls, regular, pulsing. Between noises it looks up and around.

"I think it's looking for its parents."

"Won't find them." Myfanwy's teeth worry at the pipe stem. "Left. They'll not come back for a cripple."

The chick trudges up the beach. Though each individual step looks deliberate and firm, the overall path is crooked and erratic because of the damaged wing which hangs away from its body. It passes close to them and she sees the beak – black and short, far from the subtle weapon of an adult. Its gaze is fixed on the rock pools and doesn't waver until it reaches them, then, looking around, it calls again – a fluting bleat.

"Let me feel you, child." Myfanwy balances the pipe beside her and pats the flat rock. "Lie down; that's best." Branwen looks around. "No one to see you this time of year. Not even a sailing ship. Be quick about it." Branwen lies flat, her legs from the knees downwards hanging over the edge of the slab. Myfanwy eases herself off the rock and stands between her legs. "Right then, let's see what we've got." She lifts Branwen's skirts and presses on her womb between the pelvic bones. Her eyes are closed as she rocks her palm, thumb to fingertips.

"Can anything be done?" Branwen's voice is a whisper.

Myfanwy's hands move over her for a few minutes. "No," she says at last. "Sit up now." She pulls down the girl's skirts and climbs back onto the rock, refixing the pipe between her teeth.

"Please. It was forced on me!"

"I know it. No – too late. I'm glad; hate that business. You'll have to do something to him, not his child."

"He's gone away." Branwen pulls her knuckle across her eyes, pushing them into the sockets, forcing in the tears. When she sits up it doesn't take long for her eyes to find the gull again. It's started back across the beach, following almost the same path. In the sky adults circle high up, but none seems to notice the chick. It reaches the water and goes in.

Myfanwy points with her pipe. "Look at him, like a decoy duck! There's nothing to them, you know. I held one once, fully grown it was. Someone'd had a shot at it, perfect it was, but for a small circle of red on the breast. Hollow bones they have; weighed no more in the hand than a carrot. It made a soft noise, not like a seagull. Just once it called and died between my hands, just like a sail with the wind suddenly changed. Perfect that bird was, but for the dash of red on its chest."

The chick comes out of the sea at the same place, calls for a few minutes, then returns to its journey up the beach. Though it staggers a couple of times, it seems again to be focused on the rock pools. As it passes underneath them it stops to call.

"Oh, for pity's sake – where are its parents? I beg you, let's go somewhere else!"

The bird pads on, the trailing wing making it seem drunk. Branwen slides off the rock and puts her hand out to help the older woman. Myfanwy studies Branwen's face for a moment. "Nasty birds, seagulls. One'd have your eye out soon as look at you." She pinches the girl's cheek. "Remember to eat."

Before she leaves the shore Branwen turns back once to look at the lonely figure as it trudges back down to the sea.

Cari is waiting for her by Tal's pony and cart. The pony is shaggy and fat, absorbed in a nosebag. There is no sign of Tal, though the pail of mussels sits in the back between the benches. 'Well?' Cari's expression asks. Myfanwy shakes her head and rattles her pipe around her teeth. She makes her slow way over to where a garish, hand-coloured poster is roughly pasted onto a board at the side of the road. She peers at it for a while. Cari glances quickly at Branwen before joining the old woman who jabs at the poster with her pipe. "I couldn't see the words now, even if I had the skill to make them out. I learn well, though – whole stories from the Bible word for word – some of them not fit to be heard neither. Lot and his daughters – what a tale that is!" She laughs. "Worse than the stories peddled around about the goings-on of the bawds and pimps in London. Can't make out the meaning of some of the old Bible lessons even though I've chewed on them like a cow these fifty years." She nudges Cari's forearm. "Go on – you can read it, can't you? I know what it means anyway, even if I can't read the words…"

Cari follows the writing with her finger, stumbling only a few times. "A fine diversion of bulls, bear and ass-baiting and dog-fighting and a dog will be dressed up with fireworks to augment the diversion of the spectators." Cari grimaces. "It says here that the famous bruiser Mrs Stokes won't just take on a woman, but will fight another couple alongside her husband! They strip to the waist, don't they?"

Myfanwy grunts her assent, leaning in towards the illustrations. "She'd have your eye out that one, and not with her fists!"

"You wish to see it?"

"Not I – oh no. Never go to them, or baitings or hangings. Once you've seen something with your eyes, you can't unsee it, can you? Why do I want to close my lids at night and see that? There was some pauper woman whipped behind a cart as we were on our way into town. People standing around with their knitting as she passed and that new Powell woman watching from a window." She turns back to the poster. "Anyway – look at the price of it!" She looks hard at Branwen. "You snivelling, girl?"

"Make it stop; you can stop it... can't you? Please!"

Myfanwy looks at her drily, moving her pipe from one side of her mouth to the other. "Easy enough to stop it; the hard part is for the mother to be alive afterwards. You're too late. This is no jelly to lean over the midden pit with like your moon blood. No – I'll do nothing for you, save attend on you when the child wants out." She puts a wad of leaves from her bodice into her mouth then fixes her pipe back between her lips. She stares straight ahead.

"Cari?" The older girl turns towards her. "You and Cai...? Why has the baby come in me? I felt no opening. I hated his seed! Cari?"

"If a cock even comes near your hole when it's shiny, you're in danger. Do everything else – but don't let it near you, your hole, near where you piss." Cari studies her friend then shakes her head. "But you should know this; you do know this! Why have you been such a fool? You breed donkey foals, stupid."

Branwen grimaces as Myfanwy takes her hands, eases out the tight knuckles. "You always carry two fists on the end of your arms, girl. Who do you hope to swing at, tell me that?" She laughs but it is as hollow as a hazel shell. "With a man you can do everything but sit on the end of it. That is easy to say, I know, and not always easy at all to do. Many a time it's called me like a wicked spirit calling a ship to the rocks. And they plead. Oh, how a man can plead when he carries a big red cock in his hand! I've known them weep real tears!"

"Yet you've never been with child?"

"I never said that. I've been caught – but it came to nothing." She looks sideways at Branwen as she bends to pick up her pack.

"But you ended it?"

"I said it came to nothing," she snaps. They are quiet for a while. Myfanwy hooks the tangle of stems from inside her cheek and flicks it onto the ground.

"Why do you chew that?" Cari asks. "It makes your tongue green."

"Stops the few teeth I have from hurting for a while. Hey, you girl!" She crosses to where Branwen has wandered off and is looking out to sea. "Hey!" She pulls her hair.

"Ow! Why did you do that?"

"Don't dare think of doing anything to yourself." She pokes Branwen in the belly. "There's a cauldron of blood up there; a cauldron of blood. Sticking a pig and stirring up the blood for pudding is nothing to what you'd lie in if you went prodding about. And don't think to sneak away like a cheap thief and throw it in the bog or drown it like a kitten – they'll find you, the women the worst. You had your man – now you pay."

"But I didn't want it! He took it from me. I told you, I didn't accept his seed!"

"He ravished you?" Branwen nods. "Where?"

"The Black Lion in Machynlleth"

"Where? In the stables? Where, girl?" Branwen shakes her head. Her hair sticks to her cheek. Myfanwy pushes it back, holds the girl's face in her rough palms. "You went to a room with him?" Branwen nods. "Did he drag you?" She shakes her head. "Did anyone see you go upstairs with him?" She nods again, hanging her head. "You little fool!"

"There was a mad dog – everyone was running and screaming – the men all had clubs, a boy was beating a dog on a chain, we went into the inn for safety –"

Cari rolls her eyes, "Safety!"

Branwen nods, the words tumble from her. "But then… it was not like the other time." Myfanwy kisses her gently on the forehead and turns away. "When I went to his lodgings it was different. It was I like a hunter crouched in the long grass and he the hare."

Cari's voice explodes from her. "Oh, God save us! You little fool! He has had you! He should be horsewhipped through the town; he should be taken up and gelded. God help me I could put his dirty bags between two stones and grind them to a pulp myself!"

"Shut up, you; too late for that." Myfanwy takes Branwen by the forearm and leads her to a boulder. They sit and the old woman takes her hand in both of her own. "Will you tell your father, child?" The girl shakes her head. "Then so be it." She takes a deep breath, sighs. "So, do you know when the seed came to you? When were you in the tavern?"

"It was, well, after *Gŵyl Ifan*."

The old woman nods and gets to her feet, stretching out her neck like a cockerel. "Send for me if anything happens that's wrong." She gestures towards Cari. "She'll come and find me. Careful how you hold yourself. If you stand up straight and take care with your clothes you may hide it until the end." She moves away. Turning back just before she passes the bend in the road she turns and points at Cari with the knobbed end of her stick. "And you, you've been more lucky than you know, girl – but your luck won't last forever." Still speaking she turns away, "but you won't be told, will you?"

Chapter Twenty-Four

Aт Plas Nanteos in the autumn sunshine, surrounded by a semicircle of estate workers, Master Thomas Powell, now heir to the estate, is enjoying his new home. His eyes are round with wonder as he looks from one to another.

"I did ask where's she gone? I said to you, didn't I, Jenkins?"

Jenkins smiles. "A maiden bitch can be tricky. When she's on her fourth or fifth litter she won't be bothered. She'll be only too pleased to be fed and watered and someone keeping the pups busy for her!"

His companion nods in agreement. "She went missing from the kennels a couple of days ago and I said to you, didn't I, Jenkins, the Reverend William won't be pleased. Those pups'll be worth something."

"Aye, you did, Wil."

"But happily now my father won't be displeased, indeed will never know she was missing because I found her!" Thomas hops from foot to foot as he speaks.

"You did, Sir. You did."

"I found them. I heard squeaking. 'What a strange bird,' I said to myself! John couldn't hear anything of course and he went back inside." Master Thomas rolls his eyes in disgust.

"Of course he couldn't – he's too old. That'll happen to you too one day, Sir, if you're lucky enough. Won't it, Wil?"

Thomas chuckles, "To continue the story... Oh, Cai!" The men turn as one to see the brisk figure of the bailiff coming out of the shadow of the house. "Cai, I've found her – and the pups. She's in the back of the barn." Thomas, seeming not to notice that his audience has shrunk to one, continues to tell his story to Cai. "I went to investigate the mystery, you can be sure –"

"Indeed I can."

"– and there they were, behind the wheel of the hay cart! So, I went to tell someone, but no one was about. Finally, I found Jenkins and told him to tell you. But, by the time you'd settled your affairs they'd gone."

"She'd moved them. Surely after you found her the first time she'd taken fright."

"But I didn't do anything to her. I didn't even touch her; I just stroked one of the ones furthest away. She had at least seven by my count. Anyway, then we waited quiet and I spied her out again!"

"You'll leave her alone now, Thomas. It's not good for the mother for us to be meddlesome in the nest."

"But why?"

"It can interrupt the milk, if a bitch's afeard; a sow has been known to eat her own young."

"Heavens!" Thomas' eyes are wide and round, his mouth open, "What, eat them still alive? Her own young ones?"

Cai nods. "So, stay away, will you please – she was your Uncle Thomas' favourite bitch and this is her first litter." He looks hard at the boy. "You say nothing; you don't agree to do this?"

Thomas nods. "I do... but may I go now just to look? You may accompany me to check that I keep my bargain."

"No need – a gentleman's word is enough! Anyway, I have business to complete."

Thomas looks after the retreating figure, adjusting his hat as he does so. Then, on the balls of his feet, he draws near to the barn and peeps in, soon he can resist no longer and disappears inside.

*

Early next day, Cai is fetched by Mari, the children's nurse. "Master Thomas is beyond – he won't stop crying; says he's going to fetch the keeper's gun to shoot the bitch!"

Cai goes outside. Thomas is standing in the middle of the yard howling. A few of the bystanders melt away when they see the bailiff and he dispatches those that remain to view the spectacle with a jerk of his thumb. Putting his hand on the boy's shoulder he leads him to the horse trough and passes him a handkerchief. Rather than use it, Thomas balls it up in his fist, passing it from hand to hand as he relates the story through violent sobs. "It was alright when I saw it last night; they were all perfect. I counted them all, and some you could see already, some were dog pups – and now she's moved them again and she's eaten the leg off! I saw the pup fallen on the ground and its leg in her mouth! She must be slaughtered like a sow for this – murderer!"

"Is the pup dead?"

"No, alive and wriggling, surely with the pain of it, and crying."

"Come with me."

Together they go out to the hay barn, Thomas' sobbing has turned to hiccups. Cai puts a finger to his lips, a hand on the boy's shoulder. After a few minutes, Thomas' chest is quiet. Bending down, Cai looks into his face. "You went in last night, did you?" Thomas nods, not meeting the man's eye. "Did you touch the pups, Thomas?" The boy nods his head, miserably. "How many times have you been in there today?"

"Just the one... well, two."

"Do you know why this's happened?" Thomas nods and bites his lip; tears are forming again. Cai in the lead, they enter the barn. The bitch and most of the pups are in the far corner where she's moved them. She doesn't snarl or growl when she sees them but seems to shrink away, her spine tight, body curling around her young. The injured pup is on the floor near some fallen feed bags. He's still alive and Cai picks him up by the scruff. Though it's not bleeding much now, the animal is missing one leg above the knee.

"I'll feed him, Cai; I'll feed him up – hand-feed him, like they do lambs." Cai shakes his head. "Oh, Please!" Cai gestures for them to leave the nest in peace. Out in the light the pup revives, its cries like those of a lost cat. Thomas is really sobbing now. "I wasn't rough; I didn't hurt them."

"I know you meant them no harm," the man says quietly, "but you shouldn't have been there."

"What's to be done?"

"She'll be alright now – just leave her alone."

"No, what about the pup?"

"I'll see to him."

"How will... how will you –?"

"Drown him." Thomas' sobs are beginning to attract the crowd again. Cai raises his voice to address them. "I want no one in that barn until Sunday without my permission. Let others know it. And back to work all of you – Master Thomas has a pain in his side."

The two of them go around the corner to the water butt, Cai's thumb stroking the pup's muzzle. "Look away, Thomas." But the boy shakes his head. Cai goes to lower the small body into the water but at the last minute Thomas puts his hand on the man's arm.

"No, me." He takes the pup, holding it just as Cai had done – one hand on the scruff to stop it struggling, the other under its belly to support the weight, brushes its head with his lips, and plunges his arm into the barrel.

"You can take him out now, Thomas." But the boy shakes his head vigorously, teeth gritted, silent sobs shuddering through his chest. Another few minutes and Cai speaks again; still the boy keeps his hand immersed. Finally, Cai lifts the boy's arm out. The puppy no longer looks real; nothing engaging in its blunt head; nothing distressing in the missing paw. It is nothing but a rag. "I'll take him now, Thomas."

"No, I want to do it. I'll bury him in the wood." He puts the body in his deep pocket where the water seeps from it into his britches.

Cai points, "They'll think you wet yourself!" Thomas smiles faintly. "Go on around the back then. I'll get a spade and meet you by the gate."

Thomas nods and moves away, walking awkwardly in his damp clothes.

Chapter Twenty-Five

BRANWEN STANDS IN the service yard at Nanteos awaiting instructions. It's Twelfth Night, a special time at the mansion, when a big party is held for all the household. For one night only, servants become masters; masters mingle with their servants.

For the last two years it had been Cari who had answered the call for extra help to serve so that the regular Nanteos servants could become the mansion's guests. This year, though, Cari has persuaded Branwen to go in her stead. She has dressed her friend carefully, binding her bulging body in layers of cloth and covering her in a *betgwn* and skirts several sizes too big. Even her cap is too big, falling over her eyes. "And a good idea too: no one will see your pretty face or even notice you. Speak quietly and don't look up; don't look anyone in the eye – don't even glance at a man's face. No one'll care whether it's you or I serves the party on Twelfth Night," she'd said.

"But will you not help serve after all? My father says it's an honour and might lead to better things."

Cari had laughed, grimly. "I couldn't bear to see Cai; neither would I be able to keep my mittens from the hot wine to still my nerves. I don't trust myself. It was on Twelfth Night at Nanteos that we first met – a wild, dangerous time."

"Has he tried to see you?" Branwen turns around to catch

her friend's eye, but Cari's looking down, her face hidden by her hair as she busies herself with the lacing at the back of Branwen's bodice. "Has he tried to see you since you shouted at him that time?" She turns right around and stops her friend's hand. Cari nods and tries to resume. "What did he say? Cari, what did –"

"He came to the camp; he sent messages through his friend Bryn, and presents… I don't want to talk about him." She pulls her arm out from under Branwen's hand.

"What did he say in the letters?"

"What does it matter?"

"Does he say he's sorry? What does he –"

"For pity's sake, Branwen, leave me alone, will you!"

"But he –"

"He asks me to marry him, alright; are you happy now? Yes, you may well stare."

"Marry him! Cari!" Cari holds up her hands, as if for calm. "Cai Gruffydd of Nanteos would marry you?"

Cari shakes her head. "There was no mention of going away."

"You accepted him, of course. You did accept him?"

"He didn't mean it. He won't leave Nanteos, I know it; he'll change his mind; or someone'll change it for him." Her voice falters.

"I was wrong about him."

"No you weren't and I wasn't wrong about that fiend Davies either." Cari shoves Branwen to face away from her again and finishes fastening her clothes at the back.

Branwen waits for a few moments, taking it in. He would marry her! "Cari –" She turns around and this time holds both of her friend's arms, searching her face. "You're crying!"

"No, I'm not; and mind your own business, will you. If you must know, I intend to change my mind – if he ever asks me again." Cari snatches her arms away, scrapes her hair back from her face, steps back to appraise her work. "Well, you look very odd; there's the look of a beetle about you, dainty arms and legs and a big round body under a mop cap." She smiles slightly. "Turn around for me; good, and from the back no one can see you're with child anyway. You'll do very nicely, I think."

"And what do I do?"

"Stay out of the way. There's a cook there, a fearsome woman, though Cai speaks well of her. Just do what she tells you and don't argue – oh yes, you do, if you get the chance!"

"I hope they don't keep me too long on my feet, they begin to ache now, though walking doesn't hurt me."

Cari had only shrugged. "You do what you're told. Don't let Cai see you, though he probably wouldn't recognise you."

"I wouldn't think of it. He may tell them I'm with child."

Her friend had scoffed. "He wouldn't do that, but you may embarrass him if he recognises you."

"How so?"

"You're poor, of course... and you know me – that won't impress either. Use your sense, Branwen!" Cari had smiled as Branwen nodded, the cap slipping further over her eyes. "I defy anyone to see that the peculiar serving girl is with child under all that. You are bundled thick as a cockle-woman!" Cari had kissed her and left.

So, here she is, standing at the back of the group as the Nanteos cook gives them their instructions. It is not difficult to avoid special notice; she is small, neat and is good at remembering what she's told. But inside! Once through the servants' corridor and into the main hall she is almost frozen to the spot. Everything gleams, everything shines, everything is new and polished to a glow. There is gold everywhere and mirrors, surely this light will harm the eyes! Candles beam, their light reflected back into the rooms by the plates of polished metal on the walls behind them. She had never imagined Nanteos to be so full of treasure! Both Cari and Henry Davies (God take his lying eyes) had tried to tell her, but she had not understood. The words had not really made sense.

Her job is simple; to go through to the dining room from the kitchen and back with the smaller dishes of food. As she waits for one of the kitchen maids to fill a bowl with roasted chestnuts, she studies it. A serpent rises from the side of the dish and out along the handle, first the coils of its body, then its tongue twisting four, no, six times. "Is this real silver?" she breathes to the maid.

"Course it is; don't be stupid," the girl answers.

Again and again she goes into the dining room with food; leaves with empty plates. So much wine and hot punch! A glass is smashed on the slate floor of the kitchen. No one notices, so she fetches a pan and brush. She picks up one of the bigger pieces, holding it near to the flame – polished, heavy and beautiful – how many bolts of flannel would her father have to sell to buy one set of these!

Back in the dining room they are stamping on the polished floor as three male servants, led in by the cook, carry in the Twelfth Night pudding. One of the young men helps Martha up onto a chair (surely far too good to be stepped on!) and she knocks a glass with a spoon. Here are the rules, and no one must disobey them. She pulls a fearsome face, and everyone laughs. The dried pea and bean are hidden in the cake – their finders will be Queen and King for the night.

Mistress and servants stand side by side as the partygoers are served by the cook. Some close their eyes and nibble their pieces nervously; other scan through their portions with their fingertips, feigning relief at not being the chosen ones. Branwen studies the new mistress of the house, Elizabeth. It is difficult to know whether the beauty is her own or comes from her wealth. It's the first time Branwen has seen a relatively young gentry woman up close and every movement, every garment, every piece of jewellery adds to the enchantment. When she laughs, her teeth are strong and even; when she raises her arm, diamonds flash. Branwen is next to her, watching her, when she sees her discover the pea.

"Oh, dear! Someone else must have it." Elizabeth looks around the circle. The faces are eager, lips open and wet with ale.

"Why so?" Martha steps into the space next to her.

"Well, it would be a novelty for someone else. I, well... I have the opportunity to enjoy my own way most of the year."

The older woman looks at her boldly. "That's maybe so, but it would be bad luck on all the company not to accept it." She looks at Cai, who holds the bean in his hand, his eyes fixed intently on the floor in front of him. "You must hold hands and dance for us; you must be King and Queen for this night!" He makes no move. Martha takes a step towards Elizabeth, says for no one else to hear, "Please, Mistress, the party will be spoiled – you'll bring bad luck on us all."

Elizabeth, without even a nod, moves to take Cai's hand.

Hardly moving her lips she replies, "I beg your pardon, Martha. I would not bring ill luck on this house for a fortune." Then she looks up, smiles at her guests and says in a clear voice, "Come, Sir, I mean, Your Majesty." She affects a small curtsey. "Let us dance!"

A sound, a mixture of laughter and the released sigh of relief greets them as the crowd opens to free them from the circle. The musicians strike up as she fits his hand to her waist.

Branwen keeps watching. Mistress Elizabeth's dress gleams as it catches the light. Maybe it's just the height of her heels, but she holds herself differently from every other woman in the room. Her clean hair, thick, dark and straight, shines, perhaps even with scented oil. Cai is taller than most in the room and, though he's dressed as a gentleman, moves differently from any real gentleman she's ever seen. As they dance, he lifts his partner higher, keeps her aloft for longer, pulls her closer. It is she who seems to do all the talking between them, her head tilted back, her chin white on her long, clean neck as she looks up into his face. He's smiling, though he often looks away. Even after the music ends there is a moment in which she is speaking still and he laughs before they pull apart and bow. The dance is over and Elizabeth passes her; she is wrapped in an exquisite scent, her passing like a breeze through a bluebell wood.

Someone else has been watching the pair, a lovely girl with wavy hair, different colours woven through it, from brass to chestnut. The young mistress of the house holds her hand... then she is the nursemaid or governess, surely? The young woman follows the couple intently, swaying slightly with their movements. Could she be Cai's sister, perhaps, this nursemaid of the house? But no, Cai has no brother, no sister, she is sure – and now no father either. Branwen catches the nursemaid's eye as Mistress Powell and Cai separate. The baby turns inside her but she stops her hand just in time as it moves to touch her belly. Now the young woman is watching her closely. Studying her even. She looks down quickly, busying herself with the collection of empty bowls and glasses and taking them through to the great kitchen.

"Where is the new master tonight?" she asks one of the kitchen maids as she returns with some dishes.

"Away. He's always away."

★

As the evening goes on, cook dismisses many of the visiting staff and the party for the household gets louder and bolder. Branwen is happy to retire to her bed. The mattress on the floor is surprisingly comfortable, the blankets clean. Music, cruder than before, laughter and shouting seep through the boards and under the door. 'Nanteos; stream of the nightingale.' There is something cradling about lying warm and tired, listening to a mansion full of people, with food and drink enough for all.

The following morning she is up early with the other servants. All is back to normal. The musicians are nowhere to be seen and cook, blotchy-faced, with sleeves rolled up and cap perched on the back of her head, is shouting in the kitchen. No one seems to be interested in giving Branwen her orders, but she was asked to help clear up and the wagon will not come to fetch the extra servants until later in the morning, so she gets to work. She pushes open the door into the dining room – a wanton feast indeed! Everything that could be turned upon its head has been and each step she takes towards the main table crunches. Mistress Elizabeth Powell is standing looking out of the window and turns, smiling. She has no wig or cap; in fact, she is hardly even dressed. The cold January sunshine catches the side of her face as she smiles. There is a small child in her arms, wriggling. "Morning. May I clear the table, Mistress?"

"Please do. "

She turns back to the window and Branwen can look at her without being seen. Her robe is beautiful, embroidered with flowers – not any flowers she recognises. They are too big, their colours loud, shouting their wares. Though the garment hangs heavy and looks warm, the pale cream material between the crewel work gleams, shot through perhaps with silver thread. Beyond the window the men are dragging away the Yule Log, finished now that Christmas is over. Just outside the window she can see Cai and some other men leaning over what remains of the huge trunk. She can faintly hear the axes as they set upon the tree. Elizabeth is watching intently, biting her lower lip. Her hair is the only dark thing in the beautiful room. "But why would they do that? Why would they be doing that?" Branwen realises she is being addressed. "If you please, why would they be taking pieces from the Yule Log and putting them in bags?" She gestures for her to come to the window. Branwen pulls her cap down low and joins her. "Do you have an idea? Why do you not answer, girl? You are shy perchance, I beg your pardon!"

"No, Mistress Powell, I'm not shy. I do not know."

Elizabeth starts laughing and bends to her child. "Oh, look at him, William – for goodness sake, what a naughty boy!"

A small pony has appeared across the yard, pulling a young

groom along. A stallion by the look of him, the animal is all high-legged trot and tossing head. The boy's face is as pale as the pony's flank. "Good heavens, he'll break free in a moment." She thrusts the child at Branwen and seems about to flee the room when they see that Cai has grabbed the animal by the head collar, giving him a few shakes and making him spin around him, changing direction when the horse seems to be flagging and keeping him going with a flick of the lead rein. "He makes the animal do more of what it was doing anyway, as though he wanted it to behave that way. Then of course the pony wants to stop; a most interesting technique!" She watches in silence for a few minutes, then turns into the room. "Do you know horses?"

Branwen shakes her head. Elizabeth looks at her and she looks quickly down. "Donkeys. I know donkeys, Mistress Powell."

"Then I am an admirer indeed – a donkey takes the same mastering as several horses, I've heard, and you so tiny." She returns to study the scene. The pony is back with the boy who is making his way to the stables, the animal trotting reasonably beside him. Cai has picked up the axe once more and swings at the tree. Under the burned bark, some of the wood is still clean. "No, I can bear the suspense no longer... shush William! Please oblige me... sorry I do not know your name."

"Branwen, Mistress Powell."

"Ah – lovely Welsh name." She stops for a moment, her mouth still open as if to speak, and studies the servant girl. "Good heavens, I would think that we could have found clothes to fit you better! You are positively drowning in these garments." She smiles. Branwen shrinks away from her gaze. "Ah, what was I saying? Yes, that's it, please oblige me by asking Mr Gruffydd if he'll be so kind as to visit me here and enlighten me about this business of cutting up the log with such care." For a moment Branwen hesitates, the complex words not quite making sense. Then, with a quick curtsey, she goes outside, slipping through the side door so that she doesn't get into trouble. As she approaches the men she stays close to the wall, keeping her head well down and her cap across her face. She stands for a few moments by Cai before he sees her. She has to give her message twice before he understands her properly. He laughs. She explains some more and he looks behind him towards the window where Elizabeth can just be seen. Smiling, he lifts his hand towards her, gives orders to the other men, takes up his waistcoat from where it hangs on the water tap and strides towards the house, buttoning it up as he goes. Branwen follows him into the dining room and resumes her clearing as they stand together at the window.

Mistress Powell is laughing, "Look at you, Cai Gruffydd – King of all Cardiganshire last night; a humble woodsman now in the cold light of day. Sawdust and shavings everywhere."

As Branwen turns with her pile of bowls she sees Elizabeth reach out and pick a piece of wood debris out of his hair. He laughs, combing his hands through it and bending forward to shake the sawdust away. "Shaking your mane, just like that young stallion – and on Mary's lovely carpet too!" She is laughing again, even the baby chuckling, at surely he knows not what. "Please – to put me out of my misery; the bags of offcuts – why? What do you do with them?"

"You don't know?"

"I do not. Please reveal all. We're itching to know, aren't

we, William?" Again she reaches across her child and picks a curl of wood from Cai's hair.

"We collect wood every year from the Yule Log and give it out to the farms and cottages. It's kept for luck until next year."

"I'm glad you're not here to see this," Branwen says under her breath to an imagined Cari as she takes her leave, nudging the door open a little further with her foot and slipping out into the hall, Elizabeth Powell's silver laugh ringing behind her. "Even you could not compare with her..."

Chapter Twenty-Six

WITHOUT THE INTENTION clear in her mind Branwen finds herself descending to the deep, narrow gorge of the River Einion. She stops for a moment, looking up as the late winter sun leaves the valley. A dead sheep has spread itself over the hillside which has a sickly orange tint. Below her the moss, vivid green and mustard yellow, mixes with the beech leaves, creeps from the floor and up the trunks of the trees, even along their branches. In the valley below, water spouts from everywhere, oozing up through the skin of the soil, pooling at the surface. The path slopes steep now, shale slipping under the feet. Water dapples the tiny stars of moss, feeds the feathers of grey, startling orange and sage-green lichen. From below a rumble comes up through the earth. All the noises: the birds, even the high wind in the trees, are engulfed by the river, the deep roar that enters, not by the ear but through the soles of the feet.

Her feet, as though dead at the end of her legs, slap clumsily against the ground, falling at an awkward angle on the path of loose stones. Birds sing, but it is as if their voices sound through cloudy glass. The legs move inside her skirts, regular and stiff, as though they belong to some automaton, some clockwork creature like the Turk she'd seen at Nanteos, forever moving in a circle, offering food from a brass tray.

Her hands hang crazily from her sides, filled with air, as if they could fly away from her.

The water of Llyn y Gigfran is brown, a thick froth gathers at the surface, bobbing in the shallows where the current slows. Small waves are drawn across the surface. She watches the patterns, repeating in the same place, the endless flick and curve of water. The bank is black and crumbling here – not the sticky, oily soil of the peat pools higher up; there are crystals in it, grey sand mixed into it, ready to shift at the slightest pressure. The roar of the water fills her mind. It drives through her, scraping all thought before it. Little light makes it down this far through the trees. The water calls. The river moves onwards, small waves dancing on the surface, passing the same rock, flashing white, a white spike lifting, blinding, then it disappears.

As soon as she comes to a stop the child starts churning and bothering, kicking like rabbits struggling in a bag. She lifts up her skirts, draping each side over her shoulders like a cape and now, though she cannot see it, she can feel the dome, tight as a bladder ball. She tracks the movements with her hand, reaching to grab at – a foot? What feels like a foot, struggles to get away from her grasp through the skin. "No." Her fist closes around it. Could she crush it, crush it through her belly? But then it would be club-footed – if it lived. A cripple! She lets it go, her belly churning and shifting. Has she made a wicked spell? She looks quickly upriver, shuddering. Up there is Ogof Morris, where the miners go to lay their charms. The cave goes back deep into the mountain, so deep they say those that venture in never return. Ogof Morris, the entrance to the kingdom of the *Cnocwyr* who've been mining the hills before the memory of men and who mine them still, their picks, their footsteps and even sometimes their voices to be heard deep underground, often before a flood or roof fall. Near there too the dead animal 'garden', as her father calls it. He doesn't approve. They should be caught and killed – yes; but to leave them to rot in their traps, on their chains; to hang them there above the river like that is unclean. She shudders, glances behind her. No one there. She looks quickly upstream – she would never go to the cave alone; not even in the middle of the day; not even in summer!

She is drawn to the pool below, the air clammy with invisible spray. The bank is unstable, black and crumbling, dressed with shards of slate rock. A rotten log snags her eye; it is bright orange and lumpy with fungus like some creature corrupted by pox, afflicted by blisters. She pulls her shawl tightly around her. 'What the mother's eyes look upon, so do the eyes of the unborn child.' She shudders: too much time spent with the hatter women! She finds a rocky ledge overhanging the whirlpool and stares down.

There below her something is caught in the circular current. The corpse of a rat! It lurks, bobbing as though alive, then beaten under the surface by the fall of water from above. She can see it, yellow beneath the water, hardly moving. The head is almost perfect, even the eyes still intact, lips pulled back over powerful teeth – a grimace. After a few moments more it floats up to the surface, slowly turning and bobbing, strangely buoyant, its yellow teeth set in a snarl, curved like tiny billhooks. The belly is big and bloated. Surely it would burst if someone pressed on it, but what would be inside? Bald, dead, unborn rats, sickly white, like beans in a pod; or maggots? She pulls her thoughts away from the image as the body heads towards the spout again, where it will be driven down once more until it fights its way back to the surface.

She moves away upstream, the soil under the slate chips, black and rich smelling. The roar of the waterfall is to her right now and less demanding. She goes to the edge again. A large sycamore leaf is being dragged through the shallow water across the slabs of rock above the falls. She finds herself following it down. It seems to resist, snagging on ridges in the rock, then it is pulled away, lost over the edge in the white water.

She too would bob up and down, rock backwards and forwards, her great belly breaking the surface and they would drag her out with a spike, her sodden hair ugly and loose. A cruel way for her father to find out. A magpie rattles behind her – up to its ugly business. She looks round – maybe someone... her foot slips and she lurches backwards, grabbing for a branch, it snaps and she staggers.

"Branwen!"

As she slides towards the water, struggling to get a handhold in the loose leaves, she is aware of a form coming down towards her through the trees. She seems to be going faster, the slope steeper as she nears the edge. She is almost surprised by how hard she fights to stop them tumbling in. She digs in the heels of her clogs, but that only serves to unbalance her and, instead of being thrown backwards, she pitches forward. Then a blow. Winded she lies on her back, the trees tossing overhead, rearranging the sky. For a few minutes she just lies there, heaving to get her breath. There's no movement from the child.

"What were you doing, Branwen? Why're you here?"

She shakes her head. The feeling is back in her legs. Her hands move to the mound below her skirt. Tal. She looks sideways at him where he lies next to her. He has some of her bodice bunched tight in his fist. "Why're you here, Tal?"

He gestures behind him. "We come for wood; roof props for the mine."

"Oh yes," she answers. "Yes, I see you sometimes."

"I saw you through the trees."

"You followed me?"

He is leaning over her now. "You won't see me. I call... your father has told you?"

She shakes her head. "It would make no difference even if he did let me see you; I wouldn't want to. There's nothing you can do. Go away from here, from me. I'm nothing but a lump of lead."

Tal's eyes don't leave her face. "You're lovely, Branwen. When I first saw you, you walked so lightly I thought you were a wind passing over a field." She turns her face away. "He doesn't know, does he? Your father; he doesn't know?" She shakes her head. He leans over her, finally letting go of her clothes. "You've cut yourself!"

She sits up on her elbows. A long gash runs inside her arm. She looks at it, watches the blood trickle, erratic. "It doesn't hurt." He eases off her neckerchief and moistens it from his water bag. How precisely he washes her – from the outside in, round the wound, moving ever inwards, until his hand pinches closed the two sides through the cloth. "It still doesn't hurt," she says, shaking her head.

"The white swelling. Women are strange when there's a child."

She watches him press the wet cloth flat against the cut and tie it. He sits back on his heels. "No," she says. "Keep touching me. Please, Tal. Touch me."

At first, he scratches her on the inside of her arm, running his middle finger along the line of the tendons – long, light flicks. She bends her head back, stretching out her arm, eyes half-closed. His hand moves higher, up over her shoulder, up around her head, gathering the heavy hair to one side, smoothing the length of it down in his fist, tugging on it gently. "Like a mare's tail," he speaks into her hair, breathing it in.

She bends forwards and his fingers press against her back, walking the length of her spine. "Touch me," she murmurs. He rubs hard with his fingers against her back. She struggles to pull open her bodice laces, grasping his arm, urging his hand down on her skin. "Hard!" The voice she hears is stark, thin. He bends the end of his fingers, engaging the nails against the skin of her back.

"Harder." She speaks through clenched teeth, but there is not much room for him to move his arm. She worries at her clothes, squirming, urging his hand down further. He gets to his knees, reaching as far as he can down inside her clothes. "Harder. Please!"

"I'll break the skin."

"Harder!" She groans and squirms under his nails, her movements telling him where to go; her sounds, how hard to press. He moves around to crouch in front of her. "Don't stop; please don't stop!" She begins to weep.

"Branwen!" Holding her shoulders, he shakes her. "Listen." He lifts her arm and looks under the cloth. The bleeding has stopped. "Good. Listen now." She sits up, putting her hand over the makeshift bandage. "You're eating sorrow; there's no need! We'll marry. It's nothing to me; there's no one to stop it."

"You'd marry me?" He grins. "Why, Tal?"

"Why do you think?" He sits back on his heels, takes her hand. "Would your father have me?"

Her laugh is bitter. "I think any man would do now." She shrugs. "Maybe the Reverend will take mercy on us; maybe he'll baptise my baby?" She looks hopefully at Tal but he cannot lie to her. Instead, he repeats his offer to marry her. She shakes her head. "Everyone would think the child yours." Tal shrugs. "It won't look like you – or me."

"Fair?" Branwen nods and looks away. For a while Tal too follows the water – it is almost the same from second to second as it accelerates over the slabs of rock and plunges, curling over the edge into the dark pool. Yet there are tiny differences too and it's these that keep the eye from unfocusing, sliding away. "He can have an accident any day; there are a dozen ways he could die. Mining is dangerous and he often rides the roads alone. It's easy to kill someone on these lonely roads; kill someone and melt away. There are brigands; highwaymen too. His horse may throw him. Morris' man has few friends here. Branwen?"

"No."

"It would be easy; he could fall from his horse onto a rock. Someone could cut his throat for him."

"No!"

"You wanted it from him? You want his child?" She shakes her head.

"It was too late. Myfanwy; she said it was too late."

He nods. "Will you keep the child?"

"What else can be done with it? I hate it! It feeds on me and grows like a maggot in the dark. I could kill it!"

"My people would take it; even though it's a white-footed

one, a *gajo*. But I'm glad you wish to keep it; it will have eyes like a limpet and ears like a toadstool." She laughs. He gets up and pulls her to her feet, spinning her around. "It will have fingers like a spider crab and a tongue like a flame; feet as big as a bear's –"

"And a carrot nose."

"The hair will be tight and curly as a ram's arse –"

"No it won't!"

"With hands like a peat cutter's spade."

"No it won't; it'll be beautiful –"

"With a cry like a newborn polecat –"

"No, it won't!" She's sobbing now and drops to her knees.

"And breath like Borth Bog."

"It won't, it won't..." she sobs.

Tal kneels on his haunches in front of her. "Your baby will be beautiful, Branwen; it grows there like a curled fawn." He puts his palm on her belly, "and when it's ready it'll come out into the world and look around and people will say, 'There's a lovely child for two ugly dark dwarves to spawn'." She looks at him and laughs through the tears. "How did those two stunted thorns birth a handsome oak such as this?"

She puts out her hands and he helps her to her feet. She studies his face for a moment; though the mouth grins, his dark eyes are anxious still. She has no need to marry him, pull him into her shame; it is enough that he is there. She smiles.

Chapter Twenty-Seven

CARI HAS BEEN standing in the doorway, her hair untidy and loose at the sides, ruffled by the wind which often comes as the sun goes down. "I better go for him."

Myfanwy straightens up, hands on her hips and her thumb pressed hard into the muscle at the base of her back. That pain never leaves her now. "Do it as we said – at the corner by the bridge, so he can see you from a long way off."

Cari nods and takes her shawl, kissing Branwen's clammy forehead before she goes. Standing at the bend in the road, Cari sees him at last, a tall figure, easily known by his stoop. At least he is alone tonight. She holds her ground. Evan has seen her, but has he recognised her? She raises her arm, making big, sweeping gestures over her head. He acknowledges her. Now he will know she waits for him. As he covers the distance, fast, but not running, he will have the chance to think on why she's come to meet him on the road. His mind will first go to an accident; by the time he gets to her he will have visited all the places danger lies in wait for his only daughter. Hopefully then her news will be some sort of relief. As he gets nearer, she sees for the first time that he has a limp. Walking as quickly as it is possible to do without running, his right leg looks stiff, is held straight and swings from the hip like the pendulum of a long-case clock.

He hails her and she waves again but remains still, frozen

as a woodcock in cover. "Tell me!" he calls out when he is near enough. Still she holds out. "Branwen, is she safe? She has not fallen into the wheel?"

"She's safe. Yes!" She shouts then, as loud as she can, seeing his body relax immediately, the right foot dragging on the ground for a couple of steps. She can bear it no longer and takes a few paces towards him. They meet before the bridge and he grabs her wrists in his hands. There is spittle on his grey stubble as he speaks.

"The mill then – has there been a fire?"

"Everyone is well." Then she tells him. For a moment he says nothing. His pale eyes look past her, over the river to the estuary and beyond, where the sunset burns across the sky.

"Whose child?" She shakes her head. "A boy, you say?"

"They are well. Myfanwy is with them."

He slides the pack off his back, sits on the low wall, hands resting on his thighs. His fingers knead the muscle above the right knee. Across the road a wren is rattling a warning call, darting in and out of the wall, body jerking, tail flicking.

At last he gets to his feet. "Thank you... for coming to meet me. To tell me this." He bends down as she helps him on with his burden, needing both hands to hold it as he struggles into the strapping.

*

Cari goes into the cottage first, leaving the door open for him. Branwen sits in the main bed, looking like the mistress of the house with her hair brushed and the covers clean around her. The baby is out of sight in a small crate on the floor and Myfanwy is sitting by the fire smoking her pipe. For once it is alight. "Where is he?" she speaks out of the corner of her mouth. Cari gestures behind her. "Fetch him in, girl."

Cari goes out but they do not immediately appear. With a sigh, Myfanwy knocks out her pipe and gets to her feet, but Evan is in the doorway. He goes to his daughter who, on seeing him, has started to weep, shrinking down into the bed and drawing up her knees. He puts his hand on her head and rests it there – like a priest, but saying nothing. There are tears in his eyes. Finally, "I had hopes for you," he says simply before turning away, bending with difficulty to the sleeping child. "A big lad! Branwen, how did you birth such a prizefighter?"

"Something to do with this, perhaps," says Myfanwy, drily, holding up a ladle out of one of the noxious pots arranged near the fire.

The baby is an ugly thing, eyes lost in a red, raw face. The hands are purple and wrinkled as if from the week's wash. "Take him to your breast," Myfanwy says. Branwen shakes her head, dumb tears running down her face. The baby's cry is insistent now and rhythmic, the mouth crimson and round. Inside the tongue is vibrating. Myfanwy stares hard at her. "Put your arms out for the child."

Again Branwen shakes her head. Wincing, Myfanwy crawls across the bed on her knees, holding the baby away from her body, as if wading through water. "Sit up, girl," she snaps, settling herself in front of Branwen with a grimace of pain. "My damned knees!"

Cradling the baby's head in her left palm and yanking down Branwen's nightshirt with her right, she presses the child's face at the breast. The girl recoils. Myfanwy swears and shuffles further forward. She grabs at the breast, shoving it at the screaming mouth and stuffing the nipple in. Branwen yelps as the mouth takes hold, sucking into her, through her. With a grunt, Myfanwy slumps down beside her, pulling her skirts back down and settling her back against the wall. "Look at his face," she says, quietly, but Branwen's eyes are closed as she leans back away from her breast, her face angled towards the ceiling. "You must feed the mite," the old woman says. "There's no choice about it."

Chapter Twenty-Eight

MYFANWY STAYS FOR three days. Evan is often out, visiting one house after another. "I'll tell them myself," he mutters. "They tell me my daughter should do penance; stand in shame at the front of the church and confess her sin. Hah! I say... I say to them, 'He who is blameless is not yet born'. Watch out for your own salvation!" Branwen stays inside. The breast is white and bloated – hard as a blown bladder, the nipple huge and brown. She presses it at the baby who does nothing except butt at it, wailing. "It is bigger than his mouth!"

Myfanwy laughs, "There you are, girl. You're fit to be in the boxing ring now with those." She grasps the baby firmly by the back of the head and thrusts him hard at the nipple. With her other hand she holds the breast, tugging it down hard, jabbing it at his mouth. He howls, the sound muffled as the nipple chokes him and he's forced to suck. "Don't tickle him, girl," she says as she bends over them. "You must train him, like you'd train up a horse. Don't listen to any nonsense from a baby." The mouth tugs mercilessly at the nipple. A fist clenches in her belly. "Does it hurt you?" Myfanwy snaps. She nods, miserably. "Good. The womb shrivels... don't look like that, that's what it must do!"

After a while he falls asleep. As Myfanwy picks him off the breast his arms shoot open in shock, fingers fixed tense and straight. He opens his mouth to cry but she is too quick for him, has him folded tight in his blanket and on his side in the crate, a piece of rolled material up against his back. For a moment she stays with him, one hand resting on the top of his head, the other against his side. Slowly she withdraws her hands and moves away.

*

After Myfanwy leaves them Cari comes to see her every day, bringing something tempting with her. "Will you see Tal?" Branwen shakes her head, shakes it as though wasps crowd around honey. Cari laughs. "'No' would be enough. Why not?" Branwen shakes again, folding her arms across her chest. "In time then. You have only to say the word."

"How is he?"

Cari grins. "Handsome. He's in charge of all the horses now – surface and underground."

"And Cai?" Cari whistles through her teeth, shakes her head. "Sorry... yes, I know, I promised not to ask."

"Myfanwy said you hardly spoke a word at the birth. That's not like you!"

"You're changing the subject, Cari."

"You promised. Don't... Nothing about him." She goes to peer at the baby in his crate, turns back into the room. What's it like? I don't think I could do it – even if I had a man I wanted."

Branwen shrugs. "Once it's in there..." She sits down, thumb and first finger worrying at the loose hem of her *betgwn*. "My mother came."

"Pardon?"

"My mother was with me. Just before the pains came I saw her." Cari opens her mouth to comment, but Branwen gestures impatiently. "I know she may not really have been visible, no one else could see her, I know that – but she was there, Cari, standing in the corner and her eyes never left my face. Sometimes I forgot to look for her, sometimes maybe for a long time – the pain makes it so that you can't think, somehow, but when I remembered to look for her again, she was still there, the same."

"When did she leave you?"

"Myfanwy made me look down at the baby when he was on his cord; when I looked back, she'd gone. I know now that she could come back, anytime in my life." Her friend is silent. "I did see her, Cari."

"A comfort, surely." Cari takes her hand. "But the pains, how do you bear them? I hear women screaming in the camp, worse than when a miner burns from setting gunpowder."

"It stops. That was something no one told me: between pains, it stops. At first there are minutes perhaps at a time, then close together, then it's all pain – like a cat's back legs raised up and clawing at you inside. And you can't be brave. It's not like holding your palm near to a candle flame when you're young – being brave enough to count it, before pulling away. It's in you; you can't escape it. When one was really bad, in my back, Myfanwy would take her fist and grind it in there." She rubs the base of her spine. "After he was born she showed me on the top of my thigh how hard she's been pressing – it hurt like hell!"

Cari laughs. "That woman! She smells like an old potato, but I like her."

★

A week after the birth Cari calls again, knocks hard on the door. No answer. There is no activity in the yard and the drying racks are empty. It has been that way several times over the last weeks. Not enough woven cloth to process? The prices too poor on the border? Better not raise it with Branwen and upset her. She finds her way up to her friend's room. The baby is asleep in his crate. There is a smell of sour urine. "Branwen?" She shakes her.

Branwen is conscious but drowsy. Her forehead is damp and hot. Milk seeps out of her nipples, like water from moss. Wave after wave, shadow after shadow of delicious, painful chill passes through her, like lightning over a field. She curls up, tucking everything together – her hands into fists under her chin. The same thought returns to her again and again. She seems asleep, but is too shivery and sick to sleep. Every part of her body hurts – from pricking and stabbing in her head through to the deep, dull bone ache in the joints of her fingers. One of the breasts is swollen and mottled, on fire inside.

"Branwen?" No response. "Right, I'm going for Myfanwy. Drink this before I go!" She forces her to drink water, empties the chamber pot, swills it out and strides away.

*

Later that day Myfanwy heaves herself up the stairs. This time Branwen's eyes are open and she has the baby in her arms, though she is shivering and hot to the touch. "Where's your father, girl?"

Branwen shakes her head. Myfanwy opens her shift wide and feels the breasts. "Milk fever." Branwen whimpers. "I

243

thought as much. You must put the baby to feed. He must empty the breast and clear it."

"He seems just to worry at her nipple; play with it like a terrier with a rabbit skin."

"Right, girl, sit up now; do as you're told. If this goes on much longer you could burst the breast." They pull Branwen up the bed. Myfanwy peers into the water jug. "This needs filling for a start." She thrusts it at Cari, turning back to Branwen. "You need to drink, drink like a milking cow. Every time he feeds from you, you have a drink. Eh? You understand me?" Cari returns and Myfanwy stands over Branwen until she's drained the whole mug. The baby, wailing now with hunger, is propped up on a pile of clothes next to her in the bed.

"Right, lie down on your side; roll over; no, right over and let the breast hang down to feed him. Yes... No, don't move back, the breast must be totally emptied."

Branwen winces as the baby tugs and the milk pricks through the breast as it begins to clear the blockage. Myfanwy sits on the low stool by the bed. Her face, waxy and wrinkled like an apple stored all winter, is content.

After a while the baby starts complaining again. "I think he's had it all."

"Ah, she speaks at last!" Myfanwy gets to her feet. "Come, sit on the edge of the bed for me." She sits beside Branwen and, with the flat palm of her hand, presses firmly into the breast, from shoulder to nipple. "He's clearing it," she announces, gathering the girl's damp, matted hair in her fist and holding it back from her face. "He can have a drink from the other one now. Right, sit up and sit back on the pillows."

Myfanwy scoops up the squalling child, bundles his

thrashing arms back into the cloth and gives him to Branwen. She holds him up to the healthy breast, he sucks and is soon quiet, dropping off the nipple, his mouth open. Myfanwy takes him and settles him in the box near the window. She sits on the bed and reaches for Branwen's hand. "Each time you feed now, you must feed from this breast first. Understand me? Branwen?"

"Yes."

"Good. Only when this breast is completely empty must you offer him the other. Understand me?" Branwen nods, shivering. "And feed like I showed you: the baby lying down, you over him, the breast free, not all squashed up. If you do that, there may be no more trouble; if you don't, we'll have to make a poultice for the breast or the corruption will build up in it and it will burst." She puts her hand to the girl's forehead. "Still burning... Cari, go and fill a bowl with water and find some old cloths." She makes Branwen lie still as the two of them bathe her. Cari goes to dry her. "No; let it dry itself off. She'll cool then."

"Please cover me, I'm freezing!" Branwen whimpers.

"Nonsense; when the fever cools you'll feel better. Lie there, when you're dry you can have a light shawl or something over you." Myfanwy lowers herself onto a chair by the window, kicking off her clogs and resting the soles of her feet against the wall. She mimes to Cari to go down and make food. Branwen has rolled onto her side, knees up, hands between her legs and shivering. After about ten minutes Myfanwy crosses to the bed and feels her brow. She sucks on her teeth and nods her head, pulling a light blanket across the girl as she dozes.

When the baby wakes, Myfanwy once more gets Branwen

onto her side. The baby feeds for a few minutes from the blocked breast before letting go and lying quietly, his dark eyes seeming to fix on his mother's face. "Does he cry when you put him down?" Branwen nods in answer. "You can't go lying around all day and if he's going to howl whenever you put him down, you'll have to learn a trick. You feeling better, girl?" Branwen nods.

"When will my churching be?"

"Churching!" Branwen nods. "There'll be none for you, child." Though tears form in her eyes, Branwen doesn't make a sound. "Don't you mind, Branwen. We'll do something for the little mite later. Right, let's go downstairs to the fire then and try and get some food into you." Once downstairs, Myfanwy holds a bolt of cloth in front of her, studies it, muttering to herself. "Now, do I remember how to do it?" After a couple of attempts, she grins. Crossed at the front, a sturdy band around the waist, she at last seems satisfied and holds her hands out. "Give him to me then." She thrusts one leg at a time into the shawl, taking no heed of the baby's wails of protest. Finally, the head tucked into one of the folds and pressed against her chest, she looks up and smiles. "There we are. Look, no hands!" She waves them in the air. "Now, you try." But it is not so easy to do it to another person, the baby's howls distracting them as his legs and arms are stuffed into the folds. At last he is in tight between his mother's breasts, only the side of his face peeping out 'like a squirrel from a hole in a tree'. Myfanwy laughs, turning back to the pot over the fire. Branwen walks cautiously to the settle, opening her legs wide and keeping her back straight as she lowers herself down.

She checks that her child is comfortable, bending low and

opening the folds of the material. The baby's strange musk is suddenly strong and she leans over him, her eyes closing as she breathes it in. She nuzzles his hair, matted and sour, that sour of the ewe's lambing; snuffling in the warm ridge behind his neck; like a ewe, but not gone so far. Not licking, only breathing him in.

Myfanwy turns for a moment and watches them. She smiles. "At last we can wash the birth filth off him."

Chapter Twenty-Nine

"THE ROOF'S DOWN, in Hafod level, Captain."

The men have formed a tight circle at the shaft mouth, the whimsy horse stamping and tossing his head, nervous as they close in.

"Blasting? Did someone set the shot hole wrong?" Trevelyan, Powell's Cornish engineer, looks from one man to another.

Richards, one of Powell's most experienced miners, shakes his head. "It's not gunpowder done this. It's filling up down there; like as not water's washed the props out."

"Maybe Morris' digging moved the stream, Sir?"

"Or that pond Cai Gruffydd's putting up behind the ridge's leaked?"

Captain Trevelyan holds up his hands for hush. "No, it hasn't. I was up there this morning."

"The fall's come down so they can't get back to the buckets. God help them!"

Iwan, an old miner, now only good for working the underground hand windlass for air, steps into the circle, flinging his arms wide. "The *Cnocwyr* have been warning for days. We could hear them hammering; Gwyn heard their feet marching, must have been half-dozen or so of them. Then silent. We should have got out sooner; we should never have gone in – not after that rain, not after they warned us." His eyes are wild in his lead-white face. The horse whinnies in fright.

"Quiet a minute." Trevelyan, though he can't understand the old man's Welsh, can feel the panic. He makes the calming gesture with his hands again, looks down a moment, takes a slow breath. When he looks up again his voice is calm and clear. "I need two teams: one to go down here and start digging; the other to come with me to the entrance of the adit draining the level. If the flood's not too bad we might be able to get to them that way, dig them out from both sides."

"Dangerous." Richards, leaning on his shovel, shakes his head. "Roof's so low in those old drain tunnels – crawling only in some places, and there's no air shafts put in for water drains."

"True; but we must do something." Trevelyan scans the group. "Right men, I need a team to go in – this shaft at least." Richards steps forward, followed by Gwyn, Tal and three others. "Good, thank you."

"No; not him!" Iwan, still in the centre of the circle, shouts in alarm. He looks around at the faces, his mouth open with shock, his gums lined blue with lead, the base of his teeth black. Then he moves to grab the kibble chain. The horse lurches away from him and the crank handle knocks him across the back. He stumbles. Tal goes to calm the animal.

"Get out the way, Iwan. There's men down there!" Trevelyan moves towards him.

"No!" The old man shouts again. He points at Tal, backing away from him. "They shouldn't go underground – bad luck; no, don't let him down, them with their charms... the *Cnocwyr* are afeared of them, bad luck, no –"

Richards takes Iwan by the arm and drags him away.

His shouts become sobs as he's taken behind one of the ore wagons. For a minute, none of the other men move. Then Trevelyan nods at one of the young lads. "Fetch Cai Gruffydd. You." He turns to another, "Get yourself to Gogerddan; and you, Trawsgoed. Tell them there's been a flood and the roof's down at Hafod level. All the help we can get. Cai'll know what to do."

★

It is less than an hour between the rider reaching Nanteos and the rescue party, led by Cai, setting off for the mine. The call has gone out to all the big houses, and extra wagons with equipment, horses and men are to follow.

"What's caused the fall?"

"Don't know, Cai, Sir."

"Where exactly is it?"

"Not sure, Sir – between Allt Hir and Talsarn, I think."

"God's teeth – can no one tell me more?"

Leaving the main party to follow with the wagons and equipment, Cai rides fast uphill, the cob sure-footed and confident even on the slippery terrain. He pauses at Talsarn camp. Work on cleaning and sorting the ore has stopped and the drenched workers mill listless as bullocks in a butcher's yard. He stays on his horse and they come towards him, crowding around him. He scans the group, finding a couple of faces he recognises; a couple of faces that seem animated rather than stunned. "Set up a rescue station at the dressing sheds. You, make sure they keep working the air pumps all along the tunnel."

He takes a short cut cross-country, the horse's legs

disappearing hock deep into the heather. The stream at the bottom of the valley is a torrent after the recent rain. He moves up and down the river's course for a few moments, swearing, then kicks his horse on through a pool which seems to be slow moving and he hopes not too deep. He comes out safely and urges the animal on up the steep incline, pausing by the secondary adit at the western lode. Water gushes from the entrance. Not a good sign.

Sodden men are gathered further up the hill at the vertical shaft mouth, one climbing out of the bucket as he arrives. "Well? Where's Trevelyan?"

"Gone to the main draining adit with a small team. He's hoping to reach the trapped men from that end, Sir."

Cai frowns. "Richards!" The big miner comes towards him. "Did you get near to the trapped men?"

"Couldn't get through. The fall's a big one and cut off our air. We had to turn back. Not even the candles stayed alight. We did as much as we could."

"Where is it?" He pulls a plan from his pocket, but the miner shakes his head.

"I cannot understand it."

"How far in?"

"A furlong, perhaps."

"And you say the blockage is between here and the air shaft, Richards?" He turns around and bellows at the whimsy team. "Make sure those horses are still pumping air!"

"Yes. We had no air in there. The roof must have come down between us and the air shaft."

"Good. That's good news. At least they'll have air from above – with luck." He looks at the map again, looks up. "Can any of you who've been down read a map? You – you've been down? What's your name? Tell me what you saw down there."

Gwyn steps forward. Cai peers down at him for a moment. "Gwyn, Sir."

"Sorry, lad – didn't recognise you!" Cai thrusts the map at him. Though the rain has stopped, everywhere is sodden. He pulls off his coat, spreads it on a rock and they look at the plan. "This is where we are now. Richards tells me the fall is in Ceridwen, about a furlong in."

"I don't know the names of the tunnels, Cai, nor can I tell distance underground. I'm usually with the horses. We met no air shaft though. We seemed to be travelling slightly downhill before we came across the fall."

"And right? Did the tunnel go to the right, bear to the right? Richards?"

"I think it did."

"Look, that's where I think we have the fall; that's where the nearest air shaft is." He pauses a moment. "Morris has been digging at Esgair Mwyn again?" Richards nods, his face hard. "Damn him!" Cai studies the map again. "Seven adit... When we abandoned seven adit, how much powder did we use?"

Richards speaks. "We didn't blow it. We just left it after the roof came down."

"So the old tracks are still in place, at least part of the way – as far as we know?"

Richards nods. "I think we left a couple of wagons down there too." A small circle of men has gathered around them.

"Excellent." Cai points at the map. "There's the roof fall, where we diverted the stream before – like as not Morris' men have opened it again further up and disturbed another underground stream. This is seven lode. Some of it collapsed a couple of years back but we left it – no ore in there and we didn't need it for access. But, if we can unblock it, we can get to them through this old tunnel. It's narrow, but we used to use it for air before we put the pumps in."

"Could work. I'll get some men down there." Richards is already moving. "We'll need horses and some low sledges; more wagons if the rails are still in place."

"Where's Tal? Get him to do that; he'll be able to get the animals we've got coming up from Nanteos to go into the tunnels."

"Gone, Sir. He went with the Captain to the drainage tunnel." Richards shakes his head.

Cai hesitates for a moment, then, "You; get after the Captain; tell him to meet me at seven lode. Tell him to get out of the drainage tunnel, it's a death trap. Tell them we're going to go down the old shaft instead." He looks at the boy for a moment. "What'll you tell Captain Trevelyan?"

"Get out of the drain, Captain, it's dangerous. Meet Cai Gruffydd at seven lode."

"At the old shaft into seven lode. Say it."

"Get out of the drain, Captain, and meet Cai Gruffydd at the old shaft, seven lode, Sir."

Cai flashes a smile. "Good. Quick as possible."

Chapter Thirty

IT HAS BEEN raining for days, the river brown and angry, too fierce to put the wheel to it. When her father returns from town, they must stop it, divert the water away from the wheel before it cracks. The wheel is turning strongly but the creak and screech is there again. The sound, though faster than usual, is still regular and the mind can fix on it, depend on it. Through this is another sound – urgent, chaotic, forcing her from the light doze and back into her life.

She lies on her back, her arm across her eyes. The baby is asleep. Swimming up from a doze herself, she doesn't understand the noise for a moment – banging, but the noise is in the walls – someone is beating at the door. Why? She raises the other arm and links them across her eyes, pulling each tight with her hands so that they close. The weight on the eyes is comforting. A woman shouting. Cari shouting. She rolls on to her side. It is still light, the patch of sky the pale watery pink weeping from a day-old scab. The wheel turns; in the dark behind her eyes she can see the paddles dip and slice, dip and slice – does water feel pain? They must disconnect the wheel. Cari shouts again. She could easily come in if she wanted to. There are any number of ill-fitting storehouse windows and the back door? "Hardly worth locking!" her father's always saying. There is quiet for a bit, only the groan and shift of the timbers straining against the turning wheel and the wheel – creak and screech; then from the back of the house Cari, hammering her fist on something surely, shouting out. The dogs at Tŷ Hen set up, an explosion of noise. The baby sleeps on as she drags herself downstairs.

Cari bursts in. "Is your father here?" Branwen shakes her head. "Where's he gone? Will he be back soon?" Branwen stares. "Branwen – when will he be back?"

"I don't know. Tal-y-Bont? Perhaps the road's flooded. I don't know."

Cari hesitates for a moment. "Can I have Siwan?"

Branwen nods. "But what's the matter?"

"Don't worry." Cari is already on her way through the door. "The Powell mine's flooded. We need help – and animals."

"Tal? Is he alright?"

Cari stands still a moment. "Cai is there, all will be well – though you know I keep out of his way and won't speak to him now. He never did ask me again."

"You've seen Tal for yourself?"

"Tal's safe I'm sure. I must go!"

Branwen goes outside with her. Her mind runs to questions but, since the birth, there seems a long way between a thought and the voicing of it, corridors and rooms to be lost in. She tacks up the donkey who is less than willing, planting her small hooves on the threshold before stepping out into the rain.

"Get on!" Cari, usually so patient with animals, slaps her hard on the rump with her bare hand. They leave the yard, already at a trot.

Branwen stands for a moment as they disappear into the low cloud that smothers the valley. She lifts her hand to move her hair back – it's sopping. She is soaking wet. Surprised, as if looking at another girl through glass, she looks at her hand. Water runs down and off her fingertips. Her drenched skirts hobble her as she goes back inside. Creak, grind. The mill building shudders around the great wheel. They must divert the water away and back into the river until the level goes down – she thinks this in slow motion. It's far away, a story she's heard about someone else. "The wheel pulled the wall apart and the building fell into the river." A story she's heard. She has spoken the words out loud! The child is still asleep in the cradle her father made but when she lies back on the bed and closes her eyes the sound from the wheel seems uneven – a lame peddler lurching down a long, straight road, receding into the distance.

*

At the old shaft head, Trevelyan and his team have erected a temporary winch with buckets of waste already coming to the surface. Work has gone on through the night, all but the most essential activity having stopped in all the Powell mines in the district, the visiting miners taking turns underground. Further down the hill the 'grass' men, women and children have joined in emptying the rock from the wagons and sledges coming from seven lode. Cai appears at the tunnel entrance, straightens up, protecting his eyes from the light.

"Mr Cai, Sir – a rider from Nanteos."

"Well, what does he want? Come on, for pity's sake, I haven't got all day! What does the boy want?"

"Not a boy, Sir – a man. To see you, come from Mistress Powell."

"Where is he then? Why's he sent you? I can't leave here! Send him up to me. Move!"

Even as he nods assent, the youth is turning to run back down the hillside. Cai watches him for a moment then, wedging his hat on his head and wrapping the rags around his hands, heaves himself up onto a filled wagon, throwing rocks down.

"Wouldn't surprise me if we didn't have another fall." Tal pulls up with another load. The mules and donkeys are short enough to enter the tunnels and Tal has put hoods, made from the miners' torn shirts, around their heads. Filled nosebags keep their minds off the job. "A master stroke" Cai had said when he'd heard Tal's idea for them. "Still pouring in there. Can't keep the torches lit – we just follow the rails."

Cai straightens up, glancing down the hill. No sign of the messenger. "Water's the worst enemy of any lead mine."

"Like fire is for coal."

Cai nods. "Take over here, will you – I need to get in there and look again. Maybe see where we could shore up the roof for a bit." He jumps down.

Down in the valley a rider is waving and shouting. He calls out as his horse struggles uphill. Cai swears and starts on the load from the ground as he waits.

"Gruffydd, Sir..." Both the man and his horse are beaten by the steep climb.

"Take your breath man. What is it you want? We are not idle here!"

"Master Thomas Powell, Sir; he's not to be found."

"A lost boy! You come all the way for this! Get your shirt off and help unload!"

"No, Sir. Mistress Elizabeth... Master Thomas has been

gone all night. Now it is found out. They think he came after you. Did he come after you?"

Cai has moved away from the laden sledge, gestures impatiently for the others to keep going with unloading. "Where have you searched?"

"Everywhere, Sir. The few of us left at Nanteos – we've been calling him. His pony's gone and they said you hadn't taken it with you to the mine. Everyone was saying he'd have followed you, Sir."

"No. I told him no. Fool! Has he taken a gun?"

"No."

"They checked it?"

"First thing was done. Then they said he would have followed you, but then Jacob came down from the mine to get more supplies and the mistress asked him and he said no and then she said, 'He's lost'. Well she said, 'Form a search party for him'. That was hours ago, and we went everywhere. Then she said, 'There is nothing for it; we must send to the mine for Cai to come back – he will find my son.' She said that, Sir."

Cai is still for a moment. Elizabeth's face looking up at him just before he rode for the mine. Her kiss across his cheek, light and deadly as an owl's wing in the dark. The truck is empty and Tal is already fixing the mule to the other end so he can go back in for another load. "What's the air like in there?"

Tal shrugs, "Pretty good for a tomb."

Cai crosses to the dark of the entrance, then looks up to the sky. The rain is lighter and the clouds thinning inland to reveal patches of pale blue. For a moment he is still. Tal urges the mule past him, back into the mouth of the workings. Cai stops him, holding him by the arm. "Do what you can, Tal, but keep getting them to put in the props – there can never be too many and if the water starts to rise again, even a little – get out." Tal tips his hat by way of acknowledgement and goes back into the tunnel. Cai turns to the messenger. "Have you tried the river?"

"The river?"

"By the weir. Dolydd y Castell?" The man shakes his head. "Did he take the otter spear?" Again the man shrugs, helpless. "Get back to Nanteos as quickly as you can and tell anyone who's still there to get to the river, downstream from the weir. Now!" The man's face is set in shock as Cai grabs the reins from him and throws himself across the pony.

"But, Sir – I've nothing to ride myself!"

"Get him something!" Cai shouts across his shoulder as he and the exhausted pony slide down the boulder-strewn slope.

Thomas' tearful face comes to him as he hurtles down the track. The pleading to be allowed to come to the mine after word had come of the flood and the roof fall. He had said no, of course – too dangerous for the boy; too much for him to keep him safe when he had to go in himself to determine what course of action to take – but something else too; something that was like a bruise to the touch when he thought of it now. There had been a moment as Thomas looked up at him with his hand on his stirrup, a moment in which he had wanted to thwart the boy. Wanted to say no to him, to leave him behind with his mother and ride off. And, though there had been a pang of regret to see Thomas' tears, the child's face had soon set – stubborn, resentful at not having his own way and he had stamped off, lashing out with his crop at the dogs, taking big, heavy steps back towards the house, his shoulders set stiff and hunched. Then he himself had turned away and forgotten the angry boy. The dog otter. Thomas had begged him to go with him to kill the animal. Herbert Lloyd's doing.

The pony staggers with exhaustion as Cai reaches the river at last. He dismounts downstream and walks towards the weir and the fish nets. He calls out for the boy, his voice sounding lame in the damp, still air. Wildflowers spoil the pasture everywhere, with violets hiding in the hollow at the roots of trees at the bank. The water is rust-coloured with what it has dragged down from the hills. Ridges form on the surface, minor waves like on the sea, though the spume and froth are a dirty cream rather than white. He calls again and his horse looks up from its grazing a moment. There is no sign of any other men from Nanteos; no sign of Thomas either. Up ahead around the bend is the weir. He can hear it. If he doesn't find the body of the boy now it is likely that he has not drowned, not come here to kill the fish-stealing otter and is safe, hiding out somewhere, filled with righteous spleen and intent on worrying his mother and drawing the attention and anxiety of everyone around him. Or maybe he had gone into the river earlier and been taken much further down – not trapped in the nets or caught up in the whirlpool at all…

Cai stops again, scanning the water, looking at the base of the big stones, somewhere where a body could be caught. Maybe the wilful boy had gone to see his hero Herbert Lloyd at Peterwell – or even, ridiculous though it would be, tried to find his way to London to tell tales to his father. He pulls the horse's head up again and his chest freezes: there in the long grass is a riding crop, the one with the bone fox's head. Leaving the pony to stumble on its reins he runs towards the weir. He shouts at the top of his voice, though there would be no hope of anyone hearing him above the water's din. So many times he's come here, yet today the place is unfamiliar. The nets are not visible under the volume of water. No one answers at the river bailiff's cottage when he hammers on the door, though the place seems untidy and newly-empty when he looks inside – perhaps he too is up at the mines.

At first nothing seems amiss. There are no small hoofprints or the prints of a boy's boots. He crosses up and down the bank, picking up a strong branch to help him as he wades in; to hook out a body. Nothing. The boy could have come here, seen the river was too full and ridden off somewhere else. He could have been startled by the weir keeper. He could be hiding out somewhere, listening to the anxious voices looking for him with a triumphant smile on his face. Cai hears his horse whinny from downstream and looks up for a moment. A second passes and he doesn't understand what he sees. He is looking at the animal but, though his eyes are seeing it, his mind does not. He even briefly closes his eyes but the animal is still in front of him and coming nearer – no, not his own horse; Thomas' pony. He shouts out in shock and the creature pulls up, squeals, then turns on its heels, cantering back around the bend, disappearing from sight.

*

At Nanteos, the rain has ceased and the sharp, cold white sunshine of April makes everything clear. All the hillside is dressed for spring in the garish yellow of gorse and tight white lace of blackthorn blossom and the hedges are shot through with it. At the lodge, Cai dismounts and eases the body down.

One of the men leads his horse and he walks the drive with the boy in his arms. At just twelve, Thomas is long rather than heavy, but Cai has folded his arms in towards his chest, as though he says his bedtime prayers. Bent at the knees, the child's thin legs are draped over the man's arm like a neat pair of towels. As he walks, Cai's head leans towards his shoulder where Thomas' face rests on his collarbone. Though damp, the hair is quite neat and the man can smell the river on him as he uses his own jaw to stop the head from lolling outwards. At the bend before the house is sighted, he stops to adjust the body. The men behind him, and even the animals, come to a quiet halt. He closes his eyes for a moment, lifts his face to catch the sun. A chiffchaff calls from a nearby tree, again and again the same rhythm, a nursery rhyme that never varies. At last he turns around. "Go on ahead." They hesitate for a moment but he gestures impatiently, the body still in his arms. Men, horses and a few dogs pass him and turn the bend. Cai takes all the boy's weight in his left arm. With his right hand he smooths down Thomas' hair again. The eyes are still closed and his face is calm and unblemished. He will never grow a beard now, bemoan an ugly spot. Cai finds himself humming under his breath – one of the songs the preachers peddle; at half the speed it is more lullaby than rousing call to the faithful. One of the dogs is coming around the corner, they must be coming back to find him. He takes the boy's legs across his right arm again, hitches him back to rest against his chest. As he turns the corner he sees the house – people everywhere, all suddenly stop. The dog is at his ankle, quiet and intent, looking up from time to time at Thomas' feet as they hang down. A blackbird shouts a warning, dives out of a bush and crosses straight in front of them, swerving down towards the lake and there is Elizabeth moving away from the main door and across the drive. She is wearing grey, the grey gown that is two shades lighter than her eyes. Her hair is pinned up and tidy, darker than ever in the white light. As he comes towards her, the other figures seem to shrink away and it is only her face, her eyes looking somehow past his shoulder and back down the drive, that he sees.

Chapter Thirty-One

T HE SUN WARMS Branwen's cheek, making a halo of the soft down there. She rests the wooden shame board on her tummy and it is not too heavy, though her arms are sore from stretching out to hold it for so long. The Revd Matthews has been kind to let her beg forgiveness like this; oh please God that she, and maybe even the baby, will now be clean. Her white shift moves in the sharp draught that blows under the side door. When she thinks of her baby her nipples prick and she is glad of the bandages binding down her breasts to her chest. She has done what Myfanwy said and worn the rags too – she is unclean of spirit, but to be unclean of body, in God's house and in front of them all, in such a way, would be unforgivable.

The officials move softly around Llanbadarn church – there is always something for them to be doing, though it is difficult to see what. Sharp sounds echo in the space: the slap of a Bible put down hard, like the crack of a sail. The first few are coming in now. Mostly older women, they sit in the back pews and they are talking, though no words can be heard at the front, just that their heads are curved together and that the quiet in the church is different.

Looking straight and up, over the heads of the congregation towards the large window, Branwen plays the trick that never lets her down. Staring competitions with her mother: look ahead, as if she can see, then blur the eyes, throw them out of focus. No one since could make her laugh, could beat her.

Here are the new Powells, but without their son. The boy is dead. Cold, like a shaft of lightning, runs up her back and she pictures him, floating face down, his hair undone and fingers open. She sees a mole she'd found, drowned and washed up on the bank of a flooded ditch, the soaking pelt unkempt, the body inside shrunken away from the skin.

Elizabeth Powell! Hush. Her dark dress is of such fine material that it shimmers like a black dragonfly's wing. The rows of round-moon faces turn away as the people swivel in their pews to stare at her. Some, in the seats nearest the wall, rise to their feet to see her better. Mistress Powell walks like a spirit.

A veil hides her face but the stillness is in every part of her except her feet. The Revd William's face is different. His cheeks and nose are red, looking like his older brother now. She fixes back on Elizabeth, the only face not focused on her own. Maybe she too practises the secret technique, seeming to look ahead, yet blurring her eyes so she cannot see, cannot be distracted or upset.

As the priest takes up position, Branwen unlocks herself, turns away from the sunlit window and leaves the church by the side door. No one in the aisle can see her now. Click, as she turns the iron handle, creak of hinge, slam. The graveyard is full of birds. Inside the organ starts up and the people begin to sing. Her white shift moves around her legs in the breeze. Her baby is not dead. He opens his face like a flower when he sees her, his toothless mouth wide in a smile of joy. Maybe the priest will take pity on them and baptise her son? But even if they won't take him at the font, Jesus will suffer him.

Chapter Thirty-Two

"So, this is where you go when you disappear." Cai's face is grim. "There are more people here than at a hanging!"

Cai and Mari are early and can see far into the valley below. The preachers have chosen a rocky hillside, a natural castle. Though most of the rocks are stained with moss or lichen, there is a huge one, the shape of a gravestone, which is a clean white-grey. The preacher stands behind it as his pulpit, the stone masking the bottom part of his body. He leans over it to harangue the crowd; thumping his fist on it; leans back, holding onto it for support as he gathers his voice to breathe into a crescendo which he powers forward over his listeners.

Cai stands unmoving, hands crossed over his chest. "I've never heard such a masterly performance – no player can touch him! Look at his gestures; his pauses. He turns away in disgust, only to spin around at our pleading, leaning over the rock and demanding again that we repent!"

"It is no performance! He is filled with the word of the Lord." Mari puts her hands to her ears, frantically shaking her head. "It's as though he has tightened a metal band around my head, Cai – I am not worthy, my life is full of sin!"

People from the crowd keep up a rapturous commentary, reacting to the preacher's every gesture, as though he conducts them in a choir. Some at the back can hardly hear him but are

266

transfixed by his gestures, joining in loudly when they hear "Oh yes!" and "Praise be!" from those nearer the front.

"Come to me, Lord, come inside me!" A lone woman kneels, repeatedly, one hand clutching at the front of her bodice, the other clawing at her skirts.

"I know her face... I know her, Cai. Is she not the girl that served at Nanteos?"

"At the Old New Year?"

Mari nods. "I think it is she. She tears at herself! Poor soul. What can she have done? Shall we go to her? No, wait, the preacher speaks!"

"Outside Jerusalem, at a place called Bethesda, which means 'the five gates', there was, by the sheep market, a pool. A pool touched by God himself; a pool visited by the angel, the angel who troubled the water, made it rise up." In her mind's eye Branwen sees Llyn y Gigfran, the froth moving, swirling, bubbling up, as if something would hurl itself out of the depths and grab at her. "... and there, the impotent folk," he brings his gaze down from the sky and searches the crowd beneath him, "the impotent folk," he gestures widely across them, "the blind, withered, halt, came to wait on the road, for it so pleased the Lord to make whole the first infirm person to enter the water after the visitation of the angel." He closes his eyes and lifts his face to the sky for a moment. There is not a sound from the crowd. He opens his eyes, throws his arms wide and shouts, "And I too have seen the angel of the Lord come down upon the water of this Godless county; begging of me to rinse clean these sinners, yes, those of you before me." He points to several people in the crowd. "Yes, you; and you behind him, seeking to hide – but do you not know that a man such as I who stands high on a rock looking down on you will see the hiding sinner even sharper; yes, even more sharply than the man who shields him. And Jesus asked the man how long he had been waiting at the pool; yes, our Saviour spoke to him and do you know what he said?"

He waits for so long that someone cries out, "Tell us, I beg of you!"

"And do you know how long this man had waited there, on his pallet, I ask you again?"

"Tell us," several voices cry out.

Then a lone voice. "Ten years?"

"You, who have not read the Good Book would spend till dusk guessing... No, thirty-eight years!" A moan, a gasp from the crowd. "Yes, I tell you, thirty-eight years to be saved, and Jesus said to him, 'Wilt thou be made whole?' And what did the impotent man say to him?" Again, he pauses, rocks backwards and forwards as he scans the crowd, shakes his head in exaggerated disappointment. His hands are constantly moving, like someone mending an invisible fishing net or catching at birds. "Well, what said he?"

"Yes!" the people roar. "Yes, yes!"

"Wilt thou be made whole?"

"Heal me!"

"Then rise; take up your bed and walk."

The crowd erupts in ecstasy as he steps down from the rock and comes straight towards Branwen. She moves her arms across her belly – how could he know! She looks around her in alarm as her neighbours, quivering with excitement, melt back. She sees only his face and hands coming towards her, his robe dark and blended into the hillside behind. The preacher, eyes harebell pale, seems not to blink as he stares into her face.

The air moves, sucked in by the crowd, held; there is a moan or maybe a hum from them. Someone behind her screams, short, ecstatic, like a fox in the night. Everything slips away as the preacher looms over her. His fingers are linked behind her neck, resting heavy on her shoulders; he lifts her chin with his thumbs, digging into her throat just below the jaw, tilts her face up towards his, bends over her.

"Do you seek to be saved?" People in the crowd answer for her. Again he asks and louder. "But do you want to be cured of your sin?"

She is an adit and they have lifted the holding plank. Water spouts into her, bubbles, explodes. She is not immersed in the holy whirlpool, it is inside her. He shouts again, his spittle across her cheek, under her eye. His hands have moved to her upper arms where he grips hard.

Someone near her groans. A chant has begun behind her, but she cannot understand what they say. "Help me!" Her voice is unrecognizable – another girl shouts out of her.

He bends towards her, pressing his forehead at hers. "I repeat, child. Do you want to be cured? Will you be saved of your sin?" His skull pushes at her, she is losing her balance, his hands are under her armpits now and she grabs at the front of his robes; then, like a burning branch snatched from the fire, his lips stroke hers. Her knees buckle underneath her, and she finds herself on the ground, clutching at the dirt with both hands as his palm presses down on the top of her skull. He speaks loudly in a language she cannot understand, the words regular as a bell tolling for the dead. The crowd are closing in, their warmth sour and the sound different – a growling, almost the sound of the bullring.

"Save me! Oh, take my sin, I beg you!" Her voice, but her real voice this time.

"Then sin no more lest a worse thing come unto thee." His fingers press down over her scalp, one boring into the outer edge of the eye socket; then, with a twist of the wrist, he pushes her over.

For a moment she lies with her cheek against the wet sphagnum moss, the smell of fresh apples and pine comforting, but then the hands of strangers raise her up. She is saved!

*

"He touched her! What can she have done? *Is* she the maid from Nanteos? Please, Cai; go to her!"

Though he hangs back for a moment, Mari pushes him forward and he approaches the woman. He bends to her, putting his face between her and the preacher but she strains to look past him. Though she moans and twists, her face is lit as though a blazing light shines behind it. He steps back in surprise. She is indeed familiar somehow, though there is nothing he can do for her.

"She's in rapture, Mari. Leave her alone." But Mari seems to have forgotten the girl and takes no notice as he returns to her side. Another preacher has come out from behind the improvised pulpit and stands in full view.

"There he is! Oh, when he speaks…" Her voice is already tearful. "Cai, when he speaks you feel the angel. The angel is come amongst us and Thomas, I think of little Thomas and how he disappeared the night of the flood and no one missed him – I did not miss him until it was too late and he was dead and –"

"Speak not of Thomas, Mari. I see him still." Though he reaches for her hand and draws it through his arm, he does not look at her. Instead he studies the other preacher, the man standing solid as a sculpture to his right. "So, this is Daniel Rowland – that long face and turned-down mouth, tragic with the wickedness of the world. And he who preaches now, 'tis Howell Harris, Mari?" She nods. "He has the face of a butcher or a bailiff; a twinkle of enjoyment in his eyes at least. Isn't it Harris who seeks to set up a community of believers somewhere in the south?"

"Dipping himself seven times in the Jordan, according to the word of Elisha. His cure is alluded to by our Lord and Jesus himself, oh, yes, our Lord himself. When he was come down from the mountain, great multitudes followed him. 'And, behold, there came a leper and worshipped him, saying, "Lord, if thou wilt, thou canst make me clean." And Jesus put forth his hand, and touched him, saying, "I will; be thou clean." And immediately his leprosy was cleansed. And Jesus saith unto him, "See thou tell no man; but go thy way, shew thyself to the priest, and offer the gift that Moses commanded, for a testimony unto them." And when Jesus was entered into Capernaum, there came unto him a centurion, beseeching him. And saying, "Lord, my servant lieth at home sick of the palsy, grievously tormented."' This is what Matthew tells us and you, you perhaps will go ten times to this pool and not be cured of your ailments or your sin but only on the eleventh, if the Lord chooses to bless me, his servant, to send his blessing down from heaven through his servant, like water from the falls to the wheel, maybe then you will be relieved of the burden of your sin!"

Suddenly he has bounded down the side of the low ridge

and is amongst them; their sound is a mixture of moan and roar. He's still shouting – a clear ring around him like that around a boxer – people near him cringing back to avoid the flung arms. The crowd moves down towards the stream and they can clearly see those who are to be baptised. Both men and women wait there, each wears only a white shift and is part-dragged, part-cradled by the strong handlers on each side of them as they approach the pool. One of the men is slumped between his helpers, his toes pointing downwards, gouging out a trail in the dark, mossy soil, his head thrust back, eyes rolling in ecstasy as he is part-lifted, part-dragged towards the water. Another, a small woman, is propelled easily towards the pool by her attendants, her feet hardly touching the ground at all.

One man at the water's edge takes fright and backs away, head down, whites of the eyes showing like a bullock facing the sticking pen. "No, no, Iesu, save me – I'm afeared of water!"

"Take me!"

"Lord, have me in his stead!"

The pool is so narrow that the preacher has to straddle it, only one body can fit in at a time so that the person is baptised between the preacher's legs. The keepers have a tight hold of the baptised person's torso, leaning over from opposite sides of the pool, the preacher praying in front of them, bending over the water.

"If he could only take me; wash me clean!" Mari's face shines as though with fever as she looks up at Cai. "You should have been here when they brought the people taken by wicked spirits! Howell Harris, he... oh, Cai, he took a staff and drove out the evil with a mighty prayer; they gibbered and fell to the ground kicking and foaming from their mouths. I thought I would swoon with it."

"Surely they were but old beggars and lunatics drunk on attention, Mari? Harris would have done better to buy them a loaf and some warm ale."

"No, Cai. As they say, 'These are new times; the devil must have nowhere to hide'." There is scorn in his laugh. She turns him to face her, clutching at his coat, urgently searching his face. "You won't speak of this to anyone? You won't tell them I come here – the mistress would throw me out! Jenkins told me about them, to help me after Thomas, but not even Jenkins tells anyone that he comes to hear them preach."

"It's a dangerous business. The gentry hunt the preachers like partridges, I know – and mobs attack them everywhere. Why would I tell, Mari? You do no harm here."

Chapter Thirty-Three

"THIS IS WHERE they stand Tal, wearing only their shifts, or just in shirts, the women with white linen on their heads, and he is in the water, two strong men either side because I've seen the river high and the people could be taken by the current. They take the person's arms and help them into the water. Sometimes they scream or shout out to the Lord – the water is cold, I think! The men dip them into the water, well, dip does not explain it! They go right under and he prays over them. Oh, what a voice he has, that even carries over the river. The people on the bank break into song. It is wonderful, Tal. They are cleansed, even lepers are cleansed!"

"Lepers, Branwen! What, you've seen lepers here?"

"No, not here. But Howell Harris – he said he could cleanse even lepers when he took the people down in the water to wash away their sin. I would he had taken me but I am always too late to the water; always at the back of the line."

"They are a poor and desperate sort come to the mountain to hear the Ranters."

"Not a bit! I have seen Cai, Nanteos – and the nursemaid, the one who was kind to me at the party before Epiphany." She goes to sit down beneath the tree that's green with slime. Tal flicks a couple of chicken bones away with his boot. "They bring food to the baptisms."

"I see that."

"One day I'll take him, be first in the line, wait out all night if I have to. The preacher can wash us clean, wash it away."

"He would be just as clean if you washed him yourself. Your son doesn't need a preacher to wash him. But I wouldn't choose here. I'd wash away my own sin upstream from the mine!" He laughs.

"They cast out the vile serpents." She points upstream. "They must have taken their staves and bashed down all the dead animals; pulled down all the traps. It must have been them." His face is a question. "The miners had animals there, Tal. Dead animals, caught and hung in traps and they dressed up the cave, up there, the cave, Ogof Morris, with skulls and charms." She shudders. "And now they're all pulled down. I'm sure that the preachers have done it so that there will be witches no more. The dead animals in their traps are all pulled down – I've heard it. You understand me?"

Tal reaches for her hand. "What witches, Branwen?" She shakes her head, looks quickly behind her. "These preachers you listen to, how did you come to hear of them?"

Her face is ablaze as she jumps up, telling the story with her hands. "I was before the people in Llanbadarn, I told you, the 'penance'." She looks at him. He nods, but doesn't speak. "When I came out from the service into the graveyard, the sun was out and the sky was thick with the song of birds. I put down my board and stepped away from it. My heart was so light, light as the seagull Myfanwy told about." She looks at Tal. No recognition. "Well, no matter, but light as is a bird's chest. Then suddenly a man stepped out from behind one of the graves. His face, Tal! Oh, what a face, like all the sorrows of the world were pulling on it, pulling the skin down."

"Daniel Rowland," Tal says, flatly.

"I know that now, but not then. 'Young woman,' he said, 'I see your troubles are heavy.' He looked towards the board – oh Tal, I was so ashamed! 'You don't need to carry that any more, or stand at the front of the church, in front of all the people in shame.' He even took the wand of shame and split it with his hands. He told me to come to the mountain, at the top of Cwm Einion; he told me I'd be clean and I was, oh Tal – I was! God has found me!" She looks at him, her eyes wet. "Do you believe me? You do believe him?"

Tal nods and reaches for her hands. "Shall we rest, Branwen? Come, sit down now or you'll dance all the nails from your boots!"

He takes her in his arms and they lie back – man, woman, child, dog. She puts her hand across the animal's flank and Llew presses his back into her side. Tal leans over her. She opens her mouth to his and shuffles towards him, pressing her body against him. Her nipples prick, delicious with milk – a raw sensation, a delicious ache and she feels her milk release as he kisses her deep. "Oh." She pulls away, pressing her palms hard into her breasts, but it is too late. The milk is already seeping through her underclothes and into her bodice. "Oh, I must feed him! Damn it! I'll have to wash it again… it smells so when the milk sours in my clothes."

He smiles. "Let him sleep."

"I shouldn't go long without feeding – I had milk fever."

"Let him sleep awhile."

Branwen moves up against him, fitting her still swollen body into his chest, his belly. He kisses her. Suddenly she pulls back and he groans. With a smile, she shakes her head and takes his hand. "Someone will come."

"Let them come," he says. "We are betrothed."

She kneels facing him and pulls open her bodice, groaning in relief when he takes the weight of her breast in his palm. She takes it in her hand like a skin water carrier and squeezes out a thin arc of milk. "Drink me."

Sunlight finds its way through the leaves as the breeze moves them and light flickers on the surface of the river and large stones along the bank – pulsing again and again in the same place, warming the wild garlic to release a scent.

The baby sleeps on, arms above his head, legs splayed at the hip like a dead frog. His hair is a fine fur, long at the base of his neck where his smell is at its strongest – in that hollow at the base of his skull, just behind his head. Afterwards, they watch him sleep; laughing as he purses his lips and rolls his eyes 'like a lunatic'.

"It is a rare treat to see you on your own. Myfanwy acts like a good dog – chases off the men 'sniffing around'. She is a dear friend to us now. I sometimes wonder if she and my father –"

Tal laughs. "There are always old women around a baby, but I don't think Evan would last long if Myfanwy turned her fancy on him!"

The dog stretches out in a pool of sunshine. She bends to put her cheek against his coat and he briefly raises his head, dropping it back down. His fur is warm, smelling like nothing on earth but a dog's hot fur, but his side is bony. He's skinnier than he looks under the thick long coat and she feels she may hurt him staying there. The river forms a backdrop to the sound of countless different birds – distinct in pitch, tone and rhythm from each other and, together with the faint, random swish and rustle of leaves, comforting to the ear. The baby is awake now, looking up through the constantly changing net of leaves trapping and revealing beams of sunlight. Light, shade on his face. He is babbling quietly to a low branch that shivers and bobs above his head. Branwen lifts herself onto her side, resting her head on her hand to watch her baby. She laughs. Tal leans over her shoulder, feeling her body shake with laughter as her baby coos and chunters at the branch, trying to keep from drawing his attention. He puts his palm on her belly, still not quite the same after the birth and rests his chin on her shoulder. What pleasure to hear her laughing at last, unable to take her eyes from the little boy with the fat arms and toothless smile. The baby kicks and punches air without stop, each limb moving independently, like a badly managed puppet. Tal starts to laugh too, like her, holding the sound back so as not to draw the baby's attention. She squeezes his hand, for a moment resting the side of her head on his. It is perfect.

Chapter Thirty-Four

THE SAPLING WOBBLES in the wind. Elizabeth turns, looking back at the house. "They can see us; they can see me." Cai looks at her, a question in his face. "Here, grieving for Thomas. There could be a set of eyes in each window. This…" She gestures to the plaque, the sapling. "This place is not where I shall come for Thomas; nor is the tomb at Llanbadarn."

She is quiet for a while. The young tree, bare of leaves and a stranger in the landscape, has a frail air. "A yew tree. It must be a yew tree for Thomas; not here in Mary's pleasure gardens but in the wood somewhere, somewhere I can go and visit quietly."

"Of course."

"Not far from the house; I want to see it from my window. No, not see it – then they can see me when I visit it… I want it in the wood, but near enough for me to know it's there, when I'm in bed at night. Can you do it, Cai?"

"There are plenty of young yews growing in the wood. Or do you wish to plant one yourself?"

"Let's find one. No plaque. Nothing for the world to see."

"What, then?"

She hesitates for a moment, then draws something from the pocket of her skirt. "This." It's a curl of Thomas' hair, tied not with ribbon but with some rough twine. "I found the string in a box by his bed."

"Don't you want to keep it? Have it by you?"

She shakes her head, her voice faltering. "When it's in my pocket, my fingers go to it, like they wander towards a loose thread. When it's in my jewellery box, my eye locks there – again and again I keep catching on it. If I wake in the night the box glows in the firelight. I tried putting it in the box with the Grail Cup, but even that didn't make it still."

"But why a tree? Why a yew?"

"So powerful. Every part is poison. Do you notice the space around a mature yew?" He nods. "Nothing can grow. The yew will keep him safe; quiet."

"Why don't we go now, Elizabeth?"

For a moment she looks unwilling, then, "Yes, but I have to fetch something first." She goes towards the house. Cai turns back to the tree, the hillside rising behind it. The sky is arranged in layers of grey, each layer a different shade and texture. Thomas is no more; will never canter impatient and eager, legs flapping, loose reins urging his reluctant pony on, mirroring Herbert Lloyd with his crop, nearly unseating himself at times with the big flourishes. He almost laughs, remembering the boy grabbing onto his pony's mane, hanging off the side of the saddle. "Will you ride side saddle like a fine lady, Thomas?" he'd said, half-satisfied to see the over-enthusiasm for the whip backfiring. But Thomas is no more, and Elizabeth is coming down the front steps. Though she moves more slowly now her pregnancy is advanced, unlike some women who waddle like geese when a baby's inside, the nature of her gait has not changed. She takes his arm and he draws her into his side, as much as her petticoats will allow. She lifts her chin, eyes fixed on the wood by the house. He shortens his steps for her. She glances back just before they reach the path through the trees, though she doesn't slow her pace.

"I know the tree, I think," he says.

The birdsong is thin, their footfalls almost silent – the leaves of autumn long since turned soft. The bare trees with their last, sparse leaves seem vulnerable as an old woman's skull. He looks down, worried for her, but she has changed into stout boots she'd had from the servant girl last winter. Not far into the wood, under the wall, with the lake just glimpsed below, he stops. A yew tree dominates the space, its trunk firm and straight, though eaten alive in places by the thick sinews of ivy. Nothing but ivy grows on the floor around it. Its dark green leaves are alive although, all around them, the other trees are almost bare. She looks up into the yew, layers and layers of branches climbing into the sky.

"I travelled once with William to Scotland. There they had forests of trees that never lost their leaves."

"Only the yew and the holly are like that here," he says.

"The trunk; look at it, it's like the base of a great cathedral pillar. William was keen to teach us all the proper architectural names for parts of a church. We would visit them, wherever we were, on any day – Catherine would sketch, she's so adept, but Thomas hated it. He called it the 'churchy death'. She lets go of his arm and moves towards the tree, walking all around the trunk. She stops by the one sapling surviving under the dark canopy – a tiny yew. He goes to meet her. She is holding the piece of hair again. "Let's bury it, Cai. Here." She points and he bends to make a hole with his knife – deep. He puts out his hand to take it from her but she crouches down, holding the hair to her cheek with the palm of her hand. Her eyes are closed, lips moving. Then she kisses it quickly and puts it in the hole.

As she bends forward she loses her balance, her head pitching towards the trunk but he grabs her arm and she braces against him, righting herself.

"Elizabeth?"

"I'm alright. Cover it now." She turns away, looking down towards the lake as he fills the small hole and finds a stone to go on top. He looks up; she is watching him. "Too big, Cai." He looks at her. "Someone may notice and be curious." She bends down and picks up a small, rough stone. "This is better." She nudges his stone away with her foot and replaces it, reaches for his hand as she comes back down to the path. He turns to go back to the house but she holds his arm. "I thought I may bury this too; dear Thomas." She has produced a riding crop from somewhere under her skirts and brandishes it in the air.

Cai almost laughs. "I can make another hole for it if you like, but..."

"No, I can see that would be ridiculous, and anyway, some dog might dig it up and our secret be discovered." She gives it to him and takes his arm again. "Come; let's go further through the woods until we meet the drive." Although she makes no sound, her hand returns again and again to her eyes, wiping distractedly at her tears as they move down the track. He looks away, the pain of seeing her cry! They emerge onto the drive and turn back towards the house. As they reach the lake, she stops them. "The whip please, Cai." He gives it to her and suddenly she is heading straight for the water.

"No!" He grabs at her, catching her by the back of her bodice and there is an awkward scuffle.

She fights him off. "What're you doing? Let me go!"

"No, Elizabeth!"

"Let go of my arm!" She wrestles to get away from him, but he won't let her go near the water again. She flexes against his grip a few more times. "Cai, let go of me, I beg you!" Then suddenly she gives up, relaxes into his arms. For a moment he still holds her tight. She looks towards the house. "Thank goodness for the bend in the drive!" Her tone is normal, in fact her voice even holds a smile in it. "Did you think I would…?" He relaxes his hold, though he doesn't reply. She looks up at him, her breath on his face. "But I'm past that now; and anyway, surely it's too shallow!" She is smiling up at him. "Cai, I wish only to bury Thomas' crop in the water. Please." As she takes a step back, he releases her from his arms. She takes three brisk steps towards the lake, looks back. "It seems too shallow to drown it here. There are reeds at the bank."

"Shall I take it?"

She passes it to him and waits as he crosses to the far side of the lake. She watches a heron holding its ground, in love with its own reflection. But it can hold on no more and lifts in front of the man, struggling to rise, wings, leg and huge beak uncoordinated for several beats. Cai is almost behind the island now. She sees him lift his arm, his body arching behind the throw, but she doesn't see the whip in the air, neither hears nor sees it reach the water. He comes back the same way and she walks to meet him. "Thank you, Cai." He nods. "Lose it in water."

"What did you say?"

"Oh, just something that was said to me once." She takes his arm as they go back towards the house, though with each step they move further away from one another. A buzzard circles lazy over the grassland in front of the house. "What it must be to be a bird! What they must see. Thomas would have taken a shot at it, most surely." As they reach the door, again she stops them. "You don't speak much any more." He looks down. "Why do you not speak?" He shakes his head. "Cai, you're not to blame." Taking his arms in both her hands, shaking him slightly, she looks up into his face. "Why don't you speak to me?" She waits a moment, takes a long breath. "I know what you did for me, in the summer, back in those darkest of days. Cai?" He shakes his head. "I have forgotten nothing."

"I've nothing to... there's nothing I can say. Elizabeth, leave me. Please, there's nothing to be said."

She is still for a moment, drops her arms, one hand lingering on her belly. "My back's tired. I'll go in now." But she makes no move to go.

He bows slightly. "Then I'll take my leave."

She nods. As he turns away, he hears her – "Thank you."

Elin is waiting for her just inside the hallway. "How long have you been here, girl?"

"Just now, Mistress Powell. A letter for you." She takes it as she moves away.

"Should I attend you?"

"No, I thank you."

The letter is in Mary Powell's hand. Once in her room, Elizabeth wrestles with her boots and casts off her heavy cloak, suddenly too weary even to hang it up. She has drawn mud through the house; it is even on Mary's lovely bedroom carpet. Will she ever learn! She opens the letter. Mary asks after her health, 'both in body and in spirit; especially in your delicate condition'. Once more, Mary expresses her own grief for Thomas and offers condolence. She proffers the familiar light news from London and describes the music she's playing (she is indeed an accomplished keyboard player). 'Do Edward's schemes for draining the mines flourish?' She repeats her offer to take Catherine. 'There are many good establishments for the education of clever young ladies now. I would be glad to supervise her in the capital. We would have such fine times together.' She says nothing of scandal; nothing of her dead husband. She had visited 'poor William' when he was last in London and was pleased to see him tolerably well. She ends asking after the children and servants, naming each one. A good woman to be sure, though dull.

But what it must be never to have a child... The tears come again; Elizabeth sighs, tired of weeping, just so tired of grief. She lies back on her bed, but the weight of the child pressing on her makes her feel sick. Soon she is settled on her side with a pillow under her bended knee facing the window as it grows dark. Out there, Thomas' whip lies crooked in the black water. Fish will nibble at it perhaps, before it sinks into the mud. Behind her closed eyes she can see the big yew tree, vibrating in the breeze, and the tiny sapling in its shadow. She sees the pale stone she placed there, perhaps the last thing visible as night comes to the wood and, beneath it, Thomas' hair growing cold in the dark.

Chapter Thirty-Five

As Tal, Gwyn and the horses are coming down through the woods at Cwm Einion, they hear a shout behind them. They pull up and wait for Tudor, the mole catcher, a man wide as he is tall, muscular, with a shaved head, who strides down towards them.

"I passed that girl you see; her with the green eyes. And the child. Something not right with her." He gestures back up the track with his staff.

"Here?" Tal looks behind him. "Where were they exactly?"

"On the path." He points again with his stick. "Something not right with her. Her face was as though a candle was lit behind it." He frowns; pulls hard on his pipe.

"How far up?"

"Near Llyn y Gigfran. She had a white cloth upon her head. She'd dressed the baby in some white gown – must have been freezing."

"What cloth? A cap?"

"No, I told you, a piece of cloth, like a nun would wear in a painting." He lifts his pipe away from his lips, points at Tal with it. "Thought she was yours at one time; thought you'd found yourself lucky, daughter of a fulling mill and all that. Seems not. Baby's more angel than *Sipsi*; yellow hair like an old man smoking."

Tal nods. "Thank you. Thank you for that news."

The man moves on ahead of them and Tal gathers up the reins ready to turn back. Just before he reaches the corner the mole catcher stops and shouts back at them. "Hey, mind what I said, lad. She wasn't right; something not right with her, like she had a fever on her."

A blade of cold moves through him as Tal lifts his hand to acknowledge the man before he passes out of sight. Bonnie and Sailor still stand patiently, a slight jangle of the chains at their mouths as they worry at their bits. What should he do? He only has Gwyn with him, not a hope that the boy could manage the two horses alone, gentle as they are, especially as Bonnie has her foal at foot.

"Come, Gwyn. You'll have to come with me, the horses too. I need to find her."

"The girl with the donkey, that pretty one? He said green eyes – she has green eyes, and a baby?"

Tal doesn't reply but has already turned the horses and is heading back up the track. He has taught Gwyn to ride – so much more control than on the ground, and taught him the value of having the horse from a foal. Of course, a ton of horse can do anything he likes in reality – but he doesn't know this; the trick is to make it so he never knows his own power, so he only ever sees you as the strong master you were to him when he was a foal. The boy has been quick to learn. They urge back up the quarter-mile or so to where the logging is almost finished for the day. But something's wrong; they hear shouting and a horse's terrified squeal.

Gwyn pulls up. "D'you hear that! Something's happened." The horses stop dead.

"Get on!" Tal, face grim, urges Sailor forward, turning off

the main track and down towards the river. The trees left in
the wood are leafless. Now he can see. Benjamin has fallen
all the way from the track down the steep slope, the huge log
he was dragging lying on top of him in the river. Jumping
down, he shoves Sailor's chain at Gwyn and runs through the
shattered branches, down towards the water.

"Benjamin's down!" A man shouts at him.

Tal stops for a second, holding onto a tree trunk to stop
himself from falling forwards, pointing back up through the
trees. "Get someone to hold Sailor – Gwyn has him and the
mare and foal on his own. Now!" He skids down the last
steep bank. In front of him the horse is lying on his side in
the shallow water, raising his head to scream, then sinking
back. At least eight men are working to dislodge the huge log
pinning him down – though there is no hope of them moving
it without help. "Get up there and fetch the other horses down
to shift that trunk!" Tal shouts. A couple of the men scramble
out of the water and up the bank. Benjamin screams again,
but weaker this time. Tal wades over to him. Lying on his
side, the animal's face is two-thirds underwater, though his
neck strains to lift it free. Tal, the cold river over his knees,
struggles to hold the huge head free of the water. "Help me!
Help me here!" But Hughes, the old ostler, having stepped
away from the log, makes no move. One man comes forward,
but Hughes holds the second back. Benjamin groans, but can
at least breathe properly now. Two of them are holding the
animal's nose above the water but it's not something they can
do for long.

Perhaps the horse's back is broken. "No horse could have
taken a load like this! Why did you not take care of him?" Tal
shouts at Hughes.

"Ha. A monster like him? Should have been nothing to him. Badly trained is what he is; *was* I should say."

Llew, legs flexed and body low, skulks up and down the bank, following Tal's every movement but not touching the water. Bonnie and Sailor are at the river's edge now. Bonnie chunters softly and Benjamin's ears flicker in response. Tal struggles again to lift his head. "Take over from me here – I'll harness them up." Though they glance nervously at one another, two of the foresters do what he asks, crouching forwards with knees bent, holding the horse's head on their laps above the current. "You, get hold of that foal – yes, slip a rope around him; hold him back across the chest; don't want him in the water as well."

Tal moves on and around the huge log, heaving against the chains, getting Bonnie and Sailor fastened up.

Hughes laughs, turning to a man at his shoulder. "Look at him: climbing around like a monkey, a face like one too." He spits, shouts out to Tal, "Leave the chains on them, will you, after you've pulled it off that 'orse. We'll need 'em both to get that trunk back up the bank to the track." Though he takes his time, he comes down to help fasten Bonnie to the log, refusing to go anywhere near Sailor.

"He'll have to be shot. Back's broke," one of the men says, shaking his head as he looks back upstream at Benjamin.

"Let him drown where 'e is, I say," Hughes replies, though looking all the time at Tal. "There's no gun with us here and it'll take an hour to send a runner up for Cai or some such other. Meat for the hounds at Nanteos, though shame it wasn't that bastard dead." He nods his head at Sailor.

Tal gets up on Sailor whilst one of the other men takes Bonnie's head and they move slowly forward. 'A piece of cloth, like a nun would wear in a painting.' Why would she be dressed like that up here? Tal looks behind him, controlling the horse team foot by careful foot until the huge log is no longer across Benjamin's back.

He returns to the animal's side. Standing in front of him in the water he pulls forwards and upwards on the harness around Benjamin's head, encouraging him, shouting above the noise of the river. The two men with him go behind the horse's great neck and flex against it but, though he is free of the load now, he still cannot move.

"Go for a gun, someone," Tal shouts at last, but the authority he held briefly when it seemed there was something to be done has ebbed away. The men at Benjamin's head look at Hughes as he comes towards them, lurching along the fragile bank.

"Get back to work," he says. "Leave this one to drown and get those other two buggers up onto the track with that log. Ynyshir, Nanteos – someone'll send the butchers up to get at him. He's not going anywhere."

The men hesitate for a moment. One still supports the great head on his thighs as he crouches over the water but it can't be sustained for long. Tudor's words, but even more, his tough face, frowning with worry as he looked back, determined that Tal would take note: 'mind what I said, lad. Something not right about her. Not right at all.' Branwen! The fear is like a throbbing pulse in his neck. Benjamin screams again, a strangled sound. "Stay with him, will you? Don't let him drown. I'll go for a gun myself. They'll have one at Ynyshir."

"Get away from that bloody animal and get back to work," Hughes shouts at the men in the water. Then he turns on

Tal. "You might be horse master at the mines but I'm still in charge here!"

The men look again at Tal. "I can be there and back with a gun in twenty minutes. Don't let the horse drown." Tal is out of the water now and on the bank.

"Do as I bloody well say, you; it's an order!" Hughes spits at his men. "And you –" He grabs at Tal's shirt, his fingers digging into his arm. "You –" Tal pulls away from him but the ostler grabs at him again with his other hand. Tal wrenches his shoulder away, digging him in the ribs with his elbow. Suddenly Llew darts in low, bites Hughes on the heel and, all in one smooth arc, returns to Tal's side. The man yelps, a sound that changes to a scream as he loses his balance and falls backwards. For a moment Tal freezes as he sees him topple into the shallow water by the bank, onto a slab of protruding rock where he lies unmoving. The two men supporting Benjamin are struggling towards the fallen man as the horse screams, straining to keep his head out of the water before sinking. Tal turns back only once as he scrambles upwards through the trees, Llew at his heels, a red stain growing on grey rock; the sodden men standing, looking down, helpless.

"Branwen; no!" he cries.

*

"Cariad?" Though she has dressed him specially in a clean white robe, Branwen can still smell the warm, vomit stench of old milk – turning to cheese in the deep fatty creases around his neck. She has squashed him down inside her bodice, using the stiffened frame to help hold his weight, and leaving one of her hands free to grasp at overhanging branches to steady her. Even in sleep, he holds on tight to her clothes with his fists as she picks her way down the loose shale of the steep path. Shaky, wobbling, sometimes her feet slide from under her with a sickening jolt. The precious piece of bleached linen covering her head won't stay in place and she has folded it and tucked that into her bodice too. As she moves down towards the damp cold, she can hear the river thunder in the narrow gorge. The smell of it comes towards her, the damp pelt of a dead dog fox. She stops for a moment. A scream? No, nothing, only the pounding river.

The last part is the hardest of all with the child, heavy now and almost ready to walk. It is steep and treacherous under the ferns and onto the hard, wet moss, then the crumbling black soil of the bank. She pauses for a moment to get her balance, then leaps onto the grey slab below her, right at the water's edge.

This is no slow, gentle lowland river. It is black and fast and takes her breath as her feet are covered by it for the first time, the dark, sodden moss coming away as she clutches at it, trying to steady herself as she moves away from the bank into the middle of the current, to rest on a big slab of stone. He snuffles once as she stumbles, then is still again. She lowers her mouth and nose to his head again, her lips tightening in a kiss.

There is a beach of small grey pebbles to her right and she eases herself back into the water, searching with her foot to find a steady purchase before she wades back in. Even at its shallowest point, the river is cold as iron, moving too fast, lying too deep for the sun ever to warm it. She had intended something different; had had a different vision. Both arms outstretched, the child's head resting in her palms, she would have lowered him in backwards. Like a picture in a children's Bible she had seen her hands, cupping the small head while his face looked into hers, peaceful, as the water took all the sin away. But this water was brown with peat from the mountain; there would be no looking through it at any face.

The river bullies with its roar and she can't think clearly through the bitter cold that seems to rise and smother her. Her arms cannot perform what she has imagined, his peaceful body resting along her forearm, like the raven's wing, but a sweet, sweet weight. At first the bone cold is only at her feet; then, as she wades in deeper, it seeps into her dress, growing warm, becoming easier to bear. He shudders and she stops moving. She struggles to move him down further without waking him, easing him to lie against her belly to keep him warm. His head is only just visible now, his strange pale hair, sticking straight up like dead reeds from a boggy field. He grumbles as she shoves at him; then he settles comfortably against her. What a good boy he is for sleeping! For a while they stay this way, until the water feels warm between her thighs. She moves further in, water seeping up into her dress and she feels the shock of it, running into her belly. As the water reaches his feet he starts to scream, legs kicking, fighting against her. As the cold rises, the white horror of the baby's cry stabs at her. She pushes forwards as fast as she can against the current, the ice now at her chest. She holds him tight against her, chanting the preachers' baptism prayers, the scraps she remembers, facing the torrent straight on. Suddenly she steps out of her depth and pitches forwards, hands thrashing, scrambling to regain her footing. The water is in her hair, at the back of her neck. It is not what she has intended! She makes a desperate grab at the white cloth as it floats away, but the current is moving too fast and it's lost.

She must duck down to baptise him; dip him, like the blessed in the waters of the River Jordan. But the river is too strong – again and again it knocks her back as she tries to stay under long enough to say the blessings, and she has to fight the panic to hold herself down. She struggles to the bank, knowing she must find a different place, a quiet pool, deep like this one, but calm.

Everything sodden now, she collapses back onto the flat rock. The child... There is no movement from the small body, but his fingers cling to the ties of her bodice. *"Dere, cariad."* She bends forward, trying to undo them from the lacing. *"Ga'd nhw, nawr."* She digs into the front of her clothes to pull him up a little, so there is not so much weight hanging from his fingers. He doesn't struggle as she pulls him up her body inside her clothes. *"'Na ti; bachgen da i Mam,"* she murmurs. His hands grasp the laces still. She tries to get him onto his feet; to get him to lock his knees and stand up on her thighs as she sits on the boulder. He likes to stand now, to pull himself up. But he seems to be asleep. She works to get him to let go of his grasp on her bodice; to stand on his feet. She rubs at his back through her clothes to warm him but he does not seem to want to stand up. She pulls open her stiff, sodden bodice, bending it back, trying to see his face. She strokes what she can see of his cheek. *"Der' yma, cariad."* She shakes him, getting hold of his body through the material. *"Deffra nawr; deffra."* She supports his weight with one hand, the other prizing his fingers from the cords holding her clothes. *"O, diawl, ti'n 'styfnig, cariad!"* For a moment, the strange wings of a tiny, trapped bird suddenly released stir in her chest and she cries out in hope – rich, sharp, but brief – for as she holds his head, heavy in her palm, she knows: the fingers of her son no longer grasp the lacing but are tangled in it, nothing more.

Chapter Thirty-Six

Mari and Martha drag and pull him away from the kitchen. The doctor shouts after them. "I can't, man; there's nothing I can do. She was dying even as I reached in for the child."

Once in the hallway, Cai stops, arms hanging at his sides. Mari is sobbing and he raises his hands as if to touch her face but she draws back – they're foul with gore. Putting her hands around his arm she tugs at him. Again and again she pulls him, but he takes two reluctant steps then stands, like a young bull, unwilling to accept the ring driven through his nose but unable to move away for the pain. Then she takes his hand, wincing at the blood, and draws him through the house and outside. The night air is freezing and he slumps down, holding his head in his hands, dry sobs shaking his shoulders and the muscles of his back. Mari sits next to him on the step, her leg pressed tight against his from knee to hip. She leans into him; tries to make him look at her. "Why did you attack the doctor? Why are you like this? I know your own mother died in childbed but..." Though her voice is hardly louder than a whisper, it's drenched with fear. "Cai, what's wrong with you?" Then they hear, coming out of the misty dark, formless noises, no words or reference, yet still with the power to alarm. Mari tenses, though Cai doesn't react. Now there's shouting, and a hunting dog runs out of the gloom;

swearing; the fog is clearing and glows yellow as men come up to the house with torches. Then William is suddenly in front of them, barges through the door, disappears inside. Though the men left behind are busy with the dogs, they seem reluctant to move away, forming a sullen half-circle facing the house. Some of the dogs, now restrained, bark excitedly. Cai raises his head. Roberts, the gamekeeper, takes a step forward, then changes his mind. Mari calls out, having to attempt it a couple of times before her voice comes clear. "Does he know? Does the Master know?"

Roberts nods. "Riders came for him. Found us on the road as we turned for home."

Suddenly William is behind them in the doorway; though his mouth is open he makes only a strangled gurgle. Mari scrambles to her feet and Cai looks up. "You! You have my wife's womb blood on your hands?"

Cai holds his hands out before him as though seeing them for the first time. "She's dead," he says, without expression.

William raises his whip and strikes at Cai around the back and shoulders. "You went into the kitchen! The Doctor said, he said... you touched her, you touched my wife!" Cai holds his arms up in an attempt to protect his head, but his fingers are open, like a blind man's in wind. Mari tugs at him, shouting. Cai gets to his feet as Jenkins, his head and upper body cringing away from the crop, grabs feebly at his master's arm.

Standing now, Cai looms over the two men and the whip. He looks past them, back through the door, groans and stumbles backwards, Mari dragging on his hand, pulling him away across the gravel. He stops for a moment, caught in the light bleeding from the window, looks back at Nanteos, then disappears into the fog. Mari stands, her arm still raised. William roars again and scrapes the air with his whip, calling into the dark. "Get out, get off my land – whore's son!"

*

For a moment Cai stands in the middle of the empty yard. Even his shirt and open waistcoat are covered in blood. Blood streaks his face where he's wiped at it. Though it's dark now, he raises a hand in front of him, as if to shield his eyes from the sun. He flings himself forwards to the stables, his movements strong and yet, as he runs, he is not following a straight line. His horse is broken-winded and still stands in the yard where he left it, the reins trailing in the gravel. A young groom, coming out of the stable, sees Cai and melts away.

Head down, he barges through the door, stumbles, then stands swaying, trying to focus on the line of loose boxes. Each holds a riding horse and one by one they put their heads over the half-doors. Some are chewing, others whinny softly or rumble their low greeting. Cai takes the first horse's head in his hands. It is a tall bay gelding, William's hunter. At the smell of him, feeling the warm fur, Cai sobs. The horse, alarmed, tries to pull free, but Cai is in the stable now, takes control of himself, fits the bridle to the unwilling mouth. He's ridden this animal before and the horse knows not to resist.

They move fast down the drive. Though many eyes are watching him leave, no one stands in his way. At the road he stops. To the town; the marsh; the hills?

A wagon rounds the corner, coming up from the town and, as if fleeing from it, as if he can't bear even to be near it, he turns the other way. Tall hedges on either side make the road itself almost invisible, but the horse knows its way. He reins up as the road follows the ridge above the mansion. Some light seeps from the windows of the ground floor, but it is a weak light in the cold night. As he watches, small, busy figures approach the front of the house – mummers caught for a moment, then lost to the dark.

Elizabeth is there.

His howl spooks the horse which flexes down on its haunches. Cai lets him go and they gallop the road – unable to see, the horse driven by the terrible noise of its rider.

Chapter Thirty-Seven

MARY POWELL RETURNS to Nanteos. There is no ceremony, only a groom to hand her down, the carriage moving away to the back to unload her trunk almost before she alights. She approaches the house with dread. Elizabeth – that vital, capricious woman, brought to her knees by grief and now dead in childbirth. The other remaining children – a little boy of, three, perhaps? Little William they call him. And the girl, Catherine. By all accounts a bright child with her own opinions. How they must be suffering! And the new baby, a girl. It had seemed unlikely that she would survive, though it appears Martha has taken her in hand and a wet nurse engaged.

No one is about as she goes into the outer, then inner hall. She calls out half-heartedly, shy of her own voice. It is a strange sensation; the house both disarmingly familiar, yet painfully changed. She follows the sounds into the kitchen. For a few minutes she observes the scene from the doorway without being noticed. The baby is strapped to Martha's chest, pinned there by a big well-worn shawl that is crossed over and tied in a knot at the back. The child is wailing but the cook seems to take no notice as she bends to the steaming pots. Finally, she steps into the room and calls, "It's a wonder she can breathe in there!"

Martha spins around, her face a huge smile. For a moment

it seems they will even embrace as Mary walks towards her into the room. She bends over the bundle. Only the top of the child's head can be seen, one eye squashed against Martha's chest, the other seeming to hold her gaze. "You'll build a rod for your own back carrying the child everywhere like that." She reaches out to hold the tiny hand, but the baby pulls it away.

"Not my back. Some nursemaid'll have the problem when she grows up spoilt, no doubt. The Master's around somewhere."

The child is dark like her mother and not pleasing to the eye. The spit dog barks and the child takes fright – a feeble wail, ending in a wobble. There is a smell of burning – it's the dog's coat! Mary casts about for something and grabs a tureen of brown liquid.

"That's my bloody gravy!"

But it does the trick, though dog, wall and woman are streaked with brown and the fire has almost gone out. Choking at the smoke, Martha grabs the dog by the scruff and, pulling it out of the wheel, kicks it into the yard. They stand on the kitchen step. "Well, there's a homecoming for you, Mistress Mary," Martha laughs.

"I've not often been in a kitchen before and now I know why!" She looks ruefully down at her ruined clothes and laughs. "I was taught not to as a child. Indeed, it would not have occurred to me; in London one's kitchen is in the basement. This is the second time my clothes have come to harm in here!"

"Mistress Elizabeth was always in here with us in her last days. The Master was so often away; Cai at the mines..." Mary looks at her sharply. Martha continues. "Yes, we all call him Cai here now. As I said, Cai at the mines with the trouble and the other grand ladies not coming near. She had not been well, you see." Martha stops, straightens and turns to look full at her. "She wasn't well; after the loss of young Thomas, I mean."

"Yes, I heard about it."

"You didn't come to Cardiganshire for the funeral?"

"No; I was sorry but I couldn't, being on the Continent. It wasn't possible to return in time."

Martha turns back into the kitchen. One of the maids, a thin girl she remembers from before, is already clearing up. There's no sign of the dog.

*

Mary goes to the music room, the long windows and the fine view familiar. There is a new instrument – not as good as her own, but impressive nevertheless. There is music still on the stand. She peers at it. Ambitious indeed! One of the few things they had in common perhaps. Elizabeth had been an unusual woman – rather provincial in many ways – the quaint Welsh she could never quite keep out of her voice, even speaking it sometimes, no matter who was around to hear. Yet she had been more than a younger son's wife, not a typical vicar's wife somehow. Maybe the Ynysmaengwyn blood from her mother was strong in her? There had been a strange fearlessness, maybe even recklessness about her – and to see her ride! The first time Elizabeth had come to stay at Nanteos as William's new bride she'd invited Mary to join her. Mary remembered her own hasty answer. "No, I thank you. In London there was not much opportunity, save for the great parks and I shuddered to compete with more zealous horsewomen. Besides, I was loathe to spend my money on hooves! No, thank you. I'll call for a groom to go with you." But it had been dear Edward who'd accompanied Elizabeth that time, riding (if she remembered correctly) some half-broken horse and the two had flown down the drive. In fact, had she not followed their progress from this very window, as far as the large oak on the ridge opposite?

She turns from the window to see William watching her from the doorway. But it is not the man she's known. He is diminished, even since she'd seen him in London; thin, red mixed into the whites of his eyes. "You're looking more and more like your brother," she says, coming towards him and taking his hand. The broken veins give him a ruddy appearance.

"The carbuncle is burst, Mary; the court case, so long in coming, is upon us. We will lose! If Thomas hadn't died of an apoplexy when he did, he surely would do now. Lewis Morris prevails; I tell you, he has had the ear of all and paraded himself and all the low workers of the mines through London to testify against us. We are a laughing stock!"

"I'm sure it's not as bad as you imagine, William –"

"Not as bad! Old George's already smashed the clans; he won't have any problem dealing with the Cardiganshire gentry! The Lord Chancellor says he'll send a sergeant at arms to strike us from the Commission of the Peace. They're talking of calling in the Scots Greys to protect Morris and his miners at *my mine*! I can only say that I'm glad Elizabeth doesn't have to bear witness to this and that I, as a clergyman and therefore ineligible, don't also have the expense and trouble of canvassing for election on top of all else." He takes a deep breath, seems about to continue.

"Shall we go downstairs and sit down? I'll ring for refreshment." Mary is still in her dirty travelling clothes, spiced with gravy, yet he does not seem to notice.

"Shall we sit awhile, Brother?" She finds a chair and he joins her. He is silent for a long time. She leans her elbows on her thighs and watches the flames in the parlour grate: though some are random, there is an overall pattern in terms of shape and colour, a predictability.

"I will be gone some weeks, Mary. I trust that is convenient for you?" She brings herself upright and nods at him. "You will conduct the investigation?"

"Pardon me, Brother?"

"The inquiry into her death. I do not have time for it but must see to my affairs in London. You will see the Doctor, the... well, any interested parties, ensure that right was done by her." She nods. At last there will be something for her to do. She looks again at the familiar view from the large window, one she thought never to see again. "Take Elizabeth's room, if you please." She looks at him, startled. "Your room from happier times, of course."

"No; I think not, Brother – it wouldn't be fitting."

"I beg you, take it. I'm tired of passing that door and thinking of her. Please – I've had a new mattress brought in..." He looks away. "You need have no fear, Mary – she didn't leave this world from the pink room, no indeed..." William looks again into the fire, flames catching the glass in his hand.

"I will most certainly stay in the room, if that would please you. It'll be my great pleasure." She refreshes their glasses and sits back down. For a while there is silence between them; then "Where is Edward?"

William starts. "Edward?" She smiles; a slight nod. "Edward, you say? Don't speak to me of him, Mary! Oh –" He holds up his hand as if attempting to stop a man in a fight. "Oh I know you were fond of him, though God knows why. You were good to him, I know, but we're well rid of him."

"Rid of him! What on earth do you mean? Where is he? What have you done?"

He looks at her a moment. "He's gone away."

"What do you mean? What's happened?"

"He was a marten in a hen coop –" Mary's laugh is dry, incredulous, he holds up his palm again. "No, Mary, hear me; he was spending money like water – my money, Nanteos money, he –"

"One must invest in order to profit, William. Thomas knew that. You are new to this; a clergyman not a businessman, how could you know? You –"

"Don't speak to me like a fool!" He jumps up. "You know I was much in Cardiganshire in my brother's time – at the mines with him, in meetings of the other landowners. How dare you, I –"

"Calm yourself, William." She too is on her feet. Standing in front of him she holds up her hands in surrender. "I don't seek to insult you. I know you to be a man of superior gifts; it's just that you have had much to take on and less than a year before losing your son and now your wife –"

"Let us not speak of Elizabeth!" It is a howl. Mary steps back as he flings himself into his chair, wrapping his arms about him and bending forward as though wounded in the belly.

Quietly she moves to refill his glass. "Eat something, William. Eat."

His face as he looks up at her is ravaged. "I'm sorry." Though hardly audible, it has cost him much to say it. She squeezes his hand and returns to her seat. He gestures to the desk behind him. "There, Mary – letters for him – Edward – you may do what you please with them." She nods. "The latter ones were marked 'urgent'. I've opened them. They are addressed to me anyway, well to him 'care of' myself." His laugh is bitter.

"What –"

"Read them yourself," he snaps. "He is asked for everywhere... A Sheffield owner even asks for him to join a venture he has in Pennsylvania!"

"Ah, he made an excellent impression on them when he was there studying the trade last year. It's truly inspiring what they do with the lead mines in... the 'Peak' area, I think they call it. Edward found that –"

"I care not, Mary. Do what you will about him; I care not!"

*

William returns to London and Mary wastes no time interrogating the servants about Elizabeth's death. She gathers them, in groups, then one at a time, asking the same question several times, often using slightly different words. Her detailed notes are dated, the time recorded and she is careful to be clear between any quote and her own summary. Next to the doctor, Martha is the most important witness.

"Firstly, Martha, where is Edward?"

Martha purses her lips and Elin shakes her head, her eyes wild.

Jenkins' wife, perhaps unused to being in the library, looks steadily out of the window.

William's manservant, John, volunteers. "Surely he has run away, and good riddance."

"How so?"

"Always causing trouble; who knows where his loyalties lie."

"What do you mean by that, pray?" He turns away quickly, but not fast enough to hide the smirk. "No, that will not do for an answer, I'm afraid. John is it? Turn around and face me if you please. Now." Slowly he turns around, eyes studying his boots. "Well?" He shakes his head. "No, I will not have it. An assertion has been made, or at least implied. Now must follow a proper explanation." He mumbles something. "I cannot hear you, man."

At last he raises his head. "I'm sure my Master would be happy to give you an explanation; please seek it from him yourself."

She takes a sharp breath in. He is looking her right in the eye now. It is all she can do not to lose her temper at his insolence. Has the man not heard Edward was the ward of her late husband and honoured by them at Nanteos? "Indeed I will do so." A small smile touches the corner of his mouth. "Do you not have your master's leather to clean?" He looks surprised for a moment. "Well?"

"Yes, but I…"

"Then I will not keep you. I have no need to hear any more from you. Continue with your work."

As the door shuts behind him she turns back to the women

with a smile. "What a delightful character! Interesting that the Revd William did not take his man with him on this trip to London, isn't it? Ah, where were we... This is very confusing, is it not – all these Marys, Maris and Marthas in one household!"

"It is Wales, Mistress; everyone has but one of a dozen surnames, and often uses the same Christian name too!"

"I remember it well!"

"I hear the nursemaid, Mari, is no longer at Nanteos. What of her?" Martha and Elin exchange looks. "Has she run off with some man?" Martha shrugs, a gesture which says 'as like as not'. Mary waits a moment, then continues. "You seem to disapprove of her."

"Makes more of things than need making. Can't keep her counsel."

Jenkins' wife looks quickly at Mary, as though expecting another question; perhaps wanting to hear the answer.

"What counsel? What secret?" But Martha shakes her head.

Mary waits for a few moments. Nothing more is forthcoming. "No matter for now. Right – to the cup then. As I understand, it was specifically effective in ceasing hemorrhage in women. Why was Mistress Elizabeth not offered water from the holy cup in her last hours?" They look at one another, uncomprehending. "Well?"

"We cannot understand you, Mistress. I don't understand the words." Mary explains. "We didn't know its true purpose. Mistress Elizabeth did make use of the cup, though..." Again, Mary catches a look pass between the three women.

"Yes," Martha continues, "she was very fond of the cup,

though she never drank from it – not that I know of. Oh that she had."

"Indeed."

"Mari was there through her illness after Master Thomas, and Elin was there too. They mostly took care of her when she was, when she was… unwell after the boy's accident. And Cai –" Martha comes to an abrupt stop. Mary studies the women. Jenkins' wife seems composed enough, or rather, being a heavy, dour figure, no different from usual. Martha though, does not seem herself. There is something lopsided about her stance and she shifts her weight from foot to foot.

"Do you need to leave the room for a moment?" Mary asks. Martha shakes her head. "Please sit down and be comfortable. What I have to ask you now will be painful." She has already had several chairs prepared and the women sit, brushing down their skirts at the back before they do so. "Now, if you please and beginning with you, Martha, give me an account of the last day of her life."

*

That night she invites Elin back as her maid. The pink room – her room, Elizabeth's room, is both the same and changed. The view and main configuration of the furniture, dictated by the fixtures of the room, has remained the same, though it smells of another woman, of some strange, heady scent she cannot associate with a clergyman's wife. Elizabeth was braver with her mirrors too – well, she was younger and married for her beauty not her fortune.

Elin brushes Mary's hair as she used to do, the brush in her right hand, her left hand stroking the brushed hair flat, 'oiling it' she used to call it. The ritual, which had been so familiar until less than three years ago, seems awkward now.

Mary makes conversation, complimenting Elizabeth's choice of soft furnishings until, suddenly, Elin cries, "She had the mark upon her!"

"I beg your pardon?" Mary spins round. Elin's hand remains hovering over her head; she is crying. "What do you mean?" No answer. She repeats the question.

Elin presses her finger into the outside of her thigh. "Here; the mark."

"What 'mark'?"

"Round, dark – a witching mark for sure." The girl is looking earnestly into her face. Mary is careful not to show any reaction, though she gets up smartly from the dressing table and moves to sit by the fire. Elin follows her, standing restless at her side, her voice urgent, face animated. "And then all the other things: the mines, it all went wrong –"

"That situation at the mines was happening before. Surely you must remember me mentioning my concerns when I was mistress here –"

"But it got so much worse, gunfire in the hills; men hurt – Cai hurt and then a flood and then, and then, well Thomas."

"Enough, Elin."

But there is no stopping her. "... and then everything so strange, so dark and the mistress wild..."

"Yes, with grief, to be sure!"

"... and not eating, and Cai with her... well, Cai..."

"Enough."

Mary gets to her feet but although Elin takes a step backwards, she keeps talking, her words coming even faster. "And the Revd William away in London for the court case;

and then a baby." Her voice trails off and she stands, suddenly spent.

Mary studies her for a moment. "You are tired. Please go and rest."

"But I –"

"Go and rest, Elin. In your room, if you please." She turns away and goes to the window, waiting to hear the door close. After a moment Elin leaves. Mary takes a deep breath and exhales. "Well!" She shivers, reaching for her shawl and wrapping it several times around her, pulling it up at the neck. 'A witch's mark – silly girl! And Edward again... what on earth has he done?' She pours herself some of her ginger cordial, adds a couple of logs to the fire herself and takes refuge in her favourite window seat. Poor Elizabeth, a terrible business. Mary drinks deep. "Yes," she remembers, speaking out loud. "Untimely ripped. From the womb untimely ripped."

Chapter Thirty-Eight

As Mary watches Martha change the baby she is unable to tear her eyes from the fingers, light as seaweed fronds, or the soft toes, opening and flexing. The ears are coiled and dainty like new gloves, unworn in their box.

"You can touch her, Mistress." Mary takes a step back. "Go on, she'll like it, I'd imagine."

As Martha opens the napkin, Mary gingerly strokes the purple hands. As her finger slips inside the palm the child closes her fist around it. "Oh. Oh!"

Martha looks up and smiles. "Strong, isn't she? Lanoline if you please." She gestures at the small pot warming by the fire.

"Ah, that was the smell. I'd thought it was the baby!" Mary gladly fetches it for her.

"'Tis the smell of a baby to me." Martha dips two fingers deep into the pot.

"But why put that foul-smelling stuff on?"

Martha looks at her for a moment. "Come and see."

Mary moves to look down at the child whose one leg is kicking rhythmically, like someone dancing a gavotte. "Just look at her, Martha! I think she's enjoying herself without her clothes on!"

"Of course she is. Wouldn't you?"

"Yes indeed!" They laugh.

Her sex is neat, closed like the double doors of a salon, but red, a small patch rubbed raw. "Dear, how sore! It must hurt her, surely!"

Martha is already back at work, giving a running commentary. "Wipe down on a girl child, so the dirt doesn't go up into her." Suddenly she frowns and, grabbing the baby under her armpits, holds her upright across the soiled cloth. Yellowish liquid squirts from the little buttocks.

"Oh my word!" Martha looks at her and laughs heartily. "I'm sorry, but I never did see such a thing in my life before – not being a mother myself, I suppose."

"With respect, Mistress, even had you been one, a woman in your position would hardly have been changing her child's napkins." She lies the baby flat on her back on the chest of drawers, wiping the area with warm water from the bowl. "It's only these strange times that would bring a woman like yourself into a nursery at all."

"Yes, indeed you're right. Poor child... she's frowning, Martha, look at her brow."

Martha brushes the baby's cheek lightly and she turns her head. "Ready to feed?" As if on cue the child begins to cry. "Yes, I thought so, Missy."

"How do you know what she needs? Are there different cries for different things?"

"I suppose so. With your first you have to guess a bit, but they're all the same really."

Martha picks up the child and drapes her over her shoulder. "Oh, look at her hair, Martha, hanging down over her collar like a clergyman's!"

Martha ruffles it with her fingers. "Feel it, if you wish; like the finest thread. Wish mine was half like it."

Gently she does so, but it is indeed so fine that she can hardly feel it. The child's cries are louder and Mary goes to look at the creased face, appearing over Martha's shoulder. The mouth is deep red and open, raw and jelly, like the inside of a sea anemone. "Oh hist, you, little mite!" Martha puts her finger joint to the child's mouth and she sucks down hard on it, quietening straight away. "That settles it, it's food you're after. I'll take her down to the nurse now, Mistress. The wet nurse will be in the kitchen sure as eggs, warming her dugs and knees by the fire if I'm not mistaken. Don't know why I'm doing the little one's soiled cloths and carrying her about, except that, well, I think of Mistress Elizabeth…"

Mary nods, following them from the room and down through the house. Though the child is no longer sucking on her own knuckles (a practice she's seen encouraged by Martha), she's stopped crying and watches everything intently, staring over the cook's shoulder.

Later, back in her old bedroom, Mary sits at her dressing table, takes off her wig and examines herself in the mirror. She is like a buzzard chick all ready for the drowning bucket – a fierce, stark head with fluffy hair standing on end. Plenty of grey there now, no longer matching the hair between her legs, though she has found a few there too, longer, stronger than the others. But then they'd never matched – always darker on her head than between her legs, 'and not just a colour difference, Mary; texture – and length too. Why, no woman known has been able to grow such a fine, long plait between her legs as she finds her head!' Dear Thomas – he had always been brimful of mad notions and obscure quotes and facts. What a strange education he must have had in his provincial school! He could still elicit a smile from her even now, though he'd been dead almost three years.

Would a child still be possible, should she ever marry again? Her sex feels sticky rather than slippery now. How long had it been? Looser too, a loose flap like the neck of the American bird eaten by the first settlers. She smiles grimly. She could still do her party trick however, tickling first with her fingers then rubbing with the fingers straight and clenched together. But, though the mechanism still works, delivers the same rush (those deep, wide circles of pleasure like a rock thrown into a pool), it is hard for her to keep any images of desire in her mind. Instead, her thoughts run, like a dog in a wood, through everyday things. Even as the frantic jerking bursts warm, spreading out, down her thighs and into her toes, she is actually thinking of ordering new stays. As the delicious fist clenches in her belly she calls out, then laughs – what will they think of her?

*

She has another restless night, her sleep broken again and again. A noise on the glass of the window… She has left the curtains open, as is her habit and it's quite light in her room – a moon, though not full, surely? The noise like gravel thrown again. Raindrops dashed against the window to be sure. She gets out of bed and looks out. The drive stretches clean and scoured to the far lake, though she cannot see the water itself. There is a bright moon, but it shines out of a clear sky – no sign of a cloud that would have brought rain. For a moment, as she looks down the empty drive, she imagines a figure,

Edward perhaps, looking up, raising a hand in farewell as he goes to mount a horse. Thomas, perchance, all in haste, big generous gestures, shouting instructions then waving his hat at her, even blowing a kiss in the early days of their marriage, and galloping away – too fast, churning up the gravel and the mud beneath it. The memory brings a kick of physical pain and she pushes it firmly to one side, passes water, takes a drink and returns to bed.

It takes a while for her to fall asleep again but she is once more awakened by the same sound – thrown, fine gravel or rain scattered against the glass. This time she does not get up straight away. The light has hardly changed from earlier, which must mean that her sleep was not a long one. The bedroom is disturbing – at once familiar to her as her room over those long years; its proportions agreed by her, the paper and carpeting chosen by herself. Poor Elizabeth had less than two years to put her mark on Nanteos – yet she had achieved a remarkable amount, mostly in the stables apparently, but not here, in her room. It is the scent, perhaps – Elizabeth's scent. Not a perfume, but her scent, that makes the space so unnerving and it is strong tonight. Where is it coming from? Mary gets out of bed and crosses to the wardrobe, opens it. Martha has told her all Elizabeth's clothes have been removed to a room on the top floor – that's something she must do soon: sort amongst them for things that should be kept safe for Elizabeth's daughters; parcel up and distribute those items that are not to be retained. No, there are none of Elizabeth's clothes left in the wardrobe, it's empty. So, the scent is not clinging to her clothes then, nor to the mattress which has had to be burned, Martha had told her. She turns to go back to bed, catching herself for a moment in the glass. Elizabeth had bought a long mirror, a beautiful object. This mirror and the curious japanned chest in the gallery are, she suspects, the best single items that have been added to the house in her absence. She stands in front of the glass. So typical of Elizabeth to have such a fine example! Everything she appeared in, clothing or jewellery, though not always rich or terribly expensive, was shown at its best. Elizabeth had had a natural grace, the natural grace of a sportswoman, a rider. What a strange creature she had been. The keys of her instrument were well worn, though the pedals had seemed hardly used. Apparently, according to Elin, she had used to play in her bare feet! Elizabeth's mirror surpasses even the one her own mother had had in London. In the moonlight, even she looks beautiful – her frame upright, even proud. Yet, as she looks at herself, it seems she sees a shadow behind her, just above her shoulder. The shadow becomes a face, a woman's face – Elizabeth! The pale features are angry. "It's too late; it's too late – I'm here now!" She hears her own voice, urgent, irregular, as her shawl wraps tighter and tighter around her neck. She struggles for breath, trying to jab her fingers up between the skin of her neck and the material, twisted and taut as a tourniquet. "I'm sorry, I must tell your story; I must find out what happened to you!" The face is angry, so angry, it is trying to silence her, strangling the story out of her! She struggles away and back to her bed, pulling the covers over her head. But it is impossible to sleep again; or has she been asleep all along, sleep-walking like a deranged soul? Groggy and damp with sweat, she plucks up the courage to sit up and disentangle herself from the bedclothes. There are strange sounds coming from the floor above – stamping, raised voices. Relieved to be out of her bed, she puts on her robe and slippers. Are those footsteps on the landing? She opens her door as quietly as she can and stands for a moment, just behind it. Nothing. Then, the sound from upstairs again. Quiet. She slips from her room. Ah, it is indeed a beautiful space, the windows at either end, the elegant, generous stairs, the plasterwork and arch, the step to the lovely music room. Of everything at Nanteos, it is perhaps this first-floor landing and the music room of which she's most proud. The sound of something dropped on the floor above and rolling; a cry. She crosses to the upper stairs, fastening her robe. "Help me!" She freezes: a voice behind her. The sobbing from the floor above begins again. She looks round: no one there. The landing isn't completely dark and she has no candle. Again, a voice, a breath, "Help me!" but, though she's looking along the length of the corridor, there is no one; none of the doors are open. The voice… perhaps it came from up above, night distorting distance and direction? Pulling her gown around her she turns away, going up the narrow stairs to the second floor. Female voices arguing.

The door to little William's room is open, though he sleeps on. What a blessing to be able to do so! She closes it, nevertheless. Whatever is happening further along the corridor sounds unpleasant, a situation surely not to be improved by a tired, crying three year old. She waits for a moment outside the door of Catherine's new room, then goes in without knocking.

"You had no right, no right!" Catherine's sobs are hysterical. The girl's face is swollen as though she has been stung and she flings her arms around, throwing her clothes, anything she can find, onto the floor. Elin is there, raises her hands in a gesture of defeat.

"Catherine!" Mary's voice is sharp. The girl looks at her wildly but still wails and stamps. "Stop it!" She turns to Elin. "What on earth's the matter here?"

"She runs wild!"

"I can see that. I'm asking you why? What's the cause of it? Catherine?"

"Mama's primrose," she sobs afresh. "I woke up and saw it was gone!"

Mary looks at Elin. "A dry, withered thing – I didn't even know it was a flower!"

"Mama's primrose! She gave it... to... me." The child's sobs are lower now in pitch but somehow more pitiful – the anger that had masked the pain subsiding.

Mary looks again at Elin, raising her brow by way of a question. "I didn't know. I'd come in here this afternoon to make it nice for her, tidy up a little. There were just dead stalks in the little vase – I had fresh to put in it for her."

"You threw it in the fire; in the fire, Mama's primrose." The sobs increase, seeming to shake her whole torso.

"Sit down Catherine. Sit." Mary pulls a chair away from a small table and leans on the back of it. Catherine comes towards it and slumps there, head down, hands plucking at her nightdress. "Thank you, Elin. You meant no harm. Please return to your bed." Though she shoots a resentful glance in Catherine's direction, Elin leaves quietly, shutting the door behind her.

Mary sits on the end of the girl's bed, their knees almost touching. "We will talk tomorrow about how a mistress should speak with her servants, Catherine. For now though, that is not important. Are you able to explain to me why you're so upset? Why a dead little flower meant so much to you?"

Through sobs and shudders, Catherine explains, "... and Mari knew that, and she was going to show me how to press it, but now she's gone..." Mary puts her arms around her niece and the girl reciprocates. The woman finds herself rocking them gently, the child's warm body relaxing between the shudders that still stagger through her. A flow of words comes from her, as if unconsciously, words which become a hum then nursery rhymes, partially remembered from long, long ago. At last Catherine's body is still.

"Shall we get you back into bed?"

The girl nods, uses the pot then climbs between the covers Mary holds open for her. Somewhere she knows how to do this; somehow she's remembered what to do. She puts out the candles and moves the chair to sit by the pillow, her palm resting for a while on the girl's hair. There is something strange happening in this near-dark room as her body relaxes into the chair, her own breathing slowing and falling almost into step with the sleeping girl's – her body feels warm and there is a lightness to it; when her breath comes in she feels it filling her chest and rising into that fresh empty space, her mind. Could it be that she is content? The bad dream of earlier comes again to her but it is changed. "Elizabeth, oh dear, dead young woman," she whispers to herself as Catherine's breath deepens further into sleep.

*

320

At breakfast, Martha herself is serving; there is no sign of Elin. "You don't look too good this morning, Mistress, if I may be so bold as to say."

"No, quite so."

Martha waits for an explanation. None is forthcoming. "No surprise to me; not a bit. You've lost husband, home, nephew – by marriage, granted, but still – all in less than three years." She waits again, but Mary is not to be drawn on the subject.

She says only, "Elizabeth suffered much in those last hours, as I understand."

Martha looks hard at her but Mary holds her gaze. "Have you ever been in a birthing chamber, Mistress?"

Mary shakes her head, looks down. Martha leans on the back of the chair and sighs. "Please, do sit down, Martha. There's no ceremony here – what would be the use."

The cook sits, but there is a temporary quality about it, as though the chair is not quite solid, would shift from under her in a moment. Mary smiles. "You've told me of the birth itself – remember? Your testimony in the library. Truly a harrowing account."

But Martha has more to say. "After the doctor cut her, Cai – Edward, he set upon him, taking him behind the head and pushing him over the body of my mistress, shouting all the while for him to save her, 'sew her up'. After a few moments, the doctor stopped fighting him, letting his arms go loose. I was holding the little waif who kept wailing – a thin cry, not like a baby. The more the doctor went weak, the more mad Cai became, shaking him like a dog with a young rabbit in its jaws."

Noticing the young kitchen maid lurking in the doorway, Mary suggests they go into the parlour. She settles Martha in a deep chair by the window and puts herself slightly to the side, so that anything said can be voiced without eye contact. She does not take notes. At first Martha repeats things she's said before but after a couple of minutes the conversation becomes almost a monologue. Trying to tempt Elizabeth with food. Mari's guilt. Possibly that the girl had planned to go away even before her mistress' death. Apparently, since Thomas' drowning, she had been spending more and more time with the preachers' followers, even taking Elizabeth's daughter, Catherine, with her. She talks of William bribing Sir Herbert Lloyd to take Morris to gaol at pistol point and Cai's disappearance.

"I had assumed, naturally, that Edward's... Cai's disappearance was guilt, for the death of poor young Thomas."

"And so it was!" Martha snaps.

"Yet you use the term 'cast out'? Why is he cast out? I do know however that... my husband, should he have realised his end to be so close, would have made provision for him. Happily, I too have funds. What happened here, Martha? Where, pray, is Edward?" But again, the cook shakes her head. This time her lips are set. "I see I will get nothing more out of you, Martha."

Mary gets up and goes to the writing desk, picks up the letters intended for Cai, slapping them repeatedly on the edge of the desk. "What a fool my brother-in-law is – and I do not care who hears it. This man, Thomas' son..." She holds up the letters. "... Thomas' son, for that is who he is, let us speak of things as they are now, for pity's sake. Yes he, Edward, like Cornelius Le Brun in the generations before him, will pull the Powell mines up by the hair roots and pummel profit from them if he is only given the chance! If he is given investment, he will harness water to drive the ore-crushing hammers; he will put down rails so that the ore can be moved not only inside the mine but down the slope to the barges at Derwenlas. If only William would listen! That young man told me all this, even before I went away, yet what has been done? Tell me?" She looks fiercely at Martha. "None of it! Two dead bodies..." Martha's sharp intake of breath is audible, "... a drowned boy; his dead mother – let it be spoken of in the very house in which she died."

"Please keep your voice down, Mistress Mary." Martha's finger points towards the ceiling. "The children," she mouths.

Mary looks at her quickly. "I am corrected..." She takes a breath, adjusts her sleeves. "My father-in-law was a shrewd man of business and a politician if ever there was one – I will never forget the way he wooed my mother for her hand! He made these Powells and now stubbornness will pull them down! All is debt; so much money has gone to prove the land is ours, the lead is ours and to pay for election campaigns we fail to win. There has been no mention of any significant finds of silver for ten years or more – that is Tantalus' apple, of course. Heaven help me but I tried to make my money work for Nanteos – I had better have given it to Mr Hogarth for the Foundling Hospital or to the Magdalen House!" She puts her head in her hands.

"Mistress?"

"Oh, I beg your pardon." The two women look at one another for a moment. Mary puts out her hand. "I've missed you, Martha," she says simply. "Masters and servants are not the same in the capital." Martha gets up and goes towards her and Mary takes her hand. "Yes – just as I would have imagined! Though somewhat more abrasive, you have the grasp of a High Court judge."

Martha laughs, moves back and looks steadily at Mary. "I think I know where C… Edward might be."

Chapter Thirty-Nine

A T GRUFFYDD'S COTTAGE, high in the hills, Cai sorts through a pile of rocks. Worn gloves provide some protection for his hands and he studies each stone then weighs it in his palm. There is a fierce chill in the air this high, though early bees are busy on the gorse and the April sun is bright in a clear sky. His back is to the track and he doesn't see the horse and rider, nor hear them above the fierce voice of the stream. When he straightens up and turns around they are almost at the bend in the road. Surely another desperate smallholder come to have a curse lifted? His smile is grim. The figure is waving at him, and instead of going back to work he waits for him. The rider is a youth of fourteen, perhaps, no one he's seen before.

"Cai Gruffydd? Cai Gruffydd, Sir?"

"What do you want, lad. Who are you?"

"A message, Sir."

Cai takes the mule's head collar. "Get down, will you." The boy looks over his shoulder towards the cottage and shakes his head. "Get down, I say." The boy shakes his head. His eyes roll again towards the dwelling. "You're afeared?"

The boy nods his head. *"Y Cwnjwr!"*

Cai laughs. "Don't be afraid; I'll protect you from my grandfather! Now get down. Who are you?"

The boy slides to the ground. "Iestyn, Sir. Are you Cai Gruffydd?"

Cai nods. "But I don't know you."

"I've a letter – for Cai Gruffydd." There is a noise from the cottage and the boy looks behind him, pressing himself against the mule's flank.

"Where do you live?"

"Banc y Llan, Sir."

"A hatter's boy?" Iestyn nods, turning again to look over his shoulder. "The *Cwnjwr* won't hurt you... Who sent you?"

"My mother – well, the woman from Nanteos; the fierce one with big arms."

Cai grins. "Martha. Well, what do you want?" The boy produces a letter, holding it in his palm as though it was a fine invitation on a gilded tray. Mary's hand. Cai takes it from him and immediately the boy grasps a bunch of the animal's mane ready to pull himself up. "Whoa there!" Cai takes the bridle again. "Your friend here needs a rest and something to eat; I'll warrant you do too. Come, we'll settle him and then go inside." The boy shakes his head again, the whites of his eyes showing as he spins around to face the door. "Enough of this nonsense, now." He takes the animal around the back of the cottage so that the boy can't take fright and ride off. It's a sturdy animal, used to taking the heavy packs of wool and finished hats to the border, no doubt. Lucky not to be working the ore trail. He sees to the animal then fetches a chunk of rough bread and whey milk for the boy. "Sit down to eat, lad. I said sit, will you."

Iestyn perches on a boulder and, although he keeps looking behind him at the cottage door, manages to eat the food. Gruffydd is nowhere to be seen. Cai goes inside, standing by the small window to read the letter. Suddenly the boy is on his feet and disappears round to the back of the cottage, coming back with the mule, a strand of hay sticking out of its mouth.

"Hey!" A couple of long strides takes Cai to him. "Was the bread that bad?" The boy's face is a picture of panic; he shakes his head. "Well then, why're you in such a hurry to leave?"

"Mr Gruffydd, Cai, Sir, I... the bread was good –"

"No matter." Cai laughs. "You don't expect an answer to this?"

"My mother, she said only to come straight home. To tell no one where I was going, where I'd been."

"And the pay was good?" The boy nods. Cai gives him another coin. "Don't ride downhill too fast." He tosses the boy up onto the mule and watches him ride away, then sits on the quartz boulder by the front door, his back against the warm stone. Mary. Though the letter has been forwarded on from the Sheffield manufacturer, the plan has her signature all over it. He pulls it out and reads again. After a few moments he gets to his feet and takes the envelope inside, then gets back to work building an adit with the rocks and diverting the stream away from the house.

A low chuckle behind him – Gruffydd. "The sun's gone, but here you are still. Come in now – these stones, this stream will still be here for you tomorrow." Arms crossed he surveys the scene. "A good job. Yes, I should have thought to do this years ago, before I got too old. You're an engineer still!"

Cai's smile is brief. "I'll come in soon. Go in."

But Gruffydd doesn't move. "What's in the envelope?" Cai straightens up in surprise. "Mary Powell?"

"How do you know? How do you know her hand?"

The old man laughs. "Not her writing; the gentry smell of her on the paper. Come inside."

Cai follows him, rolling down his sleeves. Gruffydd, scooping up the envelope, sits in his chair by the fire. Two metal jugs steam. Cai washes himself then joins him.

"More than a letter, I think?"

Cai nods. "She sends tickets."

"America?" Cai puts his mug down and reaches for the letter. He reads it out. For a while both men are quiet. "Two, you say?" Cai looks at him. Gruffydd repeats himself. Then, "Tickets for the passage. Two of them. Who is the other for? Perhaps she means you to take your grandfather!" His laugh is a file on stone. "When does it sail?"

"In six weeks."

Gruffydd whistles through his teeth. "Plenty of time to find her again and persuade her to come with you. Plenty of time to find what you need."

"I have not decided to go." Gruffydd snorts; takes a gulp from the tankard. "Why is that so difficult to understand?"

"You're not afeared of the sea are you? You did well on that ship, that lead ship, following the ore up to Liverpool those years ago as I remember." He chuckles. "Or maybe you're frightened of the American girls. I hear some of them can crush a bear to death between their thighs!" He laughs heartily, ending with a choking cough relieved by a swig of ale.

"It's not finished here."

"Not finished! You were finished years ago. You should never have come back after Thomas Powell sent you to school, but nothing should have kept you here after he died. Fool." Gruffydd tilts back his head and drains the flask. "Fool! Look at you now: eyes sunk into your head and heaving stones out on the hill like a pauper. I'll never forget how you looked the night you left Nanteos, riding wild out of the fog; like you were a step away from flinging yourself down an old mine shaft. Good job I was out there on the mule and stopped you. He's dead." He spits into the fire, wiping his mouth on his sleeve. "And she's dead too."

Cai looks at him for a moment, then gets to his feet. Putting the letter in his pocket and taking a heavy coat, he leaves.

Chapter Forty

MARTHA KNOCKS ON her door as she is getting ready for bed. "May I speak to you a moment, Mistress?" Mary rings for another glass, pours them both some warmed wine and moves her shawl from one of the armchairs by the fire. "I'm not happy with Catherine – she grows odd."

"Go on, please."

"Elin says she has been finding her brush and mirror all around the house. When she questioned her about it she said her Mama's doing it. 'Mama does it.' Elin said to her, 'That's a wicked thing to say!' But the child wouldn't give up her story."

"Heavens!"

"Elin told her, 'That's a wicked thing to say about your dead Mama,' but the young mistress would have none of it."

"She's a very clever young girl. The situation here has not been a healthy one for many months, so it seems. I wonder would the Revd William allow her to come with me London for a while?"

"She's had no schooling."

"No, I know. That will simply not do these days. There's no excuse." Mary watches Martha finish her glass, offers her another. "Little William? I don't see much of him – he's always in the nursery with the baby and the wet nurse. How does he fare, do you think?"

"He never was much of a talker, even when his mother was alive, but he was a happy little boy. He seems happy enough now – eats plenty, always busy as far as I can see, but he talks less rather than more, I'd say."

"I'll spend some time with him tomorrow. Thank you, Martha. How nice to have the company of another woman, however trying the circumstances. Would you care for more wine?"

*

The following evening Mary is at last free to visit William in the nursery. As she comes down the corridor she stops abruptly. William is talking to someone, his voice light. He giggles, there's a pause. She pads nearer. Again, he's talking and laughing. She smiles to herself – so long since she's heard the little boy chattering like this. She can't make out what he's saying; probably talking to one of his toys. Apparently, he puts his toys into the bed with him, now Catherine has gone to her own room. She reaches the doorway and peeps inside. He's under the covers, with his face turned away from her. The drapes are still open though it's dark and cold outside. He's still chattering, his voice animated and happy and she can hear he's talking about his pet finch. She tiptoes into the room and he sits up in bed – but not to look at her. He's still looking towards the window but has gone quiet. One of his feet is already out from under the covers, as if he's going to cross to the window, when she calls him. He looks behind him, shrinking back under the blanket as he does so.

"Sorry, William – I didn't mean to startle you." Mary sits on the side of his bed, draws the covers up around him, tucks him in. "You're a happy boy tonight. Who were you talking to?" She cannot see any of his toys in the bed. "It's lovely to hear your laugh. Were you playing with your toy rabbit?" He worms his way further into the bed and turns again to face the window. Putting her hand on his shoulder, she turns him gently to face her. "I heard you laughing just now, William. Why were you laughing?"

He smiles. "I like it, the singing."

"What singing?" He shakes his head quickly, puts his thumb back in, holding the blanket up to his face, almost covering his mouth. "Who is it that sings to you, William?"

The boy shuts his eyes tight and turns away again. When she tries once more to turn him to face her he twists his shoulder from her. For a while she continues to sit by him. Soon the sound of him sucking his thumb is replaced by the long breaths of sleep.

Apart from his cot, the main nursery is almost empty now. Thomas' proper bed has been moved to one of the empty servants' rooms and Catherine now has her own room of course. Although it's clean and smells fresh, the nursery is no longer a cosy place. William and Catherine come downstairs now, eating all their meals in the kitchen when their father's away. The baby's cot is still here, though unmade. She crosses to the window, picking up the rabbit peeping out from under the bed. There is nothing to see as she looks through the glass at the Cardiganshire night. She eases the curtains closed and leans towards the child. His lips are open, his thumb resting on the pillow, ready for use. She lifts a corner of the covers, careful not to let in any cold air, and slips in the rabbit. It will be the first thing he sees when he wakes.

Chapter Forty-One

CARI IS THERE first – at the fallen tree on the edge of the last piece of steady ground before the great bog, Cors Caron. She places herself behind a clutch of stunted willows – perfect to see, but not to be seen. Low hills surround it and it lies in a basin, malodorous, mysterious, alive with the haunting sounds of water birds.

There is a rider on the ridge. It is he, she is certain of it, though how she knows would be impossible to explain; only that a particular animal and rider have a gait as unique as any walking man. Her heart betrays her in the same old way, lurching in her chest like a horse stumbling on rabbit ruined pasture. She whispers his name; pulls at her hair to stuff it under her cap, tidies her clothes, pinches her cheeks. She loses sight of them for a while – they must be on the low road that circles the bog. Then he is there by the far track.

He dismounts, leaving his horse at a small stand of birch on high ground near the wall. She thinks she recognises the animal – Nanteos stables, surely? His coat flaps and billows around him as he comes towards her, then he stops, searching for her. He pushes back his hair and she laughs – it has grown long; he is almost an Egyptian! She steps out from behind the trees.

He crosses the rough field with long strides, as always in haste, willing the distance to disappear – but with each of his steps her dread is stronger and she fights to keep her face calm.

"This is certainly a good place to choose to meet a fugitive." He grins. For a moment it is almost impossible not to rush into his arms. His voice; that face – everything is dear to her, yet there is something different too. His eyes are shining with seeing her, yet he holds her gaze, waiting for her to make the first move. Some woman has taught him well. He's broader in the chest since their last meeting, though his face is leaner.

"James Lloyd, Ffosybleiddiaid 'wishes to refresh his stables' – we are camped nearby," she says lightly.

"Ah – I've always wanted to visit. But has not Lloyd gone to Mabws? He married an heiress, did he not?"

She looks at him sharply – that same old theme! "I think he did. He still runs the property, though. We've done well out of it."

"And what of the famous ditch where they killed the last wolves in Wales?"

"Just a good tale to tell by the fire on a winter's night, no doubt. There's no sign of such a thing in reality. The river marks the boundary between them and their neighbour."

"A pity," he says.

"You did well to find me, Cai Gruffydd."

"As it turned out I had only to ask Bryn. He was more than happy to take a message."

"'Cai asks after you... he has a letter for you. Here it is. Is there an answer?'"

He laughs. "You are still a good mimic, Cari. Poor Bryn, I think he still has a fancy for you." He bends towards her, trying to see past her hat.

She steps back. "You have grown wild in your appearance!" She cannot keep the fun from her voice. "Your hair is so thick and you even have a beard coming!"

He laughs, his hand going to his face. "Gruffydd's piece of broken glass is too small for me to fit my face in. As to hot water, he will never permit the *cawl* to be moved from its hook over the fire. As you see, I am down in the world." He mimes shaving and she laughs quickly, despite herself.

She allows herself to glance at his face – his eyes! It is too dangerous to look right at him, as though a spider has woven a deep web in the space between them and every look is a vibration. "You look well," she says at last.

"And you... look even more beautiful than before."

Her smile is ironic. "I look better now than I did, you mean? Good; maybe that is why you turned away from me before."

"That's not what I meant, Cari. Come, let's not quarrel." He looks behind him and gestures to a pile of logs. "Come, let's sit – these don't look too wet. Have you made your decision? Will you come? I must leave soon to prepare, before I'm found. I am to be hunted down it seems."

She sits next to him but is careful to be an arm's length away. "For what? Why?"

"Powell has me branded as a thief." Her face asks the question. "Which, no, I am not. But I have transgressed." He looks at her and this time she returns his gaze. "I have spent money on the mines against his express orders. The stamping machine ordered by Thomas Powell before his death –"

"I care not for your wheels and hammers. I care nothing for the mines – the miners are still poor and it doesn't seem even to make the rich happy. Look at you! All you talk of is loans, debts, 'improving'. Ha! Tal is better off out of it."

Her voice is both bitter and somehow triumphant. Her expression challenges him to ask more. What is she hiding?

"Tal's missing. Do you know something?" She laughs. "Cari?"

"It's a wise Egyptian who disappears when a man falls dead."

"Granted, but had he a hand in it? He vanished fast on the heels of the accident. The men were all questioned but few actually saw old Hughes fall; those who did said he wasn't pushed but lost his footing. He wasn't well liked."

She shrugs, looks up at him again. "As I say, wise is the fox which disappears when the hounds start to run."

"And the young mother – your friend?"

"Branwen."

"Yes, I –"

"Don't speak of her."

"I would that I'd –"

"Don't talk of it. She's beyond help now. No, Cai!" She moves further away from him. For a while each sits staring across the bog, the air between them troubled.

Suddenly he turns to face her. "What did I do to hurt you at the runaway wedding? But then at Tregaron that time –"

"Ah, the piss bucket!"

He smiles. "Yes, the piss – I thought you'd forgiven me. You asked me to stay?"

"And you turned me down!"

"I had the boy with me – where did you go?"

She looks at him sharply. "Why ask? You cared not. You could have found me if you'd tried hard enough. Myfanwy was right – I was lucky."

He shakes his head. "Your friend said you didn't want –"

"No! You cared nothing! Only for digging mine ponds and building wheels and hammers and that girl, the nursemaid with the chestnut hair –"

"Mari?"

"Yes, she. She slipped straight into step with my shadow. You missed not a beat when you found me gone."

"No, Cari. Mari was never you to me."

"Ha!" The sound is explosive, mocking. "You say that now, now she is no longer under your hand, now she's gone to follow the preachers, so it's said. And Elizabeth Powell –"

"What of her?" He is on his feet now.

She too stands, snapping her fingers in his face. "Like that she called for you." He goes to speak. "I know; they told me – two heads bent over a ledger, two horses galloping across the hill and you, playing at being her –"

"Enough! Elizabeth is dead!"

"Or *were* you her lover, stepping in whilst her husband was away?"

"Enough, Cari." Hands in his hair, he shakes his head, as though some terrible worm burrows there.

"There were even rumours you –"

"Stop!" He shakes her, his hands high on her arms. "She is dead – butchered on her own table for everyone to see; she is dead, Cari, she…" He lets her go and turns away, bent over, his hands at his face. Cari watches his back shudder. Surely, he is sobbing, though there is no sound. So he must have loved her! The thought is an iron file drawn down her spine. She sits back on the trunk, folding her arms in front of her, the palms cupped to her armpits, comforting. She looks out across the marsh. How many times has she fixed on this scene as she dreamed about the man standing before her now?

He takes a few steps away from the tree, looking out over the great marsh. She sees him pull the tickets out from his pocket. He seems to study them, as if surprised to see them in his hand. For a while he stands, only his long coat moving slightly in the wind, his body breaking the view in two: his chest, shoulders, neck and head, the sky; his lower body with the earth as background. He looks again at the tickets, moves them to his fingers, holds them up – he will let them go to the wind! A cry escapes her and he turns, seems again surprised that she is there. Does she mean so little to him now? He comes back towards her.

"I... I didn't want you to throw them away. I want you to have a chance, Cai." She is hasty to explain herself, her reaction. "Not for me, but you, you must go. Everyone says; everyone has always said it."

"Come with me." She looks up at him. The low sun is behind him and his face part-hidden, but the jaw, the hollow of his neck at the open shirt and his hand as he holds out the letter are dear to her and it is all she can do to stop herself from taking what he offers. She looks down, shaking her head, letting her face be hidden behind her hat. "Cari?"

"No!" But he holds out the ticket still. "No – I will not be second."

"There is nothing for you here! Come, Cari – even if it is only for us to part when we get to America. There is nothing to lose! Why are you so stubborn?"

"How do you even ask?"

"You do not have to love me... you need only to come. Cari?" She shakes her head. How can he be such a fool? Not trusting herself to look at him, she gathers her cloak around her and ties her hat firmly to her head. "Answer me!" He holds her wrist tight and she looks up into his face. "I... tell me... I cannot leave until I know. There is only anger in your voice; a bitter twist to your lips when you look at me. Are we nothing to one another now?"

She looks coldly down at her arm until he takes his hand away. Getting to her feet she says in a steady voice, "It's over between us, Cai. There's nothing left." But she cannot turn; cannot make her boots walk away. For a moment he does not move. Then, in what seems one fluid movement, he throws the ticket on the ground, grasps her cheeks in his palms and kisses her on the mouth. She holds herself like a stone as he steps back to search her face. Then she turns away.

He hesitates for a moment, then is gone – the long strides becoming a lope, his figure disappearing, beyond the track, out towards the wood. Only then does she let it come – the groan that becomes a sob and then a howl, lost to the wind.

Chapter Forty-Two

SURROUNDED BY PEOPLE, Mary's carriage has been forced to stop. She has been watching the column move across the hillside on the rough track at the opposite side of the narrow valley. They are mostly poor people – she can see that even from a distance, their clothes dull and shapeless. A few are mounted but the animals seem more mule than riding horse. She knocks for the driver. His face appears in the doorway, hat off, sparse hair combed by the winds.

"What are they doing up here, all these people?" she asks him.

"'Tis a hanging fair, to be sure. The judge has been busy by the look of it and there are several to be hung."

After a few minutes he manages to get the carriage going again, though it's often stalled.

As they approach the three-way crossroads at top of the hill it is impossible to proceed, the road is thick with bodies and there are even stalls selling hot food. A ragged girl comes up to the open window at Catherine's side. Her teeth are good, though her face is filthy. She holds up a tiny baby. Leaning into the coach, she thrusts him at Mary and, speaking in English with an unusual accent, "Missus, would you like him? He's called Ralph and he's only five days old. I don't want him, we have plenty of children."

"No, indeed, child. We go to London."

The girl dangles him in front of Catherine's face. "Do you want to hold him?" Catherine nods and takes the bundle in her arms. The baby is awake, but neither moves nor makes a sound. Catherine bends over him, lifting the cloth away from his face, then recoils.

"Oh, Aunt – he smells so!" she whispers.

The girl leans into the coach towards Catherine, asking again, "Do you want him?"

Catherine glances quickly towards Mary who shakes her head and says, "No. But thank you. And God bless you. We have a baby of our own."

The girl looks at her for a moment then, without fuss, takes back the child and puts it back in the box. She stands on tiptoe to see past their carriage to the traffic coming up behind them. Catherine too is on her feet, her head leaning out through the window. Suddenly she ducks back inside. "There are four fat puppies in that box with the baby!" Mary tuts. "What happens if they bite him? What's she doing with them?"

Mary hesitates for a moment. "We are going to London, Catherine, and I think you must be told of some things, for you surely cannot be kept from them. That young girl has most likely sought out this crowd in order to sell her wares."

"But..." Catherine's face has gone red. "Sell? But she wanted to give the child to us." Mary says nothing. "Was she selling her son?"

"There are many desperate women who cannot keep their babies. If only some brilliant physician could find a way to save them from birthing those they cannot or would not keep, what a blessing that would be!" She gathers her skirts and opens the door. Before she gets out, she turns around.

"Catherine, hear me now. I will have the blinds lowered on the carriage. On no pretext must you look out – not even peep around them. I will see if it's possible to pull back from here, or to proceed via another route, but it is likely that we will be stuck here for some time and there will be things you must not see. Do you understand me?" Catherine nods. A shiver runs between her shoulders. "You'll be tempted to look out. However, once the eye sees, the mind cannot forget. You will not look out; you will not defy me. I will have your answer?"

"I won't defy you, Aunt."

Mary looks at her. "I believe you, child." Then she leaves the carriage.

The tracks ahead, in every direction, are impassable. She calls the driver down and questions him again.

"The Great Sessions, Ma'am. There've been many felons waiting months – murder they've done, and other crimes, but now they've been heard, the cases, and he's had a score of them condemned. Women too, it's said."

"Move on, will you, please." The coach has come to a stop directly by one of the old gibbets where human remains hang by chains and iron bands, the body barely covered by a disintegrating, tarred shirt. "I thought a murderer was to be displayed as near as possible to the scene of his crime! Was this…?" she gestures behind her with her hand, intent on not looking back. "… was this a highwayman, perhaps?" The metal cage squeaks and groans in the wind, twisting slowly on its chain. Through the bars a skull stares out. Eyes long gone, the fine teeth leer.

"Could have been." The driver pauses for a moment. "No, I remember it. Blacksmith killed his wife and children and buried them down a mineshaft. The *Cnocwyr* –"

"What?"

"Fairy miners, Ma'am – the little people; they made a fuss with their hammers and the miners came and found the bodies. He had to make his own headdress, so to speak."

"Heavens!"

"Nasty business. Before my time on this route." He adjusts his hat and scans the scene. "No. No point in us trying to go on for a while. There'll be people coming up from the other side of the hill too. Anyways, I always rest the horses a bit when I get up here. You want some victuals?" His sweeping arm takes in many of the stalls.

"No, indeed I do not. I'll stay outside for some air, however."

"You must have seen many a hanging when you was in London, Mistress Powell."

"Not at all, though I suppose there was plenty of opportunity. I visited Tyburn only once as a young woman. Some poor woman was being burned – I cannot remember for what crime now." The driver pulls a face and shakes his head. "Yes," she continues, "I am of your opinion exactly."

"Not a proper death, burning. Shouldn't be allowed. Not in a Christian country."

"Not in any country – and I believe it is to be, soon will be, outlawed. There is also talk of executions being moved out of sight, kept within the walls of the gaol…"

"Oh, I wouldn't go that far, Ma'am. It's an important thing to see justice done and for the criminals to know there's a shaming end to them in front of all who know them."

"You are of the 'exemplar' school of justice-making, I see." He bows, though does not answer her. "Look after my niece, will you please; keep the blinds closed; for no reason must she be allowed to get out of the carriage. I'm going to see if I can rouse some official to help us through."

Mary makes her way to the edge of the escarpment and scans the scene just below her. She watches the same large group coming up from the valley. Busy chatter bubbles up from them as they strain uphill. Sometimes distinct voices separate out; many are laughing. But as the front of the group turns the final bend in the road, silence takes hold. Moving now, almost in step, they go towards the crowd already there and are soon no longer distinguishable. As if drawn by some diabolical force, she joins them.

Now she too can see. A woman stands on a cart, her torso rising above the surrounding crowd. Her back is arched strangely, neck exposed, face flattened towards the sky. A hum comes from the people, like a wet finger moving on a rim of glass, but no voice breaks ranks.

The mules are restless and the cart moves backwards and forwards. Guards, standing at intervals around it, face outwards, their pikes' dark crosses in silhouette. A man jumps onto the wagon and approaches the woman, one hand outstretched, palm facing down to quieten her, the other holding a coiled rope behind his back. Two others haul themselves up behind her and a ladder is passed up. The woman turns to face them, her hands fastened tightly behind her, pulling her shoulders back, pushing her chest forward. They hold the ladder upright, one each side, and brace against it. The first man moves close behind her and drops the looped rope around her neck. She shakes her head, resisting like a young horse, but he pushes her towards the ladder, walking awkwardly as a gundog with a woodcock in its jaws. He thrusts her, face first, against the frame as the men each side strain to keep it still. For a moment there is a scuffle: she twists and thrashes, a keening, beast sound coming from her. The people mutter, disturbed, voices at last rising distinct:

"Get up, harlot!"

"On with it, man – stop torturing the maid!"

The tethered woman struggles again as he turns her to face outwards now, pinning her down with more ropes, then fixing the one around her neck to the hook at the top of the ladder. Finally she's secured and the three of them move behind her, holding the ladder steady.

A Justice is helped into place at the front of the cart. "For the heinous and horrible murder of her bastard child, this woman be here hung by the neck until she be dead." He gestures to the men behind him and hastily climbs down.

They loosen the cords supporting her body and she begins to slide – a shallow drop, more strangulation than hanging. Her loosely-tied legs scrabble at the rungs of the ladder behind her, the tethered hands clawing backwards to find a hold. The leather shoes, too big, fall away. Her threadbare skirts ride up, giving the crowd a sight of her bare shins, dirty and thin. Isolated shouts and cries rise from people as she struggles. The men jerk the ladder upright, shaking it, so at last she hangs in air. A wave of sound, then a single woman's voice shrieking rhythmically somewhere in the crowd, regular as a turning winch. The hanging woman thrashes and twists herself, feet kicking air, just inches from the cart's floor.

At last she slumps still. A moan comes from the people. For a moment the men freeze. Then the first moves in front of her, tipping the ladder towards him. His movements are gentle, almost tender now as he holds her against him, supporting her loose body with one arm as he helps the others to untie the ropes. Finally, he lifts her across his chest, like a bridegroom on his wedding night and slowly kneels, ladder and body lost at last behind the cart sides.

For a few minutes Mary stands, unmoving. The pikemen still surround the cart, though they no longer stand in formation and several lean on their staffs. What will happen now? Will the woman's family take her body or will it be the prize of some surgeon or artist? Does she even have a family who will admit to owning her after what she's done – not just any murder, but a child! Somewhere she'd read that the executioner has the right to keep the clothes. Ha! The clothes, such as they are, and her shoes that she had fought to keep on her bare feet even as she was choking to death! A sound escapes her but no one looks at her. She is angry now, with herself for bearing witness – what was she thinking! How could she think a death here on the wild hillside would be anything different from the sordid spectacle of a London execution? The girl hardly out of her teens and surely half-crazed with fever and the horror of bearing a bastard child. Even here, when surely a significant proportion of the crowd would know the woman to be hanged, they still bought apples and new cider!

She can see the coach at the margins and makes her way towards it, relieved to see the coachman still at his post and the blinds in place. He gets down as she approaches. At first she can't hear him, the wind snatching at his words. He is still talking as he comes towards her, his hand out, fingers pinching her forearm as she stumbles over a loose stone. She can hold onto it no longer. "An abomination! That young woman was most likely out of her mind, so many are left this way by unscrupulous men. It makes my blood rage! And who ordered this; for pity's sake, should she be hanged for being poor, mad and gullible? Who would order this – it's the 1750s, not some medieval heathen kingdom!" She shoves away his hand and shakes out her skirt. The door opens and Catherine's head peeps out. "Get back inside!" It disappears. The coachman is standing, arms by his side, his face a mixture of concern and slight amusement. "Well?" He lifts his palms in a gesture of ignorance. "Who was in charge of sentencing here; do we know? Do you know?"

"Sir Herbert Lloyd I think, Ma'am. I mean," he says quickly, "I think that's what they're saying – someone came up talking to me whilst you were at the hanging."

"Hanging! It was strangulation… a disgrace. One hears nothing but the most base of things about that man. I should have been paying much more attention to matters like this, outrages like this happening on my own doorstep! I could have interceded perhaps. Ah, I am so insular here; so concerned with the domestic when there are 'causes' to be fought even here in these wild mountains!" She flings her arms out and he finds himself glancing behind him, as if a 'cause' would appear on the crest of the hill. "I must at least write letters of remonstrance when I get to London, not only to the Baronet but to his superiors, shame him into changing his ways." The man shakes his head. "What? You surely cannot condone his behaviour?" The coachman looks at her, not quite understanding her language. "What, man – you cannot agree with such a punishment? Surely you are no admirer of Lloyd?"

He shakes his head emphatically. "Not I, Mistress."

She studies him for a moment, her anger seeming, second by second, to deflate. Unseen by her, the door opens again a crack, though Catherine's head is not visible. "My apologies," she says at last. "I see that yet again I have made myself a fool; said too much and to the wrong person."

The coachman waves his hand in a gesture of denial. "You have not heard then? Sir Herbert is dead, Mistress."

"Oh! Dead you say? How so? Again you see I'm ignorant —"

"The news came to us in Cardiganshire this morning. A fellow's just been telling me." The driver smiles.

"But how? By what means? What ailed him?"

"No ailment, as far as I know. Sir Herbert often travelled with a bodyguard, they say, but not this time. He was found dead alone on the road. A journey, I think to Bath it was... I know not. By his own hand, some are saying." His eyes follow a flock of starlings on their way to roost.

It is no good; she cannot bear the suspense. "'Some are saying'? You intimate something else? Speak, man."

He looks at her then with something like irritation. When he does speak, it's slowly, with a care for every word. "I know not, Mistress. Gypsies; brigands perhaps... His throat was cut in a smile they are saying. But I know for certain nothing except this: Sir Herbert did not have many friends."

She nods. The vision of the young woman – her poor, dirty clothes, fingers clawing at the rope, comes to her again. "Yes, well... maybe his death is no unlucky thing for our poor county. Come, let us be on our way."

Chapter Forty-Three

"PUT YOUR HEAD in, Catherine; you're like a dog with its face in the wind!"

"But there's a girl up ahead walking on her own, Aunt."

"Catherine!"

Catherine ducks her head in quickly and struggles to fasten the window. "You shouldn't be walking on your own in the dark," Catherine mutters. Mary doesn't answer. She studies the view from her own window, her frown deep. "Girls should not go out alone." Catherine can tell from the stillness of her aunt's back that she's been heard.

The coach passes the figure. She's on Mary's side, slim, stiff; carrying what seems a heavy bag and wearing tough travelling clothes. Catherine wriggles in her seat, repeatedly opening and closing her fingers. The coach continues. Each square of sky is different as Mary glances from her niece, then out again. The wind will not let the sky be, hurling clouds across and across. The land is desecrated by the pits and lumps of lead mining, its contours misshapen by heaps of slag and winding gear, its natural colours blackened by the tear of a conduit, a deep shaft's mouth. "How ugly the scene is; how we have ruined it all!" she mutters.

Catherine murmurs again, louder this time. Though she is known for talking to herself, this is nevertheless aimed at Mary and the woman knows it. "There were wolves in these mountains at one time, in times past. Fierce ones, hungry for blood." She gasps in shock as Mary hammers her cane against the ceiling. The coach stops.

"There you are, Madam," Mary says. Catherine looks at her, nervous. Mary's smile is grim. "You're right; no woman should have to walk alone in the dusk. I was not wanting to have to make conversation, that's all. However, no good reason to pass a traveller on a windy night with a coach half-empty. Just make sure you don't half kill her with questions. Understand?"

Catherine's smile is broad. "I hope she doesn't smell!"

The coachman is at the window and Mary moves to gets out. "Thank you. The young woman back there; we'll wait for her and proffer a lift."

"Very good, Ma'am." He moves to close the door.

"No, I'll speak to her myself; put her at her ease. Please, return to your seat." The driver touches his hat and heaves himself back up. Mary walks towards the young woman, hailing her with a wave. The girl stops abruptly and Mary is forced to walk further than she'd intended on the filthy road. She starts talking before she reaches her. "Please don't be alarmed. Mary Powell, formerly of Nanteos." The girl looks at her sharply, taking a step back, but instead of answering pulls her hat further down on her head. Mary waits a moment, taking care not to move closer and pressurise her. "It seems by your attire that you may be going some way and it's getting dark. We have room in the carriage and are going as far as Lampeter tonight if that would help you on your way." The girl nods, shifting her pack to the other shoulder. "Please do accept a lift from us; the journey so far has been ugly enough without thinking of a young woman such as yourself being left alone here as the weather moves in."

The woman comes towards her. Though she keeps her head down, Mary can see she is as tall as herself, something rare to find in a local woman. As they walk towards the coach it is only Mary who speaks – perhaps the girl does not understand English? It was a good job, in that case, that Catherine was with them. Though the coachman offers to take her bag for her, the girl seems not to want to part with it.

Catherine's eager face itches to question her and the stranger does indeed smell – but of fresh air and damp wool rather than anything more sinister. "How far are you going?" Mary asks, careful to speak slowly and simply.

"Lampeter."

So, she does understand English, at least a little. Mary knocks for them to move on. Pack between her legs, blanket arranged by Catherine across her lap, at last the girl tilts back her hat. Her face is extraordinary! Mary half-recognises her, as though she had been used by painters for generations as a model. Her face is pale, the skin flushed only slightly from her journey. Her eyes are tawny and unusual in a face with skin like thick, new cream and are swollen and red – wind scour most likely, or perhaps she too had been witness to the dreadful business…

As the coach moves on the three sit quietly. Mary notices that Catherine is sitting on her hands and smothers a smile – it's the child's usual habit when trying to keep her mouth shut, though she still can't resist looking at her guest every ten turns of the wheels or so. The last of the sun shows itself in the clouds, a sickly orange, and Mary closes her eyes. She had not intended to feign sleep, but when Catherine starts to whisper and the stranger answers her, she continues the pretence.

Their conversation is in Welsh and indeed much of it too low for her to hear anyway, lost to the rattle and jar of the wheels, though she can pick out names and familiar words and phrases and she learns that the young woman is leaving Cardiganshire. The girl would do well, her instinct tells her. However, even with so charming an interrogator as Catherine, she does not give much away and, when asked her name, offers only "Miss Rhys". Surely there is a young man waiting for her, though an irresponsible one to let her travel alone like this! Mary opens her eyes when the coach starts to sway and jerk as they move downhill at last and the conceit of remaining asleep would no longer seem plausible.

Just before they turn off to join the principal road the girl begins to arrange her clothes. Taking off her hat she runs her fingers through her thick hair. Mary stares; never has she seen hair like this – dark, dark red, the colour of wet, November bracken. The girl sees her watching and smiles; only a small gesture, but one that changes her face. She refastens her cloak, checks her boots.

"Do you need to relieve yourself? Shall I stop the coach?"

She nods and Mary bangs hard on the roof. Miss Rhys squeezes Catherine's hand and, picking up her pack, reaches to open the door. The coachman is there first, a question on his face and a hand ready. She turns back. "Thank you for your kindness." She looks at them both then says, in good English, "I'm sorry for your sorrows; your grief." She turns and gets down. For a moment Mary is lost for words. She slides across to get out of the carriage herself but the girl has already moved away, heading towards a low hovel just back from the road.

She watches through the still open door as a small figure comes out of the dwelling. Apart from the skirt it could be a man. Bundled in rags so thick as to be shapeless, she seems but a small step from the lichen-covered boulders that surround her home. Dead furze serves as a roof and there is more smoke coming from the hole of a doorway than out of the wicker chimney. Should she remonstrate with the girl? Why would she seek the company of a woman hardly more than a beggar?

"Come on, Aunt." Catherine's voice breaks through her thoughts. "She's staying the night here – she said. Maybe she's meeting her lover?"

"Lover!" Mary laughs. "What do you know of lovers, Catherine? Too much reading my books by candlelight, no doubt." She returns to the window. The two women are together, standing in one another's embrace and most likely waiting for them to move away. "Very well." She gives an order to the coachman. "On we go. I am more than ready for a large fire and warm bed." As they leave she can just make out two white hands waving.

Catherine's eyes shine as she turns from the window, tucking her waving hand back under the blanket. "Oh, didn't she look so like a princess in rags, Aunt!"

Mary laughs. "Rags? Hardly rags, Catherine! But yes, a fine young woman – though rather more Grecian goddess in disguise than a princess, in my view. You were speaking most intimately whilst I slept, I believe... tell me, before we reach the tavern, what was her history, what her plans?"

Chapter Forty-Four

THE WOOD GROANS alarmingly, but at least he will have something to do on the passage, and some sort of privacy in the low cabin. Mary's doing, surely. He can hardly wait to open the thick package of documents, maps, drawings and plans, all carefully wrapped in oiled leather, that had been waiting for him in the charge of the captain.

Discomfort: an unpleasant, heady mixture of the sounds, smells and the writing slipping and staggering in front of his eyes. Cai puts the opened package to one side and walks out on deck. Despite the activity all around him as the ship prepares to sail, his gaze is drawn again and again to a woman who stands alone at the rails. Her back is narrow and straight, her gloved hands gripping the wood – she looks like she is fighting the ship, fighting the very sea, willing it to be still!

A strange figure somehow. She seems still to have her luggage with her and her cloak, though heavy and relatively new, is rough and unfashionable. Yet, though her attire is humble, she is here on this deck. Perhaps she is companion to a wealthy woman?

A sailor passes him and winks, gesturing with a crook of his head to the figure.

Cai looks away quickly and moves to the far side of the ship, but when he glances back the woman is still there, though bending over the side now. One of the junior officers approaches her.

Cai moves away and finds a point further towards the prow in which to watch the traffic coming aboard the ship as it prepares to depart. A small, dilapidated craft is at anchor downstream. The deck is crowded with people, many sitting and even lying down on the bare planks. Many have only small packs; others carry bedding. There are many children, as poorly dressed as the adults with them. Suddenly at his elbow is the young officer. The man introduces himself and they shake hands.

"I admire you," the man says. "I would love to emigrate myself. Perhaps one day I will make this trip as a passenger!"

"Why doubt it? I'm sure the colony has a great need for your skills. Tell me, that ship ahead of us; what is the destination?"

"Same as us, most probably. Pennsylvania."

"But the passengers – do they hope to continue for the whole passage, or do they drop off at one of our domestic ports on the way?"

"No – all aboard go to Philadelphia, I believe. That ship... probably from Rotterdam or some such continental port."

"They don't seem well enough provisioned for such a journey! Ten and more weeks at sea in front of them and already in rags!"

"The ship will provision them." The officer laughs, cynical and hollow. "Such as it is, the provisioning. Many won't make it."

"Indentured?"

"Yes. They'll need to redeem the cost of their passage once they get to the destination port. Someone'll be there on the dock to bid for them and they'll sign themselves up to work off the cost."

"An ugly business and one open to abuse, surely."

The officer nods. "The ones I feel most sorry for are those who lose relatives on the passage over and have to pay back their fares too!"

"An abomination!" They are quiet for a while, watching the activity on shore.

"I've worked that crossing twice on an indenture ship. No more, I can tell you. The stench... I fancy I can begin to smell it already, coming upstream on the breeze."

"Disappointing to think that the colonies too are ripe with abuse."

"You will find that yourself." The officer stands back and studies him for a moment. "You're one of the ones going *to* somewhere, rather than running *from* somewhere, I think. Am I right?" Cai doesn't answer him. "I am right, I think. Your eyes are on the horizon, without a backward glance. An adventurer, with nothing to hold him back."

Cai's laugh is hollow. "There's nothing to hold me, right enough; but that doesn't mean there's nothing that causes me pain to leave." He looks away downriver.

The officer seems to be waiting for him to explain but after a moment he shrugs and adjusts his uniform. "On a happier note: how do I look, Sir?" He strikes a stern pose.

Cai laughs. "Very impressive."

"I have my eye on the uncommonly handsome woman to stern. I've seen you looking at her too."

Cai smiles; why deny it? "Is she companion to some rich passenger?"

"No." The young man's smile is broad. "That's the fortunate

thing… she travels alone. Similar to your accent, I would say, though not of your class, obviously; you only have to look at the clothes. A mystery in fact. She is something of a topic of conversation amongst all us younger officers, I must admit. A most interesting project for some lucky man." He pokes his finger into his chest and grins. Then, giving a small bow, he leaves.

Cai looks again behind him. The woman is still there; now she turns and is walking away from him, her steps slow but steady; he senses she is making a great effort not to lurch about with the ship. She looks neither left nor right, holding herself stiff, leaning away from the weight of the bag which she balances on her hip. There is something familiar about her, no one thing – he has not seen her face, her hair; does not recognise her clothes. It is subtle but sure, as you know with no more than a flash of shape and colour; some unique character of movement at the edge of sight, that it is woodcock not snipe rising from cover in front of the guns. His chest clenches; the pulse hammers in his neck. She stops, lowers the bag to the deck to adjust her hat and he shouts out – one word, her name.

Also by the author:

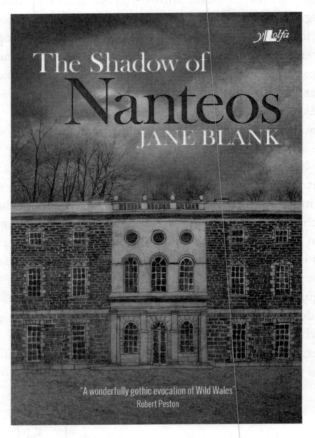

The Shadow of
Nanteos
JANE BLANK

yl Lolfa

"A wonderfully gothic evocation of Wild Wales'
Robert Peston

When William Powell and his headstrong wife Elizabeth inherit the glorious
Nanteos estate in Cardiganshire, it seems their new life is everything they
could wish for. Yet, as her debt-ridden husband is snared by the land disputes
and violence of the 1750s lead wars, Elizabeth is increasingly drawn to the
mysterious figure of Cai, the estate's handsome bailiff.

Superstition, tales of haunting, and the powerful Nanteos Grail cast their
shadow over the house and soon the family is caught up in a vicious political
and legal battle that will end in tragedy.

£8.99 (978-1-78461-171-2)

Reviews and quotes about *The Shadow of Nanteos*

Waterstones Book of the Month in Wales
Long-listed for the Historical Novel Society Awards

'A wonderfully gothic evocation of Wild Wales.'
Robert Peston

'An inherently fascinating read that showcases author
Jane Blank's exceptional storytelling skills… a deftly
crafted work of truly entertaining originality.'
Midwest Book Review

'I can't wait for the sequel. I couldn't put the novel down!'
Gwenith Closs-Colgrove
President of the Great Plains Welsh Heritage Project

'A fabulous novel. One of those titles that makes you read non-
stop. This is a worthy follow up of Blank's *The Geometry of Love*.
She is one of the best Anglo-Welsh writers of the modern era.'
Dr Alan M. Kent

'Jane Blank's thorough and meticulous research has
given us an evocative and atmospheric portrayal of cosmic
proportions. This is an imaginative world of universal import.
But it has been written with a subtle and light pen… and we are
carried along by the author's original energy.'
The late Professor 'Bobi' Jones
Aberystwyth University

'Dark, dramatic and visceral.'
Deborah Kay Davies

'A perfect book for Christmas!'
Emma Corfield-Waters
Bookish

the geometry
of love

jane blank

"The funniest, sexiest novel I've read in a long time"
NORMAN SCHWENK

Fast-paced and darkly funny, *The Geometry of Love* is set in Sheffield in the 1980s where New Romantics vie with Northern Soulers for control of the clubs and the fashion scene. The miners are on strike, Thatcher is in power, but all this means nothing to two teenage girls looking for kicks, their one aim – to lose their virginity. In the wake of their fascination with Omar, a gorgeous French-Algerian, the action moves to France. The story, however, remains one of obsession: what happens when childhood friends refuse to let go and when East collides with West in a pre-9/11 world.

£7.95 (978 1 84771 039 0)

Reviews and quotes about *The Geometry of Love*

'The teenage sexual odyssey Jane Blank describes in *The Geometry of Love* is written with honesty, verve and humour. The author has a poet's eye for detail and the frankness of the young narrator's observations accurately reflects the obsessive nature of youth. As we follow the physical adventures of Susan and Miranda, it is touching to witness the ways in which these young women begin to form themselves. The resolution of the final section is both difficult and poignant. A book to transport the reader back to our pre-sexual – and yet most sexual – selves.'

Hannah Vincent

'Blank's writing is suffused with tenderness and compassion, and her acute portrayal of the shifting emotions and unrepeatable intimacy of teenage girls is both touching and memorable.'

Suzy Ceulan Hughes
(A review from www.gwales.com
with the permission of the Welsh Books Council.)

'The funniest, sexiest book I've read in a long time.'

Norman Schwenk

'Witty and saucy.'

Bill Gallagher

Jane Blank's work has won prizes and awards and has been featured in numerous magazines and anthologies including *Planet*, *New Welsh Review*, *Poetry Wales*, *Poetry Quarterly Review*, *Western Mail*, *The Big Issue*, *Observer Magazine* and *The Independent*.

www.jane-blank.info

nanteos

BESPOKE WEDDINGS
PRIVATE FAMILY & BUSINESS EVENTS
EXCLUSIVE USE
LUXURY B&B

Nanteos Rhydyfelin, Aberystwyth, Ceredigion, Wales SY23 4LU
t:01970 600522 e: info@nanteos com
nanteos.com

CENTRAL 19-01-21